Gypsy Souls

Ivy,
Best wishes!
Tonya Royston

Tonya Royston

GENRE: PARANORMAL THRILLER/YA/PARANORMAL ROMANCE

GYPSY SOULS ~ Book Two of The Gypsy Magic Trilogy
Copyright © 2016 by Tonya Royston
Cover Design by Jennifer Gibson
All cover art copyright © 2016
All Rights Reserved
ISBN: 1539899756
Print ISBN: 9781539899754

First Publication: NOVEMBER 2016

The birds were back, but this time, a voice whispered in the wind, calling my name...

Fear lodged itself in my throat, and I froze, remembering the birds I had seen in the woods the day I had gotten lost. Just like then, they swarmed together, forming a ceiling of black overhead and crying out as they dodged each other.

"Okay, Gracyn!" Lucian called from below. "Come on down. Just take it slowly."

Grateful to have something other than the birds to focus on, I eased down the side of the rock, searching for a foothold. Finding one, I balanced on my right foot and felt around for another with my left foot. As soon as I propped the toe of my boot on a narrow ledge, a gust of wind swept through the air. At first, I ignored it. But then I heard a muffled whisper in the breeze.

"Gracyn. Come to me. I need your help."

The haunting voice faded quickly, and I stopped, not sure if it had been real or a figment of my imagination. Staring up at the sky, or what little I could see of it beyond the birds, I shivered. Then I heard the voice again. "Gracyn. I've waited an eternity for you," a woman said.

Trembling, I lowered myself, eager to get away from the eerie whispers. But my foot slid, and I lost my balance. I felt myself falling and reached for the rock on my way down, but I only ended up scraping my arms. There was nothing to grab ahold of.

Panic gripped me in that split second. I expected a hard impact and hoped I would walk away in one piece. Throwing my arms up around my head, I screamed. A moment later, I landed on my feet when a pair of strong arms wrapped around my waist. Lucian steadied me against his chest, and I reached up, grabbing his shoulders as I came to a stop, his solid touch pitching my thoughts into a whirlwind.

Gypsy Souls ~ Book 2 Of The Gypsy Magic Trilogy

All her life, Gracyn Pierce has believed in what she can see and touch. But after learning she is part of a supernatural world, she knows things are about to change.

Gracyn has no idea what lies ahead. She's nervous about her future, not sure she'll go to college one day as she hopes. In spite of the powers that have awakened inside her, she moves on as though everything is normal, studying hard and spending time with her boyfriend, Alex. She finds comfort in knowing there are others like her, particularly Lucian, the neighbor suspected of murdering his sister. As an unexpected bond forms between them, she begins to believe he couldn't possibly have committed such a horrific crime.

When Gracyn unknowingly releases an evil presence, birds turn up dead and hallucinations torment her. Then danger strikes, threatening her friend, Celeste. Gracyn does everything she can to help, but nothing prepares her for the shocking secrets exposed in the race against time to save Celeste.

Book 2 - Gypsy Souls

By Tonya Royston

1

*M*agic. That one word sent shock waves through my system. I was a witch, or so I had been told. Because of everything that had happened, from hurting my best friend's stepfather to waking up with perfect vision after wearing glasses for fourteen years, I believed it. And that was a huge feat. I was a realist. I believed in what I could see and touch, in what could be proven by fact and science. Not in magic.

Things were about to change for me, only how much, I had yet to discover. I trusted Becca and Gabriel to lead me through everything I had ahead of me now. After admitting they were also witches, they had explained that I had a supernatural connection to Gypsy, the horse Becca had given me as soon as I had arrived in Sedgewick over a month ago. Gypsy and I shared a bond, an energy that kept us young and healthy. We had been born on the same day, and we would die on the same day, but not for a very long time. Becca had indicated that as a witch, I would live for centuries. I wasn't sure if I would live as long as she had in almost four hundred years, but it seemed I would outlive a normal human life.

I still had many questions, more than I could count. The first one involved my mother who I had been told was also Becca's mother. That didn't seem possible if our mother wasn't a witch like us as Becca had explained. To make matters more complicated, Becca had asked me not to discuss our involvement in the supernatural world with my mother. That frustrated me, making me suspect there was a lot I didn't know yet.

Who else belonged to the supernatural world in Sedgewick snuck into my questions. I often thought of Lucian and his tea that cured my hangover in minutes, not to mention the day he made everyone in the hall disappear after I read his review of my painting. Every time he appeared in my thoughts, so did his criticism, bringing back my wounded pride until I forced myself to think about something else.

In spite of my curiosity to know more about being a witch, my concerns about Becca's deteriorating health overshadowed my questions. Ever since Gabriel had explained that the use of her power would wear her down until she took her last breath, I couldn't stop wondering how much time she had left. We had just gotten to know each other, and I wasn't ready to lose her.

Sunday evening as I got ready for bed, I tried to focus on something good, like knowing Sam's stepfather would never bother me again. At least that nightmare was over and Sam had her family back.

Then there was Alex, the guy who looked like a rock star even though he was in the running for class valedictorian. More importantly, he was my boyfriend. Things with Alex were like a dream come true, aside from the week he broke up with me after I got drunk on tequila. But now he was back in my life, and I had the Homecoming dance to look forward to with him by my side.

When I arrived at school Monday morning, the cool breeze and leaves splattered with orange and red filled me with anticipation of fall. The beginning of the season reminded me of starting over. Feeling like a new person, I walked through the crowd on the front lawn, the other students oblivious to the fact that my whole world had changed overnight. They chatted in groups, catching up on gossip from the weekend concert and parties. I watched them, a heavy sigh escaping my lips. I felt removed from them, and yet it didn't bother me. I might be different, but I was the same girl I'd been last week.

Inside, Alex was waiting for me at my locker, a charming smile on his face. He looked as handsome as ever with his hair pulled back into a ponytail, revealing a silver earring in one ear, and his gray shirt straining against his broad shoulders. My heart skipped a beat at the sight of him, even though less than twenty-four hours ago, we had been sitting on the front porch, shoulder to shoulder, his hand on mine.

My eyes locked with his as I approached him, feeling my worries melt away from his gaze.

"Good morning," he said, catching me in his arms and kissing me.

Closing my eyes, I wrapped an arm around his shoulders and enjoyed the touch of his lips in spite of the crowded hallway behind us. I remembered feeling self-conscious weeks ago when Alex kissed me in public, but I no longer worried about appearances. Everything felt right at this moment.

A few seconds later, he lifted away from me. I opened my eyes, instantly noticing a teasing sparkle in his.

"Hi," I said, feeling flushed from his embrace.

"How was your evening?" he asked.

"Quiet," I replied.

"Do you miss your friend?"

I sucked in a deep breath, my thoughts spinning. Of course I missed Sam, but part of me was glad to have some time to myself, at least since finding out I was something of the supernatural realm. I had a lot on my mind, and having a friend who didn't understand would have been hard. "I'll always miss Sam," I said. "She's my best friend, but things are changing for both of us and we have to get used to that."

"I hope you're happy about some of those changes." When I raised my eyebrows, Alex continued. "Considering that meeting me was a result of them."

Nothing could have stopped the smile I felt sliding over my face at that moment. He had no idea how much I needed him. His every touch, every smile, comforted me in a way I couldn't describe in words. Of all the changes going on in my life, Alex gave me a sense of peace amongst the turmoil.

"Of course, I am. And Sam knows that. But she's already looking forward to next year. We might end up at the same school, or at least in the same state, and it will be nice to be together again. But for now, I'm where I belong."

Alex seemed to miss the real meaning of my statement, but I couldn't blame him for that. He had no idea that I was a witch and that I needed Becca to guide me down this new path in my life.

With a sly grin, he pulled me closer to him. "I like the way that sounds," he said before kissing me again.

Laughing, I pulled away. "Okay. I know where your mind is this morning," I teased, untangling myself from his embrace. "But it is Monday, and some of us need to focus on school."

"We can do that later," he groaned. "I'm just trying to make up for lost time from last week. I'm going to have to kiss you twice as much this week."

As I shook my head with a grin, Derek appeared and gave Alex a swift jab with his elbow. "This guy bothering you? Because you know, he's not the only fish out there."

"Hey," Alex countered. "She's off limits. We just patched things up, so give it a rest."

"I'm only kidding. Gracyn, your friend was cute. Is she going to make another trip up here?"

"I doubt it," I told him. "Sorry."

"Aw, okay," he grumbled. "She disappeared Saturday night, anyway, after I saw her with Todd."

Todd was the quarterback of the football team and the guy Sam's stepfather paid to distract her. I felt myself frowning at the memory of Sam dancing with Todd before her stepfather dragged me away from the concert Saturday night. "Don't worry. That didn't last long," I told Derek, trying to push Sam's stepfather out of my thoughts.

"Really? Too bad you both didn't stay. There was a great party after the concert ended. Alex and I were a little bummed out that you two left, but at least he still has a chance with you."

Before I could stop them, more dark thoughts of that night flashed through my mind. Looking away from Derek and Alex, all I could think about was Sam's stepfather pulling me into the woods, my vision blurry as he knelt above me, his weight pinning me to the ground.

Uneasiness settled over me for a moment, but I tossed it aside with confidence. Never again would someone be able to overpower me. I knew what I was, and I would learn to protect myself at any cost.

My mind wandering, I noticed a flash of black out of the corner of my eye. I glanced down the hall to see Lucian making his way through the crowd, the green eyes I seemed unable to forget locked on me. His gaze steady, he stopped, oblivious to the kids glaring at him when they had to swerve around him. His light brown hair was a little messy this morning, as though he had just woken up. A gray shirt peeked out from under his black coat, and the silver cross he always wore hung around his neck.

I didn't dare look away. I wanted to approach him, to ask him how he had saved me Saturday night and why he didn't come up to the house when he had ridden over on his horse last night. But I never had the chance. After a few seconds, he spun around and headed in the opposite direction, disappearing through the doorway at the end of the hall.

"Isn't that right, Gracyn?" Alex's question snapped me out of my trance.

"What's that?" I asked, shifting my attention back to him. "Sorry. I thought I saw Celeste and I didn't hear what you said." I hated lying, but Alex and Derek were watching me, waiting for my response, and I felt compelled to explain why I had been ignoring them.

"I was telling Derek that you agreed to go to the Homecoming dance with me," Alex said.

"Oh, yes," I replied, the image of Lucian still etched in my mind. *Earth to Gracyn. You might try paying some attention to the guy who actually wants to be with you,* a voice in my head rambled, chastising me. Shoving it away, I forced myself to smile. "When is it?"

"In three weeks," Derek replied with a huff. "And those weeks are going to fly by. I just hope it's enough time for me to get back into Lacey's good graces."

"She's still not talking to you?" Alex asked.

"No," Derek grumbled with a shake of his head. "And I apologized. Several times."

Alex raised his eyebrows. "That's what you get when you drink too much and leave her to fend for herself."

"But you forgave Gracyn," Derek reminded him.

"That was her first offense," Alex explained. "You've done it to Lacey countless times. I can't say I blame her."

"Fine," he said, disgruntled. "Take her side. But if you're going to do that, the least you can do is help me figure out a way to get her back."

"Derek, you aren't seriously asking that, are you? Because it isn't that hard." Alex took a deep breath, a thoughtful look in his eyes. "Let's see, have you tried roses, chocolate, or maybe a good old-fashioned apology and promising never to do it again?"

"Never?" Derek asked in disbelief. "I'm not sure I can make that promise."

"Gracyn did," Alex added.

When Derek looked at me, I nodded. "I'm not going down that road again. That was the worst night of my life. How you can do that to yourself over and over again is beyond me."

"Someday, you might understand," he muttered, his gaze dropping to the floor.

I scrunched my eyebrows, not sure I would ever know what he was talking about. But I quickly brushed it off. "You could always take Celeste to the dance," I suggested.

Derek shot me a look that made me cringe before softening his expression with a knowing smile. "She's not my type, Gracyn. One day, you're going to see that. Where is Celeste, anyway? Last few weeks, she's looked like death warmed over."

I shrugged. "I don't know. I haven't seen her today. I just hope she's feeling better."

"Yeah," Derek said, a hint of sympathy in his voice. "No one's been killed since Lucian got back, so maybe she'll start to relax. The guy might be disturbed, but hopefully he's not stupid enough to kill again. Because if he does, he's not going to get away with it twice."

Derek's damning words made me flinch. I refused to believe Lucian had killed his sister after he had found me lost in the woods weeks ago, not to mention saved me from Sam's stepfather, something I still needed to thank him for.

"Well, this conversation just got morbid. Can we talk about something else?" Alex asked.

"Yes, but later," I stated. "I need to get organized and head to homeroom. Last week was pretty rough, and I'm behind in all my classes. I just hope I can catch up today."

"I'll help you, if you want me to, that is," Alex offered as I turned to my locker. "In fact, I'm free this afternoon. Shall I plan to come over? I can bring a pizza, and my books, of course."

"Man," Derek groaned. "You two were made for each other. I'm glad I'm not obsessed with my grades like you guys."

"Good for you," Alex said. "And what are you going to do after high school?"

"Not sure," Derek answered. "It all depends on if the band sticks together. So don't move too far away. But if that doesn't work out, maybe I'll head for the slopes up in Vermont. I could be a ski bum for a season or two."

"I'm glad you have your priorities in order," Alex said, slapping him on his shoulder. "Gracyn, I'll see you in Calculus. Derek, try to pay attention in class today."

"Why? That's no fun. I'm just here to try to get a date for the dance," Derek teased as they walked away, disappearing into the crowd.

With a smile, I resumed getting my books. Those two reminded me of brothers—as different as night and day and yet best friends through thick and thin. In spite of their constant attempts to one-up each other, their company lifted my spirits. Too bad the lighthearted mood they put me in never lasted.

—　—

Throughout the day, I concentrated in my classes, keeping up much better than I'd been able to do last week. A few times, my thoughts bounced back to the weekend and the fact that I was a witch. But before they carried me away from the lesson at hand, I scolded myself. My job right now was to catch up with my schoolwork. Being a witch was not an excuse to let my grades fall.

In History class, Celeste looked better than she had in weeks. The dark circles under her eyes had faded and she seemed more alert. When the bell dismissing the period rang and everyone rushed to the door, I followed the crowd, ignoring Mr. Wainwright who bid goodbye to the students. I still didn't like the way he looked at me, but at least he hadn't been the one targeting me over the last few weeks.

Out in the hall, I waited until Celeste walked through the doorway. Her book bag hung from her shoulder, her black sweater ending below the waist of her green cargo pants. Wispy strands of dark hair fell around her face, and she blew one out of her eyes as she headed my way.

"Hi, Celeste," I said. "How are you?"

She smiled, her expression relaxed. "Better, actually. As much as I hate to admit it, I think I'm getting used to Lucian being back."

"So you're not scared of him anymore?" I asked, falling into step beside her. We wandered through the crowd, splitting off to let someone pass between us before continuing our conversation.

"I don't know if I'd say that. I still can't handle the idea of being in the same cafeteria as him for lunch."

"Yeah. I noticed. It would be nice if you tried, though. I'm all by myself, and I'd love to have someone to sit with."

She glanced at me, a guilty look on her face. Then she stopped and we slipped off to the side to let the other students keep moving down the hallway. "I'm sorry. I haven't been a good friend to you, have I? You didn't know anyone, and I just dropped you. Please don't be mad. It wasn't your fault."

When my eyes met her hopeful gaze, I smiled, wanting to reassure her that I wasn't mad at her for being afraid. No one deserved to live in fear. After the anxiety I had felt for two weeks between the dead phone calls and the doll, I couldn't blame Celeste for wanting to hide from the world, even if it meant deserting me for lunch. "I'm not mad. I'm just worried about you, that's all."

"Thanks. I'm still worried about me, too. I've been struggling lately, but the only other option right now is to move to a new school."

"I remember you mentioned that once before," I commented. "I didn't realize it was still a possibility."

Taking a deep breath, Celeste scanned the students in the hallway before shifting her gaze back to me. "It's always an option, but the longer I wait, the harder it will be to adjust to a new school. Besides, I'd have to leave Serenity behind, and I don't think I can do that."

"Serenity?"

"My horse. She means a lot to me, and I'd miss her too much if I left. The school that has an opening right now doesn't have a stable where I could keep her."

The notion that Celeste was also a witch crossed my mind once again. Every witch in Sedgewick was connected to a horse, and I wondered if Serenity completed Celeste in that special way. *That has to be it,* a voice mused in my head. *When her parents paid a visit to Becca and Gabriel, they knew what Becca was because they kept asking her to do something about Lucian, as though she had some kind of power.*

The scene out in the driveway suddenly made perfect sense. Celeste and her parents had to be witches because there was no other explanation. I made a mental note to ask Becca about them the next time we spoke which I hoped would be tonight, as long as Becca wasn't suffering from another headache.

"I'm sorry it won't work out, but I'm glad you're staying," I told Celeste with a smile. "And I don't think there's anything to worry about."

Celeste tilted her head, her eyes narrowing. "Please don't tell me you think Lucian is innocent."

Choose your words wisely, I warned myself. I wanted to tell her he had saved me Saturday night, but it got stuck on the tip of my tongue. Even if she believed me, I doubted her opinion of him would change. "I wasn't going to say that. But he has been back for a while, and no one has been killed."

She sighed. "That's pretty much the only thing keeping me sane right now," she muttered. "I'll think about coming to lunch tomorrow, okay?"

I perked up at her change of heart. "Really? That would be great."

"Maybe, but no promises."

"That's fine. I wouldn't expect one."

"Thanks," she said with an appreciative smile. "I guess I'd better run now. Can't be late to gym. See you later." With a half-hearted wave, she turned and headed down the hall.

My spirits lifted at the thought that there was hope for her. If she stopped fearing Lucian, she might have a good year. After returning her wave, I took off through the crowd in the direction of the Art wing. A few minutes later, I rushed into the classroom as the bell rang. Out of breath, I scooted between the tables to the other side of the room only to find the desk I shared with Lucian empty. Disappointment settled over me while I took my seat, my eyes lingering on the doorway. I waited for him to walk into the room, but he never did. Instead, Ms. Friedman shut the door and launched into the roll call.

I couldn't concentrate in Art class that afternoon. Everything in the room reminded me of Lucian from his critical review of my painting to the way he made the students in the hallway disappear when he wanted to speak to me about it. Lucian was the most complicated person I had ever met, and I wasn't sure how I felt about him. Conflicting emotions of resentment over his review of my work and appreciation for his help with Sam's stepfather twisted inside me, making it impossible to follow the lecture.

Art was the only class I had kept up with over the last few weeks, so I could afford to drift away for one period. It was a good thing, too, because I couldn't shake Lucian from my thoughts. He had been at school earlier in the day, and his absence in class nagged at me. The idea that he was avoiding me slipped into my mind, but I refused to blame myself for his strange behavior.

After Ms. Friedman instructed the class to start drawing the statue of a mother and child on her desk, the sound of ruffling paper filled the room. I pulled out my sketch pad and pencils, but my heart wasn't in it. I wanted to thank Lucian for his help Saturday night, and not being able to made me feel like I had unfinished business.

In spite of my frustration, I picked up a pencil and began to draw, hoping I could forget about Lucian. For all I knew, I would never get the chance to thank him.

2

After school that day, I returned home to find the driveway empty. I wasn't surprised, but I hoped it meant Becca was getting through her day without a headache. Gabriel had left for Boston this morning and wouldn't be back until later in the week, so I had the afternoon to myself.

I spent some time in the barn with Gypsy before cleaning the stalls and putting the horses away. Knowing we shared a special connection, I felt a sense of peace in her presence. Every time she nudged me or caught my eye, I smiled. I couldn't believe how comfortable I was around her after being afraid of horses for years. Her silent company made me feel safe, especially since she had led Becca through the woods to find me Saturday night.

By the time I flipped off the barn light and stepped outside with the dogs in tow, dusk was settling in. Hazy shades of gray and purple painted the sky. A chill had crept into the air, and I knew it would only get colder as each day brought the calendar closer to winter.

When I crossed the driveway, my shoes crunching on the gravel, headlights shone in the distance. Becca pulled up and parked her SUV beside my car as I started up the porch steps. The dogs hung back, pacing along the driver's side, waiting for her. I stopped and faced the railing, brushing the dust off the sleeves of my black jacket.

Becca stepped out of the truck, her navy suit nothing like the white coat and boots she had worn the other night. I couldn't erase the image of her glowing in the moonlight as she brought Sam's stepfather to his knees. But this evening, she looked professional. A few strands of blonde hair had escaped her ponytail, framing her face, and she carried a black briefcase. After shutting the door, she walked over to the steps.

I turned as she approached, her heels clicking on the wooden planks. "Hi," I said. "How are you feeling today?"

Alert with some color in her cheeks, she looked a lot better than she had resting on the couch Saturday night before Gabriel carried her to bed where she had stayed yesterday.

Her thoughtful expression broke out into a smile. "Much better, thank you."

"I'm glad to hear that," I said, relieved.

"And how are you doing? We haven't had a chance to talk since Saturday night. I'm sorry I wasn't up to it yesterday, but I'm ready to answer your questions now." She paused, raising her eyebrows. "Assuming you have some, that is."

A soft chuckle escaped my lips. "You could say that," I muttered, my voice holding a hint of sarcasm. "I mean, I'm thankful the whole thing with Sam's stepfather is over, but I feel like I woke up in a whole new world yesterday. So yes, I have a lot of questions. Too many to count. And there are probably some I haven't even thought of yet."

"Well, we have plenty of time," Becca said, before walking past me to the door.

Her comment tugged at my heart. After Gabriel had explained that the power Becca used could eventually kill her, I wasn't sure how long we really had. But I put up a brave front and followed her into the house before shutting the door behind me. "I hope so. Can we start tonight? My mind has been spinning with questions since Saturday. I feel like I'm going to explode."

My words brought a genuine smile to Becca's face. "We don't want that to happen."

"Sorry. I can't help being a little dramatic. My reality has just been shattered into pieces. I'm not sure if you know this, but I'm the last person to ever believe in anything superstitious. And now, not only have you shown me that magic and witchcraft exist, but I'm part of it. It's going to take me a while to get used to this."

"Of course, it is," Becca said as though it was the most obvious thing in the world. She placed her briefcase on the kitchen table. "Just let me change into something a little more comfortable. I have a feeling it's going to be a long night."

"That depends on how much you haven't told me," I mused quietly before raising my voice. "No problem. I want to change my clothes, too. They're all dusty from the barn. I'll meet you in the kitchen in a few minutes."

"Okay. Do you still have the doll in your room?"

I had been trying to forget about the box stashed under my bed. The sudden thought of the package Sam's stepfather had sent to frighten me soured my mood. "Yes," I groaned.

"Bring it down. I'm going to start a fire, and I know just what to do with it."

My spirits lifted at the idea of burning the doll to a pile of ash and soot. "Can we put a hex on the guy, too?"

Becca laughed, but shook her head. "No, Gracyn. We've already stirred up enough trouble. Let bygones be bygones."

I huffed. "What good is being a witch if I can't inflict pain on those who deserve it?" After a pause and reading the knowing look in Becca's eyes, I sighed. "Oh, right. I already did that. Got it. Okay. I'll be back down soon."

Without another word, we parted ways. Becca disappeared down the back hallway while I climbed the stairs to my room. After trading my dusty jeans and shirt for navy pajama pants and a white sweatshirt, I ran a brush through my hair. Then I reached for the dreaded package under my bed. I swallowed the bile rising from my stomach when I pulled the box out, careful to keep the lid closed. The last thing I wanted was to get a glimpse of that horrible doll.

By the time I returned downstairs, Becca was digging through one of the bottom cabinets. A few clanks later, she stood up with a pot in her hands. Turning, she shifted her gaze to the box I held, recognition registering in her blue eyes. Determination swept over her expression. She placed the pot on the island and approached me. "I'll take that," she said, her hands outstretched.

"Good. It's all yours." I gave it to her and then brushed my hands off as though I could sweep away the bad vibes it gave me.

Becca carried it over to the stone fireplace and set it on the hearth. "Gabe always leaves the fireplace stocked with wood so that all I have to do is light it when he's gone." She moved the folding screen and lit a match before holding it up to the newspaper crumpled under the split logs. The flame caught onto the paper and began to grow. "There," she said, standing up and moving the screen back into place. "Just give it a few minutes to get going, and then we can take care of business."

Becca crossed the living room on her way back to the kitchen. As she picked up the pot and filled it with water from the sink, I lingered near the island, unable to pry my gaze away from the box near the fire. Knowing the doll hid under the lid unsettled me, as though it would jump out at any moment. *You can't seriously be worried about that,* I thought sarcastically. *How old are you? It's a doll, not a ghost.* As soon as the words rolled out in my mind, I shuddered. If witches existed, then perhaps ghosts and possessed dolls were real as well.

Trying to regain my composure, I looked away from the fireplace. If I was going to handle being a witch, I needed to do it with some confidence and maturity. Shaking the doubts from my mind, I shifted my attention to Becca. "Can I help with anything?" I asked as she positioned the pot on the back burner. She turned the knob, igniting the flame, and adjusted it to a high setting.

"Sure. How about getting started with a salad?"

"Yes. That I can do." *As opposed to what?* my alter ego asked. *Oh, I don't know*, I answered silently. *Maybe accepting that all this witchy stuff is real.*

I rolled my eyes at the voices pitching through my thoughts and opened the refrigerator, glad Becca couldn't see my expression. But that didn't stop the argument from raging on in my mind. *It is real. You know that from everything you've seen in the last few days. The impossible is about to become your reality. The sooner you accept it, the sooner you can adjust to this new life.*

As hard as it was, I had to admit my inner self was right. Pushing the voices aside, I piled lettuce, tomatoes and other salad ingredients on the counter.

Becca and I worked in silence for about fifteen minutes. By the time our dinner was ready, the fire across the room roared, the flames licking the soot-covered stones inside the chimney. "Don't we want to take care of the box before we eat?" I suggested as we carried plates of chicken rigatoni and bowls of salad to the table.

"No. I'd rather eat while it's hot. The box can wait." When I cringed with disappointment, Becca continued. "I'm not going to give that guy any satisfaction. He already made a mess that I had to clean up. I'm not letting him get in the way of a hot dinner. I had a long day, and I'm hungry."

I chuckled. Becca could be very straightforward at times, and I couldn't disagree with her right now. She had a good point. "Okay," I said. "I guess it can wait, then." I sat down across from her, facing away from the living room to avoid looking at the box while we ate. "This looks delicious," I said, gesturing at my plate.

"It does, doesn't it?" Becca smiled and placed her napkin on her lap. "I don't eat much when I'm not feeling well, so it's nice to have an appetite tonight. Today was my first good day in a while. I didn't have a headache, and I actually have some energy."

"Do you think you're healing?" I refused to give up hope that Gabriel was wrong about Becca's health. A part of me felt guilty about her suffering, since she had used her power to help me.

"I wish I knew. I hope so, but it's not like I can go to a doctor and find out what all of this means."

"Gabriel can't help?" I asked before spearing a piece of chicken with my fork.

"He isn't that kind of doctor. He's trained in trauma, not aging, and specifically not aging of our kind."

"What about Cadence? How is she holding up with all of this?"

"I don't understand your question."

"If you and Cadence are connected, and what happens to one of you happens to the other, then is she in pain when you are? Because as far as I've been able to tell, she acts normal when you're sick."

"That's a very good question," Becca said, a thoughtful expression on her face. "I've noticed that, too. I don't know if she doesn't feel my pain, or if she's just resilient."

"But if she doesn't feel your pain, are you two still connected?"

A smile fluttered across Becca's face. "Yes, I'm sure we are. You see, magic isn't always absolute. Sometimes things happen that are contrary to what we would expect, and we can't explain them."

"Oh," I said with a sigh, frustrated by the lack of certainty with magic. It was going to take me a long time to get used this. Trying to remain upbeat, I continued. "I guess the important thing is that you feel better today. I hate watching you deal with those headaches."

"They're no fun, that's for sure." Becca took a bite, chewing thoughtfully. When she swallowed, she focused on me. "But enough about me. What's on your mind?"

I looked up at her, arching my eyebrows. "I'm not sure where to begin. Maybe you can tell me why we're connected to horses. I mean, how did that happen? Or has it always been like that?"

"No, it hasn't been like that forever. It began in the Dark Ages of England. Witches back then weren't always able to blend into society. Misunderstood and feared, they were often cast aside and disposed of.

In the year five hundred and sixty-seven, three young girls suspected of witchcraft were abandoned by their families and sent to live in an asylum which could only be described as hell on earth. The girls were treated like filth, just like any other creature who had the misfortune of ending up there. The asylum had a stable to keep a few horses that plowed the fields and pulled the wagons into town to get supplies. But the caretaker didn't have an ounce of compassion. He treated the horses like property, barely feeding them anything and working them until they were used up. Then he slaughtered them and fed what little meat remained on their bones to the dogs."

Speechless, I felt my jaw dropping, my skin crawling at the thought of such cruelty and torture. "That's horrible. I can't even begin to imagine something so awful."

Becca nodded, her expression somber as she continued. "When one of the girls saw the man whipping a horse until it fell to its knees from exhaustion, she couldn't take it any longer. She snuck out in the middle of the night to look for the horse who had fallen. Somehow she had survived, but barely. The girl found the mare in a stall, lying on a bed of urine-soaked straw, its dirty white coat covered with bloody welts."

"Stop," I said, shuddering. "I don't think I want to know anything more. I'm sorry I asked."

Becca smiled. "I'll get to the good part. I know the beginning is horrific, but you should know this. Anyway, the girl rushed to the horse's side. She wasn't much cleaner than the horse. Her gown was frayed at the edges and smudged with soot after she had been forced to clean the asylum. Dirt caked her face, and her hair was a tangled mess. But for as awful as she looked, she refused to let the caretaker strip her of her spirit. When she crouched next to the horse, she felt a need to protect her. A force rose up inside the girl, and she bonded the two of them with a power I'm not sure she knew she had. After that, the horse grew stronger. The girl visited the mare every night to check on her. She also told the other two girls what she had done, and they each bonded with a horse in the barn. All of them flourished, becoming healthier every day."

"Then what happened?" I asked when Becca paused, relieved to learn the horse had recovered from the abuse.

Becca's expression darkened, worrying me. "The caretaker noticed, and he didn't like it one bit. He caught the girls in the barn one night and accused them of stealing food. They denied it because it wasn't true, but he didn't believe them. He cornered them, telling them they would pay for their crime. Then he began to whip them, sending the horses into a frenzy. The first horse who had been saved kicked its stall door open and charged at the man. As it struck him, the other horses burst out of their stalls. The impact of one of the doors hitting the wall caused a lantern to fall onto some hay. The barn erupted into flames, but the horses and the girls escaped unharmed."

"Where did they go?" I asked, mesmerized by the story.

"To this day, no one knows where they lived for about twenty years because they never told a soul. They hid from society until they felt confident they could fit in so no one would know just how different they were. They went on to thrive for a very long time, having families and passing their bond with a horse to each of their children. They believed that the horse would protect them. The leader, the first girl to bond with the abused horse, was my ancestor. So that is the story of how our coven came to exist. Our bond with horses has served us well, as I'm sure you understand after Gypsy found you in the woods the other night."

"I do." With no further questions about the horses, I asked the next question that had been burning in my mind since Saturday night. "Tell me about our mother. How is she not like us? I don't understand how that could be possible."

"I figured you'd ask that. Before I start, I need you to promise me that what I'm about to tell you will not cause you to hold any of this against her. Your mother has done a lot for you, and for me. She loved you like only a mother can, even though she always knew you'd learn the truth one day."

My heart dropped into my stomach and the fork fell out of my hand, hitting the table with an uneven clank. "So she isn't your mother?"

Becca's gaze shifted downward for a second before her eyes met mine again. "That's right."

The lump forming in my throat took me by surprise. Disappointment shot through me, bringing tears to my eyes, but I blinked them back. "Then we're not sisters?"

Becca reached across the table and placed her hand on mine. "No," she admitted softly. "But that's okay. We are much more than that."

Feeling betrayed by both Becca and my mother, I glared at her. "Then what am I doing here?"

"You are here because this is where you belong. You should understand that now. You couldn't possibly have stayed in Maryland after what happened with your friend's stepfather."

"Yes, you mentioned that on Saturday. But how am I like you if we're not related?"

"I never said we aren't related."

Shaking my head, I couldn't be more confused. "What?" I asked in a quick breath. "You're completely losing me here. Okay, we're not sisters, but we are related. Would you care to elaborate on that?"

"Gracyn, you were born here in Sedgewick. Your birth mother is a witch, but she knew she couldn't raise you. So Sarah, your mother, adopted you. Sarah grew up here and, through some unfortunate events, she found out about us. She was the perfect solution to a very sensitive situation. And she loves you. That much I know."

"Who is my real mother?" As soon as my words were spoken, sorrow raced across Becca's expression. "I'm getting a bad feeling about this. Is she...dead?"

Her eyes glistening with moisture, Becca nodded. "I'm sorry," she whispered.

"Oh." A moment of silence passed while I thought about the woman I would never know. The woman who had given me life. But as quickly as the sadness crept into my thoughts, I willed it to leave. There was no sense in mourning someone I had never known. "Then how are we related? Is it a connection to her, my real mother?"

With a deep sigh, Becca forced out a small smile. "Yes. Now I know this is a lot to handle."

I shifted uncomfortably in my seat, the dinner on my plate getting cold. "You think?" I asked sarcastically. "What else should I know?"

"Just that you were placed in the best hands we could find. Your real mother wanted you, believe me. But she couldn't keep you. It was too complicated."

"It would be a little easier if I knew who she was."

"I'm sure it would be," Becca agreed.

"So that's it? You're not going to tell me who she was?"

"I will, one day. You've been dealt a lot of new information lately. I don't want to overwhelm you."

"It's a little too late for that," I said, the contempt in my voice too thick to hide. "I want to know who she was. I don't think that's too much to ask."

"It doesn't change who you are," Becca replied, ignoring my request.

"That's easy for you to say."

"I know that's how it seems right now," Becca whispered before her voice grew louder. "But there isn't much to tell. She was a wonderful woman who knew the end was coming near for her. She didn't want to keep you if she was going to die."

As much as I wanted to press Becca for more information about my birth mother, I forced myself to let it go. In time, I would ask more questions and hopefully learn who she was. Perhaps I would discover more about myself in the process. But I suspected I wouldn't get more information right now, no matter how hard I pushed Becca.

"I guess I can't blame her for that," I said before changing the subject. "Tell me, who else is like us?"

"I will answer that, but first I need you to promise not to tell a soul."

"Well, considering I'm one of them, I don't think that will be too hard. Let me guess. Lucian."

"That didn't take you long. What gave him away?"

"Oh, I don't know. It could have been the tea that cured my hangover in a matter of minutes." I paused, noticing Becca's raised eyebrows.

But she didn't comment or ask any questions, so I continued. "Or it was when he cornered me in the hall and made everyone disappear last Friday. Now that was like something out of a movie."

Becca's expression fell right away, a serious look capturing her eyes. "What do you mean he cornered you?"

"Nothing, really. I was upset about something, and he was trying to calm me down."

Relief washed over her worried eyes. "As long as it was nothing serious. If he threatens you—"

"Becca," I interrupted. "Stop. He has rescued me twice now." *Three times if I count the night I drank too much.* My memory of the party was vague, but I hadn't forgotten that Lucian carried me out of the woods and gave me to Alex who drove me home. I could still see Lucian's green eyes staring down at me through my drunken haze, his expression concerned, yet disappointed. "Unlike everyone else around here, I'm not afraid of him."

"Just don't get too comfortable around him," Becca said. "He is not to be trusted as I told you before."

"Fine," I said. "But don't forget that before you and Gypsy found me with Sam's stepfather in the woods, Lucian showed up and pulled him off of me."

"I haven't forgotten that because I saw him. And I knew you couldn't have thrown your friend's father ten feet away, at least not without your power."

"If you remember what Lucian did for me, why don't you trust him?"

"There is still a lot you don't know. I can't answer why he seems to always be there when you get in trouble, but until his sister's murder is solved, he is still a suspect, even if the authorities couldn't convict him two years ago."

"What about the rest of his family? Are they all like us?" I asked, changing the subject because I didn't want to speculate on whether or not Lucian had killed his sister. The thought of it made me sick to my stomach, especially after the time I had spent with him. Something in the way he'd told me he hadn't painted anything he cared about since Cassie died made me want to believe in his innocence.

"Yes."

"Even his sister?"

Becca nodded. "Of course. Cassie was actually very special."

"Why wasn't she strong enough to protect herself? Like I did when Sam's stepfather came on to me? I remember feeling almost possessed. Power surged through my veins like fire, and I broke his hand just by squeezing it."

"She couldn't protect herself because she wasn't the one attacked."

Becca's words threw me off. I had no idea what she meant by that. "What? But she was attacked. I read about it online. And you told me she was stabbed in the heart."

"I had to tell you that because if I told you the truth when you first moved here, you never would have believed me."

I scrunched my eyebrows, my gaze locking with her steady blue eyes. "What is the truth?"

"Cassie wasn't the victim in the attack. Her horse was stabbed in the heart, instantly killing both of them."

"What?" I gasped, not sure I heard her correctly. "How could someone kill a horse with a knife? And why?" The thought that someone would viciously attack a horse was no less disturbing than the idea of a child being stabbed.

"You raise a very good point, but I don't have any answers. All I know is that another witch was behind her death."

"Lucian," I said in a single breath, although I wanted to be wrong.

"Yes," she confirmed quietly. "At least he seems to be the obvious suspect. That's why I've been warning you to stay away from him."

My heart sank at this news. As much as I didn't want to believe it, I couldn't ignore the circumstances. "Why would he kill his own sister?"

"I don't know. Sibling rivalry, perhaps? Although it doesn't make sense. As far as I could tell, he was a good brother to her."

"Then why would you suspect him? You said once before you didn't want to speculate on the matter."

Becca glanced at me, her eyes distant as though she remembered a darker time. "I don't feel it's my place to blame someone without concrete evidence. Although I will admit, even I would like to get the closure that comes from knowing who committed such a horrific crime and seeing them punished."

"But you said there are other witches in town. So he can't be the only one who possesses the strength to kill a horse in a single strike. Who else is like us and the Dumantes?"

"The Hamiltons."

"Celeste," I whispered, not at all surprised. But that didn't give me any ideas as to who could have killed Cassie. The least likely suspect in my mind was Celeste.

"Yes. And the Woodsons."

I felt as though the wind had been knocked out of me. I coughed for a moment before catching my breath. "You mean Derek?"

She nodded with a smile.

"Wow. I didn't see that coming. He's so normal. At least compared to Celeste and Lucian. Those two don't surprise me, especially since they both have horses. But Derek? I never expected that. Is there anyone else?"

"A few, but no one else you would know. Of course, that's just our coven. There are other witches across the state and around the world."

"Really?" I asked, curious. Knowing there were more like us somehow made me feel a little more comfortable about being a witch.

"Yes, there are covens all over the world. But there aren't many of us left in Massachusetts, at least not after the trials in the sixteen hundreds."

"The Salem Witch Trials?"

"That's right. They wiped out most of us. I was here in Sedgewick and I managed to keep my identity a secret, so I was spared. That's why, even though it's not the sixteen hundreds, it's very important that you don't tell anyone a thing. Humans can't know about us, not even Alex."

I nodded. The last thing I wanted was to tell Alex I was a witch. I couldn't imagine how he would react, especially after he and Derek had teased me the night we roasted marshmallows around the campfire at the lake. Now I knew how the rumors that Sedgewick was haunted had started, something Derek must also know. But Alex thought it was a big joke, and I wasn't about to burst his bubble.

"About Alex," I started. "Can I date him? I mean, is that okay?" Images of Derek with Lacey and Lucian with Zoe flashed through my thoughts. If they could date humans, I figured I could, too. But I wasn't making any assumptions.

Becca's smile put my worries at ease. "Yes, at least while you're young. We don't have any strict rules on that, although we usually end up with one of our own kind because it's hard to outlive a loved one. And that's what would happen if you married a human."

"Wow," I muttered. "Um, I think I'll stick to dating right now. Marriage seems like a lifetime away." I was more comfortable with being a witch at the moment than I was with the idea of getting married. Feeling awkward, I changed the subject again. "If you're so old, how does no one notice that you're not aging?"

She took another bite of chicken. After swallowing, she looked at me. "I've disappeared from time to time. Sometimes, I move to another town when people start to notice. Then, after that generation passes, I return with a new name. It's really not that hard. And I never leave the state."

I shook my head, not sure how much more of this conversation I could take. "Sounds like I have a lot to learn."

Becca flashed a faint smile. "I know it's complicated. The more I tell you, the crazier it all must seem to you."

"Are you trying to tell me there's more?"

"There's always more in the supernatural world. But maybe for now, we can change the subject to something a little more, shall we say, normal? How was school today?"

"Oh, no. You're not getting off that easy. I want to know about spells and using the power I have."

"We talked about that on Saturday. Yes, you have supernatural power. You will always be able to protect yourself as you did with your friend's stepfather. But it's not something we use unless we have no other choice, except for the garden, of course. We use it to survive and live in this world. Other than that, there is usually no need for it."

"Oh, I don't know. Lucian's tea sure came in handy a few weeks ago." Becca raised her eyebrows. "Care to explain what happened?"

"Not really," I said, wishing I hadn't brought it up. I wasn't about to admit that I had made a bad decision and drank too much after Alex begged me not to. The important thing was that I had learned my lesson and never again would I indulge in tequila, or any other alcohol for that matter.

"That's what I thought. Well, eat up. We have some unfinished business to take care of." Becca nodded toward the fireplace, reminding me that the doll still needed to be destroyed.

"How about if we do it now?" I asked.

Becca nodded. "Sure. I'm almost done here, although you haven't touched much of your dinner."

"Sorry. My appetite is a little off from all this stuff. Maybe once I see that thing burn, I'll be able to relax a little."

We got up from the table and walked over to the fireplace. I stood a few feet behind Becca as she moved the screen. Then she picked up the box and tossed it into the fire. The flames grabbed ahold of the cardboard, turning it from brown to charred black in seconds. Sparks shot up against the stones, as though the doll exploded inside the box.

After setting the screen back in front of the fire, Becca turned to me. "There. All done."

"Good riddance," I said, mesmerized by the flames. I watched the burning box, hoping my memory of Sam's stepfather would disappear just as quickly.

"Come on," Becca said. "You barely touched your dinner. Maybe you can eat a little more now." She gestured to the kitchen, waiting for me to lead the way.

I nodded and headed back to the table, feeling a sense of peace now that the doll had been reduced to ashes and soot. Becca sat with me as I finished my dinner and the conversation shifted to school. When I told her Alex had asked me to be his date for the Homecoming dance, she grinned, seeming genuinely happy for me.

Witchcraft and anything else related to the supernatural world wasn't mentioned for the rest of the evening. I felt as though I'd had enough for one night. I was certain I would learn more in time, but I needed to pace myself. What Becca had told me tonight would take a while to get used to. Until then, I just wanted to feel like a normal teenager, although I suspected that would be easier said than done.

3

I found it impossible to focus on my homework that night. The most upsetting part of everything Becca had told me was knowing my mother had lied to me for years. I wasn't sure how I felt about that. Anger tried to take over, but a part of me insisted on giving her the benefit of the doubt. I wanted to believe both she and my birth mother, whoever that might be, had made their decisions because they truly cared about me.

I resisted the urge to email or text my mother. She was thousands of miles away, and I was growing more independent by the day. My past flashed through my thoughts, reminding me of the differences between me and my mother. Signs that we were cut from a different mold had been there over the years, but I had never noticed until now.

As the days passed, I missed her, and I wondered if she would ever be part of my life again. Our emails and texts became less frequent. I was slow to respond to her messages, my tone distant. I knew I would have to talk to her about being adopted one day, but I wasn't ready yet.

Pushing my mother aside, I couldn't keep Lucian out of my thoughts. Knowing he was also a witch sparked my curiosity. I wanted to talk to him that week, but I never had a chance. He dodged me in the halls between classes, whether Zoe was hanging onto his arm or he was alone.

Lunch could have been an option, but the one day he showed up and sat by himself, he ran off as soon as he saw me coming. Much to my dismay, he skipped Art for most of the week.

If Lucian wouldn't make himself available at school, then I decided I would have to find him. Wednesday afternoon, I headed out to the barn and tacked up Gypsy. After fumbling with the saddle, I managed to secure the girth. Then I slid the bridle over her ears and secured the chinstrap and noseband, feeling awkward when I started to buckle one of them to the wrong strap. Becca had always made tacking up look easy, and she did it in less than half the time it took me. Gypsy had to notice the difference, but she stood still, waiting patiently while I worked.

As soon as I finished, I led her out of the barn. Her hooves clanked against the gravel stones on the way to the mounting block. The setting sun cast purple waves across the sky, reminding me I didn't have much daylight left. The air was turning cold as night approached, but my turtleneck and jacket kept me warm enough for now.

I halted Gypsy beside the mounting block and climbed into the saddle. Gathering up the reins, I nudged her with my heels and she headed across the driveway at a brisk walk. When we entered the woods, shadows stretched across the trail. A week ago, I would have been terrified to ride off alone as the sun went down. But fear was the last thing on my mind this afternoon. Determination was more like it. I needed to talk to Lucian, and if he wouldn't let me approach him at school, then I would find him. The least I could do was thank him for his help with Sam's stepfather.

Feeling brave, I squeezed Gypsy's sides with my calves. She quickened the pace until she picked up a lazy jog, her ears flicking backward as if making sure I kept my balance. I focused on her rhythm and, within a few strides, began posting to her trot. I relaxed, pushing her to go a little faster. Softening my feel of her mouth, I let out some slack in the reins to allow her the free use of her head and neck.

Good girl, I thought as she marched on ahead. *Keep up the pace, or it'll be midnight before we get home.* As Gypsy settled into a rhythm, I watched the passing trees, careful to keep my knees from hitting one. We trotted deeper into the forest, climbing hills and winding around the turns until we reached the trail opening that overlooked Lucian's estate.

I halted Gypsy in between two trees and studied the stone mansion. The pastures were empty, the property appearing void of life. No lights were on inside or outside, at least as far as I could tell. Not giving up hope that I would find Lucian, I nudged Gypsy back into a trot and guided her down the hill between the fences.

When we reached the backyard, Gypsy slowed to a walk. Occasional stomping and muffled snorting came from inside the barn, breaking through the silence behind the house.

I stopped Gypsy as an unsettled feeling slid over me. I couldn't decide if I should leave or dismount and head around to the front of the house. Before I had a chance to do either one, a man appeared in the barn doorway. He wore brown pants and a thick matching jacket. His black hair was speckled with white, his eyes the color of coal, and his olive skin weathered.

"Hello," he said in a heavy accent. "May I help you?"

I nodded with a faint smile. "Yes. I'm looking for Lucian. Is he home?"

"I don't think he has returned yet, but I don't keep track of him. I just take care of the animals."

"Oh," I said, my hopes deflated. "Well, if you see him, will you tell him Gracyn stopped by? I wanted to talk to him."

"I will relay the message if I get the chance."

"Thank you." I was about to spin Gypsy around when Diesel, Lucian's Doberman, charged around the side of the house. He ran toward Gypsy, his lip curled up, revealing his teeth, and the hair on his back standing on edge. A loud growl rumbled in his throat.

Gypsy flung her head up and quickly backed away. I braced my hands against her neck, my eyes glued to the dog.

"Diesel!" the caretaker scolded, running toward the dog and stopping when the Doberman snapped at him. Without taking another step, the man looked back at me. "I'm sorry, miss. I don't know what's gotten into him. Perhaps you should be on your way."

Nodding, I kept my eyes on Diesel for a moment. His aggressive behavior rattled my nerves, but there was nothing I could do. Then I shifted my gaze to the caretaker. "I've met him before, but he never acted like this. In any case, I'll leave now. Again, please tell Lucian I was looking for him if you happen to see him."

Without another word, I whipped Gypsy around and squeezed her sides. As she launched into a canter and marched up the hill, neither one of us looked back. When we reached the edge of the woods, she slowed before turning onto the trail. Then she surged forward, racing home.

Darkness was falling fast, the shadows sending the woods into a world of black. But the night didn't scare me as much as Diesel's odd behavior. Something seemed off. He knew me, and he had always been friendly. Why he had chased us away was just another mystery I suspected wouldn't be solved any time soon.

The next afternoon, Lucian was sitting at the desk we shared in Art class when I walked into the room. My eyes locked on him, I stopped for a moment before continuing at a slow pace. Taking a deep breath, I weaved around the other tables until I reached him. As I dropped my book bag on the desktop, I watched him, expecting him to avoid me. But he glanced my way, filling me with hope that I could finally thank him for his help with Sam's stepfather.

"Hi," I said as I sat down, my book bag the furthest thing from my mind with those green eyes studying me. He wore a white button-down shirt, the sleeves rolled up to his elbows and the silver cross hanging below the open collar. "I've been looking everywhere for you the last few days. I think we need to talk."

He nodded, his gaze drifting away for a moment. Then he looked back at me, smiling softly. "Really? What about?"

Shaking my head, I almost lost it. "You're kidding, right? Do I need to remind you about Saturday night?"

"No, of course not," he said. "But class is going to start in a minute, and I'm guessing whatever you have to say will take longer than that."

"You think?" I asked, sarcasm rising up in my tone. "Then I'll keep it short. Maybe you can explain why you've been avoiding me for the last few days."

"That's just your interpretation."

"No, I think it's pretty obvious. But I don't understand. I saw you from my window Sunday evening. Why did you ride over just to turn around and leave?"

He shrugged. "I wanted to make sure you were safe, that's all. What did Becca do with that guy Saturday night?"

"She took care of him. He won't be bothering me or anyone else for that matter any time soon. Or ever, I think."

Lucian let out a soft chuckle, amusement in his eyes. "That's not surprising. Becca is very good at what she does."

"And what exactly is that?" I asked, wanting to hear him say it even though I knew the answer.

"If I have to tell you, then I shouldn't."

The class was filling up, and the voices humming in the background grew louder. I ignored the noise, keeping my attention on Lucian. "I stopped by your house last night, but you weren't there."

"Yes, I know. I'm sorry about Diesel. He wasn't on his best behavior, and I will make sure he never acts like that again."

I wasn't sure how to react to Lucian's apology since I had been expecting an explanation for the dog's aggression. But I decided not to push for one. "Thank you," I said. "He just startled me, that's all."

"He can be a little difficult when I'm not around."

"Oh. I'll keep that in mind. So," I started before the bell interrupted me. Ignoring it, I lowered my voice. "We still have a lot to talk about."

He shook his head, his eyes shifting to Ms. Friedman. "Not now and certainly not here," he whispered.

"Then when and where?" I asked, determined to get a commitment out of him.

"Soon," was all he said before class began.

After that, I didn't have a spare minute to say another word during class. My frustration running high, I wasn't sure what he meant by soon. My idea of it was later today, but his could be within the next month. Either way, I felt like kicking myself for not thanking him when I'd had the chance.

Please, a sarcastic voice trilled in my head. *You could care less about thanking him. You're just using that as an excuse to seek him out. You seem to have forgotten his critical review of your painting. He ripped you to shreds, and then he saved your butt from Sam's step-father. So you're even. You owe him nothing. If anything, he still owes you an apology.*

Whatever my objective was, it would have to wait. Tearing my thoughts away from Lucian, I turned my attention to Ms. Friedman. Whether or not I could concentrate, I had to at least try. If only I couldn't see Lucian out of the corner of my eye, I might have had a chance to keep up with the day's lesson.

— ~

Sam called that night, providing me with a welcome distraction. I smiled when I read her name on my phone and dropped my pencil, forgetting the Calculus assignment in front of me. "Hi, Sam," I said, leaning back in the desk chair, my gaze drifting to the dark sky outside the window.

"Hi," she said. "How's your week going?"

"Good." I felt like I was hiding something from her, but the last thing I could do was tell her I was a witch. "How about yours?"

"The usual," she said with a sigh. "At least things are back to normal, for the most part." She sounded unconvinced.

"What's that all about?" I asked, suddenly interested.

"It's just weird," she began slowly. "Maybe I'm making too much out of it, but things are really odd right now."

"What do you mean?"

"Well, it's Dad."

A feeling of dread settled in the pit of my stomach. What had happened now? I couldn't wait to hear this. I just prayed it wasn't something

Becca had done. The last thing I wanted was to find out he was back in the hospital with another mystery illness. "What about him?"

"He's different. But in a good way."

Relief flooded me. "So he's not back in the hospital?"

She laughed. "No, it's nothing like that at all. He's been kind of... doting."

"Doting?"

"Yes. Always asking my mom if she needs anything. He's too nice, and it's making me suspicious."

That was the last thing I expected to hear, and it brought a smile to my lips. Becca really had turned him into a nice guy. "Maybe he just realizes what he would have lost if he had died."

"Do you honestly think that could have happened?"

"Well, he was in a coma for several weeks. I suppose it was possible, even though he seems fine now. But what I think doesn't matter. I'm sure the change in him isn't a bad thing, so maybe you should just go along with it."

"I'm trying, but it's taking a little getting used to. I mean, they had an okay relationship before, but it was more business-like. Now they're all touchy-feely, and he's bringing her roses and taking her out for date nights. Even my brother thinks it's a little over the top."

"So you're calling me to complain that your father is being too nice to your mother?" I teased.

"Yeah, it would seem so," she admitted. She paused on the other end before chuckling. "I guess I shouldn't even think about it. You're right. I mean, my mom is so happy. I don't remember ever seeing her this happy. It's like our family went from the complete pits to the other end of the spectrum within a few weeks."

"Sometimes a serious illness or a near-death experience makes people change. I wouldn't obsess over it. You've got your own stuff to deal with. Like those college applications."

"And trying to get a date for Homecoming," she added. "Speaking of which, how's it going with Alex?"

"Great. We're going out Saturday night."

"Aw, first date after getting back together. You know what that means."

"No, actually I don't," I said, thankful Sam couldn't see my grin. I knew exactly what she was insinuating, but I wanted to hear her say it.

"If I have to tell you, then you may be in way over your head."

"I was only kidding."

"I knew that. Well, have fun, but not too much fun."

I rolled my eyes with a groan. "We've only been dating for about a month. It's not that serious, at least not yet."

"Yeah. At least make him wait until the Homecoming dance."

"Sam!" I scolded as a laugh escaped me. "You know, you're going to pay for this when you find a boyfriend."

"Good. When will that happen? Can I come back up there and see that dreamy guy I danced with at the concert? I'd much rather be in your town than here with my sappy family."

"I'm afraid you have to wait for college, but it's less than a year away."

"Thanks for the reminder. I guess I'll have to live vicariously through you until then."

"I don't think you want to do that," I muttered, sounding disenchanted. Before Sam could pick up on my tone, I spoke again, this time forcing my voice to be light and cheerful. "There's still plenty of time to get a date for Homecoming. I'm sure you'll find one, and then you'll be happy you didn't end up stuck here in Massachusetts with me."

We spent the next half hour musing over Sam's potential date prospects for the dance. I enjoyed keeping the topic of conversation on her. There were many things about my new life I could never tell her, and that bothered me. I felt like I was hiding so much, but I had no choice. At least her family problems had been solved, even if she didn't know the truth. I could honestly say I hoped we never discussed her stepfather again. The memory of him unsettled me, and I simply wanted to forget all about him. I knew that wouldn't be likely, but at least for the rest of the night, my wish was granted.

4

A light knock on my bedroom door woke me up Saturday morning. After a long week of putting all my energy into my classes and homework in an attempt to catch up, I had been exhausted last night. Alex's practice session with the band had given me exactly what I needed—a quiet evening at home.

Still sleepy, I opened my eyes. Sunlight peeked around the edge of the curtain, casting a soft glow into the dark room. "Yes?" I answered, sitting up and yawning.

The door opened and Becca approached the bed. Dressed in jeans, tall brown boots, and a green shirt with three buttons at the top, she appeared ready to start the day. "Good morning. I hope I didn't wake you up."

"You didn't," I lied. "What time is it?"

"Seven-thirty."

No wonder I was so tired. It was way too early for a Saturday.

"Gabe and I are about to leave for New Hampshire. We thought it would be nice to take a drive today," Becca said.

"Okay. When will you be home?"

"Sometime later this evening. Would you mind letting the dogs out a few times and cleaning the stalls?"

"Of course not. Consider it done." She didn't even need to ask. I enjoyed taking care of the horses since it forced me to put my homework down for a while.

"Thanks." She lingered in my room, seeming hesitant to leave. "I plan to be home tomorrow if you'd like to head out on the trails together."

I nodded. "Sure. That would be nice."

"Great," Becca said with a smile. "All right then. We're leaving in a few minutes. We might get home late, so don't hold up dinner for us."

"I won't. Alex is taking me out since he had to practice with the band last night. But I'll put the horses away before I head out. Have fun today."

"You, too. Don't study too hard," she teased with a sparkle in her eyes.

"I'll try not to," I replied.

"Okay. See you either later tonight or tomorrow." She gave me a quick wave before turning and leaving my room.

As soon as the sound of her footsteps faded in the hall, I plopped down on my pillow and pulled the covers up to my chin. Not ready to face the day, I drifted back to sleep.

— ~

I woke up about an hour later and threw on a pair of jeans and a purple sweater. After pulling my hair into a ponytail, I headed downstairs. The dogs slept on their beds next to the table, opening their eyes long enough to glance at me before dozing off again. Ignoring them, I went straight to the kitchen where I grabbed a bowl of cereal.

As soon as I finished breakfast, I laced up my hiking boots and grabbed my black jacket still dusty from my time spent cleaning stalls a few days ago. Once outside, I marched across the driveway while the dogs darted ahead of me. The morning sky was clear, the sunlight shimmering above the yellow and orange leaves that circled the farm like a halo.

With nothing but my thoughts to occupy the silence, I snatched Gypsy's halter from the hook on her stall door and walked out to the pasture where she met me at the gate. She nickered softly, her reddish coat gleaming and her gaze on me as I approached. I slipped the halter over her nose, sliding the headpiece behind her ears. After securing the chinstrap under her throat, I led her back to the barn.

Five minutes later, I finished tacking up. Then I climbed into the saddle, gathered the reins and squeezed Gypsy's sides with my calves. We set off at a brisk walk, heading out on the trail. The air was crisp, and a light breeze whistled through the trees. Hues of gold, orange and red sparkled deep within the forest.

In no hurry, I kept Gypsy at a walk while listening to the birds and enjoying the kaleidoscope of fall colors. After passing the garden, we continued until we reached the gateway to Lucian's estate. In spite of my efforts to ignore the mansion, I couldn't resist peeking at it out of the corner of my eye. The three horses grazed in the field, not seeming to notice Gypsy in the woods on the other side of the fence. My thoughts instantly drifted to Lucian, and I snapped my attention back to the trail ahead. The last person I wanted to think about this morning was Lucian. I couldn't figure out why he had helped me and then barely gave me a chance to thank him in the days that followed. Confused, I shook my head, attempting to push him out of my thoughts.

Why even try? a snarky voice rang out in my mind. *He's gotten under your skin. Just admit that his green eyes and deep voice have put you under a spell. No matter what happens at this moment, you're a far cry from being able to forget him.*

I felt a scowl tug at my lips, the beautiful scenery not enough to lift my spirits. I hated it when my inner self was right.

With a huff, I shifted my attention back to the trail, determined to enjoy the day regardless of the dark thoughts rambling through my mind. Gypsy and I continued deeper into the forest, sticking to the trail. I knew better than to stray into the woods after finding myself lost and disoriented in the fog weeks ago.

Ten minutes later, we came to a fork. The last time I had been here, Becca had taken a right which led us back home, but I wasn't ready to return yet. Feeling adventurous, I steered Gypsy to the left and we headed down a hill. At the bottom, we crossed a shallow stream, her hooves splashing through the water. I grabbed ahold of her mane when she jumped up the bank on the other side and continued along the trail.

Without worrying about where the path would lead, I rode at a steady walk for about a half hour. When a clearing loomed beyond the trees up ahead, a flash caught my eye. All I could see was a white shape floating over the ground, every few seconds lifting up into the air. Curious, I guided Gypsy to the edge of the woods. We emerged out from under the cover of the trees, and I halted her in front of a post and rail fence.

A horse and rider cantered down the long side of a sand arena, approaching a jump made of white standards and red and white-striped rails set about four feet high. The horse's shiny white coat reflected the sunlight. The rider wore a black velvet helmet and tall black boots. Holding her shoulders straight and tall, she kept the horse at a steady rhythm until they reached the base of the jump. As the horse extended its neck in its approach, I held my breath. With precision, the horse soared into the air, tucking its knees up to its chin. The rider rose out of the saddle, her arms following the horse's movement and allowing it the free use of its neck to clear the rails.

After landing, the horse and rider cantered around the end of the ring before heading across the diagonal where two more jumps were set up. Without missing a beat, they approached the line. The horse lifted off the ground, clearing the first hurdle in perfect form. Then it took two steps and leaped over a second jump nearly three feet wide.

I watched the performance, my breath taken away. The horse and rider moved as though they were one. The horse's legs and belly were splattered with sand, its coat glistening with sweat. After soaring over two more jumps down the long side closest to me and Gypsy, they slowed to a walk. Still amazed, I dropped the reins and clapped.

The rider turned her head, seeming to notice me for the first time. Pleasantly surprised to see Celeste staring at me from under her helmet, I smiled. She looked so different with her hair pulled up, but her eyes gave her away.

I waved, catching her attention, and she guided her mount toward me and Gypsy. The horse's flanks heaved with each breath, but Celeste didn't appear winded at all. The reins slipped through her fingers, letting the mare stretch her neck long and low.

As soon as they stopped in front of me and Gypsy, Celeste unhooked the chin strap to her helmet, letting it dangle over her shoulder.

"Hi," she said, her eyes shifting as though she felt embarrassed from being watched. "How long have you been here?"

"Just a minute or two," I replied. "You looked incredible. That was the most amazing thing I've ever seen. Those jumps are huge."

Celeste shrugged. "Thanks, but it's really nothing. A good workout like this helps me unwind on the weekends."

"Do you do this a lot?"

"What?"

"You know, fly to the moon over those jumps," I explained with a sweep of my hand.

"Oh, no," Celeste said, stroking her mare's neck. "It wouldn't be good for her legs. But I ride almost every day, either working on our flatwork in the ring or heading out on the trails."

"I can't believe I've never ridden over here before. Maybe we can ride together sometime."

"As long as you meet me here." When I shot her a quizzical look, she continued. "I only ride out in the other direction. I won't go near the Dumantes' property."

"Got it," I said. "But I had no idea you lived so close. Why didn't you tell me?"

"It never seemed important. And I never expected you to show up here. What are you doing this far from your sister's house?"

"Just taking a morning ride."

"It doesn't bother you to pass the Dumantes' farm?"

"No," I said, my voice flat. The section of woods hidden by the fog off the trail was a different story, but I didn't want to think about that.

"It should," she muttered, her gaze drifting to the forest beyond me for a moment. "But you really have nothing to worry about."

"What do you mean?" I asked, confused.

"Nothing. Sorry, sometimes I think out loud. So, how's it going with Alex?"

I frowned, not wanting to talk about Alex. "Celeste, I know," I blurted out, ignoring her question.

Her expression softened, and she seemed relieved. "You do?"

"Yes. Becca told me. Well, she kind of had to. Things weren't making sense."

Celeste's warm brown eyes met mine. "I'm glad you know. I wanted to tell you so badly, but it wasn't my place. I knew you were like us when you didn't need your glasses anymore. How are you dealing with it? I mean, I've known what I am ever since I can remember. I can't imagine thinking I was human only to find out I'm not."

"It's been an adjustment," I said slowly. "I mean at first, I didn't know what to think."

"And now?"

I lifted my shoulders and shook my head. "Honestly, I still don't. It's going to take some getting used to. But at least I have Gypsy." I dropped one of the reins and stroked her neck. "She's great. I love having a horse. I was afraid of horses until I moved here."

"Now that's just crazy," Celeste teased.

"Maybe for you. But I fell off on a trail ride when I was young, and I never got over it. At least not until recently. So maybe we can hang out more now? I have a lot to learn. Will you help me understand all of this?"

"I can try," Celeste said. "But it's really not that exciting. It's nothing like you see on TV or in the movies. We live very quiet, uneventful lives, at least we did until—" Once again, darkness clouded her eyes as her voice tapered off.

"Until Cassie was killed," I said, finishing her sentence.

"Yes," she whispered, her gaze drifting down. A few seconds later, she lifted her eyes and a smile peeked out across her face. "I'm sorry. How do I keep doing that? Here you are dealing with a major life-changing situation, and I can't stop thinking about a crime that happened two years ago."

"It's okay. I wasn't here when it happened and I never knew Cassie, so I guess I feel a bit removed from it. But let's not talk about that right now."

"Good idea. You must have a million questions."

"You could say that," I replied with a smile. "But Becca's been great. She said I can ask her anything." *Except who my real mother is*, I added to myself. A part of me wanted to ask Celeste if she knew who my mother was, but I couldn't find the right words. "Is this why you've been so distant over the last few weeks?"

She shook her head. "No. I was just distracted by...well...you know, him. And no matter how hard I try to get past the fact that Lucian is back to stay for now, I don't think I can." Fear settled over her expression, as though she had given up trying to fight it.

"Maybe you just need more time."

Celeste shook her head. "No. I'll tell you what I need. I need Cassie's killer to be caught and punished. Until then, I don't think I'll be able to sleep again."

"I know," I said quietly. "Becca said the same thing. That catching the person who did it would give everyone in town closure."

Celeste gave a subtle nod.

I took a deep breath, wanting to shift the conversation to something a little more uplifting. "Well, you have a friend you can turn to if things get too tough."

"Really?" Celeste asked as if she wasn't sure she believed me.

"Yes, of course. And now we have something pretty important in common. I'll help you take your mind off Lucian, and you can tell me everything I should know about being a witch."

"That would be great. You know, I never had a lot of friends."

"You have one now," I declared with a smile, meeting her gaze. "So, this is Serenity? She's beautiful."

"Thank you. She means the world to me."

"You two make an awesome team. I still can't believe how amazing you looked flying over those jumps. Alex told me you compete during the summer, but I never realized how good you were."

"Thanks. It's my thing." She gave her mare a pat on the shoulder. "Speaking of Serenity, I should probably untack her so that she can go out for the rest of the day. Do you mind?"

"No, not at all. I should head home, anyway."

"Well, thanks for stopping by today. It was a nice surprise."

"You're welcome, even though I still think you should have invited me over sooner," I teased lightly.

"Sorry," she said, her tone sounding a little guilty. "Be careful on your way home."

I smiled, not worried at all. I had gotten here safely, and I trusted Gypsy to get me home. "I'll be fine. Have a good day, and I'll see you Monday at school."

After nodding, she turned Serenity around and they headed toward the gate on the other side of the ring. Gypsy and I set off through the woods along the trail that had brought us here, my conversation with Celeste replaying in my mind on the way home. I liked knowing we were both witches and I hoped we would talk more about it in the future. She seemed hesitant to say much today, perhaps because she hadn't been expecting me to show up.

We'll get to know each other better, I thought confidently. *Just give it some time.*

A half hour later, Gypsy and I arrived home. After turning her out, I retreated into the house, hoping to get a little homework done before my date with Alex.

5

lex arrived at six o'clock as he had promised. An hour before he pulled into the driveway, I brought the horses in, fed them, and let the dogs out one last time. Then I showered and dressed in jeans, a black sweater, and matching boots. My hair fell in waves over my shoulders and silver hoops hung from my ears. After dealing with Sam's stepfather last weekend, I was looking forward to a simple, predictable date. And I knew I could count on Alex for that.

"Hi," I said, greeting him as he walked up the porch steps while I locked the door. Turning, I smiled at him, once again impressed by his rock-star look with his hair pulled back and a small earring in one ear. His black shirt strained against his broad shoulders, the tails falling over the waist of his jeans. Behind him, the sun had dropped below the trees surrounding the farm, sending a chill into the air.

"Hi," he replied, an appreciative gleam in his dark eyes. "You look nice."

"Thank you," I said, closing the distance between us, my jacket folded over one arm. "So do you."

Alex stood in front of me, blocking my path to the steps. "Are Becca and Gabriel home?"

"No. They went to New Hampshire for the day and said they'd be back late."

"Good. Then we have some privacy." With a sly grin, he reached for my waist and pulled me toward him before kissing me.

I leaned against him, sliding my free arm around his shoulders. He tasted minty like he had brushed his teeth right before leaving to pick me up. His cologne smelled spicy, and his embrace felt warm and strong. I closed my eyes, savoring the moment. His chest was rock-solid, his lips soft, and his kiss mind-numbing. No matter how many times he kissed me at school, he never pulled me into a trance like he did when we were alone.

A tingling sensation rippled through my veins when his tongue touched mine. I took a deep breath, feeling my chest expand against him.

He seemed to take my sigh as a cue and lifted his lips away from mine. "Everything okay?" he asked, his voice hesitant.

"Yes," I stated. "Everything is fine. But aren't you supposed to do that when you bring me home?"

"Maybe. But I don't always do what I'm supposed to," he teased. When I raised my eyebrows, he continued. "Don't worry. I won't disappoint you later."

I let out a soft laugh. "I'm going to hold you to that."

"A little pressure. I like it," he said with a smile. "Ready to go?"

"Yes. And I'm hungry. Where are we going?"

"The Witches' Brew if that's okay. It shouldn't be too crowded now that the festival is over."

"Sounds great to me."

"Good. They make an awesome hot cider this time of the year. I think you'll like it."

"Then I'll have to try it."

"Yes, you will." Alex dropped his arms from around my shoulders and took my hand before we walked down the steps to his Jeep. After he helped me into the passenger seat, he jumped in behind the wheel and started the engine.

Ten minutes later, we arrived on Main Street. Alex had been right about the town being quiet tonight. The shops were closed, their windows dark, and streetlamps lit up the sidewalk, glowing in the early evening twilight. After parking on the street, we didn't pass a single soul on our way to The Witches' Brew.

Once inside, we found a booth along the wall and waited for menus. The hum of muffled chatter hung in the background from the handful of people sitting at tables and the bar. I glanced around, wondering if Mr. Wainwright was at the bar, but I didn't see him. As I shifted my attention to Alex, a waitress dropped off two menus and told us she would be back in a minute.

"Have you been here since the night you came to listen to us?" he asked while she walked away.

"Just last Saturday. Sam and I ate outside before the concert."

"What did she think? I don't mean just about this place, but about the whole town."

I smiled. "She was completely enamored with the town. A few days ago, she was complaining about being home. She asked if she could move in with me, but she was kidding, of course."

"Well, one weekend in this town isn't enough to know what it's like to live here," Alex said. Then something seemed to catch his attention behind me, and his gaze shifted.

"What is it?"

He shook his head, a frown flattening his expression. "I'm sorry, but you'll have to excuse me. I'll be right back." With a huff, he slid out of the booth and walked away.

I turned around and craned my neck until I saw Zoe sitting alone in a booth, her cell phone up to her ear and an agitated look on her face. Her black hair fell over her phone, her eyes scanning the bar.

Not wanting Zoe to catch me watching her, I faced forward and concentrated to pick up Alex's voice.

"Zoe, this is quite the surprise," Alex said. "I didn't expect to see you here. And alone."

"Thanks for the reminder, cuz," she said. "If you must know, I'm waiting for someone."

"Let me guess. Lucian?"

"It's none of your damn business."

"I'm making it my business, Zoe. You look miserable. What's going on?"

"He was supposed to be here an hour ago. But don't spread that around. The last thing I need are rumors circulating that I got stood up."

Alex took a deep breath and softened his tone. "I'm sorry. Really, I am. But I don't understand what you see in that guy. Do I need to remind you that he killed his sister?"

"No, you don't need to remind me that he was a suspect. But I think I need to remind you that he wasn't convicted. So drop it. He's back and we're together, I think."

"Look, I don't care how long you date the guy, I'm never going to like it. Why do you do this to yourself? He can't even show up to dinner in town? He's not good for you, and you know it."

"He's fine for me," Zoe declared defiantly. "And he'll be here."

"Really? When?"

"Soon."

"How do you know that?"

"I just do. He won't stand me up. I left him a few messages, so he'll be here."

"And you really believe he's going to drop whatever he's doing to run to you? You're the only reason he's free. Of everyone around here, the one he needs to treat well is you."

"Alex, keep your voice down. I don't need anyone overhearing you."

I raised my eyebrows wishing I could join them and find out what that meant. But I knew better. The afternoon Zoe had appeared at Lucian's when we had been working on our art project flashed through my mind. I had a feeling I wouldn't be well received if I approached her tonight, or ever.

"It's no secret you were his alibi," Alex said quietly before raising his voice. "All I'm saying is that there are lots of guys who would give anything to go out with you. And any one of them would treat you better than he does. Lucian is just using you. Can't you see that?"

"That's enough. I didn't wait an hour tonight to be lectured by you. So why don't you get back to your date and leave me alone?" she hissed.

"Because in case you haven't figured it out, I care about you and I hate seeing you miserable. He's not making you happy. I don't get it."

"He will. It's going to get better. He's still adjusting to being home. And I don't think he likes to come to town much because he knows what people think of him. I just have to be patient."

"Oh, Zoe," Alex let out with a disappointed sigh. "You really have a thing for him. Why? What do you see in him?"

"You'd never understand, Alex. Not all of us have the perfect life."

"Perfect? Is that what you think?"

"Yes, that's exactly what I think. You're in a band, you've probably already been accepted to an Ivy League college, and you're on your way to being class valedictorian. You've got a nice girlfriend and, to top it all off, you make it look easy. Well, not all of us can be perfect."

"What's with the jealousy tonight? I don't think you're seeing things clearly right now, so I'm not even going to comment on that. Now, do you need someone to take you home?"

"No," she said flatly. "I want you to get back to your date and stop worrying about me. I can take care of myself. I always have."

"You know, sometimes it's okay to let someone care about you. I hate seeing what he's doing to you. I know it's not just tonight, either. He's gotten under your skin which, for the life of me, I can't understand. I've told you before you should break up with him once and for all."

"I think I can make my own decisions."

"I'm not going to change your mind, am I?"

"When have I let you, or anyone else for that matter, make decisions for me?" she countered.

A long pause passed before Alex spoke in a softer tone. "You're right. You've made it clear that you listen to no one, even the people who really care about you." I sensed the disappointment in his voice and it tugged at my heart. "Fine. I'll leave you to wait alone. Besides, I need to get back to Gracyn. But Zoe?"

"What now?" she asked, her voice sarcastic.

Alex didn't acknowledge her bitterness. Instead, he spoke in a caring voice. "If you need anything, I'm always here. Call or text me day or night, okay?"

"Thanks," she said, sounding grateful, the contempt in her tone gone. "Now go. At least one of us has a date waiting."

That was the last I heard. A minute later, Alex returned to our table. "Sorry about that," he said, sliding into the seat across from me.

"Everything okay?"

"I'm not sure. But for now, yes. Did the waitress take our drink order?"

"No. She must be waiting for you to return." I opened a menu, but my mind was reeling over what I had just heard. A part of me felt badly for Zoe. She seemed to really care about Lucian, and yet he didn't appear to feel the same about her. Even though I hardly knew her, my heart went out to her. Lucian seemed to be taking advantage of her and that wasn't right.

Stop worrying about a relationship that doesn't involve you, a knowing voice in my head warned. *You know nothing about Lucian and Zoe, and it would be better for everyone if you stayed out of it. Unless, of course, you can't help yourself. Now that would be a disgrace. You managed to land one of the most sought-after guys at school. You'd be a fool to sabotage what you have with Alex for a guy who could have killed his sister.*

Anger at my inner self for doubting Lucian's innocence fired through my veins. Taking a deep breath, I shoved my thoughts to the furthest corner of my mind and looked down at the menu. But I didn't have a chance to scan it before I heard Alex swear under his breath.

"Well, I'll be damned. He actually showed up."

"What?" I asked, whipping around before I realized what I was doing. I caught sight of Lucian standing beside Zoe's table, his black coat hiding his tall frame and his hair disheveled, as though he'd run his hands through it hundreds of times. Turning to look back at Alex, I listened in on Lucian and Zoe.

"Zoe, sorry. Thanks for waiting."

"No problem," she said, her voice dripping with sarcasm. "Would you like to tell me where you've been?"

"I said I was sorry. I had to take care of a situation."

"A situation? Think you could spare some details?"

"If you must know, my mother's horse went down with colic tonight. I couldn't leave until I knew she was okay. I'm sorry it took so long, but I had to make sure she was stable."

"You could have called."

"I know, and again, I'm sorry. I didn't have a free moment to use the phone. I was so focused on getting her up on her feet that I couldn't think about anything else." Lucian sounded frazzled, and I wondered what that meant about his mother if her horse was sick.

Pushing my thoughts aside, I shifted my attention to Alex, pleased to see the dark expression on his face had disappeared.

"Well, she looks okay now," he said.

"Zoe?"

"Yes," he replied with a nod. "I don't like seeing her upset like that."

"I'm sure you don't." I offered him a faint smile, proud to be with a guy who cared so much about his family. But now that it seemed Zoe was okay, I hoped Alex and I could enjoy our evening. "Maybe we can get back to our date?"

"Sorry. I guess it's easy for me to fall into the big brother role with her sometimes. She puts up a tough front, but I know she's vulnerable. And she doesn't have anyone else looking out for her. If I don't do it, no one will."

"That's very sweet of you. I think it's great you care so much about her."

"Thank you for understanding. You're awesome."

I wished I could agree with him. If he knew the thoughts I'd had about Lucian, he might not think so, either. Before I could say another word, the waitress appeared. After ordering the hot cider, we turned our attention to the menus. Minutes later, she returned with the drinks, took our dinner order, and left again.

I was thankful that the conversation shifted to lighter topics for the rest of the night. I told Alex about my visit to Celeste's farm and how impressed I was with her riding talent. Then he filled me in about spending his day delivering hay and doing homework. We laughed when we realized we had both tackled the books on a Saturday afternoon, something no high school senior wanted to admit. Then we talked for hours, enjoying our dinner and each other's company.

When Alex drove me home at midnight, it felt as though he had just picked me up. Like a perfect gentleman, he walked me up the porch steps. The single light next to the door glowed in the darkness, and frigid air had taken over the night, causing me to hug my jacket around my chest.

"Cold?" Alex asked as we stopped in front of the door.

"I'm fine."

"Oh, too bad. I was going to offer to warm you up."

"I don't need to be cold for that."

"Good answer," Alex said before kissing me. When he pulled away, he smiled. "I'm really looking forward to the dance."

"Me, too."

He kissed me again and, after lifting his lips away from me, he touched his forehead to mine. "Thanks for coming out tonight. I had a great time."

"Thank you for asking me."

"We're starting to sound like an old couple that's been together too long," Alex said with a groan.

"What's wrong with that?"

"Nothing, I guess, if you like boring."

I smiled. Knowing that a supernatural realm existed and I was part of it, I liked boring a lot more than I ever expected to. But Alex couldn't possibly understand that. "You are anything but boring," I declared, my words seeming to brighten his spirits when his serious frown softened.

"Well," he said, squeezing my hand. "I should let you go in. It's only going to get colder out here tonight. I heard we're in for a frost."

"Okay. See you Monday?"

"Of course. Have a good day tomorrow and don't work too hard."

"I'm sure I will," I answered with a soft laugh as I unlocked the door. Turning, I flashed him one last smile before letting myself in. After shutting the door behind me, I leaned against it for a moment, savoring my memory of Alex. Everything about him made me happy. Tonight had been just what I needed, except for the scene with Lucian and Zoe.

With a groan, I rolled my eyes. Why did I have to remember that? Now I probably wouldn't be able to stop thinking about Zoe's bruised ego when Lucian had been late and Lucian's story that his mother's horse was sick. All I wanted was to come home from a date with Alex and think of only him for the rest of the night. I had a feeling that was too much to expect.

6

The following week began slow and steady. Celeste opened up a little and we talked more than usual between classes, although she still refused to eat lunch in the cafeteria. She seemed more relaxed with me, something I attributed to the one thing we had in common—being witches. Oddly enough, as my memory of breaking Sam's stepfather's hand and cursing him faded, I began to feel like the girl I used to be back home. I didn't feel like a witch. I still didn't know any spells or magic, and I was beginning to wonder if I ever would. I supposed I should accept that being a witch might only mean getting to live longer. Maybe Becca was right and nothing would change.

Alex found me every chance he got, taking my hand or draping an arm over my shoulders, not seeming to know whenever something was bothering me. Lucian avoided me, but that was nothing new. He had enough problems without me grilling him about witchcraft. And even if I had the chance to ask him any questions, I suspected he'd give me no answers.

Wednesday afternoon after returning home, I headed straight for the kitchen to grab a snack. As I studied my options in the refrigerator, Snow wandered in from the hallway leading to Becca and Gabriel's room. I shut the stainless steel door and looked at the dog before my eyes wandered to the corridor she had emerged from.

No way! Don't even think about it. That's Becca and Gabriel's private room, and you have no business going in there.

I opened the refrigerator again, but my thoughts lingered on the part of the house I had never seen. The possibilities of what could be hiding at the end of that hallway seemed endless. The idea that Becca and Gabriel had some books of spells or other magical things in their room snuck into my mind.

Shutting the refrigerator door, I turned, studying the dogs who now slept on their beds. Their eyes were closed, their chests slowly rising and falling. They couldn't tell Becca and Gabriel, could they? *Don't be crazy,* I scolded myself. *The dogs can't talk. How in the world would they be able to tell Becca and Gabriel if I took a quick look around their bedroom? I'll only be a few seconds. The dogs won't even know I'm gone.*

With a deep breath, I mustered up the courage to do what I knew was wrong. Then again, Becca hadn't been right to keep secrets from me. *Two wrongs do not make a right,* a pesky voice reminded me.

Oh, shut up, I told it.

Darting out of the kitchen before I could change my mind, I crept down the hall to the master suite. The door to the bedroom was ajar, and I slipped through it.

Sunlight filled the room, streaming in through two windows on the side wall. A king-sized bed with a wrought-iron frame and thick red comforter took up most of the room, the headboard centered between the windows. Nightstands with matching lamps were on each side, and a dresser and chest of drawers stood against the wall across from the bed.

At first glance, everything appeared to be in order. I studied the entire room, searching for anything that might serve as a clue. But nothing caught my eye, at least not at first. At the back of the room were several doors. I walked toward them, opening one at a time. Closet. Bathroom. Closet. I quirked my eyebrows at the last door, wondering what lurked behind it. I placed my hand on the knob, hoping it was unlocked. A breath of relief escaped my lips when I felt the handle turn.

Pushing the door open, I peeked into the room, not quite sure what to expect. A mahogany desk sat in the center, a computer screen angled on the corner. Floor to ceiling bookshelves lined the side walls. Across from the door were three tall windows covered with long curtains blocking the sunlight.

I stepped into the room, first scanning the shelves and finding mostly textbooks. Some of them were bound in leather with gold scripted lettering, appearing quite old. I ran my fingers over them, looking for witchcraft titles. But all I found were topics on anatomy, pharmaceuticals, and other medical subjects.

Giving up on the books, I walked over to the desk and tried to open a drawer in the side cabinet. My efforts proved to be futile when it didn't budge. That sparked my curiosity, but I was no expert at picking locks. I would just have to wonder what Becca and Gabriel kept in them. *Probably just some legal documents like tax returns,* I thought. If only I believed that.

Trying not to dwell on the locked drawers, I shifted my attention to the desktop. Running my hand over the wood, I studied the items spread out over the surface. Pencils, pens, a phone charger, and a small wooden box. I stopped when I noticed an amber rock cut like a diamond, its honey-color nearly blending into the wood. Mesmerized, I felt drawn to it and I couldn't resist the urge to touch it.

As soon as I did, a jolt of electricity shocked me and I snatched my hand away. My heart fluttering, I studied the stone, my eyebrows raised. Tempted to try again, I lowered my hand until it was almost an inch away from the rock. I hesitated, something telling me not to touch it again. I knew what I felt, and I wasn't ready for another shock.

Hmm, I thought. *I'll have to ask Becca about this.* Then I shook my head with a frown. *Good luck with that. How are you going to explain being in her room? You can't, so you'll just have to keep guessing.*

With a huff, I gave the rock one last glance before scanning the room again, searching for anything that would help me know more about the witches of Sedgewick. Finding nothing that caught my eye, I gave up. Defeated, I left the study and returned to the bedroom.

I was about to head into the hallway when a photograph on the dresser caught my attention. Stopping dead in my tracks, I stared at the image of Becca holding an infant with a pink cap on its head. Instead of smiling, Becca appeared sad, her eyes glistening with moisture. I studied the picture, wondering who the baby was.

My thoughts were interrupted when the dogs started barking. Jolted back to reality, I raced out of the room, hoping Becca or Gabriel hadn't come home early.

By the time I emerged from the corridor, the dogs were pacing in front of the door, barking and growling, the hair on their backs standing on edge. They began to quiet down until a knock sounded, setting them off again. My nerves frazzled, my heart took off at a runaway pace.

I rushed to the door, pushing the dogs out of the way when I reached it. "Scout, Snow! Settle down," I commanded. As soon as they stopped barking, I spoke up. "Who is it?"

"Lucian."

My pulse quickened again in spite of my fading fear. I opened the door far enough to slip outside without letting the dogs escape. Standing on the front porch, I folded my arms across my chest, my eyes meeting Lucian's familiar green ones. "What are you doing here?" I asked him coolly.

He stepped back and leaned against the railing, his silver cross necklace dangling against his gray shirt. "Take a ride with me?" he asked with a hopeful smile.

I glanced beyond him at Shade who waited patiently in the middle of the driveway, his ebony coat glistening in the sun. The reins were looped over his neck, the buckle resting on his withers in front of the saddle.

Moving my gaze back to Lucian, I asked, "Why would I want to do that?"

He raised his eyebrows and tilted his head, watching me as if confused by my hesitation. "You wanted to talk, didn't you? Well, now's your chance."

"I don't understand why we can't talk at school."

"You know that's complicated. Zoe is there, but honestly, why would you want to be seen with me?"

I narrowed my eyes, not sure what to say. "I could care less about what anyone else thinks."

"Even Alex? I heard you two are back together. I'm sure you don't want him asking any questions."

"He's not in our Art class and, besides, he doesn't own me. There are things Alex doesn't know about me. Things he'll never know about me."

Lucian didn't bat an eye at my confession. "I can relate," he said, his eyes meeting mine. "So, what do you say? It's a beautiful day."

I looked past him at the golden leaves scraping the blue sky. The air was unseasonably warm and comfortable, tempting me to accept Lucian's offer to get outside. I knew I could go alone, but the idea of riding out on my own bored me. "That's not a surprise. Every day around here is beautiful. Okay. I'll get my boots."

Without giving myself a chance to change my mind, I retreated into the house, found my hiking boots buried at the bottom of the coat closet and slipped them on. After tying the laces, I rushed back outside to find Lucian waiting on the porch exactly where I'd left him.

"Ready?" he asked.

"Yes."

He gestured for me to lead the way.

"I have to warn you," I began as we headed down the porch steps. "I've only ridden a few times, and I'm not very good."

When he didn't answer right away, I stopped in the middle of the driveway and turned around. "Did you hear me?" I asked.

"Yes, I heard you," he replied with half a smile, his steady gaze locked on me. "But I don't believe you."

"Fine," I let out with a huff. "You'll see for yourself soon enough. Where are we going?"

"There's a trail that leads to a lookout with a view extending for miles. It's beautiful, especially this time of year, and I thought you might enjoy it."

"That sounds nice. I'm sure it's incredible, and I can't wait to see it. Just go easy on me until we get there."

"You're not giving yourself enough credit. I've seen you ride. You'll be fine."

"Thanks for the vote of confidence," I said with a smile before spinning around and heading toward the barn, the gravel crunching beneath my boots. Nerves settled in the pit of my stomach. I had come a long way with my riding, even heading out twice on my own, but I suddenly felt self-conscious to ride with Lucian. I would just have to practice all that I had learned and try not to make a fool out of myself.

Once inside the barn, I grabbed Gypsy's halter and lead rope hanging from the hook on her stall door.

"What are you doing?" Lucian asked, following me down the dusty aisle to the doorway at the other end.

I shook my head in dismay. "You're not seriously asking me that, are you? I'm going to catch Gypsy so I can tack her up."

"You don't need a halter and lead rope," he stated as we walked out to the pasture.

"Of course I do. How else would I bring her in?" We reached the metal gate to the field, but instead of opening it, I leaned my arm on one of the rails and looked at Lucian, waiting for his explanation.

"Just tell her to come in. That we're going for a ride."

I narrowed my eyes in confusion. "How? She's a horse. She doesn't understand words."

"Maybe. Maybe not. But she's your horse, right?"

I shrugged, my eyes locking with his. In that moment, I realized he knew what I was. Perhaps he had known all along. Breaking my gaze away from him, I slipped into the field and secured the gate behind me. I was about to turn when I felt a hot breeze on my neck. Caught off-guard, I whipped around to see Gypsy in front of me. "Hi, girl," I said softly, stroking her cheek. "Ready for a ride?" I held the halter out and she shoved her nose into it. Then I pulled the top strap over her ears and secured the one dangling under her throat.

When I turned back to face the gate, Lucian held it open, a knowing smile on his face. I said nothing as I led Gypsy through the opening and into the barn while he shut the gate behind us.

Halfway down the aisle, I halted Gypsy and attached the crossties to her halter. Lucian appeared as I finished, his smile lingering.

"What did I do now?" I asked, my hands on my hips.

"Crossties?"

"Yes."

"Totally unnecessary. But you'll understand in time."

"Perhaps," I muttered before hanging the lead rope on the nearest hook. "Or you could explain it to me now."

"I think you already know."

With a deep breath, I folded my arms across my chest. We might as well stop beating around the bush and get things out in the open. "Yes. Becca finally fessed up and told me what I am. I also know you're just like me."

"Good. I don't want any secrets between us."

"So you admit that you have special powers?"

"Yes. It would be kind of hard to explain recent events without letting that be known."

I nodded. "I wish you had told me sooner, especially after finding me in the woods a few times."

"It wasn't my place. I knew Becca would tell you everything in a matter of time."

"So instead of telling me, you kept me guessing with tricks like making everyone in the hall disappear. Do you do those kinds of things to everyone?"

"No," he replied. "I never had a reason to. But I needed to get you to listen to me. You're not still upset about the art project, are you?"

I frowned for a moment as his harsh criticism of my work resonated in my thoughts. After a few seconds, I forced myself to let it go. "Kind of hard to remember it after last weekend. And by the way, I haven't had a chance to thank you for helping me. So thank you. But I have one question. How did you know where to find me Saturday night?"

He dropped his gaze to the dusty floor. "Why don't you get tacked up? We can continue this conversation once we head out."

Frustrated that he was dodging my question, I decided not to push for an answer right away. "Sure. I'll get the saddle."

Gypsy was clean enough that she didn't need to be brushed. I hurried into the tack room and returned to the aisle with the saddle in my arms, the girth buckles clanking from under the fleece pad folded over it.

"Here. I can help." Lucian took the pad and placed it on Gypsy's back behind her withers. Then he lifted the saddle out of my arms and placed it on the pad.

"Why don't you get her bridle while I finish with this?" Lucian suggested, sliding the girth off the saddle and attaching it to one side.

"Okay." Without another word, I returned to the tack room and emerged with the bridle hanging from my hand. As Lucian finished with the girth on the other side of Gypsy, I approached her head. After flipping the reins over her neck and removing the halter, I slid the bit into her mouth. Slipping the head piece over her ears, I sensed Lucian approach behind me.

Chills swept through me, and my pulse accelerated. Trying to ignore him, I reached for the chinstrap dangling on the other side of Gypsy's throat. I pulled it under her jaw and started to secure it, stopping when Lucian's hand clasped over mine.

My breath caught in my chest, and I jumped. Turning, I whipped my hand away from him.

"That's the noseband," he said, his expression soft. "Here. The chinstrap goes with this one." He attached the buckle to a strap hanging higher up near Gypsy's eye.

Embarrassed, I felt like kicking myself. I couldn't believe I had been so stupid. I had tacked up all by myself a few days ago, and I had gotten every buckle right. How come I couldn't get them right today? *Because Lucian makes you nervous,* a voice rolled out through my mind. Feeling a blush race across my cheeks, I shoved that pesky thought away.

"Thanks," I said with a deep breath, trying to act nonchalant. "It'll probably take me a few more times to get good at this. Saddles are a lot easier."

He grinned. "You'll get the hang of it one day."

"I hope so," I replied, reaching for the reins at the same time he did. Our hands touched again, only this time he dropped his while I pulled the reins over Gypsy's head. A tingle wormed its way through me, and I instantly scolded myself. *What's wrong with you? This is no time to let Lucian, of all people, get to you. All you want is to learn more about how he helped you and what you are. Maybe he'll know who your real mother is. But that's all. Alex is back in your life, and you don't want to mess that up. So whatever you do, keep this afternoon a fact-finding mission.*

My sights set on the driveway, I turned away from Lucian and led Gypsy out of the barn, hoping I could stick to my plan.

7

As soon as we mounted, Lucian and Shade led the way to the trail at a brisk walk. The forest was entrenched with gold that shimmered from the descending sun, the shadows adding a slight chill to the air. I paid the scenery little attention while I focused on my riding. *Shoulders up, heels down,* I reminded myself, grateful that Gypsy followed Shade in a perfect rhythm and all I had to do was concentrate on my position. I held the reins steady, keeping a soft feel of her mouth while letting her march forward.

The horses' hooves plodded against the ground while silence fell between me and Lucian. Birds chirped from overhead, and squirrels scurried across the trail and up the trees. Blue sky flickered in and out of view above the branches, and a light breeze whispered through the leaves.

Where the trail was wide enough, we rode side by side. When it narrowed, Lucian took the lead. The second time Shade fell behind to walk next to Gypsy, Lucian broke the silence. "I don't know why you seemed worried about riding. You're doing fine."

"It's just new to me. I had a bad experience with horses when I was eight years old. I never thought I'd get over my fear of them, so I'm still getting used to the fact that horses are now part of my life."

"Yes, they are. At least she is," Lucian said with a swift nod in Gypsy's direction. "What happened when you were young that frightened you?"

In as few words as I could manage, I recounted the day the trail horse had spooked, causing me to fall. When I finished, I wondered what he must be thinking. "Pretty awful, huh?" I asked, sneaking a glance at him.

"Yes," he agreed, confusion in his eyes. "But it makes me wonder what you were doing there in the first place."

"Where? On the trails?"

"No. I mean in Maryland. Clearly you belong here. With us."

His words shocked me, and I wasn't quite sure what to say. "I do?"

"Yes. Well, at least with Becca."

"This is quite a turn-around coming from the guy who told me to leave town and never look back a few weeks ago."

"I know. And don't get me wrong, sometimes I think all of you should leave, at least until—" He frowned, his voice dropping away, his last word spoken in a whisper.

"Until what?" I asked gently.

"Until Cassie's killer is found. But given the circumstances of her death, I think you're safe."

I raised my eyebrows, curious. "How so?"

He smiled faintly, looking ahead. "Just trust me."

The conviction in Becca's voice when she had told me Cassie's mare had been attacked and only another witch would have the strength to take down a horse with a knife rushed to the forefront of my thoughts. Part of me wondered if Lucian really had murdered his sister's horse, killing Cassie in the process, and this was his way of telling me he wouldn't hurt me. The whole idea unsettled me, making me shudder.

"I think I'd feel a little better if you explained what you mean by that," I said.

He turned to look at me, his sad eyes meeting mine. "There are a lot of things you can't possibly understand right now. I don't want to over-whelm you. I'd rather let Becca tell you when the time is right."

"Like how she waited until after I was practically attacked to tell me that witches exist and, oh, by the way, I'm one of them? Look, I love her, I really do. But she's not getting a gold star for being up front with me. It could take her months to tell me anything more, so why don't you just tell me what else I should know?"

"There really isn't much to tell. Cassie liked to wander through the woods for hours at a time. So as long as you don't go back into the woods alone again, I think you'll be safe."

"Believe me, I won't be leaving the trail again," I declared. "I learned my lesson." Just the thought of the fog buried in the forest beyond the trail spooked me. I didn't need to be warned because I had no intention of ever repeating that mistake.

"Good. I don't want to have to go searching for you again."

"I never asked you to," I said quietly.

"I know that," Lucian replied, flashing me a rare smile before changing the subject. "But back to your riding. You seem quite comfortable in the saddle now."

"I'm good at pretending," I explained, a teasing hint in my voice. "I'm only kidding. I am comfortable now, but it's all because of Gypsy." I dropped a hand away from the reins to pat her shoulder. "She's been extremely patient with me. When Becca said I should learn to ride, I never thought it would be so easy. I tried to get out of it at first, but she wouldn't take no for an answer."

"And now you know why."

"Yes, I do."

"Aren't you glad you learned? It's so nice out here. You can leave all your problems behind."

"Hmm," I mused. "Yes, it is relaxing. I didn't have a lot of woods nearby where I lived in Maryland. It's quite the change."

"A good one, I hope."

I nodded, taking in the surrounding scenery of gold and orange sprinkled with green from an occasional pine tree. "I think it is. I'm happy here, at least for now. I know I can never go back home, so I might as well find something to like around here." I didn't mean to sound dis-enchanted with Sedgewick, but my tone fell anyway.

"Aw, don't be so hard on us up here. This town is an acquired taste. Surely, it's not as bad as you make it sound."

"No," I admitted with a smile. "It's not. I didn't mean it like that. Besides, I have Gypsy, and she's been great."

"Of course, she has. And you know, for someone who hasn't been riding long, you have good form. You're a natural."

"I am?" I asked, surprised by his compliment. That was possibly the nicest thing he had said to me since I moved to town.

"Yes." He studied me, his eyes dropping down to my heels and back up to meet my gaze. "You're tall and fit. You were built to ride."

"Thank you."

"You're welcome. But do you mind if I give you a few pointers?"

"Not at all. Just remember I've only been in the saddle about half a dozen times."

"Well, first you need to put a little more weight in your heels. Make sure the ball of your foot is on the stirrup iron and push your heel down. A good way to practice is to stand up and stretch your calf muscles. Like this." He stood up in the stirrups, his heel sinking downward as he rose. Still standing, he nodded. "Now you try it."

I buried my hands in Gypsy's mane, leaning on them as I tried to rise, but my lower leg swung back, pitching me onto her neck. Feeling clumsy, I sat down in the saddle. "You make it look easy," I complained.

"I've been riding ever since I can remember. The reason you tipped forward is that you didn't have enough weight in your heels. Push your heels down and try again."

I focused on flexing my ankles down, feeling my calf muscles stretch. Then I stood up again, but this time I remained balanced, straight and tall. Resting my hands against Gypsy's mane, I kept my weight in my heels, finding that I didn't need to lean on her neck. "How's this?"

"Much better. You look a lot more secure now. When you sit down, try to keep your heels exactly where they are right now."

I eased back into the saddle, almost positive that my heels shifted up because the stretching sensation in my calves disappeared. When Lucian sat down, his heels remained lower than the bottom of his stirrup. "How did you do that?" I asked.

"Years of practice. You'll get the hang of it. Just work on that exercise every time you ride."

"Okay. I'll remember that. What else can I work on?"

"Well, you're a little stiff in your hips. You need to relax and loosen up. Let your hips roll with her movement."

I quirked my eyebrows, not sure how to fix that. Feeling a little self-conscious, I tried to move with the sway of Gypsy's back. "Like this?"

"Um, that's a little better. Again, just try to think about it while you're riding."

"Okay. Thanks for the tips. Although I'm not sure how much riding I'm going to do over the next few months."

"Why do you say that?"

"Two reasons. The first is I hear it gets pretty cold around here in the winter."

"That's right. You're from the south. Don't worry, after one winter up here, you'll toughen up."

"Hey," I complained good-naturedly. "I'm tough. We had cold weather in Maryland."

"But not like here."

"Okay, I'll give you that. But I still think I'm going to pick staying warm over heading out on the trails."

Lucian let out a soft laugh. "Fair enough. What's the second reason?"

"School, of course. We're only about two months into the academic year, and I'm already behind."

Lucian shrugged, looking straight ahead. "School's a little overrated if you ask me."

I studied him out of the corner of my eye, raising my eyebrows. "Having a little trouble readjusting, are you?"

"You could say that. The last two years went by really fast. I forgot what it was like to have a set schedule."

"And homework."

"That, too," he said with a groan. "But I do enough to get by."

"What are your plans for next year? College? Because I don't think you can say you want to travel the world first. From what I've heard, you already did that."

My comment pulled a smile out of him. "Yes, I did," he agreed smugly before a frown fell over his face. "But I did it alone. Maybe next time I'll have someone to share it with. Another artist, perhaps? December in Paris is amazing. We could spend the days painting and the nights strolling around the city."

His eyes caught mine as he spoke, and I felt a hot blush light up my face. Looking away, I said, "I'm sure Zoe would love to go with you."

"No," he said quickly. "I wouldn't take her."

My heart skipped a beat, and I swallowed nervously. I hadn't suspected he was talking about me until his last statement. Before my imagination could run away with me, a voice tumbled through my mind. *Don't even go there. Like it matters, anyway. Alex is the best thing that has ever happened to you, and you're not going to screw it up by putting yourself out there for some guy who didn't have a single good thing to say about your art project. Not to mention he could have killed his sister.* Even as those last words sounded in my mind, I knew I didn't believe them.

I didn't have a chance to respond to Lucian's comment. The trail narrowed, and Lucian nudged Shade into a trot. As soon as they pulled ahead of Gypsy, Shade slowed to a walk again. Lucian turned in the saddle, looking back at me. "It's going to be uphill for a while. It'll be easier for the horses to trot. And we should pick up the pace if we're going to get up to the rock and back home before dark. Are you okay with that?"

I preferred to walk, but the sun was falling and I didn't want to run out of daylight. "Sure. Just not too fast. I don't want you to lose me."

"I won't. I can hear Gypsy, so if you two fall behind, I'll turn back."

"Thanks," I muttered, not sure if he heard me when he spun around to face forward and pushed Shade into a trot.

Gypsy sprang into motion to keep up, causing me to lose my balance for a moment. Grabbing her mane, I forced my heels down again and focused on posting to the two-beat rhythm of her trot.

The trail led us deeper into the woods, heading mostly uphill. A light sweat broke out under my shirt from the exertion. Keeping up at this pace for more than a few minutes was wearing me out, but I was determined not to look like I was having a hard time.

When we emerged into an open meadow, Lucian brought Shade back to a walk. The clearing extended up the hill, the tall grass swaying in the wind like a wave crossing over the ocean. As Lucian guided Shade along the edge bordering the woods, the black horse pranced, as if ready to take off at any moment. He shook his head, snorting, but obeyed Lucian's firm hand, the reins holding him back.

"This must be where you usually let him gallop," I commented.

Lucian grinned, a rare sparkle lighting up his green eyes. "You noticed."

"Yes," I said, nodding. "He's not going to take off, is he?"

"Only if I let him." Lucian halted Shade and spun him in a circle to face me. "What do you say?"

"Oh, no," I protested. "No way. I know you say I'm a better rider than I give myself credit for, but I'm good with trotting today." I had cantered a few times—once on the way home in the rain, the second time the night Becca had dealt with Sam's stepfather, and the third time last week when Diesel had chased Gypsy off Lucian's property. In spite of that, I didn't have the confidence to gallop across an open field.

"Come on, Gracyn. You're a really good rider, for a beginner. You can do it. I wouldn't ask if I didn't believe that."

I pursed my lips together in thought. "You're just saying that."

"No, I'm not. Look, all you have to do is push your heels down and hold on. Gypsy will stay with Shade. As long as I have control of him, which I will, she's not going to run off in another direction. And she'll slow down when we do."

"I can't believe I'm actually considering this." I put the reins in one hand and stroked Gypsy's shoulder. The truth was, I trusted her. So far, our ride had gone well and I had managed to stay in the saddle. But if I let Lucian convince me to do something reckless like galloping across a field and I fell off, I would be mortified. Not to mention I had once experienced the impact of hitting the ground after being thrown from a horse, and I was in no mood to feel beat up like that again.

"Come on," Lucian coaxed. "Please. For me. You owe me, remember?" When I raised my eyebrows, he continued. "I rescued you from the woods twice, and I made you a special tea to cure your hangover."

I searched for a reason to say no, but came up empty. "Okay," I relented, letting out my breath. "I'll do it. But only if you tell me what was in that tea. I'd love to know your secret hangover cure."

"No way. I can't tell you that, or I'd have to kill you."

My breath caught on his last words. *He's only joking,* I told myself. *Or is he?*

Lucian's teasing smile faded as though he had read my mind. "Don't worry. I have other secrets I might be able to tell you. If you can keep up." Without another word, he shifted the reins to one side. Shade whirled around and charged forward, his head held high and his hooves sounding like the beat of a drum with each step.

"Great," I muttered. "Okay, Gypsy. I guess we have no choice." I touched her sides with my heels and she sprang forward into a canter. I held on, feeling the wind blow through my hair.

Gypsy and Shade seemed to canter in slow motion compared to Shade's speed the day he had carried Lucian and I home after I had gotten lost in the woods. Gypsy felt balanced, and the incline kept the horses from bolting full speed ahead. At the top, we turned and cantered across a flat field to another hill. The horses didn't break their rhythm before taking the next corner and continuing up to a summit.

As soon as we reached the highest point, Lucian pulled Shade back to a walk. Without waiting for my signals, Gypsy slowed gently, helping me keep my balance without getting thrown forward.

Lucian turned in the saddle as he loosened the reins, allowing Shade to stretch his nose down to the ground. "You survived," he said with a grin. "How was it?"

I felt a smile tug at my lips. There was no denying that our sprint up the hill had been exhilarating. "It was fine, like you said it would be." I tried to sound nonchalant, but he seemed to pick up on my excitement.

"Fine? That's all?" he asked, his eyebrows arched and a teasing glint in his eyes.

"Okay, it was a little better than just fine," I admitted.

"Maybe next time you'll trust me."

My gaze caught his, my heart thumping in my chest. I couldn't be sure what caught me by surprise more—that there would be a next time or that I should consider trusting him. Not wanting to think about either option, I changed the subject. "Are we almost there?"

"You'll see," Lucian said before turning around in the saddle.

We walked in silence for a few minutes until we reached a rocky cliff rising up along the side of the field. Lucian halted Shade, dismounted and approached Gypsy. Standing beside her shoulder, he looked up at me. "We're here. Come on. I want to take you up there." He nodded at the rocks. "It's the best view around."

"It looks kind of steep," I commented, eyeing the incline.

"There are plenty of footholds. Didn't I just tell you to trust me?"

I gazed down at Lucian to see his green eyes locked on me, expecting me to comply. I hesitated for a moment, not sure if he was asking me to trust him because he knew I shouldn't, or if he was overcompensating for the rumors circulating about him. In spite of my questions, I was certain about one thing. For whatever reason, whether it was the sadness that crept into his eyes every time he mentioned Cassie or the way he had helped me in the past few weeks, I wasn't afraid of him.

I nodded before swinging my leg over Gypsy's hindquarters and sliding down. When my feet touched the ground, I turned, suddenly noticing how close he was. My breath caught when I realized I was trapped between him and Gypsy.

"Ready?" he asked.

"I guess," I replied, fighting to calm the butterflies in my stomach. If only his shoulders weren't so broad, his features so handsome, and his eyes so mesmerizing, perhaps I could remember why I had agreed to ride with him today.

"Follow me," Lucian instructed before walking away.

I lingered with Gypsy, finally finding my voice. "What about the horses? Won't they wander off? Should we tie them up?"

Lucian shrugged as he looked back at me. Then he tossed a glance at Shade. "Shade, stay here. No running back home. Got it?" The black horse lifted his head in a quick nod, as if completely understanding Lucian. "There. They won't go anywhere. Come on. If we're any slower, we'll be looking at the stars by the time we get up to the top."

My mouth gaped open when he started walking away again. One glance at the horses who stood patiently told me Lucian was probably right. Shaking my head in dismay, I launched into a jog to catch up with him. "Do they really understand what we say?" I asked as I reached his side and slowed to a walk.

"Sort of. I don't think they understand our words, but they know what to do. Speaking to him out loud was more for your benefit than Shade's. He knows what I mean. And these horses won't leave our sides. It's their purpose to keep an eye on us."

"Oh, right. I keep forgetting that," I mused, a vision of Gypsy charging to my side after Sam's stepfather had dragged me into the woods flashing through my mind.

"Don't worry. You'll get used to it. We all do in time," Lucian said before stopping beside the rocks. "Here we are. I'll go first and you follow. That way I can pull you up if you need help."

He started climbing, placing his feet on small grooves that extended outward. The rocky outcropping seemed higher now as I stood next to it than it had from my bird's eye view astride Gypsy.

About halfway up, Lucian paused and glanced down at me. "Think you can follow? Try to put your feet where I put mine."

"Okay." Gathering my courage, I reached up to grab a small ledge and hoisted myself up. It wasn't as hard as it looked and, before I knew it, Lucian was at the top reaching down to help me up. I accepted his hand and scooted over the edge. As soon as I rose to my feet next to him, he let go of me and I gazed out at the view.

Mountains covered in thick forests, half green, the other half orange, yellow and red, formed a circle around a valley. Nestled in the center was the town of Sedgewick. The buildings along Main Street were clustered together, the tall white church steeple situated on the outskirts of town. Homes surrounding the business district were scattered between trees and open fields. The sun was dropping off to the side, its rays casting a pink glow in between the clouds.

"Wow," was all I could think of to say. "This is gorgeous. I wonder how many miles we can see from up here."

"A lot," Lucian said. He sat down, stretching his legs out in front of him as he touched the spot beside him. "Have a seat. We can take a break for a few minutes before we head back."

I lowered myself to the hard surface next to him. Staring out at the valley, I savored the silence for a few minutes. I felt like I had left the world behind, escaping everything that had happened since I had moved to Sedgewick.

"So what was in that tea you gave me?" I asked, breaking the silence.

He chuckled. "You're not going to give up on that, are you?"

"No," I stated, glancing at him out of the corner of my eye.

"I already told you it's a secret. An old family recipe."

"Don't you mean spell?" I turned my head just enough to watch his reaction.

He laughed. "Yeah, I guess I do. Knowing you're one of us is going to take some getting used to."

"Why's that? I'm just a normal girl."

"Most would define normal as being a girl who's working on finishing high school. One who will go to college, get married and have a family. I'm sure you've realized by now that your future is going to be a lot different than what you've been expecting all your life."

I pulled my knees up and folded my arms on top of them. Then I laid my cheek on my forearms, peering at Lucian. "I'm starting to see that. Will you help me understand what all of this means?"

He nodded silently.

"Becca hasn't told me much. I think she's trying to dish it out in small doses." I paused as a thought crossed my mind. "How did you know I was a witch?"

"I suspected it when I saw you riding with Becca the day before school started. We tend to be a reclusive coven. I was surprised that Becca allowed you to be so close, letting you move in with her and Gabriel. I knew there was more to it. As witches, they could never allow a human to live with them. It would be too risky. We can't afford to let humans know our secrets. And when you stopped wearing glasses and contact lenses, I knew for sure. Those glasses really threw me off at first."

"Why?"

"Because as one of us, you should have had perfect vision. I can see so clearly, I knew when you were wearing contacts and when you weren't."

"Oh," I said with a sigh. "Celeste knew right away as well. She took one look at me after my vision became clear and asked what happened to my contacts."

"She's a smart girl," Lucian commented.

"But she's still afraid of you. Should she be?"

Lucian sucked in a deep breath, shifting his gaze to the view before us. "No. Of course not." His tone was curt, as though he was insulted I had asked.

I let a few moments pass before speaking again. "I still have so many questions, I don't know where to begin."

"I'm sure you do. But I didn't bring you up here for a crash course on witchcraft. For now, let's just enjoy the afternoon. The sun will be setting soon, and then we'll have to head back."

"But..."

Lucian reached up, placing a finger on my lips. My voice fell away instantly, not from his action but from his touch that sent a fire racing across my mouth. "Shh," he said. "There will be plenty of time to talk later."

I nodded, both relieved and disappointed when he pulled his hand back to his side. Trying to forget about his touch, I gazed out over the valley, my mind a muddled mess. My questions about witches were suddenly getting mixed up with my conflicting emotions over Lucian. I had learned nothing new about witchcraft this afternoon. The only thing I had accomplished was proving to myself that Lucian had gotten under my skin. Somehow, I would have to get him out of my system, as hard as it might be.

8

ucian and I sat in silence on the rock for several minutes, looking out over the town, lost in our thoughts. I wasn't sure what to say, so I remained quiet. A part of me felt comfort in knowing that Lucian was like Becca, Celeste and me. I wondered if he knew who my real parents were, but I couldn't find the courage to ask. He still flustered me, no matter how much time I spent with him.

As much as I wanted to trust him, a sliver of doubt crept into my thoughts. *Don't be too sure of his innocence. Remember what Becca said. The person who killed his sister must be a witch because no human would have the strength to take down a horse with a knife.*

In spite of my musings, I wanted to believe Lucian had nothing to do with his sister's death. I had to, otherwise I was a fool to be alone with him. But sitting up on the rock in the quiet with only him by my side made me nervous. If I was wrong about him and he hurt me, no one would know.

Stop this nonsense! I scolded myself. *You are crazy to be up here, trusting him one moment and fearing him the next. Your constant back and forth argument over him is giving me whiplash.* Trying not to think about it anymore, I shifted my attention to the town nestled in the valley below.

"This is a great spot to paint," Lucian said, breaking the silence. "Especially on a sunny fall day when the leaves are at their peak."

"I'm sure it is," I replied, grateful that he was making small talk. Maybe now the voices in my head would stop. "How do you get your stuff up here to the top?"

"Backpack. I even bring a lunch if I come for the day."

"What about Shade? I assume you don't hike up the mountain to get here."

"No way. Of course, I ride up here. If I know I'm going to stay long, I untack him. He's spent many afternoons in that meadow."

"Do you come here a lot?"

"Yes," he said wistfully. "I mean, I used to. I was up here the day Cassie was killed, and I haven't been back since." His sentence ended in a whisper as he stared out across the land.

I desperately wanted to take his mind off what must be a horrible memory. I glanced at him, but he either didn't notice or he was ignoring me. "Maybe I can join you up here one day to paint? I'd love to see this view once the leaves have finished turning which I assume will be soon."

He nodded, seeming to be a thousand miles away, his attention focused straight ahead. I wasn't sure if that was a yes, but I didn't press the issue.

My gaze drifted back to the view, and I wondered if he had brought me here for a silent brooding that could last for hours. Then I heard him sniff. Scrunching my eyebrows, I turned to look at him. A tear rolled over the five o'clock shadow sprinkled across his jaw. "Are you okay?" I asked quietly.

He took a deep breath, shuddering. "Yeah," he said, wiping under his eyes. "I don't think I was prepared to come back here. The memory of that day is more intense than I expected."

"I'm sorry," I whispered.

Nodding, his eyes swept to the side to meet mine for a brief moment. "It's been a rough two years. You'd think it would get easier as time goes by, but it doesn't. It stays with you forever, like a knife buried in your heart that can never be removed."

"I can only imagine how that feels. I've never lost anyone I cared about, so I don't know what it's like. But I'm sure it's hard." In a brave moment, I placed my hand over his and gently squeezed.

He smiled at me, the sadness still lurking in his eyes. Then he seemed to recover and whipped his hand out from under mine before rising to his feet. "We should probably head back. I want to get you home before dark. I'm sure you have other things to do tonight." When he extended his hand to me, I took it and stood up. As soon as I was on my feet, he let go.

"I do. But this was a nice break from my homework. And from hiding."

"Hiding?"

"Yes. From all this craziness. Although I guess it hasn't been that bad since my friend's father was dealt with."

A dark shadow raced over Lucian's face. "Oh, yes, that guy. From what you told me the other day, I think Becca was way too lenient on him. It took all the restraint I had not to do any more damage after I threw him. What a low-life. He doesn't deserve the life he has after what he did to you."

I smiled at Lucian, hoping he understood I was okay with the outcome. "Perhaps not. But letting the world know what he did and ruining his life wouldn't change what happened. And if he is punished, then his family will have to pay as well. I could never do that to Sam."

"Is Sam your friend?"

"Yes. She's my best friend. Has been since we were in Kindergarten."

"She's lucky to have you. Only a good friend would give up punishing a guy like her father just to protect her."

"You're giving me too much credit. I think anyone in my shoes would feel the same way."

"I beg to differ."

Feeling a blush take over my face, I turned away with a shrug. "It's very simple. If he can't work, I don't know how she'd pay for college. And she has a brother. She'd feel obligated to help take care of him if their father ended up in jail. Besides, they already paid enough when he was in the hospital."

"Hospital?" Lucian asked, sounding surprised.

I nodded, my eyes meeting his. "Yes. It would have been nice to have known what I was a long time ago. I sort of broke his hand and cursed him. He ended up in a coma for about a month."

Lucian grinned, his eyes lighting up. "Awesome. You've got some fight in you. I feel a lot better now knowing he was punished in a way. But that must have been a little weird for you if you did all that not knowing the power you have."

"You have no idea," I said with a huff.

Another moment of silence passed before Lucian gestured across the rock to the other side. "Come on. Time to go."

"Okay," I said. Then I followed him to the spot we had climbed up and stopped, kneeling as he started to descend.

"Wait until I get to the bottom to start down," he instructed. "I don't want you to slip and knock us both to the ground."

Nodding, I watched him disappear below the edge. As I waited for him to reach the bottom, I gazed about, a little sad that our time in this peaceful spot away from the rest of the world had come to an end. Perhaps we could return someday. For a fleeting moment, I wondered if he had ever brought Zoe here. But I forgot about her when I noticed shadows circling over the rock surface. My gaze shifted up, and I drew in a sharp breath at the sight of birds soaring across the sky.

Fear lodged itself in my throat, and I froze, remembering the birds I had seen in the woods the day I had gotten lost. Just like then, these swarmed together, forming a ceiling of black overhead and crying out as they dodged each other.

"Okay, Gracyn!" Lucian called from below. "Come on down. Just take it slowly."

Grateful to have something other than the birds to focus on, I eased down the side of the rock, searching for a foothold. Finding one, I balanced on my right foot and felt around for another with my left foot. As soon as I propped the toe of my boot on a narrow ledge, a gust of wind swept through the air. At first, I ignored it. But then I heard a muffled whisper in the breeze.

"Gracyn. Come to me. I need your help."

The haunting voice faded quickly, and I stopped, not sure if it had been real or a figment of my imagination. Staring up at the sky, or what little I could see of it beyond the birds, I shivered. Then I heard the voice again. "Gracyn. I've waited an eternity for you," a woman said.

Trembling, I lowered myself, eager to get away from the eerie whispers. But my foot slid, and I lost my balance. I felt myself falling and reached for the rock on my way down, but I only ended up scraping my arms. There was nothing to grab ahold of.

Panic gripped me in that split second. I expected a hard impact and hoped I would walk away in one piece. Throwing my arms up around my head, I screamed. A moment later, I landed on my feet when a pair of strong arms wrapped around my waist. Lucian braced me against his chest, and I reached up, grabbing his shoulders as I came to a stop, his solid touch pitching my thoughts into a whirlwind.

"Whoa," he said, holding me steady for a minute. He gazed down at me, his arms still locked around my back. "What happened? I said to take it slow."

"Sorry," I gasped. My eyes met his for an instant before I looked up at the empty sky, the birds and the whispers in the wind gone. "Did you hear something a minute ago?"

"No. It's been quiet this whole time, at least until you screamed."

"That's not what I mean," I said, shaking my head. "I heard my name. Someone called for me." I studied his reaction, afraid he would think I was crazy. But I was almost more worried that he had heard the voice too, because that would mean it was real.

"Gracyn, I don't know what you're talking about. I didn't hear anything."

"Well, I did," I insisted. "There was a voice calling my name. I heard it twice. I'm not making this up. It was real. I know it was."

"Hey," Lucian said softly, unwinding one arm around my back and bringing his hand up to my face where he swiped a stray curl out of my eyes. "It's okay. There are no voices. Just me."

I shook my head again, not willing to believe him. "But I heard them. And there were birds. Hundreds of big black birds just like the day I got lost in the woods. I didn't imagine them. At least I don't think I did."

When I returned my gaze to him, my eyes met his, and I got lost in his stare. The birds and the voice became a distant memory, almost as if they had never existed, but my heart continued to race, pushing adrenaline through my veins. I was suddenly very aware of Lucian's touch. My chest was pressed up against him, and my hands still rested on his shoulders. Heat from his body made me feel flushed all of a sudden, making my head spin. The effect of his touch and his stare was intoxicating, like a drug working its way through my blood.

"Shh," he said, stroking the side of my face, his other arm still around my waist. Then he brushed his fingers under my chin and tipped my jaw upward, his eyes locking with mine. He shook his head slightly, his eyes bewildered. "Where did you come from? You're so beautiful."

I gasped nervously, fearing my heart would stop. My gaze didn't waver, and I was mesmerized by the intensity in his expression. I froze, wondering what he would do next. "What?" I asked, barely able to find my voice.

In that instant, Lucian pulled his eyes away from mine and loosened his hold on me. "I'm sorry," he said. "I don't know where that came from. We should head back now." He dropped his arms to his sides and backed up before turning his attention to the horses.

Disappointed, I took a deep breath, trying to gather my composure. The moment had passed. The birds and the whispers were gone, as was his magical touch. I would be better off forgetting everything that had just happened, which was surely a figment of my imagination, for better or for worse.

Nodding, I followed him to the horses waiting for us in the grass. When I approached Gypsy and stroked her soft neck, I realized I needed a mounting block to get on. "Hmm," I mused, pressing my lips together. I glanced around, searching for a big rock or log, but found nothing that would be useful.

Lucian looked at me as he stopped beside Shade. "What's wrong? You look confused."

I let out a long sigh. "I don't know how I'm going to get back on. I've only gotten on her from the mounting block. Unless she'll lay down for me like she did the night in the woods."

"That won't be necessary. I can help."

Great, I thought. *More close contact with him. That's all I need.* But I forced myself to smile appreciatively. "Thanks."

He walked over as I stood facing the saddle on Gypsy's left side. "I'll give you a leg up. Just reach up and jump on three."

"Okay." Placing my hands on both sides of the saddle, I felt Lucian lift my left calf, bending my knee.

"One, two, three."

Feeling weightless when Lucian propelled me into the air, I easily cleared Gypsy's hindquarters with my right leg. After helping me settle into the saddle, he let go of my calf. "See?" he said with a smile. "Piece of cake."

"Yes, thank you," I replied, nervously fumbling to put my feet in the stirrups and pick up the reins.

"You're welcome," he said before heading back to Shade and swinging up into the saddle.

We didn't talk much on the way home. To my relief, we walked down the big hill. The last thing I needed was to rattle my weary nerves with another run. Cantering up to the rock had worn me out, and I suspected I would be a little sore tomorrow.

The sun had fallen below the horizon, sending dark shadows into the woods. The birds were quiet, and a hush hung in the air. The woman's voice I had heard in the wind lingered in my memory, putting a damper on my mood. Never before had my imagination run away with me, and I suspected that hadn't changed. The voice had been real, that much I was sure of. Only what it meant was a mystery that would probably haunt me for days. With any luck, I would never hear it again, but I didn't dare hope for that. Something told me it was a warning of things to come.

When we reached the path leading to Lucian's property, he refused to turn off the main trail. Instead, he insisted on staying with me until I returned home. I tried to tell him I could make it alone from there, but my words fell on deaf ears.

We emerged from the woods, crossed the driveway and halted the horses in front of the barn door. Becca's SUV was still gone, a huge relief because I wouldn't have to explain what I was doing with Lucian. After dismounting, I slid the reins over Gypsy's head and faced Lucian who remained in the saddle. "Thanks for the ride today," I told him.

"No problem. It was fun. We'll have to do it again."

"Yes. I'd like that."

He smiled. "Do you need any help untacking?"

"No. I can manage it from here." As much as I would have liked him to stick around for a few more minutes, I didn't want him to think I was completely helpless around horses.

"Okay. Well, have a nice evening." As he nudged Shade into a walk, I started to lead Gypsy to the barn.

A few feet before the doorway, I stopped and turned. "Lucian?"

He whirled Shade around to face me. "Yes?"

"Maybe from now on, you can talk to me at school. We don't have to be strangers."

"Maybe," was all he said before Shade pivoted on his hind legs. Then he stepped into a canter and dashed off into the woods. The horse and rider disappeared instantly, but I heard the hoof beats for a few seconds until they faded away.

With a frown, I studied the shadows for a moment before accepting he was gone. As fast as the afternoon had begun, it was over. Gypsy nudged my arm, prompting me to look back at her with a smile. "Thanks for the reminder, girl," I said, stroking the bridge of her nose. "I know you're thinking about a big pile of hay. Well, you've definitely earned it."

Resisting the urge to glance at the woods one last time, I led her into the barn.

9

The next day after History class, I stopped by my locker before heading to the Art wing. Most of the other students had already made it to their next class, and only a few lingered at their lockers, seeming determined to take advantage of every last second between classes.

My sights set on Art class, I took off down the hall. I was about to turn the corner when Lucian ran up behind me. "Cutting it a little close, are we?" he asked, rushing past me.

Caught off-guard, I stopped, shocked that he had spoken to me at school. He turned and marched backward in time with my step, looking every bit as handsome as I remembered in his jeans and navy shirt. He even smiled, a playful twinkle lighting up his green eyes.

"What's this? You're talking to me here at school?" I asked, drawing in a sharp breath.

"Yes," he answered. Halting, he waited until I stopped in front of him to lean toward me. "Zoe's out sick. She's got a cold, poor dear, which means I can talk to anyone I want."

"You should be able to talk to anyone you want even when she is here."

His grin caved into a frown. "Things are not always as they should be. You'd best remember that." Then his serious voice snapped back into a lighter tone. "Well, see you in class." After whipping around, he took off with long strides.

Huffing, I launched into a run, hoping to catch up with him, but he was too fast. I couldn't believe his nerve. How rude of him to stop and talk and then leave me when we were headed to the same class. The least he could have done was walk with me. It wasn't like we were complete strangers, especially after spending yesterday afternoon together.

Why do you care? a voice in my head asked. *Aren't you forgetting what he could have done? Someone killed his sister and, until that person is caught, it very well could have been him. Besides, you're going to get quite a reputation if anyone sees you getting chummy with him. What would Alex think? Are you prepared to risk the best, no make that the only boyfriend you've ever had?*

I groaned inwardly at my inner self. No matter what I believed about the murder of Lucian's sister, I knew spending time with him would not go over well with Alex. As for Cassie, I didn't believe for a minute Lucian had committed such a horrible crime. I had seen the grief in his eyes and heard it in his voice many times including the day we had worked on our paintings and yesterday up at the rock. He was still mourning the loss of his sister, and I suspected he had loved her very much. I knew the circumstantial evidence pointed to him, but I refused to believe it, no matter how many times Becca, Alex and Celeste tried to convince me otherwise.

With that thought, I rushed into the classroom as the bell rang. Lucian was already at our desk, his head bent over his notebook. He didn't look up when I took my seat which was probably just as well. I didn't need the conflicting emotions he stirred up inside me. Perhaps I should be grateful that he preferred to ignore me or rush away from me even when Zoe wasn't at school. I had enough to worry about, and I didn't need the rumors that would come with getting to know a suspected murderer, even if I believed he was innocent.

After Art class, Alex appeared at my locker as I put my jacket on. My book bag on the floor by my feet, I turned to him, oblivious to the students filling up the hallway behind him.

"Hi, gorgeous," he said with a winning smile, his dark hair pulled back into a ponytail. His black T-shirt strained against his shoulders, and his jacket was folded over his forearm.

I felt a grin slide over my lips, my eyes meeting his. I couldn't help loving it when he called me that. "Hi. Heading home?"

"Not until I ask if you'd like to study together this afternoon."

"Thanks, but I think I'm going to pass. I want to head out to the barn when I get home, and I probably won't hit the books until after dark." I was getting more attached to Gypsy, and whether I just groomed her or took her out for a ride, I wanted to take advantage of the daylight before the sun set.

"Oh," he let out with a deep breath as though his hopes had been deflated. "I've been upstaged by a horse. Guess I've got some competition."

A dark shadow moved over me as an image of Lucian flashed through my mind. Forcing myself not to let my sudden mood change show, I shook my head with a smile and touched Alex's arm. "Don't be silly. My relationship with Gypsy is nothing compared to what I have with you." My statement couldn't be further from the truth, but Alex would never know that a supernatural connection tied me to Gypsy.

"Good. As long as it stays that way. So, how about next week?"

"Maybe. It depends on how hard the problems are."

"You seem to be doing better in Calculus lately. Are you?"

I shrugged, reluctant to explain that with everything else going on, I had started to accept I might end up with something less than an A. "Good enough, I guess."

"You don't sound too confident. If you stick with me, you'll ace Calculus," he said, a sparkle in his eyes.

Before I could respond, Derek appeared behind Alex, slapping him on his shoulder. "This guy talking about school again?" Derek asked with a smirk. "Is that all you two worry about? You know, there's more to senior year than homework, grades and college applications."

"We know that," Alex said with a huff. "Although it wouldn't kill you to take your grades a little more seriously. Once this year is over, that's it. Time for the real world to begin."

Derek rolled his eyes and laughed. He glanced at me, his enthusiasm fading for a quick moment before it returned in full force. "No, I don't think so. The real world isn't my thing."

Alex shifted his gaze to Derek. "You might say that now, but one day, you'll be sorry you didn't work harder."

"Yeah, yeah, save it for someone who needs it. I have better news, for now." A twinkle lit up Derek's blue eyes, making me curious.

"Okay, spill it," Alex said.

"I just got back into Lacey's good graces. We're on for the Homecoming dance."

"Nice," Alex said as he fist-bumped Derek. "Now we both have dates."

"Yep. Man, that was a close one. I thought she was never going to forgive me."

Alex chuckled. "How many times did you have to beg?"

"Enough," Derek grumbled. "So don't remind me." Pausing, Derek looked at me. "Gracyn, how's this one been treating you? Everything okay?"

"Yes," I said, flashing him a quick smile. "Everything's fine."

"Good. I was just checking. Because when he screws up again, I'm still available."

"Hey!" Alex cut in. "What about Lacey?"

"You know she's not a keeper. She's just someone fun to hang out with until the real thing comes along."

I shook my head while Alex and Derek began bantering back and forth. As I tuned them out, my gaze drifted to the crowd and I saw Celeste weaving between the students on her way down the hall. She was hunched over, her long braid falling over one shoulder, her black book bag matching her coat. She didn't even notice the three of us talking by my locker. She appeared withdrawn and tired again, and I made a mental note to catch up with her the next chance I got.

As soon as Celeste disappeared around the corner at the end of the hall, I turned my attention back to Alex and Derek. "Saturday night in Boston again," Derek said, glancing at me. "What do you say, Gracyn? You in? There's going to be an awesome party after our gig."

"What?" I asked looking at Alex, confused since I hadn't heard the beginning of their conversation.

"We got a last minute gig at the same place we played about a month ago," Alex explained, seeming to forgive me for drifting off. "So, want to go to Boston tomorrow?"

I hesitated, trying to think of the best way to turn him down. Like the last time they had gone, I didn't want to spend the night at a stranger's apartment with a bunch of guys, even if Alex was one of them. "That's probably not going to work. I have some shopping to do this weekend for the dance."

"Oh," Alex said, a knowing look in his eyes. "Then by all means, do what you need to do. And I'm sorry we can't hang out this weekend. It just came up today. Derek got the text about an hour ago. We can't pass up this chance. It's a really big deal to be called back to this place. The crowd must have liked us."

"It's okay. I'm happy for you guys. Don't worry about it. I hope it goes well."

"Thanks, Gracyn," Derek said. "You're really cool about all the gigs we do. Alex could never keep a girlfriend because they didn't like being left alone on a Saturday night."

"So is that the reason you stay with me?" I asked, casting a sly glance at Alex who turned bright red.

"No, that's not all of it," he said, conviction in his voice. "But for the record, it is awesome that you're always cool about the band's schedule."

"Well, it will give me time to catch up with Becca this weekend. We don't see each other much during the week."

"Yes, you should take advantage of it because I'm not sharing you next weekend," Alex teased, catching my eye.

Seeming to grow bored, Derek checked his phone. "Hey, Alex, I just got a text back from Justin. The guys want to practice tonight. Please tell me you can spare two hours from your homework."

"I suppose," Alex said as though his answer had been dragged out of him. Then he flashed a grin my way. "See you tomorrow?"

"Of course," I replied.

He planted a kiss on my lips before he and Derek took off. I watched them for a minute, happy they had been called back to play in Boston again. They worked hard, and the band was good. Besides, I never minded getting a weekend to myself.

Turning back to my locker, I resumed sorting through my books. After shutting the door, I reached down to grab my book bag when Celeste approached. "Hi, Gracyn," she said.

"Hi. I didn't know you were still here. I saw you going the other direction a minute ago."

"I know. I didn't want to interrupt since you were talking to Alex and Derek. Derek tends to run away whenever he sees me," she explained, sounding sad and defeated.

"I'm sure that isn't true," I countered, silently scolding myself for the white lie. It certainly was true because he had admitted to it. But I tried not to dwell on that thought and quickly changed the subject. "What are you doing Saturday night?"

She shrugged, shaking her head. "Nothing, as usual. Why?"

"Want to come over? We can get a pizza and have a girls' night. What do you say?"

Celeste looked shocked. "Really?"

"Yes. Why not? We need to hang out together more, especially since we have some pretty heavy things in common."

A hesitant smile formed on her face. "Yes, we do. Okay. Sure. That would be nice."

"Great. Do you need a ride?"

"No. I can drive over."

"Then come around six. I'll order the pizza."

"That sounds great. Thank you." Her brown eyes glistened as if she was about to cry. Then she took a deep breath, composing herself.

"What are friends for?" I asked, my eyes meeting hers. "Are you heading out to the parking lot?"

"Yes."

"Then we can walk together. Let's go." Side by side, we wound our way through the crowd to the school entrance. If I couldn't spend Saturday night with Alex, Celeste was the perfect second choice. I couldn't wait to ask her questions about witchcraft. If I was lucky, she would tell me how to cast spells and work magic. But beyond that, it felt good to have a new friend. I missed Sam, and even though Celeste could never replace Sam in my life, she was probably the best new friend I could ask for.

10

I woke up to a steady rain beating down on the roof Saturday morning. With a yawn, I sat up, gazing about the dark room that had been my home for over a month now. Soft light dim from the clouds snuck in through the window, twisting around the curtain. I sighed, the rain washing away my hope to ride Gypsy out on the trails today.

After getting up, I approached the desk, leaned over it and pushed the curtain aside. Thick fog hung low and heavy, hiding the treetops, a sign that the rain would linger all day.

Faced with a day trapped inside, I grabbed the white hoodie draped over the back of my chair. Putting it on, I wandered into the hall, instantly smelling coffee.

"Hmm," I mused. Hot coffee would taste so good on a cool, damp morning.

When I reached the bottom of the stairs, Becca was sitting at the table, the newspaper sprawled out in front of her. Beside it sat a mug, steam rising from her coffee. "Good morning," she said, her attention focused on an article while she bit into a pastry.

"Good morning. The coffee smells great," I said, passing her on my way to the gurgling pot on the counter.

As I filled a mug, I heard the paper crinkling behind me. Then Becca spoke. "Sorry. I just wanted to finish reading something."

After dashing some creamer into my coffee, I turned and leaned against the counter, my hands curled around the warm mug as I lifted it to my lips. "No problem. When is Gabriel coming home?"

"Not until tomorrow," she replied, shifting sideways in her chair to look at me.

"Wow. It seems like it's been a long week for him."

"It has. He had to cover for some of the doctors who filled in for him the other week when he took time off. That's pretty normal for his schedule. It surges every now and then."

I nodded in understanding, my gaze wandering to the half-eaten pastry on Becca's plate. "What's for breakfast?"

"An apple turnover. There's more in the pantry. Help yourself."

"Thanks. I think I will. That looks really good." I placed my mug on the counter and went directly to the pantry.

"Any plans for today?" Becca asked when I sat down next to her with my coffee and a pastry.

"I was hoping to ride, but it doesn't look like that's going to happen," I replied before taking a bite.

"Not if you want to stay dry," Becca commented with a grin.

"Yeah," I agreed, rolling my eyes. "Nice weather. Why couldn't it wait for Monday?"

"It never does," Becca said as she folded the newspaper and pushed it to the side of the table. "Well, I have an idea if you're interested."

"That depends. What is it?"

"Let's get out of here for the day."

"Where do you want to go?"

Becca grinned, amusement gleaming in her eyes. "Shopping. There's a mall in the next town. I haven't been over there in a while, and I could use a few new things to spruce up my wardrobe for the winter. What do you say?"

"That would be perfect. I need to get a dress," I replied with a smile. At least I could take advantage of the rain to get ready for the dance next weekend, and shopping had been my excuse to turn down Alex's invitation to go to Boston tonight.

"A dress?" Confusion swept across Becca's face before a knowing look replaced it. "Is it Homecoming already?"

"Yes. Next Saturday."

"Wow. Time has really flown by. Before you know it, the holidays will be here. I take it you're in. How soon can you be ready to go?"

"Within the hour."

"That's perfect. It'll give me enough time to clean up."

"What about the horses?" I asked, my thoughts shifting to Gypsy.

"I already turned them out. They love this weather."

"Really?" I asked, surprised.

"Oh, yes. We'll probably see three huge mud balls out in the pasture when we leave."

I laughed. "Lovely. Well, I can help with the stalls later as long as we're home by five. Celeste is coming over at six to spend the night."

"That's great. I didn't know you two were such good friends."

"I'm working on her. After all, we have a lot in common."

"Yes, you do," Becca agreed with a nod. "And we can talk more in the car. Right now, I need to get ready. The mall opens at ten, and it'll take us almost an hour to get there."

Becca stood up and headed for the sink with her dishes in her hands. I took another bite of the apple turnover, my thoughts on our plans. I had never enjoyed shopping like some girls, but today would be different. I had a mission—to find the perfect dress for next weekend's Homecoming dance. This was just what I needed. A day away from the farm and all reminders that I was a witch. A day to feel like a normal teenager. If only it would last forever.

— ◡ —

My trip to the mall with Becca turned out to be extremely successful. I found a knee-length black dress and strappy sandals with glittering rhinestones that matched the jewelry I picked out. Becca bought a gray suit for work at a fraction of the original price. We ate lunch at a Mexican restaurant in the mall, and not once did we talk about anything supernatural. Instead the horses, Alex, and my classes dominated the conversation. For those few hours that seemed to pass all too quickly, I felt almost normal. Just a teenager out to find the perfect dress to impress her date at a school dance.

Celeste arrived at six o'clock that evening as planned. I heard her car while setting out plates and napkins for dinner as Becca kept me company from where she sat at the island with a glass of red wine. When the doorbell rang, the dogs charged across the living room and stuck their noses around the window curtains, whining.

"I'll get that," I announced, finishing with the table before I crossed the room and opened the door. "Hi, Celeste."

"Hi," she said, seeming a little shy. Under her black coat, she wore a cream-colored sweater, the complete opposite of the black she wore almost every day. Her hair flowed in smooth waves over her shoulders, and an overnight bag hung by her jean-clad hip.

The dogs nosed their way outside, sniffing her boots and prompting her to smile. Leaning down, she rubbed Scout's head between his ears. "Hey there, Scout," she said softly. Then she looked up at me, explaining, "I know them."

"You've been here before?"

"Of course. A couple times. But I haven't been back since Cassie died." Her voice fell, ending in a sad tone.

The last thing I wanted to talk about, or even think about for that matter, was Cassie. Forcing myself to smile, I gestured to the living room. "Come on in. It's getting cold out there. The pizza should be here soon."

She walked in, the dogs following her, and I shut the door. "Hi, Becca," Celeste said, approaching the island.

Becca smiled at her. "Celeste, my dear, you look good. How are you?" She embraced Celeste in a hug, letting go a moment later.

"I'm fine, thank you."

"How's your mom?" Becca asked. "Everything going okay over at your place?"

"Yes. We're getting ready for winter like everyone else."

Becca nodded. "I heard it could be colder than usual with more snow this year."

"I heard that, too," Celeste replied.

"Wait a minute," I interrupted, joining them at the island and turning my attention to Becca. "When were you planning to tell me? It's already going to be colder than usual for me."

Becca smiled. "And that's why I didn't tell you. I didn't want you to worry."

"You'll be fine. I'm sure Alex will keep you warm," Celeste piped up with a teasing grin.

My cheeks feeling hot, I ignored Celeste's comment. "Can I take your bag and coat?" I asked her.

"Yes, that would be great." She handed me her overnight bag before taking off her coat. "Thanks," she said as soon as I reached for it.

While Celeste turned back to Becca, I scurried about, first dropping the bag beside the stairs and then hanging up her coat in the front closet. When I returned to the island, Becca and Celeste were chatting like old friends. They paused, giving me enough time to find out what Celeste wanted to drink. Playing the part of the hostess, I prepared two glasses of ginger ale with ice before joining Celeste and Becca.

"Here you go," I said, placing one of the glasses in front of Celeste.

"Thanks," she said before taking a sip.

"What are you girls up to tonight besides eating pizza?" Becca asked.

"Oh, we'll probably hang out upstairs or watch a movie," I said.

"Sounds good. I might join you for the movie if that's okay," Becca said.

I looked at Celeste, and she nodded. "Of course, that's fine," I said.

"Celeste, how is Serenity?" Becca asked. "Have you ridden in any competitions this fall?"

"No. I stopped when school started. We did so many over the summer that I wanted to give her a break."

Becca smiled, looking at me. "You should see these two in action. They're incredible."

"I know," I said. "I took Gypsy out for a trail ride last weekend when you went to New Hampshire, and we ended up at Celeste's farm. I got to see them flying over some pretty big jumps, and it was amazing."

Celeste's face turned red, and she dropped her gaze to the counter. "It's really no big deal," she murmured.

"Yes, it is," I said. "You're the best rider I've ever seen. I don't think many people can ride like you."

A thoughtful expression fell over her face, but before she could say anything, the doorbell rang. The dogs scrambled up from their beds and ran across the room again. "Pizza's here," I announced before approaching the door.

After paying the delivery boy, I took the pizza and shut the door. The box was hot as though the pizza had just come out of the oven, and it smelled like garlic and warm bread. I carried it back to the table where the three of us sat down for dinner. With Becca joining us, I had to save all my questions about witchcraft for later. There would be plenty of time for that when Celeste and I could be alone. Instead, our time at dinner felt more like eating with a parent than a sister. Becca asked Celeste polite questions, keeping the conversation on lighter topics such as school and horses. I quickly grew bored, realizing that Becca and I had talked about the same subjects earlier in the day. I couldn't wait to get Celeste alone and move on to far more interesting topics, like spells and magic.

When we finished eating, Becca offered to clean up and chased us out of the kitchen. Celeste and I headed upstairs to get her settled in for the night before we picked out a movie.

As soon as we entered my room, I shut the door. Celeste stopped in front of my bed, studying the room. "Wow. This is really nice. Did Becca do all this, or did you decorate it after you moved in?"

"Becca did it. She's awesome," I said, walking past Celeste and sitting sideways on the edge of the bed.

"Yes, she is. I've always looked up to her."

"She's very fond of you, too. She was worried about you when Lucian first moved back to town."

"Really?" Celeste asked, her eyebrows raised.

"Yes. But I didn't bring you up here to talk about Becca."

"Then why did you invite me over?" Celeste looked shell-shocked, as though she feared the real reason she was here.

"Because it's nice to have a friend," I said knowingly, a teasing smile on my face that collapsed when I confessed my ulterior motive. "And I want to know how our magic works. Becca has pretty much left me in the dark when it comes to that."

"Of course, she has. Winter is coming, and we only use our power in the spring and summer for growing. I'm sure she'll ask you to help next year."

"So that's it? You know, being a witch is kind of boring. Can't you teach me some spells or show me how to use magic?"

Celeste paused thoughtfully before a smile formed on her face, a rare sparkle in her eyes. "All right. I have an idea. I'll show you something really cool if you promise to keep it a secret."

"I can do that. What is it?"

"It's hard to explain. And even if I did, you probably wouldn't believe it unless you saw it."

"Okay. Now I'm really curious."

Celeste smiled. "We'll need a knife or scissors. Something sharp."

My excitement faltered for a moment. "Why? We don't have to cut ourselves or anything like that, do we? I don't like blood."

"No. Not at all."

"Promise?" After she nodded, I went to my desk, opened a side drawer and pulled out a red-handled pair of scissors. Then I turned and held them up. "Will these work?"

"Yes, that's perfect." She reached out and took them from me, clutching the handles in her palm. "Is the door shut all the way?"

I glanced at it, noting that it was. "Yes."

When I looked back at her, my eyebrows raised, she smiled. "You won't want any of them to get trapped in the house. They'd make an awful mess, not to mention drive the dogs crazy."

"What are you talking about?"

"What I'm about to show you. Are you ready?"

"Um, I guess so." I suddenly wasn't sure what I was in for, but nothing should surprise me anymore.

"Good." She walked past me to the nightstand and began rummaging through my pillows on the bed.

"What are you doing?" I asked.

"Just making sure these came from..." She pulled off a pillow case and tossed it aside before examining the pillow. "Yes, this one will do." With the scissors in her hand, she sat down on the bed and placed the pillow in front of her.

"You're not making any sense at all."

Celeste put a finger up to her lips. "Shh." Then she opened the scissors and stabbed the pillow, ripping a huge hole in it. Determination set deep in her eyes, she scooped out a handful of feathers and dumped them on the bed.

"What are you doing?" I asked, my voice rising, only to be quieted by the stern look she flashed at me.

She focused on the feathers as she pushed the scissors and what was left of the pillow aside. Then she held her hands over the pile, a soft light emitting from her fingers. The glow extended down to the feathers, consuming them in a bright yellow ball. I squinted from the light, holding my breath when the feathers rose into the air, hovering above the comforter.

Celeste spoke a few words I didn't understand, and sparks shot out from the light. Each of the feathers suddenly turned into a white dove. Within seconds, the birds were flying about the room, their chuckling noises and fluttering wings drowning out the silence. Celeste held up a hand, and one of them landed on her finger, its small talons gripping her.

"Wow!" I exclaimed. "How did you do this? They're amazing!" There must have been at least fifty doves, some flying about, others landing on the dresser, chest of drawers, and desk. A few of them perched on the headboard, seeming very comfortable to be trapped in the room with me and Celeste. I ducked when one of them swooped too close to my head, missing me by a narrow margin.

"It's magic. You asked to see something, and I showed you."

"But you just turned those feathers into doves. I don't know what I expected, but it wasn't this." I gestured to the birds with a sweep of my hand.

She shrugged as if her actions were as routine as getting dressed in the morning. "It's nothing, really. In fact, this is what my mother and I do in the spring. We use the feathers from the previous year's chickens and turkeys to bring a new flock to life."

"It's most definitely not nothing, Celeste. All my life, I've only believed in science and fact. I like understanding how things work. So how did you do this?"

"I already told you. It's magic."

"Okay," I said with a huff, my frustration growing. "Let me start with the obvious, then. Were those dove feathers in my pillow? Because I didn't think they make pillows from dove feathers."

"They don't. Actually, those feathers came from our farm. If we turned every feather back into a chicken or a turkey, we'd have a serious overpopulation problem on our hands. We'd never be able to manage that many birds. Besides, it takes a lot of power to do this and we only have so much of it. We use the extra feathers to make things like pillows and comforters. My mom sells them every year at the harvest festival."

"But," I started, my mind churning with more questions. "If the feathers were from chickens and turkeys, how did you turn them into doves?"

"With a little concentration, I can turn them into any species of bird I want. Besides, I didn't think it would be cool to have a bunch of chickens running around your bedroom. What would we do with them? At least the doves can be released out the window."

"So the bird the feather came from doesn't determine the species you bring to life?"

"No. I just have to pick what I want to create and focus." A guilty smile spread over Celeste's expression. "We're not supposed to play with magic, but I haven't always followed that rule. I learned how to turn feathers into all different kinds of birds a long time ago."

"Like what?"

"Well, for starters, chickadees and woodpeckers. One time, I managed to get a snow owl. That was my favorite."

I shook my head, not sure what to say. I was speechless, still stunned by the birds buzzing around my room in a blur of white. "What do you do with them?"

"Release them, of course. I don't think woodpeckers or owls would make a good meal."

"What?" I gasped, shocked she would even suggest that.

Celeste laughed softly. "Gracyn, don't look so horrified. Where do you think the chicken on your plate comes from?"

Wrinkling my nose, I watched one of the doves perched on the headboard peck at its chest before raising its head, its beady black eyes taking in the room. "I don't like to think about that."

"Well, you should," Celeste said. "Especially now that you're here. Our ways are quite different from the rest of the world. You see, poultry used for our sustenance are brought to life by magic. When it's time to harvest them, their lives are taken away by magic. It's painless. They feel no fear and are never harmed in any way during their life."

"Oh. Well, that's good to know, I guess."

"You don't sound very convinced."

"Sorry. I just never thought about farming before."

"Most people never do. But here, we're different."

"Yes, you certainly are." I glanced around the room, wondering how long she planned to keep the doves in my room. "You're not going to put these doves to sleep now, are you?"

She shook her head. "No. There's no reason to. We can open the window and let them fly away."

"Will they be okay? I mean, it's cold and dark out there."

She nodded. "They'll be fine. I would never send a creature out to its demise."

"Okay." Still amazed at the birds fluttering about my room, I went to the window and raised the bottom pane as high as it would go. The birds flocked through it at once, the last one to leave seeming reluctant to launch itself off Celeste's finger. As soon as they were gone, quiet settled over the room. Not a feather remained, and fortunately, neither did any other deposits from the birds. My room was as clean as it had been minutes ago.

"Pretty cool, huh?" Celeste said with a grin while I shut the window and leaned against my desk.

"Yes. I've never seen anything like it."

"Please don't tell anyone what I showed you. Like I said before, we aren't supposed to play with our power. Although, it's kind of fun to break the rules from time to time."

"Can I learn to do that?"

"I'm sure you could, but it will take a lot of practice. You might want to start with learning to help Becca and Gabriel grow vegetables in the spring. I'm sure they'll need your help. By adding your power, they'll be able to increase production."

"That seems kind of boring. I'd rather make chickens out of feathers. I remember hearing that the Dumantes raise cattle. Do they do it the same way your family produces poultry?"

Celeste's carefree expression darkened the moment I mentioned our neighbors. But she seemed to recover quickly. "Not entirely. The cattle are bred just like any others. The Dumantes use their power to keep the grass rich and healthy for the cattle to graze on all year. They have a fifty-acre field hidden in the woods off to the side of their estate that they use for a hundred head of cattle. The field keeps the herd well fed. But the cattle are put to sleep in the same manner we process the chickens. It keeps the animals free of pain and fear and is very peaceful. I wish—" Her voice dropped off, a faraway look sweeping over her eyes.

"What do you wish?" I asked, prompting her to continue.

"That all animals produced for food could be processed the same way. It's a cruel world out there, but we are small in number and we can only handle producing what we need. What little is left goes to the town." Celeste paused with a sigh before her expression brightened. "Do you have any other questions? About being a witch, that is."

"Of course I do. Probably too many to count. But most of them are pretty insignificant. Except for one."

"What's that?"

"Do you know who my mother is? Becca told me I was adopted, and she won't tell me who my real mother is."

Celeste shook her head. "Sorry. I didn't know you existed until you showed up at school. Did Becca explain why she wouldn't tell you?"

"Just some lame excuse that it's history and not worth bringing up. Maybe it isn't worth it to her, but I think I have a right to know how I came into this world, especially now considering the woman who took care of me my whole life isn't who she said she is."

"I haven't met the woman you knew as your mother, but did you two have a good relationship?"

"Yes. The best. We never had any problems."

"I'm sure if she said she loved you, she did."

I smiled, glancing across the room at the picture of my mom and me at the beach on my dresser. "Yes, I think you're right. And from all I've learned over the last few weeks, I get why she couldn't tell me, but I feel like Becca is still keeping secrets from me."

"Becca is the oldest and most trusted witch in our coven. If she won't or can't tell you, you have to trust her. I'm sure she has her reasons."

"I've been trying to tell myself that," I grumbled, feeling frustrated again. Sensing that I wouldn't get any new information out of Celeste, I changed the subject. "Okay, I don't want to obsess about this all night. What do you want to do now?"

"I don't know. Maybe watch a movie. As long as it has nothing to do with witches."

"Deal," I shot out. "Come on. The TV is downstairs. Let's go." I waved for her to follow me as I walked to the door. Smiling, I led her down the stairs, although I wasn't sure how I could concentrate on a movie after watching Celeste bring a pile of feathers to life. That had been way better than any movie ever made.

11

The rain cleared out of the area sometime during the night, giving way to a blue sky the next morning. After Celeste left, Becca didn't have to ask twice when she invited me out for a morning ride. I jumped at the chance, rushing up to my room after a quick breakfast to get dressed and put on my boots.

Outside, the air was cool and crisp. Puddles filled dips in the gravel, the sun's reflection shining on the surface. The grass and leaves glistened with leftover moisture that would surely dry within the hour. Zipping up my jacket to ward off the chill, I stopped on my way to the barn, admiring the fall colors of gold, orange and red which seemed brighter now since the dark clouds had gone.

While Becca saddled Cadence, I tacked up Gypsy without needing to ask for help. A hint of pride swelled in my heart, my confidence growing stronger. After buckling the girth, I secured the bridle straps, smiling with satisfaction when I connected the last one. As usual, Gypsy stood still, waiting for me to finish before we headed outside.

As soon as Becca and I hopped on from the mounting block in the driveway, Becca and Cadence led the way along the trail. Gypsy and I followed behind while the dogs ran ahead, veering off into the woods a few times only to return to the trail moments later. Unlike the day they had run off, not a single deer could be seen. At least now, I knew better than to follow the dogs if they took off after an animal or anything else that caught their interest. Instead of worrying about them, I relaxed and enjoyed the scenery I was beginning to love.

We rode in silence along the familiar trail. The horses splashed through puddles while the wind blew through the leaves, sprinkling us with leftover rain.

"Where are we going?" I asked as we passed the opening to what was left of the garden. The rows of vegetables had been cut back, the apple trees picked clean of their fruit with only leaves remaining that would soon fall.

Becca shifted in the saddle, looking back at me. "I thought we'd just take the trail that circles back to the barn. You don't want to be out too long, do you?"

"No," I replied with a sigh. "I have to hit the books for the rest of the day as soon as we get home. That's what I get for taking a whole Saturday off."

She smiled. "I figured as much. Want to trot a little?"

"Sure." I picked up the reins and pushed my heels down as Lucian had shown me. Lucian. He kept creeping back into my thoughts, no matter how hard I tried to forget him. I couldn't count the number of times I had envisioned every moment of our ride up to the rock a few days ago. Somehow, he had gotten under my skin and I seemed unable to get him out of my head. Whether it was his mesmerizing eyes or the feel of being in his arms when he had broken my fall, I might never know. And now, we were about to pass by his estate. That was just what I needed, another reminder of him.

Focus, I told myself as Gypsy picked up a trot. My thoughts shifted to my riding and I sank my weight into my heels every time I rose up out of the saddle. As soon as I felt comfortable posting, I shortened the reins, keeping a soft feel of Gypsy's mouth.

We trotted through the woods for about twenty minutes. The horses didn't bat an eye at the puddles, splashing through them and splattering their legs and bellies while maintaining a steady pace. The farther we went, the thicker the forest became. Patchy sunlight swayed across the path with every breeze that lofted through the leaves overhead.

When we reached the top of a hill, Becca slowed Cadence to a walk, giving the horses a chance to catch their breath. The reins slipped through my fingers, allowing Gypsy to stretch her head and neck down. Holding the reins with one hand, I stroked her shoulder with the other.

"It's beautiful out here," I said as the horses began their descent down a hill.

"Yes, it is." Becca took a deep breath, her shoulders rising and falling. "I wish I could ride out here more often. Although, it hasn't been the same since Cassie was found."

"Thanks," I groaned. "I didn't need to be reminded of that."

"Yes, you did. You should never forget about what happened. You need to be vigilant. I told you before not to come out here alone."

I rolled my eyes, remembering how quickly I had forgotten her warning the day the dogs had run away. "You also told me you think I'm safe from whoever did it. I'm starting to get a little confused. But maybe we can talk about something else. Like the dogs." I looked around, seeing no sign of them in the still underbrush. "Where are they, anyway?"

The ground leveled off, and Becca stopped Cadence before whistling. Then she waited. A black bird launched into the air from a low tree branch, its fluttering wings breaking the silence. As soon as it disappeared, the quiet returned. "Scout! Snow!" Becca called. When they failed to appear in a few moments, she shrugged. "They may have gone home. Let's keep going." She nudged Cadence, cueing her to resume walking.

The mare took two steps before sliding to an abrupt halt, her head jerking up, her wide eyes alert. Becca straightened her shoulders at once and sat deep in the saddle, trying to push Cadence forward. Ignoring Becca, Cadence started backing up, scooting her hindquarters right under Gypsy's nose. When she bumped into Gypsy's chest, Gypsy had no choice but to step backward.

"Easy girl," Becca muttered. "What is it?"

"Becca, what's going on?" I asked.

"I don't know," Becca replied, her voice quiet. She clucked to Cadence, squeezing the mare's sides with her legs. "Come on, Cadence. Let's keep going."

Becca's attempts to coerce the mare to resume walking failed. Cadence snorted as she tossed her head, her mane swaying against her neck. Then she pawed the ground, refusing to move forward. Gypsy seemed to pick up on Cadence's apprehension, her ears flickering, her attention focused on the woods as if she was listening to every sound.

Then Cadence whinnied, her shrill cry sounding fearful. She hopped up with her front end, not consoled at all by Becca who stroked her neck, encouraging the mare to move forward. Instead, Cadence pivoted around on her hind legs, prancing in place when she faced Gypsy.

Gypsy took small, jittery steps backward, not seeming sure what to do. "Becca," I said, panic clutching my heart. "What's wrong?"

"I wish I knew. But if they don't want to keep going, there's no way I can force them. We have to trust them." Becca appeared to be trying her best to sound composed, but the intensity in her eyes gave her away. Whatever the horses sensed, it rattled Becca. I had never seen her so unnerved before. "We need to go. Turn Gypsy around and let's get out of here."

Gypsy didn't waste a single moment. She whipped around and galloped off, only slowing over patches of mud to avoid slipping. I grabbed her mane and hung on, ducking below low-lying branches that flew by. The wind blew through my hair and sent a cold blast against my cheeks, but I tried to ignore it as the woods passed in a blur. I wished I knew what we were running from, although perhaps it was better that I didn't know. I had never seen Cadence or Gypsy scared like this before, and the panic in Cadence's eyes sent a chill over me.

Gypsy led the way back to the house at a gallop. She splashed through puddles, the spray often reaching my face and arms. But I didn't care. I simply wanted to get back to the house where I could feel safe. About halfway home, the dogs emerged from the woods and ran ahead of us, skirting around the sloppy sections that the horses trudged through without batting an eye.

After passing the garden, Gypsy broke into a trot. She took a few steps before slowing to a walk, her hooves sliding on the soft ground for a second until she caught her balance. Then I lifted my shoulders and turned to face Becca.

"Does that happen often?" I asked, out of breath from holding on to Gypsy for dear life. I had never felt so out of control since I'd started riding her, and it had taken all of my strength to stay with her.

"No," Becca stated. "Never."

"Oh," I said with a sigh, turning to face forward. I wasn't sure whether to shrug it off as a one-time thing or worry that it was a sign of something bad to come. Before I could make up my mind, we reached the driveway. Gypsy shuddered with a deep breath, seeming a little relaxed as she walked toward the barn, her hooves crunching on the stones.

We had just halted in front of the doorway when tires rolling over the gravel sounded in the distance. A moment later, Gabriel pulled his BMW into the driveway and parked next to Becca's SUV. He hopped out of the car, his golden hair shining in the sun and dark sunglasses hiding his eyes. Dressed in jeans and an untucked white shirt, he smiled as he shut the door.

He approached us, taking off his sunglasses and revealing the amusement in his blue eyes. "Wow! What happened to you girls?"

I looked down at Gypsy, noticing for the first time the mud splattered up to her neck with globs clinging to her mane. Gypsy breathed fast, her sides moving in and out quickly.

"We had a little situation out there," Becca explained as she slid off Cadence. "Something spooked the horses, and they insisted on running home."

"Really?" Gabriel asked, his grin fading while a serious look swept over his face. "Where were you?"

"Just on the trail that loops around the property," Becca replied. "I have no idea what got them so riled up, but I knew I wouldn't get Cadence to go any farther. She was pretty freaked out."

"Hmm," Gabriel mused. "Well, they seem calm now. Maybe I can ride out later and check it out."

Becca nodded. "I'll go with you."

"Becca," Gabriel started, his tone sounding like he was about to object.

"Don't try to stop me, Gabe."

"Fine," he relented before a small smile appeared on his lips. "It looks like you need a good hosing. Shall I do the honors?" he teased.

"That's quite all right," Becca replied, seeming unamused. "I'm glad you find this so funny."

"I don't. But until we get to the bottom of what happened out there, you should clean up."

"Good idea," Becca said. "Would you draw me a hot bath while I put Cadence away?"

"Of course. And I'd hug you right now, but..." Gabriel gestured to Becca who glanced down at her muddy shirt and jeans.

"What? Don't you love me enough to see past the dirt?"

Gabriel smirked before leaning in to kiss her lips. When he lifted his head, he smiled. "Better now? At least not all of you is covered in mud. Now let me get that bath started for you while you girls hose down the horses. I'll meet you inside." He grinned one last time before returning to his car and opening the trunk.

After dismounting, I followed Becca and Cadence into the barn with Gypsy by my side. She stopped beside me in the aisle while I folded my arms across my chest. "Are you really going back there to see if you can find out what scared the horses?" I asked as Becca backed Cadence into the wash stall.

"Yes. Why? Want to come with us?"

"No, I think I'll pass. Just promise you'll tell me if you find anything."

Becca pulled the saddle off Cadence and approached me, the girth buckles clanking until she stopped. "Of course," she said. Then she disappeared into the tack room, returning empty-handed to begin un-buckling Cadence's bridle.

"Please tell me you won't change your mind. Whatever it is, I can handle it," I insisted, unconvinced she meant what she said.

Becca stopped, leaving the chinstrap dangling when she turned to me again. "You sound like you don't trust me."

"No, that's not it. I just feel like sometimes you don't tell me everything because you're trying to protect me. You haven't even told me who my real mother is. Was she an evil witch?"

Becca let out a deep breath with a smile. "No. I assure you, that's not the case."

"Then tell me who she was."

"Maybe one day. It's a long story, and we don't have time for it now. Gabe is waiting for me, and I have to clean up Cadence."

"Fine," I said. I had a feeling Becca would dodge my questions every time I asked about my real mother. But I wouldn't stop trying to get more information about her. I could be pretty persistent when I wanted to be, but today wasn't the day to press the issue. "I mean it about the woods, though. I really want to know what was out there."

"We'll see," she said, making me suspect once again she wouldn't keep her promise. "Just do me a favor and don't ride out on your own again. I know you've gained a lot of confidence and I think that's great, but I want to find out what we might be dealing with first."

A heavy feeling of dread fell over me, but I nodded and tried not to appear frazzled for Becca's sake. "Okay. I won't."

"Good. Well, let me finish with Cadence and then you can use the wash stall to hose off Gypsy. It's warm enough that they can go out wet."

"Okay," I said with a nod.

Without another word, Becca resumed unbridling Cadence. I turned to Gypsy, lifted the saddle flap and unbuckled the girth, trying to move on as though everything was fine. But nothing could be further from the truth, and I had a feeling that my worries would linger for the rest of the day, if not longer.

After turning Gypsy out in the pasture, I headed back to the house. I couldn't wait to get out of my dirty clothes and wash the mud off my face and forearms.

My phone was ringing as soon as I walked into my bedroom. Grateful for a distraction, I rushed over to the dresser, wondering if it was my mother calling. Maybe hearing about Russia would help take my mind off today's ride. Even though I knew she wasn't my biological mother, I had depended on her for as long as I could remember, at least until I had moved to Sedgewick. I still thought of her as my mother, and I wasn't ready to write her out of my life.

When I reached for the phone, I read Alex's name right away. "Hi, Alex," I said after swiping the screen, hoping he wouldn't sense any apprehension in my tone.

"Hi. Miss me last night?"

Hearing his voice prompted a smile to work its way onto my face. "Always," I replied, feeling a slight flush come over me.

"Good answer. So what did you do?"

I almost laughed, imagining his reaction if I told him Celeste had come over and shown me how she could turn feathers into birds. Instead, I said, "Stayed up too late watching movies and eating popcorn. But I also went shopping and got a dress for the dance."

"Nice. Is it hot? It is, isn't it?" he teased, his mind seeming to slide into the gutter.

"If by hot, you mean short and tight, then not really. But I like it, and I hope you will, too."

"As long as it's on you, I'll love it."

"Are you just trying to score points?"

"Yes. Is it working?"

"No. Because you're already the best thing that has happened to me since I moved to town."

Silence lingered for a moment before Alex responded. "Really?" he asked as though he didn't believe me.

I wondered right away if I had said too much. He had no idea I was dealing with a supernatural world entirely new to me. "Yes. But about the dance, I haven't gone to many. So go easy on me, okay?"

"They aren't that hard, Gracyn. We'll have a great time, you'll see."

"I hope so," I said quietly. Perhaps a fun dance with Alex was exactly what I needed.

"Okay, what's going on? You sound distracted again. You do that a lot, you know."

"Sorry. It's...well, I just got back from riding with Becca, and I'm covered in mud."

"Mud?" Alex asked with a laugh.

"Yes. And I'm glad you find that so funny."

"It's just hard to imagine. What happened?"

"The trails were soaked from the rain yesterday."

"I'm sure they were. Well, I'll let you go. Call me later tonight if you want to talk again, okay? Or if you get stumped on a Calculus problem, although then I might have to come over and help you."

"And by help, you mean—"

"Making out in your room," he stated matter-of-factly.

"That's what I thought," I said with a smile. Suddenly, I felt a lot better. He knew just how to take my mind off what worried me.

"So seriously, call me. I'll be around."

"I will, if I need help, that is," I assured him.

After a quick goodbye, we hung up. Silence fell over my room as memories of the horses' fear on the trail returned to the forefront of my thoughts. Hoping Becca and Gabriel would get to the bottom of it soon, I tried to comfort myself.

It could be nothing, a voice in my head stated. *It was probably an animal, and all this worrying is for nothing.* As soon as the words ran through my mind, I pushed them aside. *Cadence is a four-hundred-year-old supernatural horse. Something tells me that anything normally found in the woods wouldn't bother her, not even a bear or coyote. No, she picked up on something today, and only time will tell what it is.*

With that thought, I headed into the bathroom, longing for a hot shower to wash away my concerns with the mud, although I doubted it would be that easy to forget the horses' fear. My nightmare had only just begun, and I might as well get used to spookier times ahead.

12

As soon as I saw Lucian enter the Art classroom Monday afternoon, my heart accelerated against my will. I had spent more time than I cared to admit thinking about him over the weekend. The image of his intense green eyes, rugged good looks and strong frame had been impossible to forget since we had ridden up to the rock nearly a week ago.

I looked down at the desktop from where I sat, silently scolding myself. *You have got to get a hold of yourself. Lucian is not the one you want, Alex is. So just get over whatever he's doing to you and start thinking about Alex. Besides, you have bigger things to worry about—like whatever spooked the horses yesterday.*

Just like that, my mind snapped back to yesterday morning. I vividly remembered the panic in the horses' eyes, and I still had a burning desire to know what had caused them to act so frightened. Becca and Gabriel had ridden out on the trail yesterday afternoon, but they found nothing. Not even the tiniest clue. At least that was what they had told me. I considered asking Celeste if she knew what it could have been, but she looked like she wasn't sleeping again. One look at the haunted glaze in her eyes this morning had been enough to convince me to keep yesterday's events to myself.

Shifting my gaze up, I saw Lucian walk across the room, veering around the tables until he reached the seat beside me. I smiled, catching his eye while he hung his black jacket on the back of the chair and sat down. His expression remained hard, curiosity burning in his eyes.

My smile faded as his stare bore into me, his eyebrows raised. I took a deep breath and skipped any semblance of a greeting. "I need to talk to you," I said, my voice hushed.

"Really? You don't say?" he rolled out, his gaze drifting about the room.

Ignoring his indifference, I huffed. "I'm serious. I don't know where else to turn. Things are getting really weird."

"And you expect me to be surprised by that?"

"Yes, actually, I do. I need someone to talk to."

"What about Becca? Have you talked to her about whatever is bothering you?"

"Of course. But she's been vague, as usual. Besides, if she had the answers I'm looking for, do you really think I'd be coming to you?"

He sighed, shifting his eyes back to me. "Good point. Fine, we can talk. But not here."

Before I could say another word, the bell rang, piercing through the chatter in the room. Although I wasn't happy I'd have to wait for Lucian to be ready to talk, I focused my attention toward the front of the room. Ms. Friedman stood behind her desk and launched into the afternoon's agenda as soon as the whispers quieted down. I opened my notebook, watching Lucian out of the corner of my eye and cursing the disappointment fluttering through me when he didn't glance my way. Instead, he focused on the teacher as if he could care less that something was upsetting me.

He has no idea what's on your mind, I reminded myself. *So give the guy a break.*

Class crept by slowly that afternoon. I tapped my pencil several times, wishing Ms. Friedman would wrap up her lecture and give us our assignment for the week. She loved to start Mondays off by studying the work of a famous artist before assigning a project for the week. I didn't mind learning about Art history, but I enjoyed painting a lot more. Losing myself in a new project always helped take my mind off life in Sedgewick which seemed more like a fairy tale lately.

As soon as the bell rang, I let out a long sigh of relief before looking over at Lucian. "So, when can we get together?"

He shrugged. "I'm not sure. I'll have to let you know later."

"How about this afternoon?" I asked boldly.

"Sorry. I have plans." A smile slid over his face, a wicked sparkle in his eyes. "You're not going to ask me to teach you spells again, are you?" he whispered.

"No. This is something else. Okay, if today is out, what about tomorrow afternoon? I can ride over."

"No," he said a little too sharply. "Please don't do that. Remember what happened the last time you showed up unannounced?"

"Yes, of course. And you never explained what that was all about. Diesel never acted like that before."

"He gets very territorial when no one is home. He's usually inside, but the caretaker let him out that night for me. I can't be sure it won't happen again, although you'll be fine as long as I'm home."

"Good. He can be a little intimidating." I shook my head, realizing Lucian's dog worried me far less than whatever unknown threat the horses had spooked at a little over twenty-four hours ago.

"I've got to run. I'll catch up with you later, okay?" Lucian said, a faraway look sweeping over his expression.

"Fine," I muttered as he jumped up, grabbed his jacket and book bag, and took off. He probably hadn't even heard me. *Great*, I thought. *Once again, I have no one to talk to. Alex knows nothing about any of this, Celeste is always a world away, and Becca acts like it's no big deal that the horses freaked out at something. Maybe it's time I bought an Eskimo suit and moved to Russia.*

"Gracyn. Is everything okay?" Ms. Friedman asked, breaking me out of my trance. The room had emptied, and only the two of us remained.

"Yes. I was just getting my things." After grabbing my book bag off the floor and stuffing my supplies in it, I stood up, pushing my chair behind me. Then I rushed out of the room, hoping she couldn't tell that I had just told a huge lie.

Lucian didn't keep his promise that week. We only saw each other briefly in Art class, and he never offered up a time and place to talk. I didn't ask him again, either. He seemed to be avoiding me which was nothing new, and if I had to beg for his help, I didn't want it.

The only other time I saw him was in the hall between classes, but with Zoe hovering close by, I knew better than to get near him. I pretended it didn't matter that he had blown me off, and I focused my attention on Alex. As the week wore on, I slowly forgot about whatever might have scared the horses and put my energy into my classes. No good would come from worrying about something that may not even exist.

On Friday, the other students seemed louder than usual, their anticipation of the Homecoming weekend filling the halls with excitement. I'm not sure how he did it, but Alex talked me into going to the football game with him that night. I never went to the games back in Maryland, but I figured some changes would be good for me. Sitting next to Alex under the tall lights with his arm around my shoulders and listening to the cheering crowd ended up being a far better choice than staying at home wondering what weird thing would happen next.

When Alex dropped me off, he planted a quick kiss on my lips before promising that the dance would be amazing, a sly grin on his face and a twinkle in his eyes. With a smile, I nodded and then headed inside. By the time I climbed into bed, I was tired and relaxed. I wanted to get a good night's rest so I could thoroughly enjoy Saturday night. Hoping to dream of only Alex, I closed my eyes and felt my smile linger until I fell asleep.

The next morning, I woke up with a dull ache just above my eyes. I sat up in bed, rubbing my forehead while I squinted at the morning light streaming in through the window between the open curtains. The pain seemed weak, and I didn't think anything of it. I was sure a few aspirins would take care of it. I had never gotten bad headaches before, aside from the one triggered by tequila, and I hadn't had a drop of alcohol to drink since that horrible night several weeks ago.

Brushing off my thoughts of the slight discomfort that would probably be gone in a few hours, I shoved the comforter aside and stood up, ready to face the day. I had eight hours to kill before I needed to start getting ready for what I hoped would be a night to remember. Just thinking about Alex as my date for the dance made my heart swell with happiness. I could forget about everything tonight—the witchcraft I didn't know how to use, the unexplained panic in the horses' eyes from last week, and Lucian's odd behavior. Because tonight, none of it mattered.

I spent the morning in the barn, grooming Gypsy and helping Becca with the chores. As the day wore on, my headache grew stronger, in spite of the aspirin I had taken. I returned to the house around noon and ate a hearty lunch, hoping that would get rid of the discomfort. To my dismay, nothing made me feel better. What had begun as a dull ache escalated into a sharp pain. Even resting in bed for most of the afternoon didn't help.

At five o'clock, after drinking more caffeine than one should probably consume in a week and taking six aspirins, I felt far worse than I had when I'd woken up this morning. The pain extended above my eyebrows, making my head feel like it was caught in a vice being cranked together.

I finally sat up in bed and glanced at the open closet where my new dress hung under a plastic cover. Tears of disappointment filled my eyes. I wanted to enjoy tonight so badly, but I wasn't sure how I could with the crippling pain in my head. I swallowed the lump forming in my throat and took a deep breath, determined to endure the agony. There was no other option. I couldn't break my date with Alex. He would be crushed. Getting stood up for a dance like Homecoming was the kiss of death for a senior. I would never forgive myself if I hurt him like that.

After a hot shower that failed to wash away the pain as I hoped, I got ready for my date. The roar of the hair dryer made my head pound even more, but I refused to let it beat me down. I managed to brush my hair into soft waves, apply some makeup, and slip into my dress. Then I added a rhinestone necklace and matching earrings to my ensemble.

I paused in front of the mirror, pleased with everything except the tortured look in my eyes. My dress fit perfectly, the V-neck top giving me a hint of cleavage and the hem ending right above my knees, showing off my legs. Black worked for me, making my strawberry blonde hair seem lighter and enhancing my blue eyes. On any other night, I would have been overflowing with excitement. But it was impossible to enjoy a night while suffering with an excruciating headache.

I tried to smile, but it was useless. How I would hide my misery from Alex, I had no idea. If he knew that it felt like a jackhammer was pounding into my skull, surely he would insist I stay home and rest. After disappointing him the night of the party when I had gotten drunk, I still felt like I needed to make it up to him. Tonight had to be perfect. Taking a deep breath, I prayed for the strength to let me get through the dance without letting Alex see just how uncomfortable I was.

Grabbing the tiny black purse that contained my phone, ID, and cash, I marched out of the room in my high heels, ready to get the night over with.

Why is this happening? I thought. *This isn't how a dance should begin—with me wishing it was already over.* I shook my head, annoyed and in a bad mood. When I reached the bottom of the stairs, the dogs trotted over to me. I hesitated, not wanting them to smudge my dress with their wet noses.

Becca must have read my mind because she called to them from where she stood in the kitchen. As they returned to the table and plunked down on their beds without another glance at me, Becca whistled. "You look gorgeous. I love that dress on you. It's fun and carefree."

"Thanks," I said, mustering up a faint smile on my way to the island. I sat down on one of the stools, wincing from the sharp pain splitting my head in two. "Ow." I reached up, rubbing above my eyebrows as I must have done hundreds of times today.

"Are you okay?" Becca asked.

"Yes," I lied. "I just have an annoying headache that won't go away. But I'm fine."

"Are you sure?"

"I think so," I said with a nod, wanting to change the subject. "What are you and Gabriel up to tonight?"

"We're just going to stay in. Gabe went into town to run some errands, and he's picking up a pizza for dinner while he's there."

At that moment, the doorbell rang, sending another splintering jab into my skull and breaking my attention away from Becca.

I sucked in a sharp breath. My head felt like it was shattering into pieces, the pain becoming almost unbearable. I leaned my elbows on the granite and dropped my head into my hands, closing my eyes for a second.

"Gracyn," Becca said softly, sounding concerned. "Your date is here."

I looked up, feeling light-headed. "Right. I'll get the door."

As I stood up, Becca shot around the island and wrapped her fingers around my wrist. "You don't look okay. How bad is it?"

I tried to shrug, my gaze drifting to the door to avoid meeting her eyes. "I'm not going to lie. It hurts. But I have to be tough tonight. For Alex." I looked back at her, hoping she understood how important it was that I went to the dance, no matter how much I was suffering.

Her expression softened. "Well, do you want to take something? I have some Tylenol."

"No, thanks. I've already tried just about everything. Nothing has worked. Unless you want to give me something stronger like the medicine Gabriel gets for you. Do you think I could try that?"

"I can't give you one of those pills without checking with him first. I wish you had said something earlier when he was home."

"I didn't want to bother him. And it wasn't that bad a few hours ago. It got much worse this afternoon."

"You are never a bother to either one of us. Well, if you want to wait until he gets back, that's certainly an option."

"No. Alex is here, and I don't want to make him wait any longer than I already have." I stepped away from the island when another thought occurred to me. Stopping, I glanced at Becca. "Please don't say anything to Alex."

She frowned as though she didn't like my request. "Fine," she said after a long pause. "I won't. But you have to smile a little, or he's going to know something is wrong."

"I'll try." I made an attempt, although it felt weak. "How's this?"

"Better," Becca said, although I wasn't convinced.

Without another word, I went to the door and opened it, realizing it was going to be a long night.

Alex stood on the porch, his hair pulled back into a ponytail without one strand out of place. An earring glittered above his dark jacket, and his gray tie stood out against his white shirt. He smiled, holding out a white corsage. "Wow. You look amazing. I don't think I've ever seen you in a dress."

My heart soared from his compliment, and my headache disappeared for a second. "I don't think I've seen you in a suit, so I guess we're even."

"I hardly think we're even because I doubt you have any idea what you're doing to me right now," Alex said in a low voice, a gleam in his eyes.

I felt a blush race over my cheeks and I looked down, a little embarrassed. I hoped Becca hadn't heard him, but at least his words distracted me from the pain for a minute.

"This is for you," Alex said, stepping closer to me. He carefully pinned the corsage below my left shoulder, smiling at his handiwork. "It looks perfect."

I ran my fingers over the soft petals as Becca approached us. "Okay, you two," she said. "How about a picture?"

I started to object when I noticed Alex beaming. "That would be great," he replied, pulling his phone out of his pocket. "Can you get a few for me, too?"

Alex and I stood together, his arm draped over my shoulders. I tried to relax, hoping I didn't look as bad as I felt. After Becca snapped a few pictures, she set her camera aside and took several more with Alex's phone before giving it back to him. Then we turned to leave.

"Have a great time," Becca said.

"We will," Alex replied. "Thanks again for taking some pictures."

After we stepped out onto the front porch, Becca closed the door behind us. Alex took my hand and we walked along the boards until we reached the steps. "Alone at last," he said, squeezing my hand.

When I looked up at him, he stopped. "Is it okay to kiss you before the dance?" he asked.

I paused, wishing I could enjoy his attention. But tonight, all of my energy was consumed fighting the pain.

He seemed to assume that my silence meant yes and slid his arm around my waist, pulling me against his chest before placing his lips on mine.

I stiffened immediately, oblivious to his touch because my headache returned in full force, making every breath I took feel like a living hell.

"Everything okay?" he asked, his eyes searching mine.

"Yes," I whispered, feeling badly for lying. "I just don't want to mess up my hair and makeup. Besides, Becca's inside and Gabriel could pull up any minute. It would be a little awkward if they saw us kissing on the porch." My excuse was lame since Becca and Gabriel never held back their affection for one another around me, but I had to say something.

"Okay," Alex said. "I wouldn't want to make you uncomfortable."

"Thanks." I smiled weakly until the sharpest pain I had felt all day seemed to shatter my skull. "Ow!" I gasped before I could stop myself.

"Gracyn, are you okay?"

"Yes," I replied quickly. *Think fast,* I told myself. *Don't ruin this for Alex. Just make something up before he realizes the truth.* "It's these new shoes. The straps are a little tight. Maybe I can loosen them in the car."

"Well, we can't have you hurting from them tonight." In a swift movement, Alex scooped me up, wrapping one arm around my back and lifting my knees with the other.

I curled my arm around his shoulders, wanting to laugh and cry at the same time as he carried me down the steps to his Jeep. When he put me down next to the passenger door, I glanced up at the dark sky. The light from the full moon hovering above the trees washed out the stars.

"Wow," I said. "Look at the moon. I can't remember the last time I saw a full moon. Of course, back in Maryland, it was hard to notice the moon and stars at night because of all the city lights."

"Well, we don't have any of those around here."

"I've noticed."

Alex smiled. "What do you like better? The city or the country?"

"I haven't decided yet. The jury's still out."

"Ah," he mused. "Then I have to keep working on you."

I laughed. "It's nothing personal. There are things I miss about home." My mother, feeling normal, and not knowing witches and magic existed topped the list. "But there are other things I really like about Sedgewick."

"Might I be one of those things?"

"You really are fishing tonight, aren't you?"

"Damn right." He leaned toward me, dropping his voice to a whisper. "You look really sexy in that dress. You probably shouldn't know what went through my mind when I first saw you." His breath tickled my skin, causing me to forget my headache for a moment. But my reprieve ended a second later, reminding me that the pain was unshakable.

"Then don't tell me," I said, my eyes suddenly filling with moisture. *Don't cry now! You're almost in the car. Just keep up the convincing performance. You're doing great. And remember, this is for Alex. He deserves to have an amazing time tonight, and you don't want to ruin it for him.*

This could have been such a wonderful night. I loved the way Alex made me feel between his warm smile and strong touch. I could get lost in his arms tonight if it wasn't for my headache.

Alex seemed to sense that something was off and pulled away from me. "You're not upset, are you?"

I shook my head. "No. Of course not."

"Good. Because sometimes I don't get you."

I raised my eyebrows. "Don't overanalyze things. I already told you I never went to the Homecoming dance back home. I'm just a little nervous right now."

"You shouldn't be. It's just me, remember?"

"You're right," I said with a sigh. "I should relax."

"Yes, you should. We have a long night ahead because things won't end when the dance does."

"Remind me again what you're talking about." I quirked my eyebrows in mock confusion, then bit my lower lip to keep from laughing.

"I'll remind you right here, right now." His smile faded as he stepped closer to me and trailed his fingers down my back to the curve of my butt, continuing down until his hand stopped at the top of my thigh.

"Okay. Got it. I won't forget again," I said, a fire racing through my veins from his touch.

"Good." He backed away and opened the door. As he helped me into the seat, a cold wind blew and I shivered for the first time since coming outside. I hadn't even noticed the chill in the air against my arms because Alex had been so close, keeping me warm. Or was my headache jumbling the thoughts in my mind, causing me to forget something as simple as my coat?

Before he shut the door, he must have read my mind. "Do you want to get a coat?"

"No," I said, shaking my head. The cool air actually felt good. Maybe it would help relieve the pain. "I'll be fine. If I get cold, you can warm me up."

"You can count on me," he replied, a look of anticipation in his eyes before he shut the door. I watched him walk around the front of the Jeep, hoping I hadn't given him a false hope for tonight. As much as I liked him, I felt a little guilty for using him as a distraction. At least I seemed to have hidden my headache from him in the ten minutes since he had arrived. Unfortunately, I had several more hours of pretending to go.

When Alex jumped in on the driver's side and started the engine, I leaned back, feeling the pain grow stronger again. One thing was certain. It wasn't going away any time soon.

13

As soon as Alex led me through the doorway to the dark gym, the loud music pushed my pain to a new high. Voices rang out all around us, and a disco ball twirled from the ceiling. Speckled lights circulated over faces, suits and shimmering dresses of all colors. I could barely keep up with Alex, and if he hadn't been holding my hand firmly, he probably would have lost me. I bumped into the other students, muttering "Sorry" about fifteen times while we squeezed through the crowd until Alex found Derek and Lacey.

"Hey, guys!" Derek called when he saw us, a huge grin on his face. "Where've you two been? We were beginning to wonder if you were going to show up."

Alex fist-bumped Derek. "Hey, man."

Derek ran his eyes up and down the length of me and whistled. "You're lookin' good, girl. I don't think I've seen you in a dress before."

"If you have, you're dead meat," Alex warned. "Because I know I haven't."

They both stared at me, and I smiled nervously, my headache causing my vision to blur. When Derek and Alex started talking again, Lacey joined in, but I didn't hear a word they said. The music and voices surrounding us seemed to be getting louder.

I focused on trying to keep my balance in my high heels, hoping it would take my mind off the pain. Slowly reaching my threshold, I was desperate to hold myself together. If I couldn't tolerate the pain any longer, the night would be ruined. I inched closer to Alex, grateful he still held my hand. I tried to listen to the three of them, but I couldn't concentrate. I wasn't sure if I could last another ten minutes, let alone a few more hours.

When Derek and Lacey whirled around and disappeared into the crowd, Alex turned to me. "Want to dance?" he asked.

"Um, sure."

He flashed me a grin before pulling me through the crowd. Music pulsed from the speakers, and everyone in the gym danced in tune to the beat, the disco lights rotating over their smiling faces. I seemed to be the only person here who felt like crying.

When we found some space near Derek and Lacey, Alex spun around to face me. He started to let go of me, but I squeezed his hand. Instead of releasing me, he slipped his arm around my waist. "Is this how you want to dance?" he asked, his chest pressing against mine.

I nodded and wrapped my arms around his shoulders, drawing in a deep breath when I felt moisture filling my eyes. *No!* I thought. *Don't do it. Be strong. You can hang in there. It's just a few hours.* I gulped, trying to hold my tears at bay and forcing myself to stay composed as my eyes wandered, scanning the crowd behind Alex.

Everyone in the gym was a blur until a pair of familiar green eyes locked in on me. Lucian. He was the only person in focus. His hair was neatly combed, his jaw clean-shaven, and his black suit presumably of the highest quality and very expensive. He watched me for a moment, a thoughtful yet concerned look in his eyes. When Zoe swayed up to him, her dark blue gown shining under the speckled lights, she slid her arms around his shoulders, holding him close, commanding his attention.

A sharp pang of jealousy struck my heart, and I looked away. Silently scolding myself for caring who Lucian was with, I tripped in my high heels and clutched Alex's shoulders to keep from falling. He steadied me against his chest, locking his arms around me.

I shook my head, unable to stop the tears from rolling down my face. "I'm sorry," I whispered before pressing my forehead against his jacket. "I can't do this. It hurts too much."

Alex stopped moving to the music, oblivious to the other kids dancing all around us. "Gracyn," he said, his voice and expression full of concern. "What are you talking about? Is it your shoes again? Because I'm sure you can take them off. No one will care. They probably won't even notice."

I wanted to tell him the truth, but the words got stuck in my throat. The alternating lights and shadows swarmed around me, making me dizzy. The pain had me in its clutches, squeezing my head from side to side. "No, it's not my shoes. I've had a headache all day, and it's getting a lot worse in here from the music and the crowd," I explained, feeling guilty that I had given up trying to tolerate the pain because now our night would be ruined. "I'm sorry." The words escaped in a whisper before my eyes closed.

Feeling weak, I hoped Alex wouldn't let go of me. Within seconds, an arm slipped around my back and another one slid under my knees. Then I was floating through the dark, passing by the sea of students. When we reached the door, Alex rushed me out into the bright hallway where he put me down on a chair.

Stooping in front of me, he rubbed my upper arms. "Gracyn, why didn't you tell me when I picked you up?"

Before I could answer him, a paper cup filled with water appeared in front of me, and I took it. As I sipped it, Lacey sat down beside me, her red dress falling below her knees. Her brown hair had been swept up into a twist and sparkling earrings dangled from her ears. "You almost passed out in there. Are you okay?" she asked with a concern that seemed out of character for her.

Dismissing my surprise at her compassion, I finished the water. Then I handed the cup back to her. I dropped my chin, staring down at my dress. Sifting my hands through my hair, I shook my head. "No, I'm not."

When I looked up, my eyes met Alex's. "I'm sorry," I repeated, my voice cracking.

"It's okay," he said softly. "I just wish you had told me you weren't feeling well."

I took a deep breath, letting it out with a shudder. "I didn't want to ruin tonight."

"So you elected to suffer instead?"

I nodded, blinking back my tears.

"You'd do that for me?" he whispered, reaching up and tracing the side of my face with his fingertips.

"Of course," I answered.

When Alex didn't respond right away, Lacey fumbled with her small black purse. "I have some aspirin," she announced, whipping out a tiny pill bottle. "Here, maybe these will help."

I shook my head as she dumped two pills into her hand. "Thanks, Lacey. But I already tried that. Not to mention nearly an entire pot of coffee. I probably won't sleep for days." That was ironic, because I just wanted to sleep so I wouldn't feel the pain any longer.

"You sure?"

"Yes. You wouldn't happen to have any strong sedatives in there, would you? Something that could knock me out?"

Lacey dropped the pills into the bottle and twisted the cap back into place. "No. Sorry. Well, I hope you feel better, but I need to go find Derek. He's probably wondering where I disappeared to." She stood up, excusing herself before returning to the gym.

I frowned, shifting my attention back to Alex. "What should we do now?"

"Well, that's really up to you."

I sighed, not sure what to say. Stalling, I asked, "Can I get a little more water?"

"Of course," Alex said. He reached for the paper cup before jumping up and hurrying away. As soon as he was gone, I bent my head, pushing it against my hands. But every time I tried to fight the pain with pressure, no amount of rubbing gave me even the slightest relief.

As I stared down at my dress, a shadow appeared in front of me. I assumed it was Alex returning until I looked up to see Lucian studying me, his eyes worried. "I saw Alex carry you out of the gym, and I thought I would check on you. What's going on? Are you okay?"

"Do I look okay?" I asked, wondering why he cared after blowing me off all week.

"No," he said softly, either completely missing the sarcasm in my voice or choosing to ignore it. He kneeled before me and reached up, placing his hands on my forehead and my cheek. "You don't feel feverish. Tell me what hurts."

Looking up, I caught his intense gaze. My frustration with him suddenly crumbled, and I pointed at my forehead. "Here. You wouldn't happen to have some of your miracle tea with you, would you?"

"No, but even if I did, unless you drank half a bottle of tequila or whiskey, it wouldn't work."

"Then what good are you?" I meant it as a joke, but when I smiled, the stabbing pain returned, causing me to wince.

He shook his head, his expression solemn and sincere. "You need to get some rest. You shouldn't have come out tonight, not if you were in this much pain."

When I shifted my gaze up at him, Alex returned with my water. He sat down and handed it to me. "Thank you," I murmured, taking it from him.

"Alex, Gracyn really should go home," Lucian said.

"You don't need to worry about her," Alex replied, his voice flat. "I'm perfectly capable of taking care of her. You have your own date to tend to."

I whipped my head toward Alex, cringing inwardly at his cold tone. I placed my hand on his forearm, my eyes locking with his, silently begging him not to make a scene. "It's okay. He's only trying to help."

With a nod, Alex slid his attention back to Lucian, his expression hard and suspicious. Before he had a chance to say a word, an irritated female voice broke through the silence that had fallen over us. "Lucian. I didn't come to the dance stag, and I don't appreciate being left alone."

When I looked up, Zoe was standing across the hall. Her arms were folded across her dress, her icy blue eyes flashing with anger. The last thing I needed right now was her bitterness. Ignoring the scorn she cast my way, I turned to Alex.

All I could think about was getting out of here. Nothing else mattered. Not Lucian or the jealousy that snuck into me every time I was reminded of his relationship with Zoe. I had even lost hope of enjoying the night with Alex, the one I should be thinking about.

Lucian took a deep breath as if irritated and rose to his feet, not bothering to turn around. "A little patience and understanding wouldn't kill you, Zoe," he said.

A scowl on her face, she huffed and whipped around, her ebony hair sweeping across her shoulders. She disappeared into the gym, but Lucian didn't follow her. Instead, he focused on me. "Sorry about that. She can be a little insensitive sometimes. Alex, you're a nice guy. Too bad your cousin doesn't have the same traits."

"She may not be perfect, but she is your girlfriend," Alex reminded him.

Lucian ignored Alex's comment and extended his hand out to me. "Come on. I'll walk you out."

I glanced at Alex, worried he would become defensive again. "That's okay," I said quickly. "I can go with Alex."

Lucian raised his eyebrows. "You sure?"

I nodded. "Yes. I'll be fine."

"But he had to carry you out of the gym."

"That's because the music and the crowd made me a little dizzy. I'm fine now. I can handle getting back to the car."

"Yeah, Lucian. I got this." Alex stood up, facing Lucian. His shoulders straight and tall, Alex narrowed his eyes. "Just get back to Zoe and keep her happy."

Lucian glanced my way, sympathy lurking deep in his eyes. "Well, I tried. Take care, Gracyn." Then he gave Alex a swift nod before returning to the gym. I assumed he would track down Zoe, apologize and make things right with her. The thought of the two of them back in each other's arms for the night made me want to throw up, and I instantly scolded myself for caring. Where did that come from? *Even in pain, you can't stop obsessing about him. It's just as well. If you can't manage to get through a party without getting drunk or a dance without getting sick, Alex is going to give up on you. And quite frankly, I don't blame him. You don't deserve him.*

My thoughts cut through my heart like a knife, but only because they spoke the truth. I shook my head, trying to blame my feelings on the pain.

"Hey," Alex said, breaking me out of my thoughts. "Are you ready to go?"

"Yes," I declared quietly. When he reached down to me, I took his hand and stood up. The blood seemed to rush out of my head, and I clutched his arm, my vision becoming blurry again for a moment.

"Whoa," he said, wrapping an arm around my waist. "Easy. Take your time."

"Thanks."

With his arm holding me close, he led me down the hall to the front door, stopping briefly to toss the empty cup into a garbage can. Then we stepped outside into the night.

The soft light from a few lampposts was just enough for us to see the stairs leading to the parking lot. At the bottom, Mr. Wainwright approached. He wore a pressed suit, his hair brushed into place and the five-o'clock shadow sprinkled over his jaw less scruffy than usual. "Aren't you two supposed to be heading in the other direction? The dance is this way." He pointed at the school.

I shook my head, noting the concern in his eyes. "I'm not feeling well," I explained.

He scrunched his eyebrows as if not sure what to think. "Really? You must feel pretty bad if you're leaving the dance when it's barely started."

At that moment, the pain struck again, squeezing my forehead above my eyebrows. "It was just too crowded and loud in there," I whispered.

"I'm sorry. I don't know what to say except I hope you feel better soon. If there's anything I can do, let me know."

His offer left me feeling a little embarrassed. Even though I knew he was trying to be nice, I didn't understand why he seemed to care. "Thank you, but I think I just need to rest."

"Okay." Mr. Wainwright looked at Alex. "I take it you're going to make sure she gets home soon?"

"Yes. Becca and Gabriel should be there, so maybe Gabriel can give her something for the pain."

A dark shadow raced over Mr. Wainwright's expression at the mention of Becca and Gabriel, but he recovered quickly and nodded. "All right. Well, I need to get inside. I promised to chaperone tonight, and I'm running a little late." Shifting his attention to me, he smiled softly. "I hope you feel better, Gracyn."

"Thank you," I said before averting my eyes away from him.

When Mr. Wainwright continued on his way to the school, Alex and I headed across the parking lot. The reflection of lights glinted in the car mirrors, twinkling in the night. The full moon had risen high in the sky, a purple glow surrounding it against a veil of black. I couldn't believe such a beautiful night was about to be wasted because of a stupid headache.

We had almost reached Alex's Jeep when a breeze sent goose bumps racing over my arms and legs. I shivered, grateful when Alex pulled me closer to him. "Cold?"

"A little. But it actually feels good." Either the cold temperature or the fresh air seemed to give me a little relief. The pain lessened, but I didn't dare hope that the torture was over. I suspected any reprieve I got would only be temporary until the morning.

Alex helped me into the Jeep before hopping into the driver's seat. A comfortable silence lingered between us on the way home. I leaned back, watching the shadows fade in and out across the road leading us home.

When we arrived, Alex parked in front of the house, shut off the engine and turned to me. "Feeling any better yet?"

I wanted to lie and tell him yes, but I couldn't. "Not really." I sighed, staring out the windshield at the front porch lit up by the single light beside the door. "I'm so sorry about tonight. We just can't catch a break, can we?" I asked, wondering what he must be thinking.

"Maybe not, but I still like you."

"Good. Me, too," I said, my voice low as I shifted my gaze to him, searching his expression for a sign of forgiveness.

"Well, you should get inside. You need to rest." He reached over, touching my hand. "Come on. I'll walk you to the door."

Alex jumped out of the Jeep and met me on the other side. With his arm locked around my shoulders, he led me up the front steps. The lights were on inside the house, and I hesitated at the door. "What?" he asked.

"Becca and Gabriel are up."

"Of course they are. It's only eight-thirty."

"They probably thought they wouldn't see me before they went to bed." I frowned, feeling like the lamest girlfriend in the world. It was bad enough Alex, Lacey and Lucian had seen me lose the battle against my pain tonight, and I didn't want to have to explain it again, even though Becca knew I wasn't feeling well earlier when Alex picked me up. With a sigh, I leaned against the door, savoring the cool air.

"Don't you want to go in?" Alex asked.

"Not really."

"Why not?"

"Because it's a little embarrassing," I admitted.

"Gracyn," Alex began. "You need to stop feeling badly about this. It's not like you can control it. Besides, maybe Gabriel can give you something to help you sleep."

"I know. But—"

"But?"

"I don't know him very well yet. And I don't want either one of them feeling sorry for me." Wanting to change the subject, I walked across the porch and leaned my arms on the railing. I gazed up at the sky, admiring the moon.

Alex approached behind me, wrapping his arms around my sides. He leaned his chest against my back, sliding his chin over my shoulder. A new wave of goose bumps ran over my skin, but these came from his touch, not the cold. He rubbed my upper arms, his hands warming me up.

For a fleeting moment, I considered returning to the dance, but there was no guarantee my reprieve would last all night. The pain had reached its height at the dance, and I wasn't prepared to fight it again.

Whipping around, I faced Alex. "I'm sorry about tonight. I really am."

"Shh," he whispered before kissing my forehead. He ran his hands down my arms and back up, resting them on my shoulders under my hair. "It's okay. But if it makes you feel better, you can make it up to me later."

"At this rate, I'll owe you for the rest of my life."

"I'm sure that's not going to happen," Alex said with a smile. "Are you ready to go in now?"

"No. I think I'm going to stay out here a little longer. The cool air feels good. You can leave. You should go back to the dance and have fun."

"It won't be the same without you. I'm happy to hang out here with you for a while."

"Thanks. But I don't think I'll be very good company. I kind of want to be alone for a while."

"Okay," he relented. "I'll call you tomorrow to see how you're feeling. Just promise me you'll go inside soon. I don't want you catching a cold. You don't even have a coat on, and it feels like it's getting colder by the minute."

"Okay *Dad.*"

Alex laughed softly. "I'm serious, but only because I care about you. In any case, I'll leave you alone now. I hope you feel better soon."

"Thanks. So do I."

"Goodnight," he said.

"Goodnight, Alex."

He turned, walked down the steps and jumped into his Jeep. After he started the engine, the headlights shining in the darkness, he backed away from the house and drove down the driveway, leaving me alone.

As soon as the Jeep disappeared, a hush fell over the night. My pain returning, I rubbed my forehead and glanced at the front door, hesitant to go inside and explain what I was doing home so early. Without a second thought, I rushed down the steps to the driveway. I stopped at the bottom, my attention focused on the barn. I suddenly longed for Gypsy's silent company on this night of disappointment. Images of the other kids laughing and smiling back at the dance tugged at my heart. That was where I should be, having the time of my life with Alex. Instead, here I was, suffering and miserable.

My mood falling to a new low, I felt a tear roll down my face. A sudden desire to see Gypsy, stroke her soft neck and read the unspoken sympathy in her eyes came over me.

I began to make my way across the driveway, but walking on gravel in high heels was nearly impossible. Every step was a challenge until I shifted my weight to my toes, not letting the stones throw me off balance.

I was only halfway to the barn when something white in the woods caught my eye. *Snow?* I wondered, surprised that one of the dogs would be out here alone when Becca and Gabriel were inside.

I turned and approached the edge of the trees, searching for whatever I had seen in the shadows. I had almost reached the woods when I saw it again. I halted, my jaw dropping at the sight of a white wolf. Bigger than a dog, it paced between the trees, its stride stealthy. I blinked a few times, not sure if I believed my eyes. But the wolf remained in my sights, weaving around the bushes, seeming nervous.

I concentrated on breathing, my limbs feeling heavy as though I was paralyzed. A breeze whispered through the leaves, causing the wolf to shimmer in the moonlight, its body appearing translucent like that of a ghost. I sucked in a sharp breath, mesmerized. At first I thought I was imagining it, but the wolf continued to flutter in and out of focus.

I couldn't tear my eyes away from it. I stood still, watching it stop and turn in my direction, its yellow eyes locked on me. An icy chill shot through my veins, and something told me I should run, but the message never got through. Instead, I remained where I was, my attention focused on the wolf as I waited for its next move.

14

The white wolf stared at me from where it stood in the shadows. I expected it to threaten me with a growl, but it remained silent as it crept toward me. The wind whipped through it, causing the apparition to wave like a flag. A small voice in the corner of my mind told me to back away, but my feet felt as though lead weights had bolted them to the ground. The wolf came closer, captivating me, the intense but non-threatening expression in its eyes turning my fear into curiosity.

"Please help me," whispered the same voice I had heard the afternoon at the rock. "Follow my friend. She will bring you to me."

I gasped in surprise and looked around, but found no sign of anyone in the darkness. When I shifted my attention back to the wolf, it stood within an arm's reach. As my gaze locked on the golden eyes staring up at me, the pain that had tortured me all day vanished.

"What are you?" I murmured, shaking my head in disbelief. I extended a trembling arm out to it and attempted to stroke the fur between its ears, but my fingers passed through the illusion. "How is this possible?" I wondered out loud. "What do you want?"

"To return," the voice replied. "I need you, Gracyn. You're the only one who can save me."

The wolf shook its head, then backed up a step. It turned halfway, but stopped to watch me, as if expecting me to follow. "Please," the woman begged. "You must come tonight or the portal will close until the next full moon. The pain you felt today is nothing compared to the agony I've been in for centuries."

I sucked in a sharp breath, scanning the darkness and wishing I knew who the voice belonged to. It intrigued me, but at the same time, it scared me. For a second, I considered running back to the house, and instantly, the stabbing pain returned. I closed my eyes and reached up to touch my forehead.

"You're hurting," the woman said. "Come to me, and I will get rid of your pain."

"How?" I asked, opening my eyes and staring at the wolf.

"Just trust me," she replied.

I hesitated before making a decision. "Fine," I whispered. "Tell me where to go."

"Follow the wolf."

As if in a trance, I took a step forward, approaching the animal. It whirled around and trotted into the woods, heading for the trail. I followed as quickly as I could, my high heels wobbly on the gravel.

Reaching the path, I entered the forest, grateful for the even footing. The wolf led the way, occasionally glancing back at me, its body shimmering in and out of focus. I had gone about fifty feet when thunder roared out from the barn, as though someone was trying to break down the door. Then a loud whinny shrieked through the night. Gypsy. I skidded to a halt, my heels digging into the ground. Turning, I looked behind me for a moment, the silence returning.

I wasn't sure if I should keep following the wolf. As I hesitated, the pain struck again, putting an end to my relief. *You can't stop. Do what she says. It's the only way to get rid of your headache.* Whipping around, I saw the wolf far ahead in the distance. I launched into a jog, immediately hitting an exposed tree root and falling to my knees. My hands caught my fall, my fingers digging into the soft earth. With a deep sigh, I stood up, brushing the dirt and leaves off my dress. Worried I would trip again, I kicked off my shoes.

Leaving them on the side of the trail, I took off after the wolf. The moment I headed in its direction, my pain subsided as the woman promised. The cold ground beneath my feet was a small price to pay to escape my headache.

After racing past the garden and the trail leading to Lucian's estate, I caught up to the wolf. It ran ahead, often stopping to wait for me to catch up. Every time it peered at me, its yellow eyes glowed in the moonlight and its expression remained docile.

A few minutes later, the wolf darted off the path and into the woods. I stopped and stared into the darkness, wary about leaving the trail. The last time I had ventured into the woods flashed through my memory. If I got lost in the fog, I doubted Lucian would find me again since the dance wouldn't end for several hours. I was on my own tonight.

Hesitating, I studied the hillside. I couldn't be sure if this was the exact location on the trail that led to the fog, but I knew it was close enough. Unsure, I stood at the edge of the trees. The wolf had disappeared in the distance, causing me to linger a moment longer.

Before I could head back down the trail toward home, the wolf appeared in the shadows, a scornful look crossing over its eyes as if scolding me.

"No, I can't go there," I explained in a hushed voice, as though the wolf understood.

The wolf gave a subtle nod before it felt like a hammer pounded into my skull. Tears welled up in my eyes, and I fought to keep my composure, biting my lip to keep from crying. "Okay. I'm coming. Please, just make the pain stop."

Without another thought of heading home, I launched into the woods, the wolf in my sights. The underbrush scraped my arms and legs, and I winced when a thorny branch caught onto my panty hose, ripping a hole in the nylon. I slowed down, stepping gingerly on sticks and rocks that battered my feet. By the time I caught up to the wolf, my feet felt bruised. "Are we almost there?" I muttered.

"Yes," the voice said, louder now. "You know where we're taking you. You've been there once before."

"No," I protested, halting on the hillside when chills trailed down my spine. She had just confirmed my suspicions that she was taking me back to the fog, the one place I had pledged never to return to. "I don't want to go back there."

"It's okay, my dear. You're safe as long as you come with us. You will be protected, I promise. But if you don't..." The sinister tone in her unfinished sentence made my skin crawl.

What am I doing? I thought. *Following a ghost wolf out into the middle of nowhere? All for what? Because I can't handle a measly headache?* Deciding to turn back, I whirled around only to feel shooting pain again. The intensity brought me to my knees as I clutched my head.

A pile of damp leaves broke my fall. Kneeling with my hands pressed up against my forehead, I realized I didn't have the strength to fight. *Just do what she tells you. It's not worth suffering.*

Rising to my feet, I swallowed. "Fine," I declared. "Just tell me what to do so I can get this over with."

"That's the spirit," the voice whispered, her soft tone returning as though she was pleased with my compliance.

The wolf floated down the hill toward me, an impatient look in its eyes. I nodded and marched ahead, continuing deeper into the woods. I followed the wolf through the underbrush, our pace slower than it had been on the trail. I pushed the branches aside, determined to keep going since there was no turning back.

After what felt like an eternity, we reached the top of the hill. The air grew colder, the black night giving way to fog that glowed in the moonlight. Clouds draped over the trees, hiding the tallest branches. The birds I remembered from several weeks ago were absent, leaving the land in an eerie silence as I trudged through the white veil of mist.

"Are we almost there?" I muttered, annoyed when the wolf ran far ahead, making it seem like we were heading into the middle of nowhere. "You never warned me that we were running a midnight marathon."

The voice never answered me. Left with no choice but to keep walking, I followed until I emerged into a clearing. I stopped, my heart falling into my stomach at the sight of tombstones rising up from the leaves covering the ground. A picket fence surrounded the small area, its paint chipped and its boards rotting from decay.

Pulling myself together, I walked into the graveyard and approached a headstone. Vines crawled over the front of it, the leaves dead and brown. The slate was riddled with cracks in the engraving that read, "Esmerelda, 1410 – 1622." I didn't bat an eye at the dates. Becca had lived far longer than that.

I walked over to the next stone which, like the first one, was cracked and covered in dead brown ivy. "Igor, 1388 – 1617," had been carved on the surface. I ran my fingers over the top, feeling the cold rock before glancing about, searching for the wolf.

I spun around, spotting it near the fence across from me. Forgetting the tombstones, I hurried over to it, my mind set on taking care of whatever was expected of me and getting home, if I could find my way. But I couldn't worry about my sense of direction now. Until I finished with whatever I had been brought here for, going home wasn't an option, unless I wanted to suffer.

The wolf led me to a stone building at the far edge of the graveyard directly across from the gate. Approaching the door, the wolf apparition rose into the air. After fluttering in and out of focus, it exploded into a cloud of tiny white particles. They extended into a long row like a ribbon waving in the breeze. Then it slithered into the building through the crack between the door and the wall, disappearing from sight.

Left alone, I froze. The cold air sent goose bumps racing over my skin, and I wrapped my arms over my chest, rubbing them. Not a single sound could be heard. I huffed, searching for a sign that would tell me what I had been led here to do.

"I could use a little help," I said, hoping the woman who had spoken earlier would hear me. "What do you want from me?" When I received no response, I threw my arms up, frustrated. "Seriously? You brought me up here in the dark and the cold just to let me stand around? Please tell me what you need me to do so I can go home."

I waited, suddenly worried I had been brought here to be hurt. Maybe I was a sacrificial lamb. Could that be what had happened to Cassie? Had she been tortured by a headache, only to find relief when she followed the orders?

If only there was a sign. Something to indicate why I was here. At that moment, I heard a faint whimper. My breath caught in my throat and I listened carefully, wondering if I had imagined it. But then it came again, this time a little louder. When it continued, I looked suspiciously at the door to the stone building, my eyebrows scrunched and my head tilted.

The property looked like it had been untouched for years, if not centuries. Dead ivy covered the stone walls and cobwebs dangled from the roof corners in a crisscross pattern. Dirt and dust caked the single window built into the side next to the door. A rusty knob was welded into the stone, a latch above it at eye-level secured with a padlock.

When a scratching sound began from inside the building, my breathing became shallow and I stared at the door. Not sure what to do, I approached it. When I came within an arm's reach of the handle, I paused. "Hello? Is someone in there?" I called.

The scratching sounded again, but faster, as if someone or something was frantically trying to dig out of the building. Then a loud whimper cried out from behind the door.

Flustered, I felt adrenaline pulsing through my veins. My heart rate picked up speed, pounding in my chest, and my thoughts became a whirlwind. Someone or something must have been left in the stone building to die. I had to help, but how? The door was locked, and I certainly didn't have the key.

"You don't need a key," the woman said, her voice floating through the air. "You, Gracyn, are the key."

"What?" I gasped, feeling hopeless. "But that's impossible. It's locked. I don't know what you expect me to do."

"Open the door, Gracyn. You're the only one who can set me free. Go on. Touch the lock. It will open for you."

This is crazy, I thought sarcastically. *And maybe I'll find my true love in there.* This whole thing reminded me of a fairy tale—a sick and twisted one at that.

Figuring I had nothing to lose since my night was shot and I couldn't return to the dance, I grabbed the padlock, expecting to tug on it and prove a point when it didn't budge. But as soon as my hand wrapped around the metal, it disappeared, and I was left holding my hand in a fist.

"I wasn't expecting that," I whispered, rolling my eyes. Hesitantly, I reached down for the door knob, not sure whether to be scared or relieved when it turned right away.

I gave the door a gentle tug, opening it. The hinges creaked as though they hadn't moved in years. Dust rose up in front of me, filling my lungs. I coughed several times from the tickle in my throat, waving to clear the air. When the cloud dissipated, I stepped into the building, searching the darkness for the source of the scratching and whimpering.

A dirty animal lay in a heap on the cement floor, its eyes closed. It looked like a dog, or maybe a little bigger. It was hard to tell from the matted fur clumped over its frail body. It appeared dead, but that couldn't be possible if it had been scratching and whimpering minutes ago. Then I noticed the slightest movement of its chest.

I knelt beside the animal, and it stirred, straining to lift its head. I studied it closely, noticing that its white fur was covered with a thick layer of dirt and dust. When its eyes opened, I jumped back at the sight of the same yellow eyes that belonged to the ghost wolf.

It gazed at me, pain buried deep in its expression. Tears welled up in my eyes, sympathy for this creature that had been locked up and left to die filling my heart.

Oblivious to the cold floor against my feet, I was overwhelmed by the urge to relieve the animal's suffering. But first, I needed to know it was real, not some transparent illusion that would fade away any minute.

Without a moment of hesitation, I placed a hand on its neck, cringing at the feel of its grimy fur.

The wolf glanced back at me, the intensity in its eyes scaring me. But I kept my hand on it, slowly sifting my fingers through its fur until I touched a cold metal collar locked around its neck. I gasped when it disappeared just like the lock had minutes ago.

The wolf took a deep breath, a vibrant glow lighting up its eyes before it leaped to its feet. Knocked backward, I fell onto the cement floor, my eyes never leaving the animal as it transformed right in front of me. The skin sagging over its emaciated frame filled out with muscle and substance, the dirt and grime melting away to reveal a healthy white coat.

Captivated, I watched in awe as the wolf came back to life. I couldn't tear my eyes away from it. It stood tall, its posture straight, its body appearing strong. If I hadn't witnessed the transformation, I never would have believed it was the same animal that had been lying in a heap seconds ago.

The wolf caught my eye and gave me an appreciative nod before sprinting out the door in long strides. In a blink, it was gone, leaving me alone in the decrepit building.

Remaining on the floor for a moment, I stared at the open doorway, my mind drawing a blank. I couldn't believe what I had just seen. *Believe it*, a voice shot out in my head. *And get used to the fact that this crazy stuff is part of your life now. Celeste can turn feathers into doves, and apparently, you can bring dying animals back to life.* Trying to put magic out of my thoughts, I wondered if I had accomplished what I had been brought here to do. If so, I assumed I could return home now.

"Yes," the voice said, drifting into the building from outside. "You may go. And thank you, my dear. You have ended centuries of suffering."

"Just no more headaches, please," I said, but received no response.

After a few seconds of silence, I stood up and walked outside. I staggered for a couple steps, overwhelmed by dizziness. My eyelids heavy, I fought to stay awake and headed across the graveyard, my sights set on the opening in the picket fence.

Fog swirled over the ground while I wandered around the tombstones. My feet felt like they were dragging a ton of bricks, and my headache was long gone, replaced with fatigue. I had only reached the middle of the graveyard when my eyes closed. Then my knees gave out and I fell to the ground as my world went black.

15

When I opened my eyes, I sat up in the most comfortable bed I'd ever slept in. I blinked a few times, not recognizing the pale purple comforter and four-poster bed. The white furniture matched the carpeting, and the walls were the same purple as the bedding. Ruffled curtains framed the windows, allowing sunlight to fill the room.

My gaze swept about, stopping to rest on several pictures propped up on the dresser. Curious, I shoved the comforter aside and slid off the bed. Still wearing my dress from the dance although it was now wrinkled and smudged with dirt, I approached the dresser, my attention captivated by the photographs.

The first one in the row captured a girl who appeared to be about eleven or twelve years old sitting in a meadow, the setting sun casting a yellow glow over her golden hair. Her green eyes sparkled, and a silver cross hung from her neck.

I could have stared at that picture for hours, but I forced myself to move on to the next one. In it, the same girl sat astride a pure white horse, her posture tall and confident. Wearing jeans, her long hair pulled into a ponytail, she rode bareback. A dazzling smile on her face, it was the cross pendant attached to her necklace that caught my attention once again.

A portrait of the same girl standing between Lucian and an older man, their father I presumed, had been positioned on the corner of the dresser. A lump formed in my throat as I realized that the girl in the pictures must be Cassie, and my heart broke when I thought of her untimely death. How anyone could have taken the life of a child was beyond belief.

Trying to distract myself, I scanned the room until I noticed the painting of a white church lit up under a winter sky hanging on the wall. I approached it, drawn to the soft brush strokes of the snow-covered hills.

The sound of the door opening behind me interrupted my thoughts. Turning, I watched Diesel trot into the room and stop when his gaze met mine, causing my heart to thump. Afraid he would growl at me as he did the day I had ridden over to find Lucian, I backed up a step. He remained where he was, his head tilted to the side, his curious dark eyes making me feel self-conscious in my wrinkled dress.

Crossing my arms over my chest, I waited for the Doberman to come closer, but he never did. Instead, a familiar deep voice came from the hallway. "Diesel. Get back here. Didn't anyone tell you it's rude to walk in on a girl before she gets up?" Lucian said.

"It's okay," I called. "I'm awake."

The door swung wide open, and Lucian appeared. Freshly showered, he wore a white button-down shirt that fell over the waist of his jeans. "Sorry about that," he said. "Diesel must have forgotten his manners."

"It's fine. As long as he doesn't attack me," I replied.

"He won't."

"Good," I said with relief. Then, forgetting about the dog, I glanced at the crumpled comforter on the bed, memories of the wolf in the graveyard rushing back to me. "What am I doing here?"

"I found you out in the woods, again," Lucian explained, an added emphasis on his last word. "I'm getting a little tired of that, you know. Want to tell me what happened? I thought you were going home to rest."

"I was. But—" My voice trailed off as I wondered what he would think if I told him a voice in the woods had lured me to a hidden graveyard by controlling my pain.

"But what?" Lucian's green eyes met mine, the concern lurking in his stare unmistakable. "You can tell me anything, even if it sounds crazy. You should know that by now."

I sighed, not sure he'd believe a story about a ghost wolf and one that magically came back to life from my touch. "Sometimes I don't know what to tell you," I said quietly, wanting to ask him why he had blown me off last week when I wanted to talk. But I decided against it, letting that go. "Remember when I heard a voice the day we were up at the rock?"

"Yes."

"Well, I heard it again last night after I got home. But this time, she told me she needed help and asked me to follow a wolf into the woods."

"A wolf?"

Meeting his gaze, I nodded.

"And you did it?" Lucian asked, seeming disappointed with me.

"Only because my headache went away as soon as I went after it," I said with a huff.

"Really?" He appeared interested, but not ready to believe me.

"Yes. And trust me, I tried to turn around several times, but then my head started to hurt again. And I don't mean just a small pain I could tolerate. Each time, it was like someone hit me with a hammer." I'm not sure why I felt compelled to explain, but I wanted him to understand I hadn't ended up in the woods again by choice. I had learned my lesson the first time and, had I been in control, I wouldn't have gotten lost again.

"Then what happened?"

I shrugged, shifting my gaze down to stare at the floor. "I ended up in the fog like last time. Before I could try to find my way home, I must have passed out."

"So you got rid of your headache, but did you ever find out what the voice wanted with you?"

I hesitated, deliberating how much to tell him. Finally, I decided the less he knew, the better. Besides, I just wanted to forget about the wolf and that would be difficult if I talked about it. "No."

"Well, I found you in the graveyard. You might try to stay out of there next time."

"I'll try," I said with a roll of my eyes. "It would have been nice if someone had warned me there was a cemetery in the woods. Finding out in the middle of the night was a little unsettling. So if there's anything else I should know, maybe now is a good time to tell me."

Lucian shook his head. "No, that's the only thing hiding up there."

"Good. I don't need any more surprises." I took a deep breath, ready to change the subject. "Why didn't you take me home when you found me?"

He raised his eyebrows, a knowing look crossing over his face. "I didn't want to show up on Becca and Gabriel's doorstep in the middle of the night. I had a feeling I wouldn't be well-received, especially if I was carrying you."

"So you brought me here instead?"

"Yes. I figured you needed your sleep. And this room has been empty since Cassie died," he said softly, sadness sweeping through his eyes.

Nodding, I returned my attention to the pictures on the dresser. "Is that Cassie?"

Lucian walked across the room and stopped beside me, his attention on the pictures. "Yes."

"She was beautiful."

"I know. And her beauty went far beyond her appearance. She had one of the purest hearts of anyone I've ever known."

I took a deep breath, my shoulders rising and falling. "I don't know how anyone could hurt her. It's really awful. I'm so sorry." Turning away from the dresser, I looked up at Lucian who stood inches away from me. "Tell me about her."

"She was everything you would expect of a young girl. Sweet and caring with a love for animals, especially her horse, Angel. She also loved the church."

"Really?"

"Yes. Ever since she was young, she was fascinated with the music, the candles, the cross, and, as she got older, the scripture."

I shifted my gaze to the painting. "That explains the picture. It's amazing."

"I made that for her."

"You did?" I asked, turning back to him. "I thought you didn't like painting still life."

"I don't. But I wanted to make something special for her."

My gaze drifted to the silver cross hanging over his shirt. Without thinking, I raised my hand and touched it. "And this?"

"It belonged to her. It's the same one she's wearing in the pictures. I wear it to keep my memory of her alive."

Tears filled my eyes when I heard the grief in his voice. Blinking, I nodded, waiting for him to continue.

"I had it engraved on the back. See?" Lucian lifted his hand to pick up the pendant, his fingers brushing against mine. I whipped my hand away while he turned the cross over. The inscription on the back read, "RIP Cassie."

Swallowing, I looked up, and my gaze locked with his. Moisture glistened in his eyes. "I noticed you wear this a lot, but I had no idea what it meant," I said.

"I wouldn't expect you to. Few people understood just how special Cassie was."

"I'm sure she was special, but tell me more about church. I haven't seen Becca and Gabriel go to church once since I moved here. Do we, I mean witches, go to church?"

"We can if we want to. It's not forbidden or anything like that. It's more of a personal preference. We tend to live by our own code, although it's similar to many fundamentals found in the Bible. Cassie preferred the church over everything else. It's unusual for one of us to be drawn to religion, but it's not out of the realm of possibilities."

"Why do you think she liked it so much?"

"I don't know. I tried to figure it out, but I gave up years ago. Perhaps it gave her a sense of peace and belonging, something she couldn't find here at home. That's why I painted the church scene for her. I gave that to her for Christmas the year before she died."

"I'm sure she loved it."

"Yes, she did. She said she would never take it down. And now, as long as I'm alive, it will never leave this room."

A moment of silence fell between us. I glanced at the unmade bed, feeling a little guilty for sleeping in a room that now seemed to be a shrine. I wondered if everything in it had been left in place since Cassie had died, each item holding a cherished memory for Lucian.

I struggled to find something to say, but Lucian beat me to it. "Well, I'm sure you don't want to hang out in my sister's bedroom all day. How about if I take you home? You must be ready to change out of your dress."

Glancing down at the dirty, wrinkled material, I nodded. "Yes. I must be a complete mess." I ran a hand through my hair, trying to smooth out the tangles, but it was hopeless.

Lucian's eyes grazed over me, his expression softening. Without saying a word, he looked down at my feet. "What happened to your shoes?"

"I kicked them off on the trail because they were hard to walk in and I tripped. I think I remember where I left them. I'll look for them later today."

"Would you like to borrow a pair of tennis shoes to wear home? My mother left a lot of her things here. Let me grab some, and we'll see if they fit."

He never gave me a chance to answer. Instead, he turned and disappeared down the hallway, leaving me alone with Diesel. Ignoring the dog who no longer scared me, at least for today, I let my eyes drift around the room. I couldn't help wondering why Lucian had given me Cassie's room for the night. The house was huge, and I imagined it had at least one guest room.

Just be thankful he didn't put you in his bed, a voice rattled off in my mind. Pushing the idea of being in Lucian's bedroom far out of my thoughts,

I approached Cassie's bed and straightened the comforter while waiting for Lucian to return.

As I placed the last decorative pillow against the headboard, Lucian spoke behind me, causing me to jump. "You didn't have to make the bed. I would have taken care of that."

I spun around, smiling appreciatively. "It's the least I can do after you found me last night. I'd probably still be in the graveyard if you hadn't brought me home. I'm guessing it isn't much nicer during the day, either." The thought of spending the night on a bed of leaves in the cold surrounded by tombstones marking the graves of deceased witches made my skin crawl.

His lips hinted at a small smile before he held up a pair of canvas tennis shoes in one hand. "Here. See if these fit," he said, giving them to me when I approached.

Taking them, I noticed my black purse in his other hand.

"And I almost forgot to give you this," he said, holding it out to me.

I slipped into the shoes that were a little tight before reaching for my purse. "Thank you. Did I drop this in the woods? Because I don't remember even carrying it."

"No, you left it on the bleachers in the gym. I found it after Alex took you home. That's why I left the dance early to find you. I figured you were feeling much worse than you let on."

Guilt wormed its way through me. "Guess I couldn't fool you." I toyed with the zipper, my thoughts shifting from Lucian to Becca, wondering if she had left me any messages when I never came home.

"Don't worry. I didn't open it. It's not my style to go through girls' purses."

"I wasn't thinking that," I said quickly. "I was just wondering if Becca went out of her mind not knowing where I was all night."

"You might want to check your phone, then. Maybe you can give her a quick call to let her know you're okay before we leave."

I unzipped the handbag and grabbed my phone. Tucking the purse between my arm and my side, I swiped the screen. It lit up right away, but there were no messages. Not a single voice mail or text. "Hmm," I mused. "That's odd. Nothing."

"Nice sister," Lucian said, immediately noticing my raised eyebrows. "What? In case you haven't noticed, she doesn't exactly like me. But then again, neither does anyone else in town. She probably thinks you stayed out with Alex. Believe me, if she knew you were here with me, she would have sent a search party out to look for you."

I cringed inwardly at the reminder that the town citizens believed he had taken Cassie's life. Even though I wasn't convinced of that, I knew her killer was still on the loose. A quick dose of fear rippled through me before a heavy sadness replaced it. Being in her room and seeing the pictures of her, not to mention the despair in Lucian's eyes when he talked about her, tugged at my heart even though I had never known her.

My thoughts shifting back to Becca, I glanced at Lucian. "Then maybe I need to have a talk with her because I think I can choose who I'm with. You've had plenty of chances to hurt me, and yet all you've done is help me. She should know that by now. And if she doesn't, she will as soon as she finds out you spared me a cold night in a graveyard."

"I'm not sure that's going to be enough to clear the suspicion that I killed my sister," he said, his voice low and bitter, a frown flattening his lips.

A lump building in my throat, I touched his forearm. He flinched, snapping his cold stare up to look at me, as if shocked by my gesture. "Lucian, I—" I started to tell him I believed in his innocence, but he jerked away and cut me off.

"Don't worry about it. I've been living with these demons for over two years now. I knew they would only get worse when I returned to town." He paused, taking a deep breath. "But I'm sure you don't want to stand around in my sister's room wearing last night's dress trying to comfort a monster. Come on, I'll take you home."

The sarcasm in his voice tore at my soul. "I don't think of you as a monster," I said, not sure if he heard me when he turned and walked into the hallway. Left with no choice but to follow him, I headed out of the room, the tight shoes squeezing my toes with each step I took.

I followed Lucian down the staircase in the two-story foyer, the grandeur of the shimmering chandelier seeming wasted in a house haunted by the memory of a little girl taken from the world at such a young age. When Lucian led me outside into the brisk autumn air, the blinding sunlight seemed to wash the doom away. We wandered down the sidewalk to where his Range Rover was parked in the driveway. I went around to the passenger side, noticing that Lucian didn't offer to help me get in. *Alex would have at least opened the door for you,* a voice reminded me, as if I needed convincing that Alex was the right guy for me. *He's a perfect gentleman, and yet you can never seem to keep it together when you're with him.*

I will soon, I promised myself. *I'm going to make up for last night.* Shutting out my inner voices, I slid into the front seat and closed the door.

After the short drive home through the woods lit up with leaves of red and gold, we pulled into Becca and Gabriel's driveway. Lucian eased the SUV to a stop beside my car and turned off the engine as Gabriel stepped outside onto the porch. He scanned us with his crystal clear eyes, a scowl on his face.

I stepped out of the Range Rover and walked around the front of it, meeting Lucian on the other side. We hesitated, watching Gabriel rush down the steps, his footsteps on the wooden planks cutting through the quiet morning.

"What's going on here?" he asked, approaching us. His black shirt made his golden hair seem even lighter in the sunlight. He narrowed his blue eyes, an icy glare in them.

"I'm just making sure she gets home safely," Lucian explained.

"How noble of you," Gabriel said, his words dripping with sarcasm. Then he shifted his attention to me. "Gracyn? Everything okay?"

"Yes. I'm fine," I assured him. "Where's Becca?"

Gabriel's stone cold expression softened. "She's not well."

"Another headache?" I asked.

"Yes," he confirmed.

At least now I knew why she hadn't called or texted me when I never came home last night. "Oh, no," I muttered with dread. "Are they ever going to end?"

"I wish I knew," Gabriel replied.

Lucian's jaw dropped, his gaze darting from me to Gabriel. "Becca's not well? How long has this been going on?" he asked, alarmed.

"It's none of your business," Gabriel shot out.

"I think it's everyone's business," Lucian countered. "We already lost Cassie. We can't lose Becca, too."

"Don't you think I know that?" Gabriel gritted out, his teeth clenched. "Besides, you're one to talk."

Sparks brewed in Lucian's green eyes. "Whatever you think about me, you're wrong. This is neither the time nor the place to go into what happened in the past."

Gabriel relented, although he didn't seem too happy about that. "Fine. So what happened last night? Care to tell me what Gracyn's doing with you?"

Anger simmered in Lucian's expression, but he remained stoic. "I found her in the woods around ten o'clock. She had passed out and it was late, so I took her back to my place. I didn't want to wake you or Becca."

Gabriel slid his gaze over to me, his reaction calm. "Gracyn, what were you doing in the woods? Weren't you supposed to be at the dance?"

"It's a long story," I murmured, not sure how much I wanted to tell him. With careful deliberation, I kept my memory of the wolf and the woman's voice to myself. I had yet to decide how much I should reveal, and I just wanted to sort out what had happened before I attempted to explain it to anyone. A part of me hoped I could forget about it, but I had a feeling that wish would never be granted. "I had a headache. It seems that Becca isn't the only one who gets them now. Do you have any idea what could be causing them?"

Gabriel shook his head thoughtfully. "No, I don't. Sorry."

"I just hope mine was a one-time thing," I said. "But knowing what Becca's going through worries me. I'd really like to talk to her. Is she up?"

"No. I gave her a sedative so she could rest comfortably."

"Another one?" I asked. "Perhaps drugging her isn't the answer."

"And you would rather watch her suffer?" Gabriel challenged. "She takes them willingly. Feel free to ask her about the pain the next time she's up. You just experienced something similar. Imagine if you had to live with it for days on end."

"Of course, I don't want her to suffer," I said quickly. "It's just that sedatives seem a little extreme. Isn't there something she can take for the pain that allows her to function?"

"There was. But her headaches have been getting more severe and lasting longer. I'm doing the best I can. I've consulted with a neurologist whose only recommendation is to send her in for a CT scan. And we all know that won't give us any answers."

"Oh," I said, my hopes deflated. "Okay. I know you're just trying to help her."

"You may be trying to help Becca," Lucian started. "But what about the rest of us? How long were you planning to keep this to yourself?"

"This is a family matter. Stay out of it, Lucian," Gabriel warned. "As long as Becca's alive, everything is fine."

"But these headaches could be a sign," Lucian said. "She's older than any of us, and she's lived longer than any witch in our coven which means she's probably on borrowed time right now. You should not be withholding information regarding her health from the rest of us. My father would not be pleased."

"Leave him out of this. I'm handling it."

"By doing nothing except treating her symptoms. Tell me, Gabriel, are you waiting for her to die? What's in it for you?"

Without a word, Gabriel lunged at Lucian like a strike of lightning. In a flash, he pinned Lucian up against the Range Rover, his hand gripping Lucian's throat. "I don't like what you're insinuating," Gabriel hissed. "Considering your family history, you have no room to talk. I ought to just end you right here, right now. Good riddance if you ask me."

Lucian glared at him, his muscles tense. "Go ahead and try. I'll fight you to the bitter end and take you down with me."

Silence hovered between them, their eyes locked on one another in a heated stare. After a moment, Gabriel released him and backed away. "You'll get what's coming to you. I'll see to that. One of these days, you'll pay for Cassie's death." Done with Lucian, Gabriel turned to me. "Gracyn, you might want to be a little more careful in selecting your friends. Don't trust this one. You need to watch your back."

I wasn't quite sure how to respond. Gabriel didn't seem to realize that I hadn't chosen Lucian. Fate kept bringing him to me, even though he avoided me whenever he had the chance. "I'll keep that in mind," I said.

"Make sure you do. Now, are you coming in?" Gabriel asked.

"In a moment," I told him.

He nodded before tossing one last glare at Lucian. Then Gabriel spun around and retreated up the steps. As soon as he disappeared inside, I looked at Lucian. "I'm sorry about that," I said.

"You don't need to be sorry. It's not your fault. I'm just sorry you have to hear the suspicion and judgment everyone has. You may not believe me, but I didn't kill my sister. I loved her. Our family was pretty dysfunctional, so Cassie and I were closer than most siblings our age."

A wistful glaze swept over his eyes, making me want to reach out and comfort him. But I resisted that urge. "I believe you," I said, realizing the truth in my words as they tumbled out of my mouth.

His eyes brimmed with gratitude. "You have no idea how much that means to me. Now, you'd better go."

"Okay. Well, thank you again for finding me last night. It was nice to wake up in a warm bed instead of a cold cemetery."

"You're welcome. Just promise me one thing."

I raised my eyebrows, not sure I wanted to know what he meant. "What's that?"

A faint smile slid over his lips. "That you'll stay out of the woods for a while. I'm getting a little tired of rescuing you."

"I'll try."

"No, don't try. Just do it," he said before opening the door to the Range Rover. "I mean it this time."

"Fine," I relented. Backing up, I watched him slide into the driver's seat and turn on the engine. Then I gave him a quick wave before he drove away.

As soon as the Range Rover disappeared around the bend, I charged up the steps and into the house.

Gabriel jumped in front of me as I was on my way to the stairs to head up to my room. "Gracyn," he said, a parental tone in his voice. "I have to say, this was quite a surprise. I'm afraid to ask what's going on. You left with Alex, and you returned home with Lucian."

"Lucian explained what happened. I didn't stay out all night on purpose."

"That doesn't matter. What does matter is that you stay away from him. The last thing we want is to bring you home in a body bag. He's not the company you should be keeping."

I could never believe that would happen, but I knew better than to try to convince Gabriel that Lucian wouldn't harm me. "Fine. I'll be careful."

"Good. Now I'm not going to mention this to Becca when she wakes up. I'm actually glad she's too out of it to know who brought you home. She doesn't need anything else to worry about these days."

"I understand."

Gabriel's stern expression softened, a faint smile appearing in its place. "You know, we just care about you. You've got a long life ahead, and we would hate to see anything happen to you."

"Me, too." I glanced at the stairs behind him. "May I go now? I'd really like to change and get started on my homework."

"Of course." Nodding, he moved out of my way.

Without looking back at him, I rushed up the stairs, ready to throw myself into my assignments and forget all about the last twenty-four hours.

16

My day was quite uneventful compared to the previous night. I showered, grabbed a bite to eat and holed myself up in my room with a pile of textbooks and homework. It wasn't until my phone rang at three o'clock that I realized I had barely come up for air.

Grateful for the distraction, I reached for my phone on the desk from where I sat, my laptop flipped open in front of me. Alex's name flashed across the screen, and I smiled. Hearing his voice was probably the best way to take a break from my assignments, not to mention the memory of the wolf in the graveyard haunting me. After swiping the phone, I put it up to my ear. "Hi," I said, my gaze shifting to the window. Gold leaves sparkled against the blue sky, swaying in a passing breeze.

"Hey," he said softly. "How are you feeling?"

"Better," I answered, trying to sound upbeat. My answer was honest, at least partially. The physical pain from yesterday was gone, and I felt recharged and full of energy. But as time ticked by, images of the cemetery snuck into my mind when I paused between paragraphs of my English essay and while contemplating the next step to the Calculus problem I happened to be working on at the time. The wolf chipped away at my nerves, and the suspicion that there was more to it than just an animal in need of rescue nagged at me. I tried not to speculate on where it had gone or what havoc it could be wreaking. Instead, I told myself it had probably slinked away into the woods. Unfortunately, my common sense didn't let me rest with that notion. That's what a normal animal would do, and this wolf was anything but normal. It was a supernatural creature, magically brought back to life from my touch without a bite of food or sip of water.

Pushing the wolf out of my thoughts, I tried to concentrate on Alex when he replied. "Good. I really hated watching you suffer. If I had known how bad it was, I would have told you to stay home before we left."

"That's okay. There was no way to know the loud music would make it worse. But I'm fine now. Did you go back to the dance last night?"

"Yes. But it wasn't the same without you." Disappointment hung in his voice, and a pang of guilt jabbed at me. "I left early to go to Justin's party, so the night wasn't a complete waste."

"Well, I'm so sorry."

"Stop apologizing," Alex said, his tone forgiving. "At least I got to see you in your dress which, by the way, was very sexy. Nothing wrong with starting the evening off with a little eye candy."

"Back at you," I replied, smiling at the vision of Alex in his suit, a flirtatious twinkle in his dark eyes.

"Speaking of getting dressed up," Alex began. "Let's plan a night out soon so you can wear it again. You promised you'd make it up to me. And even though you don't have to, I want you to."

I thought of my wrinkled, dirty dress hanging in the closet. As far as I had noticed when I hung it up, it hadn't been torn and just needed a dry cleaning. "Definitely. You're on."

"Awesome. I'll have to come up with an idea of where we can go."

"Please do," I said, feeling a grin tug at my lips. "You really are the best, you know that?"

"You're pretty great, too. So, how's your day going?"

I sighed. "Lame. I've just been doing homework."

"I'd ask if you'd like a break, but I still have to write my paper for Lit. Did you finish yours?"

Frowning, I thought about the unfinished draft saved on my laptop. "I'm working on it," I said vaguely. "But let's not talk about homework. I want to think about something else. Do you have any gigs coming up?"

"No. Derek's trying to book a few more clubs, but he hasn't gotten anything lined up yet. We might play another night or two at The Witches' Brew this month. We'll see."

"I hope so. I want to hear you guys play again. I missed most of your set at the festival."

"Yeah," Alex groaned. "Don't remind me."

"Why?"

"Because I'm still kicking myself for how I treated you after the party."

"Okay, now it's your turn to stop apologizing."

The line on the other end went silent for a moment before Alex spoke again. "Do you think we'll ever get a break?"

"What do you mean?"

"It just seems like every time we get together and I think we're going to have a great time, things fall apart. First it was the party, and now the dance."

I couldn't blame him for wondering about us. I had started doubting that our relationship was going to grow, but I would never reveal that to him. "I don't know," I said with a sigh.

"Well, I know last night was no one's fault. Maybe the third time's a charm. I guess I'd better start brainstorming on ideas for our next date. It has to be epic."

"Sounds good to me. And by epic, you mean..."

"A quick dinner followed by a make-out marathon."

I laughed, shaking my head. "At least you're honest."

"Of course. I mean, I managed to get the new girl to go out with me, and I haven't even gotten to second base with her yet."

"Oh," I teased. "Is that what this is all about?"

"Yes," he declared. "What else would it be about? All work and no play is beginning to wear me out. Okay, I know we need to have that date.

I don't know where we'll go or when, but I'm going to make it happen. Promise me you'll wear your dress again, okay?"

"I already promised you that. I want to wear it again. I can't believe I got all dressed up for nothing." Except the night hadn't been for nothing. The wolf got what it wanted, although I doubted it cared about what I had been wearing. Trying to push the cemetery out of my mind for the hundredth time that day, I sighed. "Well, I guess we both should get back to the books."

That earned me a loud groan. "You just had to bring me back down to earth, didn't you? All right, I got the message. Meet me before class tomorrow? I need a little bit of what I missed last night."

"Yes. But you'd better get your mind out of the gutter. You have work to do."

He laughed, and then we said our goodbyes. As I placed my phone on the desk, I studied the treetops touching the sky outside the window. My thoughts drifting back to last night, Alex became a distant memory. The woman's voice rang out in my head, leaving questions in my mind. Who was she? Or better yet, what was she? She had talked about being set free, but I had released a wolf. Did the voice belong to the wolf?

I rolled my eyes as a sarcastic voice rambled through my thoughts. *A talking wolf? Now, that's a good one. Things around here just go from crazy to freaking unbelievable.*

After a pause, the voice in my head continued. *Believe it. So far, you broke a grown man's hand and cursed him. Your vision was corrected overnight, and Lucian cured your massive hangover with his magic tea, not to mention made everyone in the school hallway disappear for five minutes. Then you found out witches exist, and oh, by the way, you're one of them and you have a supernatural connection to a horse. So yes, a talking wolf fits right in.*

Don't listen to all that, I told myself, giving my thoughts a mental kick. *Just concentrate on your homework.* Reaching for the mouse, I moved it to wake up my laptop. The document lit up the screen, but I failed to focus on the words. Instead, all I saw was the emaciated wolf coming back to life.

Nothing frustrated me more right now than not being able to talk to Becca. She was the only one I felt I could turn to, and yet she was struggling with her own demons.

I needed to know if the wolf was real. Without thinking through my plans, I logged off my laptop and shut the screen. Leaving it on the desk, I ran downstairs and grabbed my hiking boots and jacket from the coat closet. Then I left the house, thankful Gabriel wasn't around to ask me where I was going.

I hurried down the porch steps and across the driveway, noticing that the sun had fallen halfway to the horizon in the western sky. The air was cool and crisp, the breeze stinging my face and hands. My sights set on the barn, I ignored the cold. After bringing Gypsy in from the pasture, I tacked her up, managing to fasten the bridle buckles correctly on the first try.

Before leading her outside, I paused by her head, my eyes locking with hers. I pictured the cemetery draped with fog in my mind. "If you can see my thoughts, you know where I need to go."

She tossed her head, nickering softly.

"Good," I murmured, stroking her face. "I knew I could trust you." Then I led her out of the barn to the mounting block.

As soon as I climbed into the saddle and slipped my right foot into the stirrup, Gypsy set off at a quick walk. I gathered up the reins as she headed for the trail, her hooves rattling the stones beneath them. When we entered the forest, the quiet resumed. Shadows stretched across the path in front of us, the sun now shielded by a canopy of leaves. I noticed my dress shoes where I had left them beside a patch of ferns last night and made a mental note to pick them up on my way home.

The trail had become so familiar to me that I knew when to expect the hills and turns. Without hesitating, I nudged Gypsy into a trot, anxious to get to the graveyard before the sun went down, as if it mattered in the fog.

After about ten minutes, Gypsy turned off the trail and marched into the woods. She darted between the trees, often swerving to miss them. I focused on keeping my balance, ducking to avoid being battered by low-lying branches.

We continued up a hill, snapping twigs and skirting around the thick underbrush. The air grew colder when we entered the fog, and

Gypsy slowed to a walk. The birds and scampering squirrels now gone, all was still and quiet in the mist except for the sound of Gypsy's hooves rustling through the fallen leaves.

A shiver rolled through me, the barren tree branches appearing dead and making my skin crawl. I was tempted to turn back, but I refused to let my fear send me home before I had a chance to look for any clues about the wolf. The scenery reminded me of that fateful day Lucian had found me here. The thought of him made me pause for a moment. If something happened this afternoon and he came to my rescue once again, I'd feel like a complete fool. But my anxiety vanished almost as quickly as it had appeared when I realized Gypsy would make sure I got home safely.

The fog thickened, but Gypsy didn't let it phase her, keeping her pace steady as she climbed up the hill. I tried to see through the cloud, but it was nearly impossible. Somehow, Gypsy avoided every tree with room to spare in spite of the low visibility.

When we entered the clearing, the mist lifted, exposing the tombstones that rose up from the ground within the fenced area. "Whoa," I said, gently pulling back on the reins.

Gypsy stopped, but I remained in the saddle and studied the graveyard. It was exactly as I remembered it—old, decrepit and haunting. The stones were faded, some crawling with dead ivy that looked so brittle, it would shatter into pieces if touched. My eyes swept across the cemetery until I spotted the stone building, its door hanging open a few inches.

My attention focused on it, I dismounted. Leaving the reins to rest on Gypsy's withers, I ran my hand along her neck until I reached her head. "Stay here," I told her before walking through the gate.

Dead leaves crunched under my feet as I made my way to the building. Approaching it, I pulled the door wide open. The room was empty except for the rusted chains on the floor. I entered the dark room, running my fingers over the cold stone wall, my mind flooded with images of the wolf laying in this very spot less than twenty-four hours ago.

After a few minutes, I retreated outside and scanned the graveyard again, the eerie silence haunting me. Gypsy stood where I had left her, waiting patiently while I searched the grounds. I paused, trying to decide what to look for next, when a black bird swooped down from the sky and landed in the woods. My gaze followed it to a flock gathering on the ground at the edge of the clearing beyond the fence.

Curious, I left the cemetery and began making my way to them. My heart accelerating, I felt a wave of apprehension wash over me. I wasn't sure what to do, but I hadn't come this far to give up and go home. Something had attracted the birds, and I was determined to investigate it, regardless of the fear raging through my veins.

What are you going to do if they attack you? my alter ego asked.

They're birds, not monsters, I thought, huffing at myself. *Besides, Gypsy is here. I have to trust her. She'll give me a sign if she suspects anything will harm me. She never would have brought me here in the first place if it was too dangerous.*

My sights set on the birds, I walked quickly, not paying attention to my footing. Halfway across the clearing, the ground fell out from under me and I tumbled into an open pit. When I stopped at the bottom, bracing my hands against the soft earth, my pulse raced. Crumbling dirt surrounded me, exposing a few tree roots.

What is this? I thought, digging into the ground with my hands and letting the soil sift between my fingers. When a worm appeared in my palm, I dropped it and whipped my arms back to my sides. *Ew. I wasn't expecting that.*

Wrinkling my nose, I rose to my feet. The hole was about four feet deep, extending in a circle roughly ten feet in diameter. A few leaves littered the bottom, but otherwise, it appeared as though it had been dug within the last few hours. I couldn't begin to imagine what might have opened up the earth. Little monsters from horror movies flashed through my mind, and I cringed. Now was not the time to let what little imagination I had run away with me.

Trying to remain calm, I climbed up the side. As soon as I hoisted myself over the edge and stood up, I brushed the dirt off my jeans. Gypsy approached, her eyes showing concern. "I'm fine," I told her, stroking her neck. "But thank you for coming. This place is getting creepier by the minute." I took a deep breath, apprehensive about getting close to the birds now. A part of me wanted to jump back on Gypsy and get out of here.

In the end, I won out over my fear. With a deep breath, I marched over to the edge of the woods where the birds gorged on something, at least when they weren't pecking at each other. One of them extended its wings, letting out a loud cry when another bird got too close.

Feeling numb, I stopped behind them, my gaze dropping to a dead deer being picked apart by the hungry birds. It lay on the ground, its glassy eyes open, its tongue hanging out of its mouth. A rack of antlers jutted up from between its ears. The hide was clean where the birds had yet to rip it open, and I wondered how long it had been dead.

I tried to scoot in between the birds and shoo them away, but one hammered its beak against my calf. "Ow!" I cried, backing up until I stood behind the birds, realizing this might be as close as I could get to inspect the carcass.

Not ready to accept defeat, I turned and whistled to Gypsy. As if reading my mind, she charged over, whinnying loudly. She slid to a stop, toppling over the birds. They shrieked and fluttered their wings, dispersing into the trees in a commotion that sent feathers flying.

My gaze dropped to the deer, my stomach turning with nausea at the sight of the organs distended from its open belly. I fought back the saliva that pooled in my mouth, swallowing hard.

Composing myself, I studied the carcass. A huge hole opened up its body cavity, the hide torn, frayed and bloody. The birds had pulled its intestines out, and pieces were missing where they had nibbled. Looking away from the carnage, I walked toward the deer's head and knelt beside it. "This would all be much easier if you closed your eyes," I said quietly, more to calm my nerves than anything.

My eyes roamed down its throat to its chest where another hole had been dug open. Blood pooled on the ground before an empty space where the heart used to be. The wound appeared fresh, the puddle bright red. I had no idea what had killed the deer, although I suspected whatever had gotten to it wasn't human. A hunter would have slaughtered it with a gun or bow and arrow, and there was no evidence of either weapon. And no hunter would have left so much meat to rot.

A tingle of fear trailed down my spine. My only saving grace was Gypsy who stood beside me, ready to protect me if needed. A bird cried out, and I glanced up. They perched on nearby branches, their beady eyes on us, waiting for us to leave so they could return to their meal.

Fog swirled around me, coming in waves from the graveyard, and the air turned colder. I folded my arms across my chest and spun in a circle, searching the surrounding area as the visibility faded. Upon making a complete turnabout, I stopped short. A pair of yellow eyes glowed roughly twenty feet away from me on the other side of the deer. A low growl rolled out, making my heart leap. Gypsy jerked her head high into the air, her ears flickering, a frantic look in her eyes, the whites around them showing. Snorting, she pawed the ground with her hoof.

I took a deep breath, forcing myself to be brave. But my courage didn't last long when the wolf darted toward me. Gypsy leaped over the deer, charging at the wolf with her head down and her ears pinned. It took one look at her and whipped around, disappearing into the woods.

When Gypsy returned to me, she nudged me hard, as though trying to tell me it was time to get out of here. "I know," I said, my eyes still glued to where the wolf had vanished. "You're right. Let's go." Turning to her, I reached for the reins as she dropped her knees to the ground. With little effort, I pulled myself up into the saddle and found the stirrups while Gypsy rose to her feet. As soon as I squeezed her sides with my calves, she launched into a quick trot.

I gathered up the reins and ducked down close to her neck. Then I gave her a swift nudge with my heels, pushing her into a gallop. Closing my eyes, I grabbed a thick chunk of her mane. "Take us home, girl," I said, not sure if she heard me in the wind. But it didn't matter. She didn't need to hear me. I knew she understood, and I trusted that she would get us out of here. Holding on for dear life, I never looked back.

17

It didn't surprise me that Becca was still sleeping when I returned home from the graveyard. After untacking Gypsy and putting the horses away, I retreated to my room. Gabriel was packing for Boston, and Becca would be in bed for the rest of the night from the sedatives. Once again, I found myself alone with a lot on my mind. A few weeks ago, the crank calls and doll had turned my world upside down. Now, I had to live with the knowledge that I had released a supernatural wolf from a crypt. I wasn't sure which plight was worse.

I resumed working on my English essay, but several times, I went to the door, debating whether or not to tell Gabriel everything. Each time I touched the knob, about to head downstairs, I changed my mind. What I had to tell him seemed crazy. And talking about the wolf would only make it seem more real.

In the end, I slinked back to my desk, forcing myself to finish my assignments. Part of me wanted to forget about the cemetery and the wolf. I kept telling myself that a wolf was no big deal. It had thousands of acres to roam with plenty of prey to feed on. But my attempt to convince myself that it would keep to itself and not bother anyone failed miserably. I suspected that no good would come from the wolf. I had to tell Becca as soon as I had the chance, but I had no idea when that would happen.

The next morning Alex found me in the parking lot before school just as he had promised. "Good morning," he said as I slipped out of my warm car only to shiver in the autumn air.

After shutting the door, I turned to him, my book bag hanging from my shoulder over my coat. "Hi."

He flashed a smile, looking as handsome as ever, his black shirt and jacket matching his hair. The feather pendant of his necklace caught a ray of sunlight, but I ignored it, my eyes locking with his instead. "You look a lot better than you did Saturday." When I shot him a quizzical look, he continued. "I mean you don't look like you're in pain now."

"That's because I'm not," I replied, wanting to direct the conversation away from the dance and my headache. "Did you finish your paper yesterday?"

"Barely. It was not fun. How about you?"

"Let's just say I have something to turn in, but I'm not sure how good it is."

"Good," he said with a soft laugh. "Then you won't bust the curve because I'm going to need it on this assignment."

"Just remember that the next time you write a kick-ass essay. It's hard for the rest of us to keep up with perfection."

"So, you think I'm perfect?" Alex gloated with a grin.

I rolled my eyes while he slid an arm around my waist and pulled me up against his chest. "I was talking about your work," I clarified. "No one's perfect."

"Hmm," he mused, his eyes twinkling. "Perhaps this will change your mind." He ducked his head down, his lips touching mine.

I sighed, closing my eyes, my body relaxing. All I wanted was to get lost in his kiss and let it wipe away all that troubled me. But out in the parking lot on a cold Monday morning, the moment only lasted a few seconds before Alex lifted his head and backed away. Without a word, he wrapped his arm around my shoulders and led me across the pavement, the heat from his body lessening the chill. We skirted around the cars, then stopped to look both ways before crossing the lane of traffic.

When we reached the sidewalk, we headed up the cement stairs on our way to the school, now finding ourselves part of the crowd. Halfway to the front door, Derek approached and launched into a conversation with Alex about plans for the band. They stopped on the lawn, letting waves of students pass to get to the door.

Hoping they would finish up soon so we could head inside, I remained beside Alex, his arm still draped over my shoulders. But my attention drifted away when I noticed Lucian and Zoe strolling hand-in-hand down the sidewalk toward the stairs. She beamed, a winning smile on her face as she leaned against him, seeming oblivious to the serious look on his face. Her long black hair hid her coat collar, her jeans meeting brown boots at her ankles. She exuded a confidence that I envied. Or did I envy her because everywhere she went, at least at school, Lucian wasn't far behind? Even though he scowled now, his green eyes cold and a frown squaring his jaw sprinkled with a five-o'clock shadow, he paid more attention to her than to anyone else.

I knew I should look away, but my eyes were glued to him. The crystal clear memory of being in his sister's bedroom yesterday morning ran through my mind like a movie stuck on one scene. Never before had another person's emotions ripped at my heart the way seeing his love for his sister had. Drawn to him due to reasons I couldn't explain, jealousy struck me the longer my gaze followed him and Zoe.

When a pang of guilt shot through me, I returned to reality. How could I dare even think about Lucian when I had a heartthrob like Alex on my arm? Tearing my gaze away from Lucian, I shifted my attention back to Alex, barely catching his last words.

"No way," he said, his words rushing out on a long breath. "That's a huge club. You mean they'll really have us?"

"No," Derek clarified. "I mean they might let us audition. There are no guarantees."

"But at least we have a chance."

Derek scoffed at him. "Hundreds of bands audition for a chance to play there. We'll be lucky if they let us finish one song."

"Man, you're negative. I'm just trying to stay optimistic. You might try it someday."

"We'll see," Derek grumbled, causing me to glance at him. He met my gaze, his eyes narrowing for a quick moment.

My breath hitched, and I wondered what that look was all about. Until now, Derek had showered me with plenty of attention, usually to flirt, much to Alex's dismay. I made a mental note to ask him what was on his mind, but only if I had the opportunity to talk to him alone.

The moment ended a few seconds later, and we began heading toward the school. When we entered through the double doors, the hallway was a flurry of activity. Students were going every direction, crowding the halls and filling the air with chatter. A few groans rang out, typical of a Monday morning.

I walked with Alex and Derek until they reached their lockers. After a quick goodbye, I left them and set off through the crowd on my way to my locker. But I saw Celeste before I reached it and stopped. "Hi," I said, leaning against the locker next to hers.

She shuffled books around on the shelf, her back to me. After a few seconds, I cleared my throat. "I said hi," I repeated, projecting my voice over the others.

Celeste spun around, seeming startled. "Oh, sorry," she said quietly, her voice withdrawn. "I didn't hear you."

"Everything okay?" I asked.

She took a deep breath. "Yes. I just overheard some other kids talking about the dance and it reminded me that I didn't go. But you did. How was it? Did you have a good time?"

A weak smile fluttered over my face. "Not quite."

"Oh, no," she said, seeming alarmed. "What happened? Is everything okay between you and Alex?"

"Yes," I assured her. "Everything is great with Alex. It's nothing like that. I had a horrible headache all day Saturday and, by the time I got to the dance, I ended up leaving right away. It was pretty much a disaster."

"Ouch," she said, cringing. "I'm sorry. I'm sure you were looking forward to it. That must have been a huge disappointment."

"It was." The memory of the graveyard and the wolf resurfaced in my mind. No matter how hard I tried, it seemed that I wouldn't be forgetting them any time soon. Burying my thoughts in the corner of my mind, I forced myself to smile. "But it's over, and today is a new day."

"You don't have another headache, do you?"

"No. I'm fine." Today marked day two of being pain-free, something I hoped was permanent.

"That's good." Celeste finished packing books in her bag and shut her locker. "Well, I'm done here. I should get to homeroom."

"Yeah. Me, too," I said.

On that note, we parted ways and I ran down the hall to my locker. The other students were starting to filter into their rooms, and I needed to hurry if I didn't want to be late.

— —

I managed to survive my classes that day, but my thoughts were a world away. I even started to run out of History class, oblivious to Mr. Wainwright asking me to hold up. If the boy in front of me hadn't turned around and said something, I never would have known I was being asked to stay. Part of me preferred to ignore Mr. Wainwright, but as soon as I knew he was trying to get my attention, I felt obligated to acknowledge him.

"Gracyn," he said, his soft brown eyes scanning me. His dark green shirt was tucked into his khaki slacks, but the long scruff covering his jaw and chin was back. "I won't keep you long. I just wanted to see how you were feeling."

"I'm fine," I answered politely.

"I trust you made it home okay Saturday night."

"Yes. Alex was very helpful."

"Good, because I was a little worried. I thought about calling Becca, but that wouldn't have been a good idea."

"Why not?" I asked. If Becca wouldn't tell me what had happened between them, maybe I could get Mr. Wainwright to explain it. "I tried to ask her about you after we met at the bar before school started, but she dodged my questions."

Dropping his gaze to the floor, he sighed. "That doesn't surprise me. I know she's very happy where she is right now, but that doesn't mean I don't care." He looked up, meeting my eyes with a forlorn glaze in his.

"I don't understand."

"I'm sure you don't. I'm sorry I brought it up. I never wanted to drag you into this mess. I'm just glad to see you feeling better." He glanced at the door. "And I don't want to keep you. You should probably get going to your next class."

"Okay. Thanks," I said softly, watching him shift his attention to a pile of papers on the desk. Not waiting for him to say another word, I escaped out of the room. Locking my book bag against my hip, I sprinted down the hall to the Art wing.

Lucian was sitting at the desk we shared when I got to class, but he never looked my way. I sat down next to him as the bell rang, painfully aware of his presence. He seemed larger than life this afternoon. For weeks, he had been the mysterious, dangerous guy everyone whispered about. The rumors about his role in his sister's murder had unsettled me from the beginning. Even when I wanted to believe in his innocence, it had been hard to look the other way. But not today. After waking up in Cassie's room yesterday and listening to him reminisce about her, the grief still alive in his eyes, I saw him in a different light. Now, nothing could convince me he had killed her.

When class was dismissed, I hoisted my book bag up onto the desk and unzipped it. Before I had a chance to pack up my sketch pad and pencils, Lucian grabbed my wrist, clamping it down on the desktop. I whipped my eyes up to his, surprised.

"Wait," he said quietly.

Confused, I arched my eyebrows in silence. Then I nodded, prompting him to let go of me. After tucking my things into my bag, I remained seated. The classroom emptied, the other students paying us no attention. As soon as the last girl left, Lucian asked, "What happened?"

"What are you talking about?" I asked, startled.

"You're upset today. I sense fear and apprehension coming from you. Why?"

I shook my head in amazement, wishing I knew how he could get into my head and read my emotions. "Um, I don't know how to answer that."

"How about starting with the truth?"

"Well, the truth is, I'm fine. Really," I replied, hoping he would let it go.

He took a deep breath, as though he didn't believe me. "You sure?"

"Yes," I insisted. When his stare seemed to penetrate my soul, his eyes nearly accusing me of lying, I huffed. "Okay, you win. No, I'm not completely fine. If you must know, I'm still a little shaken up over passing out in a graveyard in the middle of the night. It's starting to give me nightmares. Any normal person would be a little freaked out from that for a few days."

"You're not normal."

"Thank you for reminding me of that, but the last I checked, neither are you."

"Nope. I never wanted to be, either," he quipped, a rare sparkle lighting up his eyes.

I tilted my head, studying his smile. The curve of his lips loosened his square jaw, relaxing the frown that always seemed set in stone on his face. A playful gleam swept over his eyes, drawing me to him like a moth to a flame. "You are full of surprises sometimes, you know that?" I asked.

He lifted his eyebrows. "I'll take that as a compliment." He paused, his grin fading. "So, aside from the nightmares that I'm sure will go away in time, was there any other fallout from the night? Did Gabriel get over the fact that I brought you home?"

My thoughts darkened at the memory of Gabriel lunging at Lucian in the driveway. "Yes, of course. He's just worried about me. It's hard to stay angry with him when he's trying to protect me."

Lucian nodded, a solemn faraway look settling over his expression. "He doesn't need to protect you from me. Maybe one day, both of you will realize that."

The cold glare returning to his eyes, Lucian stood up. "Well, I should be going. Have a nice afternoon, Gracyn." Then he was gone, crossing the room in long strides before disappearing into the hallway and leaving me alone.

So much for the small talk, I thought, frustrated Lucian hadn't given me the chance to explain that I didn't believe anyone needed to protect me from him.

Grabbing my book bag, I stood up and walked out of the room, hoping I could set the record straight with him soon.

Later that afternoon, I heard Becca pull into the driveway while I was brushing Gypsy in the barn. Tempted to rush out and greet Becca, I held back, not sure what to tell her about Saturday night. As I continued the brush strokes over Gypsy's red and white coat, Becca appeared in the doorway.

Leaving Gypsy's side, I approached Becca, stopping a few feet in front of her. "Hi. How was your day?"

She offered a soft smile, seeming a little tired. A black coat covered her gray suit, the collar hidden by her blonde hair. "Pretty status quo. I'm so sorry, though. I never had a chance to ask you how the dance was. I had another rough weekend."

"I know, so you don't have to apologize. But I don't understand. You seemed fine when I left."

"I was. The last thing I remember is being struck with a headache around eight o'clock that night. It hit really fast, and Gabe didn't think I should wait to take the medicine and a sedative. But I don't want to talk about that. I want to know how the dance was. You and Alex looked amazing. Did you have a nice time?"

I shot her a quizzical look. "Gabriel didn't tell you?"

Her smile faded instantly. "Tell me what?"

"I couldn't handle the loud music and crowd. Alex and I left the dance early."

"I'm sorry to hear that. Where did you end up going?"

"We came back here," I said, averting my eyes to the dusty aisle floor. "I couldn't come in and face you. I just wanted to be alone."

Becca raised her eyebrows, silently prompting me to continue.

"So I went for a walk in the woods." The wolf lingered on the tip of my tongue, but somehow I couldn't get the words out to explain that part. I was so worried Becca wouldn't believe me that I lost my nerve to mention the wolf. Instead, I told her I got lost again, and the pain took over, making me pass out. I ended my monologue with the confession that Lucian had found me.

When I finished, I glanced at Becca, the worried look on her face reminding me of a parent about to scold a young child for doing something dangerous. "Gracyn," she rolled out. "You need to stop getting yourself in trouble like that. Need I remind you that Cassie died in those very same woods and whoever did it has not been caught?"

"No," I said, feeling a blush race across my cheeks. "But I thought you said you believe I'm safe."

"I did, and I still believe that. But there are things about our world that are complicated. I'm just asking you to stay out of the woods. Please, can you promise me this is the last time it will happen?"

"Yes," I said quietly, nodding. *Tell her about the wolf,* a frantic voice shot out in my head. *You have to tell her. Maybe she knows something about it. You shouldn't keep this from her.* I agreed with my inner self, but as soon as I opened my mouth to say something, the words got stuck in my throat. Speechless, I stared at Becca.

"Good. Well, I'm going to head inside and change. If you'll finish up with the horses, I'll get dinner started."

"Of course," I replied.

When Becca turned and left the doorway, I stood where I was, fuming at myself. I had just wasted the perfect opportunity to tell her about the wolf, and the last thing I wanted was to bring it up at dinner.

Determined to forget about the wolf, I turned around to face Gypsy, my attention focused on the barn chores and nothing else.

The rest of the evening was exactly what I needed. Dinner with Becca talking about school and Alex. Then a hot shower to wash away the barn dirt followed by a successful attempt to finish my homework. By the time I climbed into bed, I felt as though the wolf had been left behind in the dust.

I fell asleep expecting my alarm clock to wake me up the next morning. Instead, when my eyes opened, I found myself standing beside the graveyard fence. Sunlight streamed down through the trees, lighting up the cemetery. The grass around the tombstones was lush and green, the picket fence solid white. Cassie skipped through the yard, humming to herself with a carefree smile on her young face. When she stopped, she whistled and a white horse appeared at the gate.

She approached the horse as Lucian walked up beside it. He wore a white button-down shirt, his hands hidden behind his back. Neither of them seemed to notice me from where I stood beyond the fence on the other side of the cemetery.

Their eyes locked on each other, not once did they look my way. When Cassie approached Lucian, he knelt down. She launched herself into his embrace, hugging him. He wrapped his arms around her, exposing a knife in his hands. A ray of sunlight glinted off the blade, the spark flashing like lightning.

At that moment, I shot up in bed and recognized the familiar shadows in my room. My pulse pounded hard and fast, my fear lingering with the vision of Cassie and Lucian in the cemetery, the knife in Lucian's hand permanently etched in my thoughts. *It was just a dream. A very bad dream,* I told myself, trying to find some comfort.

Still feeling unsettled, I lowered myself onto the pillow. I took deep breaths, hoping to steady my heart and fall back to sleep. But when my eyes closed, a howl shot out through the night. Wide awake, I jumped up, ran to my desk and opened the window a few inches. Peering outside, all I saw were the stars twinkling in the midnight sky. I was about to shut the window when something white flew through the air.

Curiosity whipped through me. Without hesitating, I hurried out of the room, careful not to make a sound. My feet bare, I rushed down the stairs in my pajamas. The dogs slept soundly on their beds, not moving a muscle from my flurry of activity.

I went straight to the front door and flipped on the outside light before stepping onto the porch and searching for a sign. But all was still in the dead of the night. I looked to both sides, swiping a stray lock of hair away from my face when the wind blew. Studying the night shadows, I saw nothing out of the ordinary.

It must have been part of the dream, I told myself. *That's all. A figment of your imagination.* I almost believed it until I wandered over to the stairs and spotted a white clump at the bottom.

I ran down the steps and dropped to my knees, studying the object. "What in the world?" I mused, my voice fading when I noticed wings, a beak and tiny talons. The dove's eyes were closed, the feathers on its chest stained with blood.

Swallowing, I looked up and gazed into the night. "Who's out there? What do you want?" My questions cut through the silence, and I suddenly prayed that I wouldn't get an answer. I wasn't sure I wanted to know what was out here. My skin crawled at the thought of an evil presence killing birds for no good reason.

Composing myself, I retreated into the house and rushed to the kitchen, retrieving a pair of dishwashing gloves and a plastic bag. After pulling the gloves on, I returned to the steps and deposited the dove into the bag. I tied a knot in the handles, then carried the bag out to the barn where I dropped it in the garbage can before heading back to the house.

As soon as I stepped inside, I locked the door. My nerves a complete wreck, I returned to my room and slipped into bed, sure that getting back to sleep would not come easy.

18

As expected, I tossed and turned for the rest of the night. When the early dawn light peeked in through the window, I knew that my failed attempt to sleep would punish me all day. Tired and drained, I managed to throw on a pair of blue jeans, a black sweater, and matching boots. After pulling my out of control curls into a pony-tail, I covered up the dark circles under my eyes with a little makeup, hoping no one would notice how exhausted I was.

At school, Alex stopped by my locker before homeroom. "Good morning," he said, his backpack slung over his denim jacket. "Oh, no, another sleepless night?"

"Is it that obvious?" I asked with a sigh.

He nodded, sympathy in his soft smile. "Don't worry, I get it."

"You do?" I asked, feeling my eyes widen. For a moment, I wondered how he knew about the wolf. But then a voice of reason tumbled through my head. *Don't be ridiculous. No one knows anything, including the one person who should know—Becca. You still haven't told her, only why I can't figure out.* Without trying to defend myself to my alter ego, I turned my attention back to Alex.

"Yes. We talked about a make-up date, but I never formally asked you. So, Gracyn," he began, reaching for my hand. "If you're not busy, will you go out to dinner with me Saturday night? There's only one condition."

"What's that?"

"You have to wear your Homecoming dress, of course."

"I thought that was the whole idea," I said, feeling a frown take over when I remembered that my dress still hung in my closet, dirty and wrinkled. I would have to drop it off at the dry cleaners tonight and hope it would be ready by Saturday.

"But?" he asked slowly.

"No buts," I replied, flashing him a reassuring smile. "I just want to get it cleaned, and I should be able to take it into town tonight."

"Sounds like a perfect plan," he said, mischief twinkling in his eyes. Then he slid his arm around my waist and pulled me to him. He leaned in and kissed my lips, first lightly, then bolder, deeper, sending a familiar heat through my veins.

Gathering my wits, I backed away, unraveling Alex's arms from around me. I glanced out at the crowded hallway, thankful no one seemed to be paying us any attention. I was about to look back at Alex when my eyes met Lucian's cold green stare from across the hall. My cheeks feeling hot, I whipped my gaze away from him, trying to push him out of my thoughts.

Smiling, I caught the sparkle in Alex's dark eyes. "You are too much," I said. "Glad to see your intentions haven't changed."

"Never!" he quipped.

I laughed, stealing a quick glance across the hall to see that Lucian was gone. Relief fluttered through me, and I felt free to give Alex my undivided attention. "You do realize today is only Tuesday, don't you? Saturday night is five days away."

"You love to crush my spirits, don't you?"

"No, I'm just being realistic. Besides, you have work to do this week. Study first, play later."

"But a little fun in between never hurt anyone."

"You're not going to let me have the last word on this, are you?"

"Nope," he replied good-naturedly.

"What happened to the audition Derek was trying to line up? Did anything ever come of it?"

"Not yet, though I'm sure Derek will let me know the minute he hears something. If it happens, then great, I'll go and play my best. But if not, no big deal. I've got too much to do right now like get ready for our date Saturday night."

I sighed, sincerely appreciating him for being in my life right now. "Sounds good to me." After flashing him a grateful smile, I turned back to my locker and continued sorting through my books, optimistic that Alex and my classes would keep my mind off the dead dove for the rest of the day.

— ~

My trip to the dry cleaners to drop off my dirty dress proved to be unnecessary. After the owner promised it would be ready Saturday morning, Alex had to break our date since Derek pulled off getting an audition for the band. Their Saturday afternoon in Boston meant Alex would never make it back to Sedgewick in time for dinner.

Alex showered me with apologies nearly all week. I assured him I wasn't upset, hiding my disappointment behind a winning smile. I tried to convince myself I would have more time to study over the weekend, but I only ended up worrying that being home day and night meant anything could happen. I wasn't sure I could handle the wolf or another dead dove, but hopefully I would at least be prepared if more mysteries took ahold of the upcoming weekend.

Saturday morning, Becca popped her head in my room while I sat on my bed, a book resting against my propped-up knees. "Gabriel and I are heading out to the store. Is there anything you need?" she asked.

I looked up from the words spanning the open pages in front of me. "No, I'm fine."

"Okay. We should be back in an hour or so." Then she shut the door behind her, leaving me alone.

A few minutes later, I heard the dogs barking downstairs followed by a knock on the front door. Sighing, I put my book aside and jumped up. Wearing blue pajama pants and a gray sweatshirt, I rushed out of my room and down the stairs. When I reached the door, the dogs paced in front of it.

I slipped around them until I was close enough to glance out the peephole. My rebellious heart skipped a beat at the sight of Lucian. I opened the door as the dogs pushed their way outside, circling him. His green eyes slid down to my feet before rising to meet my gaze, an amused look on his face. In his light brown shirt and jeans, he looked handsome, his unshaven jaw adding a rugged touch. The silver cross hanging over his shirt glinted in the morning light, taking my breath away when it resurrected my nightmare from the other night.

Forcing myself to forget the image of Lucian hugging Cassie with a knife in his hands, I looked at him, curious. "Haven't you ever heard of a phone?"

"Haven't you heard of saying hello before jumping into your questions?" he countered with a teasing smile.

I was caught off-guard for a moment, remembering our last encounter which ended with him giving me the cold shoulder. His mood swings really kept me guessing. But his grin was contagious, and I felt one slide over my expression. "Hello, then. Is that better?"

"Much."

"Good. Glad we got that out of the way. But seriously, it wouldn't kill you to pick up the phone and call me before you come over. That way I could at least make sure I'm dressed."

"I never expected you'd still be in your pajamas at ten-thirty." He paused before adding, "And you haven't given me your phone number."

"Good point. Fine. If you're going to keep doing this to me, then I will. But that aside, what are you doing here?"

"I wanted to invite you out for the day. The weather is absolutely gorgeous, and I'd hate to waste it spending the day alone." When I didn't answer immediately, he asked, "So? What's it going to be? A boring day here by yourself, or something more interesting with me? Unless you already have plans."

Tempted to say yes right away, I resisted. "No, no plans. And it depends. Where are you going?"

"It's a surprise."

"Really?" I asked, my eyebrows raised. "I think I've had enough surprises lately."

"Well, this one will be nothing like those. Promise."

"Why can't you just tell me where you're going?"

"Because I don't want to spoil it. Besides, it's nothing spectacular. You might even laugh if I told you. It'll be much better if you see it for yourself when we get there."

"I wouldn't laugh," I assured him.

"Let's just say it could ruin my dark and dangerous reputation," he said, lowering his voice with a sparkle in his eyes. "But I'll give you a hint. It's something I did with Cassie every fall before she died, and I haven't been back without her. Until now, I wasn't ready for the memories. But after talking about her a few times, I think I can handle it."

I didn't need long to deliberate his offer. My curiosity ended up getting the best of me. "Okay. You convinced me. I'll come with you. Just give me a few minutes to change."

"No problem. Make sure to wear good walking shoes and bring a jacket because it's still a little chilly."

"Got it." I gestured to the open doorway. "Would you like to wait inside?"

"That's okay. I'll hang out here. Just be quick. I waited until Becca and Gabriel left to come over, and I'd like to go before they get back. You know they won't approve of you leaving with me."

The truth in his words soured my mood. I didn't like feeling as though I was sneaking off, but Becca and Gabriel would no doubt frown upon any time I spent with Lucian. The fact that he wouldn't tell me where we were going made it even worse, but I'd never be able to explain to them how I felt safe with him amidst the rumors circulating around town. "I can do that. Give me five minutes, maybe even less." After flashing him a smile, I dashed into the house.

I ran upstairs and flew into my room where I ripped off my pajamas and slid into a comfortable pair of jeans and a black sweater. There was no time to shower, wash my hair and tame it with a blow dryer. Instead, I brushed it as best as I could before pulling my unruly curls back with two clips. A quick dab of makeup completed my preparation.

As soon as I returned downstairs, I grabbed my hiking boots and laced them up. With a denim jacket folded over my forearm, I emerged onto the front porch.

"That was fast," Lucian commented from where he leaned against the railing. "I'm impressed."

"It's one of my many hidden talents," I quipped before rounding up the dogs and ushering them into the house. Once they were inside, I shut the door and locked the deadbolt. "Okay. Let's go because I'm really curious," I said, dropping my keys into my purse.

Lucian gestured for me to lead the way down the porch steps. "After you."

I rushed ahead of him, heading across the gravel to the passenger side of his Range Rover. I was about to open the door when he approached behind me, reaching out to grab the handle. My breath hitched, my heartbeat taking off in a frenzy from the heat radiating off his chest. Turning, I glanced at him out of the corner of my eye. "Thank you," I said when his gaze met mine, causing me to forget everything except his intense stare.

"You're welcome. Now get in," he instructed.

I nodded before hopping into the Range Rover. My pulse slowed when he shut the door, the short minute alone giving me a chance to compose myself. I buckled the seat belt while he circled around the front of the SUV and got in behind the wheel.

After turning on the engine, he backed up and drove down the driveway. As soon as the barn and house disappeared in the rearview mirror, I reached into my purse.

"What are you doing?" Lucian asked.

I whipped out my phone. "Texting Becca to let her know I'll be out for the rest of the day. I don't want her to worry when she gets home and finds me gone. Even though she's given me a free rein since I moved in and doesn't try to keep tabs on me, it's the right thing to do."

"Where exactly are you telling her you'll be today?"

"I'm not. She doesn't need that much detail. I'll just explain that a friend stopped by and I won't be home until later," I said, feeling a frown set in over my face. I hated hiding the truth, but I didn't know what else to do. No one, aside from Zoe, seemed to think of Lucian as anything other than a murderer.

I quickly drafted the text, hit send and then shut off my phone. "There. Done."

Lucian turned onto the road, and a kaleidoscope of red, orange and yellow foliage whipped by. "Good. Maybe when I bring you home safely, you can tell her I was the one who stole you for the day."

"Hmm, we'll see," I muttered thoughtfully. "Why did you ask me to join you today?"

"Because I couldn't think of a good reason not to."

"What about Zoe?"

"She went to Boston with the drill team to visit a dance studio and then take in a performance tonight. She won't be home until tomorrow. Besides, she wouldn't appreciate where we're going. It's not her thing." He paused, sliding his eyes my way, a soft appreciation in them. "I'd rather take you. I can't share these memories with just anyone."

I swallowed, chills rushing over me from the emotion buried deep in his voice. "But you hardly know me."

"I think I know you well enough."

"Really?" I asked when I recovered from my shock. "And how do you know it will be my thing?"

"Because it involves art, in an abstract, indirect and elementary sort of way."

"Art? Wait, you did this with your little sister? I'm not following you. The more you tell me, the more confused I am."

"Good. You'll just have to keep guessing until we get there."

I shook my head. "You really are insufferable this morning."

"I know," he said with a grin, his eyes shifting my way again.

"Okay. So, how long do I have to wait before I know what you're up to?"

"About forty-five minutes."

"That long?" I asked with a groan.

"Don't worry. The drive will go by fast. Just relax and enjoy the scenery. This is peak New England foliage at its best."

I settled into my seat and gazed out the window. The woods lining the road looked like they had been lit on fire. Bright sunshine enhanced the golden hues, and a clear blue sky peeked out from beyond the branches overhead. Sighing, I watched the glorious fall landscape as we sped along the country road. I had no idea what the day would bring, but I was determined to enjoy it.

19

Nothing could have prepared me for what Lucian had planned. We drove past the town limits and into the country. Open fields of corn stalks and baled hay rolled out in waves between wooded patches. Occasional houses and barns dotted the landscape, often surrounded by pastures of grazing cattle and horses.

Neither Lucian nor I said much. As if reading my mind, Lucian turned on the radio, instantly finding a station that played everything from classic rock to current hits. The music soothed me, allowing me to relax and enjoy the ride.

About forty minutes later, Lucian slowed the Range Rover to a crawl and pulled into a gravel driveway centered between two rows of fire-engine red maple trees. A rustic wooden sign reading "Country Meadow Farms" had been staked into the ground at the entrance. Post and rail fencing stretched out behind the trees on each side of the driveway. Truck-sized round hay bales were scattered throughout one field, a menagerie of livestock including horses, donkeys, ponies, goats and a solid red steer in the other. A fuzzy black and white pony trotted up to a sway-backed sorrel gelding, nipping at him until he lunged at it, ears pinned flat against his neck. The pony ducked just in time before darting away, as if having learned its lesson.

By the time I tore my eyes away from the amusing pony, we had reached a store at the end of the driveway. Half empty tables and chairs had been set up on the front porch, and a huge red barn towered above the store beside it. A pumpkin patch and open area with tractors and hay bales converted into playground accessories extended beyond the buildings. The parking lot was full of minivans and SUV's. Families with young children from toddlers to first-graders, wandered about the property. Some parents pushed strollers while others carried babies as they kept a watchful eye on their older children who took off for the tractors.

After taking in the surroundings, I turned my attention to Lucian as he parked the Range Rover next to a minivan. "What is this place?"

"A farm. Halloween is only two weeks away, and I don't have a pumpkin yet. I'm guessing you don't, either."

I laughed, shaking my head. Never would I have guessed he was taking me to a country farm to pick out a pumpkin in the company of families with young children. I suspected we were the only childless people here. But he had explained he used to come here with Cassie, so in that respect, it made sense. "No," I replied, smiling. "But this is still very unexpected."

"Good. I like to surprise people." He paused, leaning across the console toward me. "Listen," he said, dropping his voice. "Today is our secret. I don't want this getting out."

"I won't tell a soul," I assured him.

"Good," he said, sounding relieved. "Now, are you ready to have some fun?"

"I guess so. Just promise me you're not going to drag me out onto the playground. I'm not five."

His eyes scanned over me, his smirk growing. "I noticed. And no, I wasn't planning to climb on the tractors. There's a corn maze on the other side of the play area. I thought we'd get some exercise first."

I raised my eyebrows. "Well, that sounds interesting. Okay, I'm in."

I hopped out of the Range Rover and shut the door. Lucian appeared a minute later and, when I turned to him, the sun nearly blinded me. His hair reflected the light, a few golden streaks woven through shades of light brown. His green eyes twinkled, his expression carefree. For the first time since I had met him, he actually looked happy.

"Ready?" he asked.

I nodded.

"Follow me," he said before turning and leading the way across the gravel driveway.

We passed families slowly making their way to the play area, their small children holding them back at a snail's pace. A toddler who couldn't have been older than two wearing a wide-brimmed denim hat waddled for a few steps before tripping. His hands shot out, catching his fall. Then he stood up without a care in the world and trudged on ahead, escaping his father who rushed over to help.

"I think we're the only people here without kids," I told Lucian.

"That's okay. This place has the best pumpkins around. Last I checked, they don't discriminate against single people like us. And the maze is a lot of fun. Cassie and I got lost in it last time." His smile faded for a second at the mention of Cassie.

"Getting lost was fun?"

"Yes," he said as we started walking across the lawn. His expression turned solemn when silence passed between us. In the distance, children laughed and shrieked, climbing like monkeys on the equipment.

After a few moments, I asked quietly, "Everything okay?"

He nodded. "I was just remembering that day. It was a lot like today. Clear sky with a gentle breeze."

"Did you bring her here by yourself?"

"Yes. My mother was in Hawaii, and I don't remember where my father was. Somewhere around the world," he said, a hint of bitterness in his voice.

"I'm sorry to hear that. But you must have been an amazing big brother to take time out of your weekend to come here. It's not exactly a high school hang-out."

"I never cared about being popular, and I certainly never worried about what anyone else thought. I always did my own thing, and I still do."

"What about your mom? Was she away a lot?"

"Yes. Before Cassie died, she came home about once a month. But ever since the funeral, I don't think she's been back one time. I visited her in Hawaii about a year ago, but that's the last time I saw her."

"That sounds awful. For both you and Cassie. I can't imagine my mom taking off like that." The thought of my mother reminded me that I didn't know who my birth mother was. My mood dampening, I crushed those thoughts with a single blow. I refused to waste a gorgeous day wallowing in my self-pity.

"My mom was dealt a pretty rough hand in life. I kind of understood because I was older, but Cassie never did. It was much harder on her, and I think that's why I tried to give her some childhood experiences that all kids should have."

Blinking back tears, I imagined Lucian here with his little sister, taking her hand while they wandered through the field, searching for the perfect pumpkin. "That's very impressive. I'm sure she knew how much you loved her. She must have appreciated all you did for her."

"I hope so," he said wistfully. He sniffed, then took a deep breath and nodded toward the hand-painted corn maze sign. Shaped like an arrow on a crooked piece of wood, it pointed toward a wall of dried-up corn stalks. "We're almost there. The entrance is around the corner."

Lucian led me to the opening and we entered the path. I stopped inside, feeling a little claustrophobic from the tall stalks towering over me on both sides.

"Hmm," I mused, glancing about. "Does anyone come out of this alive?"

Lucian laughed. "It's just for fun. Don't worry, you'll be safe with me."

I slid my gaze his way, meeting the sincere look in his eyes. His expression held a daring hint, as if challenging me.

I swallowed nervously and nodded. "Fine. Let's go."

"After you."

Leading the way, I looked back over my shoulder. "Great. So when we get lost, you can blame it on me?"

"Of course," he teased.

I shook my head and pressed on, determined to make it through this as quickly as possible. Shadows crossed the path ahead, the stalks to the side shielding the sun. I picked up a brisk walk, only slowing when we came to a fork. After a moment of deliberation, I continued down the right path.

Lucian followed closely behind me, the sound of his footsteps seeming louder as we walked deeper into the maze, leaving the shrieking children on the playground far behind.

"So," I said, breaking the silence between us. "Am I the only one besides Cassie you've brought here?"

"Would it impress you if I said yes?" he asked, raising his eyebrows when I tossed him a smile over my shoulder.

"Maybe," I said before looking straight ahead, my smile never fading. Something felt different between us. I suspected he didn't let many people get to know him, and yet he had opened up to me. He seemed to have let down his guard, causing the mystery shrouding him to crumble. I wondered if he needed to share his memories of Cassie with someone. Someone who hadn't been around when she had died. Someone who didn't judge him or look at him like he was the monster who had put Cassie in the grave.

We reached another fork and this time, I turned to the left, forging deeper into the maze. The path seemed endless, and I wondered how long it would take to find our way to the other end. A breeze whispered through the stalks, the cool draft raising the hair on my forearms. Folding them over my chest to ward off the chill, I picked up the pace.

The corridor curled to the right, and I met my first dead end. Stopping, I sighed with defeat. "Okay, this is going to be harder than it looks," I said, whirling around to find myself alone. "Lucian?" I called, but received no response in the silence. "Lucian!" I repeated, a little louder this time.

My pulse quickening, I gazed ahead at the path cutting through the corn stalks. *He must be playing some kind of joke,* I thought. "Come on, Lucian. This isn't funny!" I shook my head, starting to feel irritated.

With my next step, the light overhead dimmed. I looked up to see dark storm clouds rolling across the sky. With a deep breath, I tried to ignore them, but I couldn't help wondering where they had come from on such a beautiful day boasting of clear blue skies.

Swallowing, I halted, the dead silence sending a chill up my spine. A tendril of smoke drifted past me from behind and I whipped around. Flames cackled in front of me, burning the dry corn stalks. My heart falling into a sheer panic, I jumped back. The fire waved, its orange and yellow glow nearly blinding me. Heat seared my face, creating a sheen of sweat on my skin.

I wanted to run, but stopped at the sight of the wolf within the flames. Its yellow eyes were locked on me, its white fur standing out against the fire.

Closing my eyes, I took a deep breath. *This isn't happening,* I told myself. *I don't even smell smoke. It's a trick, and a really good one.*

When I opened my eyes, the fiery image was gone. The corn stalks rose up around me, not a single flame igniting them. The smoke had cleared, giving way to the blue sky overhead, and a patch of sunlight sparkled on the path in front of me. Relief ran through my veins, slowing my pulse to a normal pace.

Not wanting to linger at the dead end making me feel trapped, I took off in the direction I had come from. When I turned the corner, a pair of arms reached out and grabbed me, bringing me to a halt. Looking up, I met Lucian's gaze and shuddered. "Where were you?"

"I told you I heard a child crying and I was going to try to find out what was wrong. Didn't you hear me?"

"No," I said firmly, worming my way out of his grasp. "I didn't hear a thing. And normally I can hear everything."

"Of course, you can."

Frowning, I didn't want to speculate on why I hadn't heard Lucian or the child. In the wake of the disturbing image of the fire and the wolf,

I wanted to forget all of it. The knowledge that I'd been so mesmerized by something that wasn't even real made me feel out of control and completely out of touch with reality.

"Gracyn," Lucian said when I remained silent, lost in my thoughts. "Why is your face so white? You look like you just saw a ghost."

Flashing my eyes at him, I debated whether or not to tell him about the fire. After a quick moment of silence, I decided not to. I didn't want to sound crazy. "I was just a little spooked when I realized I was alone and trapped. But I'm fine now. Did you find the child?"

"Yes. It was a little girl. She got lost in here and was all alone. I took her back to the store and left her with someone who works here. They'll make sure she finds her mother."

"You were awfully fast."

"That's because I ran back to the maze. I didn't want you to get lost, too."

"Thanks. Well, I'm glad you helped her. I'm sure she was happy to get out of here which is what I want to do because I'm feeling a little claustrophobic."

"Okay. We can go. And I promise not to disappear again." Lucian reached for my hand, but I snatched it away at his slightest touch. He flashed me a disappointed look, the rejection in his eyes tearing at my heart.

I shifted my gaze to the ground, feeling guilty for pulling away from his gesture. Alex appeared in my thoughts, reminding me that my actions were justified and sending a new round of guilt through me. Perhaps I never should have agreed to let Lucian take me out today. *Don't be silly*, a voice scolded. *You're at a farm for families with young children, not on a romantic date. Don't read more into this than there is. You're still dating Alex, and the last I checked, Lucian is still dating Zoe. You can just be friends with him. After all, he's like you, and you need someone you can talk to when your world turns upside down.*

Reassured that it was okay to be here with Lucian, I offered him a soft smile, but my concession was too late.

"I guess we should go. Maybe this wasn't such a good idea after all," Lucian said quietly.

He ripped his gaze away from me before taking off. I watched him for a moment, then ran to catch up, hoping to get our day back to what it was—an escape to the country with a friend.

In silence, we backtracked through the maze and walked out through the entrance. I felt as though I had been set free from a cage as soon as the corn stalks were left behind, opening up the vast sky above. The store and barn could be seen across the field, the tractor play area sprinkled with carefree children climbing to their hearts' content while their parents lingered on the outskirts, keeping a watchful eye on their little ones.

Lucian continued making his way to the parking lot in long strides, and I jogged to keep up with him. About halfway across the lawn, I noticed a little girl tugging on her mother's shirt. She wore jeans and a white turtleneck smudged with dust, her brown hair falling over her shoulders in two long braids.

"Mommy," she said, pointing to Lucian. "That's the man who helped me."

Upon hearing her, Lucian and I stopped. The woman approached, her brown eyes brimming with relief. Her auburn hair hung from a ponytail, her jeans and white blouse matching the little girl's clothing. "Excuse me," she said. "Are you the one who found my daughter?"

Lucian nodded, his eyes wandering to the little girl. "Yes, ma'am."

"Thank you," she said, her tone appreciative.

"It was nothing. Anyone would have done the same thing," Lucian said before dropping to his knees in front of the girl. He offered her a gentle smile. "Hello again. How old are you?"

"Five."

"And what is your name?"

"Alicia," she replied, seeming mesmerized by him.

"Well, Alicia, what did you learn today?"

"Never to leave my mommy."

"That's right. Because next time, there might not be someone who can help you. I'm glad you're safe now. Just promise me you'll stay close to your mother at all times from now on."

"I will," she said, beaming. Without a moment's notice, she wrapped her arms around him. He hugged her, gently patting her back between her shoulder blades.

"Your husband is a wonderful man," the woman said to me, breaking me out of my trance.

"What?" I asked, speechless for a second. When I finally found my voice, I explained, "Oh, he's not my husband."

"No? I'm sorry. I just assumed that. You two look good together, if you don't mind me saying so."

My breath caught in my chest, the moment seeming surreal. Her comment and the vision of Lucian embracing the little girl as a father would hold his daughter moved me. Taking a deep breath, I pushed my emotions aside. I couldn't allow my heart to get swept away. I still didn't know Lucian very well, although that was starting to change, maybe faster than I wanted it to.

"No," I replied. "I don't mind. I'm just glad he was able to help."

"Me, too. That was the scariest five minutes of my life." The woman stepped toward Lucian as he let go of the little girl and stood up. "Thank you again. You're a good person, and I'm grateful you were here to help." She shook his hand before turning to her daughter. "Okay, Alicia. Are you ready to pick out a pumpkin?"

"Yay!" the little girl shrieked. "Bye, mister!" Then she and her mother walked away, heading for the pumpkin patch.

Alone with Lucian again, I looked at him, noticing the thoughtful smile on his face, his eyes following the girl and her mother.

"What are you thinking?" I asked, wondering if he'd heard the woman assume we were married.

"This is the first time since I moved back when someone didn't assume the worst about me. It's nice to get away from Sedgewick for a day and not be viewed as a murderer."

A lump forming in my throat, I realized how much that meant to him. Back in town, everyone feared him, but here, he was just a random guy no one knew.

"I'm sure it is," I said, touching his arm. When I dropped my hand, I grinned at him. "Now listen, you promised me a pumpkin today. I think it's time you follow through with that."

His smile widened, his green eyes holding my gaze. "I did, didn't I? What are we waiting for? Let's go."

20

After selecting two plump pumpkins from the field, Lucian and I carried them back to the store where he refused my offer to cover the cost of mine and paid for both of them. Then we hauled the pumpkins out to the Range Rover and tucked them behind the back seat before returning to the store for lunch. The deli inside had everything from meats, a variety of cheese, homemade pies, and apple cider. Lucian and I selected made-to-order sandwiches and took them outside to an empty table on the porch.

Once we were seated, I took a bite of my turkey sandwich. The parking lot was packed and people were scattered everywhere from the play area to the pumpkin patch. A teenage girl led a pony around the lawn, giving rides to children. On the other side of the driveway, a farm guide supervised a group of boys and girls feeding the donkeys and horses over the fence.

I took in the view, watching families come out of the store with pumpkins in their arms, the children by their sides beaming from a day of fun-filled country activities. My eyes shifting to Lucian, I grinned. "You know, this is the last place I expected you to bring me today."

"I figured as much. I hope you're enjoying yourself, at least since we left the maze."

I didn't let my thoughts of the fire sour my mood. "I am, much more than I probably would have anticipated had you told me where we were going. It's nice to get away from Sedgewick for the day."

"I know what you mean," he said before pulling his phone out of his pocket. Dropping his gaze to it, he scrolled over the surface with his thumb. When he stopped, he propped it up in his hand, the front facing me. A picture of Cassie sitting in one of the tractors, a carefree smile on her face as her blonde hair blew in the breeze, lit up the screen.

"When was that taken?" I asked.

"About six years ago. She was nine in this picture."

"Really?" I glanced up, meeting Lucian's eyes. "How old were you?"

"Thirteen."

"How did you bring her here when you were so young? Or did you grow superhumanly fast and get your driver's license years before the rest of us?"

He laughed softly. "No, I assure you I was very much a boy then." His grin faded, his expression appearing wistful. "We had a driver to take us anywhere we needed to go. I was old enough to keep an eye on Cassie, so the driver usually waited for us in the car wherever we went."

I arched my eyebrows, impressed he had taken care of his sister at such a young age. "That's very noble of you. I thought most thirteen-year-old boys just want to play soccer and get dirty."

"Not all of us. I was always very protective of Cassie, even when I was young. I don't think I ever did anything the typical boy does."

That didn't come as a surprise. I watched him turn the phone around and fiddle with it before flipping the screen to face me again. This time, the picture showed Cassie a few years older standing outside the corn maze. "This one was taken the year before she died. She was almost twelve, and she kept telling me she was too old for this place."

"She sure seems to be having fun," I commented, studying the grin on her face. In her blue jeans and purple shirt, she looked just like the girl in the pictures I had seen in her room a week ago. The cross dangled over her chest, the silver glinting in the sun.

"That's because she was teasing me, telling me I dragged her here as an excuse to relive years past when she was little. She liked to call me an old soul trapped in a young body. Probably because I was often like a father to her." He paused, sorrow falling over his expression.

"You were an awesome brother," I said, hoping to distract him from his sadness. "A lot of kids wouldn't take time out of their social life to do things like that with their little sister."

"She meant a lot to me. Our parents had some problems, and I wanted Cassie to have it better than I did when I was young."

"Really?" I asked, curious to know more.

He nodded as he placed his phone on the table. Picking up his sandwich, he took a bite, his gaze drifting away from me.

Wondering if I had touched on something he didn't want to share, I opened the bag of chips on my tray and sipped my soda. A few seconds later, Lucian swallowed the bite in his mouth before breaking the silence. "My parents had a pretty turbulent marriage. When I was young, they were still trying to patch things up. They were too busy with counseling sessions and weekend trips to the Cape to do things like this with me. When Cassie started school, they realized there was nothing left of their relationship to save. Instead of trying to resolve things, they both ran away, in different directions, of course."

"I'm sorry to hear that. I never had a father, just a mother. But she was very good to me. We were always together, at least when she wasn't working and I wasn't in school."

"Well, things were very strained at home. It was almost a relief when Mom left for Hawaii. Cassie took it pretty hard, so I felt like I needed to be there for her. I think it's one of the reasons she was drawn to the church. She wanted to feel like she belonged somewhere. Although she always had Angel."

The thought of Cassie's horse brought another question to my mind. "So, if your mom and dad are gone a lot, how does that impact their horses?"

Lucian shrugged. "It weakens the bond a little, but they do okay. Just like I did when I was gone for a few years. It's better to be here, but it doesn't hurt to be away. You should know since you never knew Gypsy existed until you moved here."

"Oh, right," I said, remembering the night Becca had revealed my connection to Gypsy. "So, did Cassie love fall and Halloween?" I asked, changing the subject.

"Not as much as Christmas. When she was eight, she started taking it upon herself to decorate the house with anything she could find. Lights, wreaths, and her favorite—homemade paper snowflakes. Another tradition of ours was to cut down a Christmas tree every year."

Smiling at the image of Lucian trudging through a snowy field to find the perfect tree for his little sister, I asked, "Is there anything you didn't do for her?"

My question had been innocent enough, but it caused a frown to fall upon his face. His eyes shifted away from mine as a dark shadow raced across his expression. "Yes. Save her from a monster."

"Hey," I said quietly, reaching across the table to touch his hand. When he looked up at me, I continued. "You can't blame yourself for what happened. It's not your fault."

He sighed deeply, his eyes filling with moisture and glistening in the bright sunlight. "I know, but I still do. I should have been there for her. I should have known where she was at all times."

"She was twelve, right?"

"Yes."

"No one would expect you to stay with a twelve-year-old every minute of the day."

"I keep trying to tell myself that. But she was special. I should have been more careful."

"Of course she was." I squeezed his hand before pulling back and taking another bite of my sandwich. It was time to talk about something a little less depressing. "You told me this adventure had something to do with art. Are we going to get to that at some point?"

A grin slid over his face, erasing his sadness from a moment ago. "Yes. As soon as we finish eating, we can head home. We have some work to do when we get there."

"Work?"

"Mm-hmm," he murmured, picking up his sandwich.

"Care to explain?"

"Nope," he said before taking a bite.

I groaned. "Why am I not surprised? You sure like to keep me guessing."

"Yes, I do," he said with a gloating smile. "Now finish your sandwich so we can get going. I have everything we need set up at home."

"Okay. I guess I'd better eat fast because now I'm curious."

"Sounds like a plan," he said.

After lunch, we hopped into the Range Rover for the drive home. Lucian turned on the radio and we talked a little between songs, mostly about the farm, the weather, or something equally as boring.

A few times, I glanced at him, noticing how he watched the road with his intense green eyes. The cross necklace dangled against his light brown shirt, reminding me of how much he must have loved Cassie.

About halfway home, images of the flames and the wolf jumped into my thoughts. Pushing them away as quickly as they appeared, I scolded myself for letting my mind conjure up the one unsettling moment of the day. *Just forget about that. It was probably your imagination acting up,* I told myself.

Not quite, another voice argued. *I have never had hallucinations like that before. Something is going on, and sooner or later, I'm going to have to come to terms with it. I can't keep it a secret forever. I need to tell Becca, and soon. I'm not going to let this wolf torment me any longer.*

Closing my eyes, I tried to think of something else. Immediately, the memory of Lucian hugging the little girl back at the farm popped into my mind, which was much better. I could still see the appreciation in her mother's eyes. When her assumption that Lucian was my husband came to mind, I shook it out of my head. This was neither the time nor the place to let myself get carried away with the idea of dating Lucian. I was in a relationship with Alex, and clearly, Lucian still had Zoe in his life. Even if there was a remote possibility Lucian and I would get involved, just thinking about him in a romantic sense made me twinge with guilt.

When we pulled up to Lucian's house, he parked in the driveway and turned to me. "It's time," he said before getting out of the Range Rover. I slipped out on my side and met him at the back where he opened the cargo area.

"Good. Because I'm dying to know what you have up your sleeve."

"Get your pumpkin. We've got some carving to do."

I laughed. "Is that what this is all about?"

"Yes. I take pumpkin carving very seriously. I used to get really creative. One year, Cassie made me design a horse head on her pumpkin. It was actually pretty good, if I don't say so myself."

"Wait," I said thoughtfully. "There are still two weeks before Halloween. Won't they get all dried out and rot if we carve them today? My mom never let me carve a pumpkin until a day or two before Halloween."

"I'll take care of that. I promise you it will stay fresh for weeks. So let's get to work. I already have an idea for mine."

"You seem a little too eager," I said, watching him curiously.

"I haven't done this since Cassie died because I was never here for Halloween. This one will be for her."

"Oh, okay. But I'm not very good at this. I'll probably just do a face with triangles for eyes and teeth."

Lucian raised his eyebrows. "Surely you can come up with something better than that."

"Like what? I didn't exactly prepare for this today, and I'm drawing a blank on ideas."

"Well, think fast then," Lucian said before reaching for his pumpkin which measured nearly eighteen inches in diameter.

As he stepped back from the SUV, my phone buzzed from where I had left it in my pocket after checking for new messages on the way home. I pulled it out and read a text from Alex. *The audition went great! On our way home now. I'll call you later.*

"Everything okay?" Lucian asked, breaking my attention away from the phone.

"Yes, it's fine. The band had an audition in Boston today. Alex just wanted to let me know he's on his way home now."

"Oh yes, Alex. How's that going, anyway?"

"Fine," I said in a tone that meant I didn't want to talk about it. After returning the phone to my pocket, I reached into the SUV's back compartment for my pumpkin. Wrapping my arms around it, I propped it up against my chest. As I stepped back to clear some room for Lucian to shut the overhead door, conflicting emotions tumbled through me.

I felt like kicking myself. Here I was spending an entire day with Lucian and I had barely thought of Alex. To make things worse, I felt drawn to Lucian, the grief that consumed him from losing his sister eating away at my heart.

The door came down with a thud, snapping me out of my trance. "Follow me," Lucian said before leading me to the front door. He managed to unlock it with the pumpkin balanced in one arm. Then he opened the door and we marched inside, heading straight to the kitchen where newspaper covered the table.

Setting my pumpkin down, I inspected the other items on the table. A big bowl and spoon had been placed next to a pair of black markers and two knives. The knives made me flinch, reminding me of Lucian holding one in my nightmare. An ounce of doubt whipped through me, and the notion that Lucian had killed his sister made my skin crawl.

Stop letting your imagination get the best of you, I thought. *Lucian loved his sister, and he has proven it over and over again. You can't keep second-guessing him. Either you believe he's innocent and you're safe with him, or you don't. And if you don't, then shame on you for accepting his invitation today.*

When the rant in my head ended, I took a deep breath, acknowledging my inner self had a good point. Determined not to let fear creep into my thoughts again, I watched Lucian pick up a marker.

"Ready to start drawing?" he asked, handing it to me.

"I guess so," I replied, hesitation in my voice as I took the marker from him.

"Before we get started, would you like something to drink?"

"Sure. What do you have?"

"Well, Cassie used to drink apple cider when we came home from getting our pumpkins," Lucian said on his way across the room to the refrigerator.

I looked at him, feeling an amused smile slide upon my lips. "You know, I'm beginning to get a complex here. I feel like you're using me to bring Cassie back to life for a day."

Lucian glanced at me from the other side of the island. "Believe me, when I look at you, the last person I see is Cassie. You are quite different. It's just nice to have someone to share my memories of her with, that's all. But you are definitely not my little sister."

"Okay. Good. I was just checking," I said, a little embarrassed. "Apple cider would be great. Thank you." Turning back to the table, I pulled the cap off the marker and held it up, poised to start drawing even though my creativity seemed to have escaped me.

A moment later, Lucian approached behind me and reached around my side to put the glass of cider on the table. I whipped around, my nerves rattled by his presence so close that I felt the heat from his body.

"Your cider," he said, nodding to the glass.

I backed up until my thighs touched the edge of the table and glanced at the drink. When I shifted my gaze back to Lucian, the intensity in his green eyes caused me to shudder.

"What?" I asked, mesmerized once again by his stare.

"Thank you for coming with me today. It means a lot. You're the only person who seems to believe in me." He lifted his fingers to the side of my face, tucking a loose strand of hair behind my ear.

My breath hitched as a line of fire erupted under his touch. I swallowed hard, fighting for every ounce of composure. "I'm pretty sure Zoe believes in you, too."

His gaze remained locked on me, the mention of Zoe not making a dent in his focus. "I'm not even going to go there. Zoe is nothing like you, little witch," he whispered, leaning toward me.

His lips hovered above mine, his breath tantalizing me. He stopped so close, his eyes studying me, a storm brewing in them. My heart fluttered out of control, a fire pulsing through me. In that instant, I felt removed from reality. Every time his eyes met mine or he touched me, a burning desire tore through my soul. Now was the moment I would give in to those feelings. I waited, breathless, captivated...

My phone rang from inside my pocket, and I jumped, breaking my eye contact with Lucian. Alex popped back into my mind, pitching a healthy dose of guilt into my conscience. Slowly, I looked back at Lucian as the ringing stopped. "I think we should get started on the pumpkins, or we're never going to finish today."

He drew in a deep breath before stepping back. The distance between us gave me room to breathe, and I didn't dare reflect on the moment that had just passed. Instead, I sighed with relief.

"Fair enough," he said before picking up the other marker. Without another word, he started to draw the face of a young girl on his pumpkin.

We spent nearly an hour on our pumpkins. After we drew the faces, Lucian cut the tops off and we scooped out the seeds and filling. Then we worked in silence on the carvings. Mine, a simple jack-o'-lantern face with triangular-shaped eyes and teeth, was done in about ten minutes. But Lucian took a half hour, paying careful attention to every line and curve. By the time he was done, the silhouette of a girl, her hair hiding one side of her face, had taken over the pumpkin.

After we finished, Lucian took me home. When I got out of his Range Rover, he remained in the driver's seat, barely looking at me. The pumpkin in my arms and my purse hanging from the crook of my elbow, I glanced at him. "Thank you for today. I had a great time."

He turned and flashed a faint smile, the first one I had seen since our awkward moment in his kitchen. "I'm glad. Well, see you around."

I nodded and shut the door. As soon as Lucian drove away and the Range Rover could no longer be seen in the twilight, I headed up the front porch steps, realizing I had about two seconds to come up with an explanation for the jack-o'-lantern in my arms.

21

Monday morning at my locker, I found myself alone while the other students crowded the hallway behind me. After hanging up my coat, I began organizing my books, unsuspecting that something was amiss. But after a few minutes, I stopped and turned, Alex's absence perplexing me. He usually greeted me by now, often in the parking lot before I made it into the building. It wasn't like him to not find me. My curiosity getting the best of me, I left my book bag on the floor and scanned the sea of students.

I looked to the right, craning my neck to look over the heads bobbing up and down. The other students bustled with activity, slamming lockers and giving each other high fives. Nowhere in the crowd did I see Alex. Whipping my gaze to the left, the scene before me didn't change. Still no Alex.

I was about to give up when I caught sight of Derek at his locker, his attention captivated by a girl I didn't recognize. Tall with long red curls, blue eyes, and a black leather jacket open wide enough to reveal her curves outlined by a black shirt, she exuded a cool confidence.

Raising my eyebrows, I wondered who she was. Derek seemed smitten, confusing me. He had just patched things up with Lacey, although it wouldn't surprise me if they had flipped the off switch on their relationship again.

Personally, I hoped he would change his mind about Celeste one day. She was always alone and hadn't even attempted to find a date for the Homecoming dance. I knew she had been heartbroken, knowing he had taken Lacey. There was no telling how she'd feel if she learned one more girl had jumped in front of her. I scowled at the thought, my frown deepening when the students down the hall moved out of the way and I saw Alex standing next to Derek and the new girl.

My thoughts of Celeste's nonexistent love life faded as rejection took over my mood. Jealousy zapped me, a little like how I felt every time I saw Lucian with Zoe. But this was different. This was personal. Alex was my boyfriend, and I didn't appreciate a new girl, especially one as gorgeous as this one, stepping in.

Relax, I scolded myself. *He's probably trying to hear every word so he can tease Derek later. Derek is surely going to fall over himself trying to impress this girl.*

Forcing myself to smile, I spun around to shut my locker and grab my book bag. Then I made my way down the hall, weaving in between the students, my sights set on Alex, Derek and the redhead.

When I reached them, the new girl shifted her attention from Derek to me, causing him to stop talking mid-sentence. He and Alex looked my way, and suddenly all eyes were on me. "Hi," I said quietly, feeling a little shy in front of my audience.

"Hey," Alex said, wrapping an arm around my shoulders and kissing my cheek. "I was just about to start looking for you."

"Sure you were," I teased, enjoying his affection.

"We just met Maggie. She's new. Maggie, this is my girlfriend, Gracyn," Alex said.

A little unnerved by her stare, I forced myself to smile. "Nice to meet you. Welcome to Sedgewick."

"Thank you," she replied, her voice as smooth as honey. "These two were just telling me that this town is haunted. Maybe you can tell me the truth. Is it?"

I felt my eyes roll as I tossed Alex and Derek a knowing look. "You guys are mean," I scolded. "At least you let me settle in before you started messing with my head. Maggie probably hasn't been in town more than a few days."

"They told you the same story?" Maggie asked.

"Yes," I confirmed. "But don't believe it. None of it's true." *Unless you're a witch,* a pesky voice reminded me. *Then there's no telling what's going to happen.* At this point, accusing the white wolf of haunting me didn't do it justice. Pushing my memory of the flames and the wolf in the maze aside, I offered Maggie a faint smile.

"Good," she let out with a long sigh. "That's all I needed."

Shifting my attention to Alex, I caught his eye. "I was wondering where you were this morning. So scaring the new girl took priority over me?" I asked with a pout, pretending to be upset.

He smiled and gave my shoulders a comforting squeeze. "Sorry. I was going to come find you in a minute."

"Sure you were," I teased.

"No, seriously, I mean it. You know I feel awful about last weekend. I wanted to make sure you're free this Saturday night. Our date is getting a little overdue."

Grinning from ear to ear, Derek winked at Alex. "You know, make-up dates are the best."

I felt a hot fire race across my cheeks and looked down, a little embarrassed.

"And I should know," Derek continued. "Since Lacey and I are making up all the time." He flashed a coy smile at Maggie who seemed oblivious to him, her eyes locked on me.

Her intense stare made me nervous, and I tried to ignore her, as hard as it was.

"I mean, we used to make up all the time," Derek explained. "But our relationship is starting to give me whiplash, so maybe it's time I find someone new. Maggie, what do you say you let me show you around this week, and maybe even over the weekend?"

She slid her eyes away from me and smiled at him. "I'd love that. You are such a gentleman to take pity on the new girl."

My jaw nearly dropped, my gaze taking in her tight jeans and even tighter black shirt which accentuated every curve under her jacket. She was drop-dead gorgeous with a fierce confidence that commanded attention, not sympathy.

"Maggie, I guarantee you my offer is not a pity party," Derek assured her. "In fact, by the end of the week, you'll probably have a dozen offers. I figured I'd get mine in first."

"You are too kind," she replied with an appreciative smile.

"No, just honest," he said before an awkward silence fell over the four of us.

I could have thrown in a remark about Derek hitting on all the new girls since he had flirted with me when I moved to town, but I held my tongue. Instead, I smiled at her. "So, Maggie, where are you from?"

"Boston."

Her one-word answer made me suspect I would have to prompt her to reveal anything more than exactly what was asked. "What brought your family to Sedgewick?"

"Nothing. My family didn't move here, just me. My father had a stroke last week, and my mother passed away when I was little. So I'm staying with my grandparents for a while."

"Oh, no. I'm sorry to hear about your father," I said. "Is he going to be okay?"

"The doctors think so. It's just going to take some time."

"When did that happen?" Derek asked, his eager expression replaced with concern.

"A few days ago. I stayed alone while he was in the hospital, but then I had to pack up and move...here." Her voice lowered on the last word, as though she wasn't thrilled with her new home.

"Man, that sucks," Derek said, completely falling for her disappointment. "You had to trade Boston for this hole-in-the-earth town. Well, don't worry. It's not all bad. I promise."

Her expression lit up. "I'm sure it isn't, as long as it's not haunted," she threw in with a grin as if her worries about her father had disappeared into thin air. "And who better to show me around than you, right?"

"Of course. Now you're talking," Derek replied.

"I know it's only Monday, but what's going on over the weekend? Anything fun?" she asked.

"I think there's going to be another bonfire at the lake," Derek said, glancing at Alex, his eyebrows raised.

"I heard that, too," Alex confirmed. "But it will probably be the last one of the year, and the last party always gets busted. I bet everyone chickens out at the last minute."

"Well, if they don't, then count me in," Maggie said. "You'll introduce me to everyone, won't you, Derek?"

He smiled, mischief twinkling in his eyes. "I'd rather keep you all to myself." When she sighed, he quickly recovered. "But I suppose that would be selfish of me. So yes, I'll make sure you meet everyone who matters. But you also have all week to make friends. By Friday, you could know the whole school."

"I doubt it," she said before turning her attention to me and Alex. "So, Alex and Gracyn, if Derek finds a party, are you guys coming, too?"

"Probably not," Alex replied. "We have a date Saturday night." He squeezed my shoulder, putting a smile on my face.

"Don't mind him," Derek teased. "He's not as much fun as he used to be. But I'll stay out until the sun comes up with you, honey."

Maggie tossed Derek a smile. "You are too good to me," she said before her gaze drifted away from him. Her eyes locked on the students, a thoughtful look crossing over her expression.

I glanced down the hall to see Celeste rushing through the crowd. Her black coat and pants were no different than always, but her eyes were bloodshot with dark circles under them. Her brown hair hung from a loose ponytail, and she pushed a stray lock out of her face as she hurried around the other students.

Turning my attention back to Maggie, I watched her, my curiosity getting the best of me. But I didn't have a chance to say a word when Derek jumped in.

"Don't mind her," he said, giving a swift nod in Celeste's direction. "She's a little odd. She won't be someone I'll be introducing you to at the party."

Maggie shifted her gaze to Derek. "Well, that's a shame. It looks like something is bothering her. I'll bet she could use a distraction. Poor girl. What is her name?"

"Celeste," I replied, not sure what to think of Maggie's interest in her. "And I think I'm going to go check on her. She looks pretty tired this morning." I turned to Alex. "See you in Calculus?"

"Of course. Just don't let Celeste bring you down today. We have some catching up to do this week, and I don't want you worrying about anything, or anyone."

His words brought a smile to my lips. "Got it."

"Good," Alex said before placing a light kiss on my lips. Then he lifted his arm from my shoulders. "Now go find her before she disappears."

After saying a quick goodbye to Derek and Maggie, I took off in the direction Celeste had gone. I found her at her locker, her back to the crowd while she rummaged through the books on the shelf. As I approached, one fell to the floor with a thud.

"Damn!" she muttered, her eyes clouding up with tears of frustration.

"Here, I'll get that for you," I said, bending down to retrieve it. Straightening up, I held it out to her. "Celeste, you look awful."

She grabbed the book, tearing it out of my grasp. "Gee, thanks. Good morning to you, too," she said in a sarcastic voice before turning her back on me.

I wasn't about to let her ignore me. "Celeste, what's going on? You seemed to be doing great over the last few weeks, and now this? What happened?"

She whipped around to face me. "Please don't worry about me. I don't need any sympathy."

"That's not what this is," I insisted. "You're my friend, and when you show up looking like you haven't slept in a week, I'm going to be concerned. That's what friends do."

"I'm sorry. You're right. And thank you. I'm not used to someone being so nice."

"Now will you tell me why you're so upset?"

"I feel a storm coming," she whispered. "I'm in trouble, worse than you could ever imagine." She met my gaze for a moment, her bloodshot eyes locking with mine.

After a quick second, she snapped her gaze away and turned back to her locker. "Who am I kidding?" she muttered, raising an arm up to the shelf. "No one's going to take me seriously. I know evil has returned to Sedgewick, but it's probably going to take my murder to get anyone to believe me."

Ranting, she shuffled her books around. Her coat sleeve slid to her elbow, exposing huge scratches along her forearms. Shocked, I drew in a sharp breath as I caught her wrist and pulled it to me. She tried to break away, but I had a strong grip on her. After a moment, her arm became limp and she allowed me to inspect it. Long red scratches and dark purple bruises covered her skin. Without a word, I reached for her other wrist and pushed her sleeve up, revealing similar injuries.

"Celeste!" I gasped, my voice panic-stricken. "What happened to you?"

She looked at me, her bottom lip quivering for a split second before she whipped her arms back to her sides. Her sleeves dropped to her wrists, hiding the marks once again. She took a deep breath, composing herself. "Remember the doves?" she asked, lowering her voice as she glanced at the crowd for a moment.

"Of course."

"Well, they're dead."

The image of the lifeless dove I had found after waking up from my nightmare flashed through my thoughts. "All of them?"

"No," she answered, shaking her head. "Only five, but that seemed like a lot."

I cringed. It had been awful to find one dead dove, let alone five. Shaking the idea of any number of dead birds out of my mind, I watched Celeste. "But what does that have to do with the marks on your arms?"

"Last night, I had another nightmare. It's the first one I've had in a few weeks. Serenity got upset and woke me up."

"How?"

"She was whinnying from her stall. She can be pretty loud when she wants to be. So I got up, and that's when I noticed my arms were a mess. By the time I got out to the barn, she had kicked a hole in her stall door. She was pawing at it trying to get out. She scraped up her legs pretty badly."

"Oh, no. That sounds awful. Is she going to be okay?"

Celeste nodded. "Yes. We both are. These wounds are superficial, and they should heal in a day or so."

"Good," I said, relieved Celeste didn't seem worried about her injuries. "Now tell me more about the doves. Where did you find them?"

"Right outside the barn door."

"Do you know how they died?"

"No. They were bloody, though. Something must have gotten to them, although it could have just been an animal."

"But what animal kills for no reason? I mean, wouldn't it have eaten them? It seems odd they were left behind like that." Just like the one I had found at the base of the porch steps.

The renewed worry racing across Celeste's expression shot a pang of guilt through me. "I guess it's not impossible, though," I added quickly, hoping to see her relax.

"No, but you're right. It's not normal behavior for a wild animal. That's why I think it's a sign of trouble coming."

"What kind of trouble?"

"I don't know," she said slowly. "Although I wish I did. All I know is it's not good."

I wondered what she would say if I told her about the dove I had found, but I knew it would only upset her more. Keeping that to myself,

I offered her a small smile. "Well, there's nothing we can do about it today. Did you tell anyone about this?"

"No. I'm still in a bit of shock."

"Maybe you should."

She shrugged, a distant glaze sweeping over her eyes. "I'll think about it." Then she turned to her locker and resumed gathering her books, her back to me.

"Well," I said, getting the feeling Celeste didn't want to talk any longer. "I guess I'd better get to homeroom. See you later."

I saw her nod before I walked away. The other students in the hallway were a blur. Celeste's comment about the dead birds being a sign of trouble on the way hit me hard. Knowing the wolf I had released was still at large sent a blast of fear through me. As much as I wanted to blame it for the carnage, I held back. I couldn't be sure of that. And until I could prove it, I had no choice but to wait and try not to worry about what would happen next.

I saw Lucian several times that day, but once again, he ignored me. Even in Art class, he never looked my way, locking his cold stare on Ms. Friedman instead. But when the bell rang, he grabbed my wrist before I could stand up.

I turned to him, my eyebrows raised. "What?" I asked with a frustrated huff, in no mood to play any more of his games.

"How are you?" he asked, a concerned look in his green eyes. "I'm sorry I haven't had a chance to say hello today."

"How nice of you to wait until the last class of the day to tell me."

"You know I can't be seen with you here," he said, his tone warning me not to question his motives.

"Yes," I said with a long, drawn-out sigh. "Zoe. God forbid she sees you talking to someone else." I rolled my eyes, painfully aware that his fingers were still curled around my wrist. I silently cursed the faint tingle crawling up my arm. No matter how hard I fought to not let him send my emotions into a whirlwind, I lost that battle every time he was near.

Maintaining my composure, I took another deep breath. "You can let
go of me now."

"You're not going to take off, are you?"

"If you must know, I have a lot of homework to do tonight. But I'll
stay for a minute if you make it fast."

He smiled softly, releasing me at once. "You haven't answered my
question."

I moved my arm to my lap, thankful to be free from his touch. "I
know. I just didn't think you cared."

"You should know me better than that by now," he said, his gaze on
me holding steady. "You have done something for me no one else could
do. You helped me bring my memory of Cassie back to life in a way I
never thought possible. I'm grateful to you, and yes, I do care."

His words struck a chord in my heart, rendering me speechless for a
minute. Gathering my wits, I quickly recovered. "I'm glad I could help,
although I'm not sure how I did it."

"By being the gentle soul you are and not buying into the propaganda."

"I have always been an independent thinker," I confessed with a
smile.

His eyes met mine, appreciation shining in them. "You have no idea
how glad I am that you are and that you're here."

"I'm happy I could help. And I'm fine. Thank you for asking."

"You sure?" he asked, seeming skeptical.

Celeste's battered arms flashed through my mind, but I didn't think
she'd appreciate it if I told Lucian about her nightmares. "Yes," I assured him, feeling like I was lying.

"Good. Well, I'd love to stay, but I actually have to go."

"Of course," I said, glancing away from him as a familiar disappointment rushed through me. I reached down for my book bag, the sudden
urge to get away from him striking me. I knew he meant he needed to get
back to Zoe, and the reminder of his relationship made my blood run
hot with jealousy.

You need to stop this infatuation, a voice in my head reprimanded me. *How
many times do you need to be reminded you are dating Alex? He's the best thing that ever*

happened to you. Do. Not. Ruin. It. I hoped I could heed my inner self's warning, although it simply depended on whether I would listen to my head or follow my heart.

Unable to make up my mind, I bid Lucian a quick goodbye and watched him walk out of the room, his broad shoulders and haunting green eyes a mere memory as soon as he disappeared around the corner. Alone, I gathered up my things, prepared to return home and work the afternoon away.

22

Over the next few days, I attempted to reclaim my sanity. I didn't want to think about magic. I forced myself to forget the wolf locked in the crypt and the image of it in the flames. Instead, I focused on my classes and filled out a few college applications. Thinking about life after Sedgewick gave me something to look forward to. College seemed like a lifetime away, but I hoped it would give me a reprieve from the supernatural world.

Things started to settle down, and that helped. Celeste withdrew again, which didn't surprise me, but I left her alone. Lucian ignored me, or pretended to with an award-winning performance. I caught his eye a few times, but he quickly looked away. Alex was a life-saver, as usual. He took me out for pizza Tuesday after school where we worked on our Calculus assignment. We hadn't spent much time together since the dance, and I realized I had missed his company more than I expected. His dark eyes and warm smile comforted me in a way nothing else could, at least not lately.

The new girl, Maggie, walked through the halls like she owned the school. She made many new friends that week, including the entire football team. Overnight, she became the talk of the school. Rumors circulated about where she was from and why she had moved to town, but I didn't pay them any attention. The new girl was hardly something I cared about right now.

Thursday afternoon between classes, I made my way through the crowded hallway, oblivious to the other students. Their chatter faded into the background when I saw Celeste at her locker. I turned in her direction, but a flash of red cut me off. I stopped dead in my tracks, my jaw dropping when Maggie intercepted me. She approached Celeste, starting up a conversation with her at once. Celeste beamed from the attention, smiling at something Maggie said.

Hidden from their view by the other students, I strained to listen to Maggie and Celeste, my curiosity getting the best of me.

"I hear you're a really good rider," Maggie said. "My horse got here a few days ago. I'm keeping her at the Four Oaks boarding stable on Marshall Road. Is that near your house?"

I raised my eyebrows, not sure if I was more surprised that Maggie rode horses or that she'd struck up a conversation with Celeste.

"Yes," Celeste answered. "It's about half a mile from us."

"Great. Do you want to head out on the trails sometime?" Maggie asked.

"I suppose we could," Celeste replied slowly, sounding a little hesitant.

"Perfect," Maggie said, not missing a beat. "How about this afternoon? It's a beautiful day for it."

"Okay. I'll tack up as soon as I get home."

"What's your address?" Maggie asked.

Celeste rattled off her street name and number. "Do you want to write it down?"

"No. I have an excellent memory. I'll ride over. Meet you there in about an hour? Will that give you enough time?"

"Yes," Celeste replied with a nod.

"Then it's settled. I'll see you soon." When Maggie turned away from Celeste and headed into the crowd, her eyes met mine. She smiled coyly, seeming pleased she had won over Celeste, one-upping me.

I looked away at once, my jealous streak punching me where it hurt. Celeste and I had never ridden together, although neither one of us had made an effort to meet up on the trails. In spite of that, I felt betrayed knowing Celeste had taken to Maggie so quickly. *Maggie charmed everyone at school this week*, I reminded myself. *Why would Celeste be any different than the entire football team, the cheerleading squad, and Derek?*

My mood falling, I tried to ignore my wounded pride. Heading to my locker, I considered asking if I could join Maggie and Celeste on their ride today. On second thought, I suspected three would be a crowd. Accepting defeat before I had even put up a fight for Celeste's friendship, I approached my locker and whipped the door open, the books on the shelf now my main focus for the rest of the day.

Thursday afternoon might have been a disappointment, but it paled in comparison to Friday. When I returned home from school, the driveway was empty as usual. Gabriel was in Boston again and Becca was at work. I hopped out of the car, prepared to change my clothes and get out to the barn before the sun went down. But after racing up the porch steps, I stopped as soon as I saw the front door cracked open. I had been the last one to leave this morning, and I distinctly remembered shutting and locking it.

My heart plunging into my stomach, I pushed the door wide open and looked inside. Everything was still in the dimly lit family room. The dogs who usually rushed to my side when I returned home were nowhere to be found. A feeling of dread swept over me, and I wondered if they had escaped.

Hoping I was wrong, I walked into the house and shut the door behind me. My heart fluttering with fear, I studied every piece of furniture, looking for anything out of place. But everything appeared to be in order. Even the magazines on the coffee table were in the same position I remembered from this morning—stacked on top of each other and angled out like a fan.

Convinced that nothing in the family room had been moved, I proceeded to the kitchen. My gaze instantly fell on the dogs who slept peacefully on their beds beside the table. A little worried because they didn't seem to notice me, I sighed with relief when I saw their chests moving up and down.

"Scout. Snow," I said, wishing they would wake up. Having their company, even hearing their nails tap against the floor as they walked around, would make me feel safer after finding the door ajar.

"Come on, guys," I said, dropping my book bag on the kitchen table with a thud. "Wake up."

Scout snapped his eyes open and scrambled to his feet. As he nudged my legs, Snow woke up and trotted over to us.

"That's better," I said, petting them between the ears. "You guys had me worried there for a moment. Everything okay? The door was open." I shook my head, silently chiding myself for talking to the dogs like they understood me. I continued petting Scout while Snow slurped up water from the bowl tucked under the island ledge. I began to relax, assuring myself that everything was fine. I had to assume I hadn't closed the door and locked it as I thought. Or perhaps Becca had run home during the day and forgot to lock up in her hurry to return to the bank. Whatever had happened, surely there was an explanation.

Taking a deep breath and pushing my worries out of my mind, I grabbed my book bag and rushed upstairs to change my clothes, eager to spend the rest of the afternoon with Gypsy before the sun set.

The next morning when I wandered downstairs still wearing my pajamas, Becca was standing in the kitchen, a coffee mug in her hand. "Good morning," she said with a smile. "I was thinking about making waffles. Want one?"

"Hmm," I mused. "I'm not sure. I have a big date tonight."

"Really?"

I approached the island and sat down on one of the stools. "Yes. Alex is taking me to dinner since we got cheated out of the dance."

"That sounds nice." She paused before putting her mug down on the counter. "Well, I want one and I know Gabriel will have a few when he gets up, although that won't be for a while since he got home after midnight. So it's settled. And there will be plenty if you decide you want one." She bent down behind the island, standing up with a waffle maker in her hands. After placing it on the counter, she pulled a can out of the pantry and grabbed a bowl from an overhead cabinet. She measured the mix, then added water. With a whisk, she began whipping up the batter. "It sure got cold last night. We're in for a hard freeze tonight, so make sure you take your coat with you."

"I will." I watched her for a moment, my mind a world away from the waffles she was making. "Can I ask you something?"

Becca looked up from the bowl, seeming curious. "Sure. What's up?"

"Am I going to college, or am I wasting my time filling out applications?"

She smiled, glancing down at the mixture she continued whipping. "Yes, of course you can go to college if it's what you want. You don't have to stay in Sedgewick forever just because you're one of us. A lot of us do because it's what we want, but look at Lucian's parents. They're gone all the time."

"Okay. Good. Because I really want to go to college." The wolf, the dead dove, and the open door from yesterday lingered on the tip of my tongue. *Tell her now,* my inner self ordered. *This is the perfect opportunity. But be quick in case Gabriel gets up soon.* The voice in my head was right. I needed to tell Becca, and now was as good a time as any. I opened my mouth, but Becca spoke before my words came out.

"Just break it to Gypsy gently. I know she's grown quite fond of you, and I'm sure she'll miss you."

The will to explain the events of the last few weeks escaped me at that moment. "I'll miss her, too. But I'll always come back."

"Be sure you do. She's been a lot happier since you've been here."

"Really?"

"Yes. She gets out more. She used to stay home when Gabe and I rode out on the trails."

"I'm glad to hear that. I enjoy riding her."

Becca finished mixing the batter as the waffle maker beeped. She opened it, waited for the steam to clear, poured the batter over the griddle, and shut the lid.

"But, back to college," I said. "Now I don't know what to do about my mom."

"What about her?"

"She set up a college fund for me, but I'm not sure I feel right using it now."

"Gracyn," Becca said firmly. "Your mom loves you. If she set aside money for your education, she'll want you to use it."

"It just feels weird now."

"It shouldn't."

"It would feel better if I knew who my real parents were."

"Why? Even if you found them, they would be strangers to you. Your mother is still there for you. I never wanted you to turn away from her. And I'm sure she doesn't want that, either."

I nodded, grateful for the reminder that my mother was still my family. "Thank you for saying that. You're right, and I'll remember that. At least I have time to plan for college." *Which means time to be harassed by the wolf. Tell Becca! Tell her now!* I glanced at her, at once realizing I didn't want to dampen the mood this morning. *Later,* I promised myself before changing the subject. "What do you have planned for today?"

"Not much. We're expecting a hay delivery. It's time to stock up for the winter."

"Already?"

"Oh, yes. You never know what the weather will do around here. We could be seeing the first snow soon."

"Yikes. Halloween isn't even here yet, and you're talking about snow?"

"You'd be surprised how fast those flakes start falling. The trees are starting to lose their leaves. Winter is right around the corner."

"Then I need to finish my college applications. Guess I know what I'll be doing today, after I pick up my dress from the dry cleaners, that is."

"Good. You seem happy lately. You must be looking forward to tonight."

I mentally rolled my eyes. If only Becca knew I had released a wolf from a crypt and started seeing hallucinations.

She would know if you told her.

And ruin her day? That would just be mean.

Ignoring the argument in my head, I flashed Becca a winning smile. "Yes, I am. Alex has been so patient with me. I hope tonight is perfect. We haven't had the best luck lately."

"I'm sure that will change." The waffle maker beeped, and Becca opened it. She lifted the golden waffle and slid it onto a plate before pouring more batter over the iron and dropping the lid.

A semi-sweet pastry scent filled the air, making my mouth water. "You know," I said. "I think I'm going to take you up on your offer for a waffle this morning."

Becca's eyes met mine and her lips curled into a grin. "I had a feeling you'd change your mind."

— ◦ —

My day was fairly quiet. After picking up my dress in town, I returned home to find a tractor trailer in the driveway delivering the winter supply of hay. I managed to maneuver around it before heading inside to work on my college applications.

Sometime after the truck left, I spent an hour grooming Gypsy, grateful for her soothing company. My mind wandered as I ran the brush along her red and white coat, first picturing Alex and imagining what the evening would bring. But when the wolf invaded my thoughts, darkening my mood, Gypsy stomped her front leg and snorted. Forcing the haunting images out of my mind, I smiled at her and watched the concern in her eyes fade away. Still amazed at how she seemed to read my thoughts, I concentrated on Alex and our date that would begin in a few hours.

By six o'clock, I had finished getting ready for what I hoped would be an evening to remember. After a hot shower, I had dried my hair, brushing it into smooth waves that fell over my bare shoulders. My black dress looked as though I had never traipsed into a graveyard wearing it. Clean and pressed, not a smudge of dirt remained on it.

As I slipped into my shoes, a knock tapped on the front door followed by the dogs barking. Without another thought, I grabbed my small purse packed with my phone, keys and lip gloss, and rushed downstairs as quickly as I could in my high heels. After pushing the dogs away from the door, I whipped it open.

My smile collapsed at the sight of Lucian standing on the front porch, the setting sun behind him glowing above the distant treetops. "Well," he said with a smug grin. "You look nice. You didn't get all dressed up on my account, did you?"

I hovered in the doorway, not sure how to react to this unexpected surprise. "What are you doing here?"

He shrugged, his green eyes locked on me. He wore black from head to toe, the silver cross standing out against his shirt. "I was bored, so I thought I'd take a ride. Then I ended up over here. It was all Shade's idea."

I peeked around him to see his black horse waiting in the driveway. The stirrups hung loose against the horse's sides, and the reins were looped over his neck, partially hidden by his long mane. "You expect me to believe that?"

"If it helps my case."

"No, far from it. Now, if you'll excuse me, I need to get my coat." I started to shut the door, but stopped when Lucian curled his fingers around the edge, bringing it to an abrupt halt before it closed. "Really? You're going to push your way in after ignoring me most of the week?"

"I was hoping we could talk."

"Well, you'd better make it fast because Alex will be here any minute," I said. After releasing my hold on the door, I headed toward the coat closet. Cold air drifted in through the doorway, reminding me of the falling temperatures.

I grabbed my long coat and turned around with it folded over my arm. Lucian had let himself in, leaving the door ajar behind him.

I raised my eyebrows. "Shouldn't you be with Zoe? I mean, it is Saturday night."

"She's going to a party at a football player's house. It's not really my thing, although I told her I might stop by later."

"Then you should be getting ready."

"I will when I feel like it." He paused, his eyes studying me as his steady expression softened into a smile. "That dress suits you. I hope Alex realizes how lucky he is."

My cheeks felt hot at that moment. Shifting my gaze away from Lucian, I unfolded my coat. "Thank you," I muttered, sliding my right arm into the sleeve.

"Wait," Lucian said as he rushed across the room. He walked around me, stopped, and reached for my coat. "Where are my manners?"

Before I realized what he was doing, he pulled the coat up over my shoulders as I stretched my left arm into the sleeve. Then he swept his hand under my hair, his fingers grazing the back of my neck and sending a jolt of electricity through me. My breath caught for a moment while he tugged my soft curls out from under the collar, letting them fall as soon as they broke free.

Turning my head slightly, my eyes met his. "Thank you," I said, noticing his soft gaze and wishing he wasn't so close. A fire erupted in the pit of my stomach, pitching my heart into a frenzy. Once again, those haunting green eyes captivated me. My attention on him, I tried to read the emotion buried deep within his stoic expression. Whether it was desire, jealousy or concern, I couldn't tell. No matter what occupied his thoughts, he flustered me, especially after ignoring me for the last few days at school.

A knock at the door broke me out of my trance. I whipped my head around to see Alex standing in the doorway, confusion registering on his face. I felt my cheeks burn red hot and took a deep breath, gathering my composure. Alex could never know Lucian had gotten under my skin, and I had a scant few seconds to pull off a convincing performance.

"Alex," I said with as bright a smile as I could muster. Rushing toward him, I felt a wave of relief from the distance separating me and Lucian. Silently cursing him for being here when Alex arrived, I forced myself to remain calm. My heart still pounded, but now with the hope I could get through this awkward moment. I approached Alex and stopped in front of him, searching for forgiveness in his eyes.

"Everything okay here?" he asked, sounding unsure as he reached for my hand, his touch warm and comforting.

"Of course," Lucian said smoothly, walking toward us.

"I wasn't asking you," Alex responded coolly, glancing at Lucian before looking back at me.

"Yes," I assured him. "Lucian was just leaving." I snapped my gaze to Lucian, narrowing my eyes for a moment. "Weren't you?"

"Not really, but I will if you insist."

"I do insist. I'm leaving, and I'm pretty sure you don't want to be hanging around when Becca and Gabriel get home."

"Good point," he said. "Have a nice night, you two. Alex, be careful with this one. She's not one to mess with." Lucian shot me a knowing grin before turning and disappearing out the front door.

Before I could say a word to Alex, I heard hooves clamoring on the gravel. The clattering sound faded until silence returned, filling me with a renewed sense of peace.

"What was that all about?" Alex asked, his dark stare on me unwavering. He didn't seem angry, just confused and a little worried.

I squeezed his hand. "Nothing. I'm not really sure what he was doing here." At least my answer was honest. And I really wished I understood what purpose Lucian had sought by coming over tonight. Perhaps he was lonely, or he had taken an interest in me beyond that of friendship. My last thought spun up my heart again, a complete betrayal to the amazing, gorgeous guy about to whisk me away for what I hoped would be a wonderful night.

How dare you hope Lucian likes you as anything more than a friend! If Alex doesn't buy into your 'I don't know and I don't care why Lucian was here' attitude, you deserve any bitterness he harbors.

Shamed by my inner self, I pledged to get the evening back on track. "I certainly didn't invite him over. He just showed up."

"I didn't realize you knew him well enough to let him inside."

"We did an art project together a few weeks ago. And since he lives next door, we've run into each other a few times out on the trails," I explained, hoping it was enough to satisfy Alex's curiosity. "Ready to go?"

"In a minute. I'm worried about you."

"Why? I'm fine."

"You are, now. But you can't let your guard down with Lucian. Do I need to remind you—"

"That he killed his sister?" I finished for him.

"Yes."

"No, you don't need to remind me everyone thinks he killed Cassie." I couldn't keep referring to her as Lucian's sister. Now, every time she was mentioned, I pictured her sparkling green eyes and dazzling smile from the photographs in her room.

"Gracyn, it's not what people think. It's what we know. Please tell me he hasn't convinced you he's innocent."

"That's not possible. I'm not the kind of person who's easily swayed. I just know I have to trust the authorities. If they didn't have enough evidence to convict him, then he must not be guilty." My eyes wandered away from Alex, a wave of sorrow washing over me as it did every time I thought of Cassie. Her untimely death broke my heart. She had been so young and had so much to live for. Lucian had lost a beloved family member. No one seemed to realize how much grief and pain he still carried in his heart.

"He really has gotten to you," Alex mused, his voice disappointed.

"No," I shot out a little too quickly. Softening my voice, I continued. "Don't you remember when I drank the tequila at the party? He found me after I passed out."

"I remember."

"Well, he can't be all bad if he helped me."

Alex shrugged, his eyebrows raised.

"What about Zoe?" I asked. "She's still dating him. Maybe you should be more worried about her."

"Trust me, I am. But no one is going to get Zoe to change her mind when her heart is set on something. She's quite stubborn. Believe me, I've been trying to get her to dump him for weeks."

"Guess you need to try harder," I said, a faint smile forming on my lips. "Okay, can we stop talking about this now? You promised me an amazing night, and I don't want to start off on the wrong foot. Maybe we should start over."

Alex smiled and pulled me near him. "I like the way you think. So Becca and Gabriel are out?"

"Yes," I replied with a sly grin.

"Good." Without another word, he lowered his head and kissed me.

My eyes closed the moment his lips touched mine, erasing any doubt I had that tonight would be anything less than perfect. How Alex managed to clear my conflicting emotions about Lucian, I'd never know. After a minute, I pulled away. "Should we get going?" I asked.

He let out a sigh. "I suppose so. I made reservations, and I don't want to be late. How are you feeling tonight? No headache, backache, or any other pain that will prevent you from having a great time?"

I laughed, but a fleeting thought of Lucian dampened my spirits for a split second. I felt my smile fade and forced it to return before Alex noticed. "No. I feel great. I've been looking forward to this all week."

"Me, too," Alex said, a sparkle in his eyes. "So let's go."

I nodded and, ready to leave all thoughts of Lucian behind for the night, leaned against Alex as we walked out the door.

23

lex drove to the edge of town and turned into a gravel driveway leading to a quaint restaurant surrounded by woods. Lights glowed inside the white colonial building, shining in the twilight dusk. The parking lot was half full, the Mercedes, BMWs and Jaguars indicating an upscale clientele.

Alex pulled up next to a silver sports car at the end of a row, his Jeep towering above it. As he slid out of the driver's seat, I waited for him to meet me on my side. After opening the door, he extended his arm to me. I took his hand, grateful for not only the support as my heels wobbled over the stones, but also the warmth from his touch. The temperatures had fallen quickly, the bitter air nipping at my legs through my stockings.

We hurried around the cars on our way to the restaurant. Inside, a hostess wearing a black dress, her blonde hair pulled up into a twist, seated us in a cozy dining room. Flames flickered from the fireplace, licking the soot-covered stones. About half of the tables were occupied, the other guests creating a soft hum of voices. Alex and I had a table in the corner, a single candle casting shadows on the crisp white tablecloth. My coat now hanging on the back of my chair, I was pleasantly warm, the frigid air outside forgotten.

"This place looks great," I said, admiring the horse paintings that hung on the walls without even glancing at the menu in front of me.

Alex smiled, the gleam in his dark eyes causing my heart to swell. "This restaurant has an excellent reputation. The food is great."

"Have you eaten here a lot?"

"Yes," Alex answered. "Many times. My father actually proposed to my mother right here in this room a little over twenty-five years ago."

"Really?" Between the fire, candles and ambient light, the room had a romantic touch. "That's very sweet." Then a thought crept into my mind, causing my smile to fade. "Um, you're not planning—"

"No," he said with a chuckle. "I'm not going to propose to you. At least not tonight."

"Good," I let out on a long breath before realizing how that must have sounded. "I mean, not because I wouldn't like that, but because I'm definitely not ready for marriage. Maybe in a few years or so. Right now, I just want to get through this year." *And keep my sanity,* I added to myself.

Alex smiled, studying me. "You don't have to explain, trust me. We're in high school. I haven't thought about getting married to anyone yet. I just want to graduate and start college."

"Me, too," I said. "Whew. That was a little awkward."

"No, just honest. Why don't you take a look at the menu and decide on something for dinner?"

"Now that I can handle." Relieved, I looked down at the entrée selections, my stomach grumbling. I hadn't eaten much today since my anticipation of the evening had held my appetite hostage.

A few minutes later, the waitress appeared and took our order. As soon as she left, Alex gave me his undivided attention and took a deep breath. "Finally. It was beginning to feel like we'd never get to make up for missing the Homecoming dance. Thank you for coming."

"Thank you for giving me a second chance," I told him. "I still feel awful about everything. I know I'm not—"

I didn't get the chance to finish my sentence because Alex reached over and pressed a finger against my lips. "Just stop right there. You are perfect in so many ways, and the fact that you don't realize it, in spite of your twenty-twenty vision, makes you even more perfect."

I felt heat spread through my cheeks and looked down, relaxing a little when he pulled his hand back to his side.

"Am I embarrassing you?" he asked, a twinkle in his eyes.

"Not as much as I'm about to," a deep voice said from behind me.

Alex and I looked up at the same time to see Derek approaching, his fingers laced through Maggie's. Derek's dark suit made his blond hair seem lighter while Maggie's long red curls fell over her bare shoulders, the ends blending into her shimmering red dress. Alex's jaw dropped, and he huffed, not seeming happy when they stopped beside our table. "Derek, Maggie. What are you two doing here?"

"I wanted to take Maggie out on the town tonight, but she insisted on getting dressed up. She missed her Homecoming because of her dad," Derek explained.

"So you weren't kidding when you said it was over with Lacey?" Alex asked, sounding frustrated.

"No. I was dead serious. She was getting way too moody. Why should I have to deal with that when Maggie and I hit it off so well? Anyway, we never expected to see you guys here. Mind if we join you?"

"Not at all," Alex said, his teeth clenched.

Oblivious to Alex's annoyance, Derek hailed a busboy who helped him move a table and two chairs next to us. As he and Maggie got settled, Alex leaned across the table. "I'm really sorry about this," he whispered. "I swear, I never told him where we were going tonight for this very reason."

"It's okay," I said, trying not to let my disappointment show. First Maggie had swooped in and befriended Celeste, and now she and Derek were crashing my date with Alex. As much as I hated to blame her since I didn't even know her, I couldn't help feeling like she was encroaching on my territory.

"There," Derek said, prompting me to look away from Alex. Now sitting beside me across from Maggie, he flashed a satisfied grin. "That's better. What are you two drinking?"

"Soda," Alex answered sharply. "And that's all. Don't even think about using your fake ID in here. I'm not about to get kicked out."

"Once again, there you go taking all the fun away," Derek complained. When Alex shot him a scowl, he softened his tone. "But I'll hold off, at least until after dinner."

"So, Derek," Alex began. "I never thought I'd see you in here. Care to tell me how you ended up picking a classy restaurant over a seedy bar?"

"It wasn't my idea. Maggie picked it," Derek explained.

Maggie nodded, speaking for the first time since she and Derek had arrived. "Yes. I did a little research on the internet to find the best place in town. The reviews convinced me to try it. It sounds amazing," she said in a smooth voice.

"It is," Alex assured her as the waitress returned with our drinks. After placing them in front of me and Alex, she proceeded to take Derek and Maggie's order.

Ready for a moment alone, I quietly excused myself. After winding around the tables, I followed the short hallway leading to the front entrance and slipped into the ladies room.

My eyes adjusting to the bright florescent lights, I went straight to the sink and washed my hands. As I dried them with a paper towel, I lifted my gaze to the mirror, pleased to see my hair still falling in soft waves over my shoulders, only a single stray lock out of place. I swiped at it, tucking it behind my ear. With a sigh, I glanced down at the sink, my thoughts heavy. Once again, it seemed my date with Alex was destined to fall flat.

Determined not to let Derek and Maggie ruin the night, I looked up and gasped at the redhead staring back at me in the mirror. My heart leaping from surprise, I drew in a long breath and spun around to face Maggie.

"You scared me," I said. "Are you always so quiet?" Summoning my composure at that moment was nearly impossible as Maggie studied me with her intense blue eyes, unsettling me.

"Only when I want to be," she replied, her voice low and steady.

"Oh, well, you're pretty good at it," I said with a faint smile, trying to lighten the mood.

"You look very nice tonight, Gracyn," she said, stepping closer to me.

I backed up until my legs bumped against the counter. Curling my fingers around the edge, I met her gaze. "Thank you. So do you."

"I do love this dress," she said, her eyes dropping before she looked back at me. "I feel free in it. Like the chains of yesterday are finally gone. I actually owe you a thank you."

"I have no idea what you're talking about."

"You will, one day. But not tonight." She started to turn, but stopped. "By the way, I've been meaning to ask why you're with Alex."

"I don't understand."

"I see the way you look at Lucian. How Alex has missed the love-struck glaze in your eyes every time Lucian walks by is beyond me. You might try being a little more subtle next week."

My blood ran hot with anger. How dare she make an assumption about something that didn't involve her? "You're reading something that isn't there. I know Lucian, but it's not what you think. He's my neighbor, and we're in the same Art class. We had to work on a project a few weeks ago, that's all."

"If that really was all, you wouldn't be trying so hard to convince me it's nothing."

"Look, I don't like what you're insinuating, and I really don't appreciate being cornered here in the ladies room. So if you'll excuse me, I'm going to finish washing up." Without waiting for her to say another word, I spun around to face the sink, hoping she would leave. As I turned on the faucet again, her low voice rose above the running water.

"Go ahead and do that. But I know what happened at the pumpkin farm last weekend and, well, let's just say one could feel the heat between you and Lucian. You know you want him. Admit it," Maggie whispered from behind me.

"What?" I lifted my head up at once, glancing in the mirror to find the space behind me empty as if she had vanished into thin air. My pulse picking up speed, I whipped around in time to see the door swing shut. Alone, I took a deep breath, her words echoing in my mind.

I felt flushed all of a sudden as panic swept through me. Every second of that day rolled through my thoughts—the drive out into the country, the families with young children, and the confining corn maze. I didn't remember seeing Maggie anywhere, and she would have stood out in that crowd with her red hair and model looks.

Confused and frightened, I remained at the sink for a few minutes, wondering how she knew about last weekend. *You probably missed seeing her because you were too caught up with Lucian and those gorgeous green eyes,* a knowing voice said, silently scolding me. *How she knows about last weekend isn't the problem. The question is what's she going to do about it? So get back to your date before she breathes a word to Alex.*

The last thing I wanted was to return to the table where Maggie was waiting. But I had to face her. I wouldn't allow her to sabotage my relationship with Alex. Gathering every ounce of my courage, I took a deep breath, preparing to fight for what I wanted more than anything right now—a night to enjoy with my boyfriend.

Snapping out of my trance, I turned the faucet off. Holding my head high, ready to defend what was mine, I walked out of the ladies room, determined to make this night a success in spite of Maggie.

By the time I returned to the table, Derek and Maggie were sipping their drinks. Smiling at Alex, I took my seat across from him, trying to ignore Maggie who sat next to him. Out of the corner of my eye, I saw her red hair and sensed her sly smile, but I didn't dare look at her. I refused to give her the satisfaction of knowing she had rattled me.

"I was just telling Maggie that you two have something in common," Alex said, breaking the silence.

"Really?" I asked, nearly choking on my own breath.

"Yes. You two are the only girls who have moved to Sedgewick, at least since I've been in school. And you both ended up here within a matter of months. Not to mention that you both have red hair. Are you sure you two aren't related?"

My jaw dropped, my thoughts blank.

"Hmm," Maggie mused. "You never know. Stranger things have happened."

Curious, I raised my eyebrows and looked at her. "What are you saying?" I asked coolly.

"Just that it can sometimes be a very small world," she replied.

I glanced away, not wanting my expression to reveal the way she unnerved me. "I would think we'd know if we were related," I said with a sigh, trying to act bored while the thought of my unknown relatives swept a renewed uneasiness over me. I didn't know who my blood relatives were, except Becca, although I hoped I would someday.

"Well, I think it's awesome," Derek chimed in. "Two hot girls in just a few months. I was getting bored with the locals. Fate has been good to me. At least the second time around." He shot me a grin loaded with mischief and winked.

Derek's teasing helped take the edge off, bringing a smile to my lips. "What would Lacey think if she heard you say that?" I asked.

"I don't care," Derek answered, flashing a sly look at Maggie. "Don't worry. She's history. You're the only one on my mind now."

"I wasn't worried," Maggie assured him. "You're quite the catch. I'd be more worried if you didn't have a girlfriend or two in your past."

Derek beamed, his face turning pink. "Okay, you're embarrassing me. I think I like you even more now," he said before leaning across the table and kissing her.

A little uncomfortable, I looked at Alex, grateful for the smile he tossed my way. "The food should be here soon," he said. "Hungry?"

"Yes," I replied, realizing at once that I wasn't. Maggie's appearance in the bathroom and insinuations about my feelings for Lucian had chased my appetite away. And now, seeing how she had Derek wrapped around her finger when I believed she wasn't trustworthy, turned my stomach. *You'd better find your appetite,* my inner self warned. *Nothing says 'I'm not having a good time' like picking at your food. For Alex's sake, you will eat and pretend to enjoy every bite.*

Fine, I answered, knowing my alter ego was right. Keeping things together with Alex depended on my convincing performance tonight.

Before I could think of anything else to say, Derek pulled his lips away from Maggie and eased back into his chair. Maggie struck up a conversation with questions about the restaurant, listening with interest when Alex told her his father had proposed to his mother in the dining room we were sitting in. Thankful to focus on something as innocent as Alex's parents, I remained quiet, hoping the conversation would remain on anything other than my weekend with Lucian.

About ten minutes later, our entrees arrived. After the waitress placed our dinners in front of us, she left with the tray and folding stand. I picked up my fork, the creamy chicken pasta before me resurrecting a sliver of my appetite.

"So what's up with that guy, Lucian?" Maggie asked before I took my first bite. Just like that, what little appetite I had gotten back disappeared.

Setting my fork down, I watched a dark shadow race over Alex's expression. "I'd rather not talk about him. I don't want to spoil our dinner," he replied, his gaze on me.

The memory of Alex arriving to pick me up while Lucian helped me with my coat crushed my hopes that tonight would end well. Surely that moment had just returned to the forefront of Alex's thoughts as well.

"You won't," Maggie stated. "I'm pretty hungry. Nothing could ruin my appetite." Proving her point, she cut a piece of prime rib, speared it with her fork, and raised it to her lips. Chewing quietly, her mouth closed, she smiled, the look in her eyes suggesting she still expected an answer to her question.

"Then let me put it this way," Alex said. "You're better off not knowing."

"Yeah," Derek grumbled. "Let's not ruin the evening."

"You're just sore because Zoe's still with him," Alex threw out at Derek, earning him a scowl.

"And you're happy about that?" Derek shot back.

Tension filled the air between them before Maggie broke the silence. "Sorry. I didn't realize the guy would upset you two that much. I just couldn't help asking. He's the mystery guy at school. You know, older, dark—" She paused, flashing a suspicious look my way. "And sexy."

"Maybe to some," Derek muttered between clenched teeth. "But the last I checked, being a murderer isn't something most people find attractive."

"I keep trying to tell Zoe that," Alex said with a huff.

"Hmm," Maggie mused, her steady gaze still on me. "How about you, Gracyn? What do you think of the guy?"

The three of them locked their eyes on me, flustering me. Heat rushed through me, and my blood boiled from being put on the spot. I swallowed hard, resolving to keep my composure. Feeling the pressure, I decided the best way to handle her question was to speak the truth.

"If you ask me, his family situation breaks my heart. I realize everyone around here thinks he killed Cassie, but he wasn't convicted. I have to assume there would have been enough evidence to put him behind bars for life if he had done it."

Alex opened his mouth as though he was about to disagree, but I continued, not giving him the chance to interject a word against Lucian. "I know you guys think he did it, and that's fine. We are all entitled to our own opinions. I'm just telling you my thoughts." I glanced at Alex, surprised to see a look of understanding in his eyes.

"When you put it that way, it's hard for us to argue," he said. "Just be careful."

I nodded before looking down at my plate, realizing my dinner was getting cold. I picked up my fork and twirled a piece of pasta around it.

"Is that all?" Maggie asked, her icy stare challenging me.

"Yes," I replied.

"Really? Because it seems to me you know Lucian better than you're letting on. Call it intuition, since us girls can pick up on those things."

My eyes narrowed, my disgust for her rising into my throat. For a brief moment, I was grateful Alex had seen me with Lucian tonight. He wouldn't be surprised by my explanation. "He's my neighbor, and he's in my Art class. So I've gotten to know him a little. Last I checked, that's allowed. But instead of talking about someone who isn't here to defend himself, maybe we should find out a little more about you. We hardly know anything except that you're from Boston. Maybe it's time you fess up and tell us what skeletons you're hiding."

As my rant ended, I ignored the shocked looks Alex and Derek shot me. I watched Maggie, waiting for her answer.

A smile broke out over her face. "Well, Gracyn, that was quite the speech for someone who has barely spoken since we got here."

"Can you blame me after you and Derek crashed our date?"

Her eyes narrowing, she paused for a moment. "Fine. I'll answer you. Of course I have a thing or two in my past I'd like to forget, not to mention keep a secret. But since you seem intent on confessions, I'll spill it. I haven't always made the best decisions. Several years ago, I stole something, and let's just say I paid for my mistake."

Derek studied her, his reaction blank. After a few seconds, he smiled. "What really happened? Did you take a piece of candy from a store when you were five?"

"Not quite," she said. "If you must know, I stole a book. A very valuable book."

"And?" Derek prompted.

"And I'm sorry it happened. It was a huge mistake, and it cost me dearly. I lost a lot of things I cared about because of my actions." Dropping her gaze, she took another bite of her prime rib.

"So you learned your lesson," Derek said, reaching out to touch her arm.

She nodded, her head still bent. "Yes, I did." She sounded ashamed, but when she glanced at me, I saw nothing but satisfaction in her eyes, the regret in her voice appearing to be an act.

Taking a deep breath, I looked away, my instinct not to trust her growing.

When I shifted my gaze back to Maggie, her expression had softened, showing remorse. Derek and Alex seemed to fall for it, but I didn't believe it for a second.

"So, Gracyn, you asked and now you know," Maggie said. "But what about you? If we're sharing our skeletons, it's only fair you tell us what you're hiding."

My eyes locked with hers, I refused to back down. She had turned the tables on me and asked a fair question. The only way out was to give her what she wanted, even if it wouldn't be what she expected.

I glanced at Alex. "She's right. I had a secret when I moved here, and I think it's something you should know."

"Gracyn," he said, his voice filled with concern. "This doesn't sound good."

The memory of that stormy night with Sam's stepfather caused tears to well up in my eyes. I usually wasn't so dramatic, but the effect seemed to be working. Alex and Derek stared at me, their expressions worried. "Before I left Maryland to move up here, I had a situation with my friend's stepfather."

Alex drew in a sharp breath as his fork fell to his plate with a clanking sound. "What?"

Composing myself, I continued. "He drove me home one night. It was late and a storm moved in, so he pulled into an alley to wait for the rain to stop. And then he made a move on me."

Anger raced across Alex's face, followed by sympathy. "Why didn't you tell me?" he asked softly.

Meeting his gaze, I smiled faintly. "I just wanted to forget about it. I wanted to pretend it never happened."

"I'm almost afraid to ask—" Alex started.

I shook my head. "Don't worry. He didn't get very far." A smile snuck out on my face. "I'm stronger than I look," I said with a grin, earning me a knowing look from Derek.

"So you're okay?" Alex asked.

"Yes," I assured him. "I am. I don't want any pity here, okay? It's over, and it taught me I can stand up for myself when I need to."

With a satisfied smile, I picked up my fork, my appetite making a sudden comeback. As I twisted pasta around it, a voice rang out in my head. *Very clever,* it said. Confused, I looked up, not sure where those words had come from. Assuming I had imagined them, I took a bite of my food.

I felt Maggie's stare on me, but I refused to pay her any attention. As far as I was concerned, her game was over and I had won. She couldn't bring Lucian up again without making herself look really bad after I had shared the painful memory of being a victim.

"Well," Derek said, breaking the silence. "That was pretty heavy." He tossed a smirk at Alex. "Your turn."

"No way," Alex said between bites. "I'm good. But your date started it, so how about you go?"

"Fine," Derek relented with a sly grin. "But my skeletons are hardly a secret. Everyone knows I've had a bit too much to drink a few too many times."

"And you never learn your lesson," Alex said. "You'd better be careful, or you're going to end up like Mr. Wainwright."

"No way," Derek quipped. "He got whipped. I'll never let a girl mess me up that badly."

"Famous last words," Alex joked.

From there, the guys resumed bantering back and forth, their incessant teasing lifting the mood. I said little for the rest of the dinner, focusing on my entrée instead. I suspected Alex would ask more about Sam's stepfather later when we were alone, but until then, I wanted to finish my meal which happened to be one of the best chicken pastas I had ever tasted.

24

Relief swept over me when Alex and I bid goodnight to Derek and Maggie outside the restaurant. The tension I held bottled up inside instantly escaped like the air being sucked out of a balloon.

"Alone at last," Alex said, draping his arm over my shoulder while we walked down the sidewalk to his Jeep. Shadows from the glow of light posts scattered around the half-empty parking lot stretched across the ground.

"I know. That was pretty disappointing," I commented as my eyes adjusted to the darkness. Fatigue began to settle over me, the bitter cold air making me feel more tired. Sitting across from Maggie and worrying she would tell Alex about my day with Lucian at the farm had drained me more than I expected.

"But that's Derek. Sometimes he doesn't know how to take a hint."

"Yeah. I'm beginning to see that." We approached the Jeep and I stopped, turning to Alex. "But I don't blame him. His date definitely seemed to be in charge."

"His dates are always in charge," Alex said with a smile. "Unless there's alcohol." He paused, his grin fading as concern brimmed in his dark eyes. "But I don't want to talk about Derek and Maggie. It's you I'm worried about."

"Me? Why?"

"Because of what you went through with your friend's father. Why didn't you tell me about that?"

"It never seemed important. I mean, I was here and he was back in Maryland. Besides, he didn't hurt me. I took care of it." If only I could tell Alex I had punished Sam's stepfather by breaking his hand and cursing him.

"That doesn't matter to me. He obviously intended to. If you don't mind me asking, who was it? You've only mentioned one friend since I met you. Was it Sam's father?"

I glanced away, my eyes drawn to the glare of the parking lot lights shining in the car mirrors. But all I saw was Sam's stepfather's sleazy smile the stormy night he had put his hand on me. Nausea pitched my stomach into a roll, sending bile into my throat. I swallowed it back and looked at Alex, not answering him.

"It was, wasn't it?"

I nodded. "Yes. But he's not her real father."

"I think you mentioned that once. Real or not, he never should have touched you."

"The important thing is he never will again." I smiled, remembering that Becca's spell would ensure his loyalty to his wife from now on.

"I have to ask, although I'm betting the answer is no, did you report him to the cops?"

Shaking my head, I recognized the disappointment in Alex's eyes.

"Why not? The guy deserved it."

"Well, for starters, I was eighteen, so technically, he didn't break the law. And when I said no, he backed off." *Only after you broke his hand,* a sly voice stated. "Besides, what about Sam? If I accuse him of coming on to me, it would tear her family apart."

"Is she close to him?"

"Not particularly. But her mom and brother are. Something like this would devastate them, and Sam would be impacted, no matter how she feels about him. I could never do that to her."

"So you let him get away with it to protect your friend and her family?"

"Pretty much. But don't think I'm that forgiving. I broke his hand, so at least he suffered some consequences."

Alex's jaw dropped open. "You did what?"

I shrugged like it was no big deal, realizing I needed to explain fast even if it meant telling a small white lie. "I slammed the car door on him and his hand got caught in the way. Oops."

"Remind me never to get on your bad side. But wait a minute, didn't he bring Sam up here a few weeks ago when she came to visit?"

"Yes," I said, frowning at the memory of him dragging me into the woods. Then the image of Becca pointing the knife at his throat brightened my spirits. "He did. And he still had the cast on. But everything turned out fine. I think he learned not to mess with me."

Alex smiled, chuckling. "You're a tough one, aren't you?"

"When I have to be."

"Well, you never have to be tough with me," he said. "If anything ever goes too far, all you have to do is ask me to stop."

"I know," I assured him. "I've always felt safe with you."

"Good. Because you are." He paused, rubbing my upper arms. Even through my thick coat, his touch felt nice. "Well, it's pretty cold out here. Are you ready to go? Ben is having a party tonight. We could head over to his place."

"Yes, I'm ready to go. But I'm not really in the mood for a party now," I answered honestly.

"No?" he asked, sounding defeated.

"Sorry," I replied, shaking my head. "I think dredging up everything about Sam's stepfather killed my mood."

Alex let out a long sigh and leaned his forehead against mine. "We can't catch a break, can we?"

"Maybe next weekend?"

"Yeah, sure," he grumbled with a grin. "Just keep teasing me. You're killing me, you know that?"

A sudden pang of guilt dove into my heart, tempting me to go with Alex to the party. But if I went, I knew I wouldn't be much fun. "I'm sorry."

"It's okay. It's not your fault some jerk made a move on you. I'm sure it isn't easy when you're reminded about him. But for the record, I'm glad you told me."

I felt a weak smile slide over my lips, my eyes meeting his. "You are? I never wanted to burden you with my problems."

Alex lifted his head away from me, reached around my waist, and pulled me against his chest. "You are never a burden. And knowing this makes me feel a lot better. Sometimes I get a vibe from you I don't understand. Like you're here with me, but your mind is miles away. Now it makes more sense."

There was a lot more on my mind than Sam's stepfather, but I simply nodded. "I hope you never thought it was you."

He smiled. "I did a few times. But I also knew you were worth not giving up on." With a gleam in his eyes, he planted a kiss on my lips. When he pulled away, he studied me. "So we'll keep taking things slow. And I'll drive you home." He released my waist, took my hand in his, and walked me around to the passenger side of the Jeep.

After helping me into the seat, Alex hurried back to the other side and hopped in behind the wheel.

"What do you think of Maggie?" I asked as he started the engine.

"I'm not sure yet," he said, flipping on the headlights and backing out of the parking space. "Why?"

"I don't know. She doesn't seem like an average high school student," I explained, hesitant to tell Alex I didn't trust her.

"No. That's pretty obvious. But she's new and maybe she's trying a little too hard to fit in. It wasn't long ago you were the new girl."

"Yes, I know. Although you made it awfully easy for me." My comment earned me a wide smile. When Alex looked back at the road cutting through the dark woods, I continued. "But I didn't have the whole football team wrapped around my finger in a week."

"Maybe you didn't try hard enough," Alex quipped.

"Ha, ha," I said with a groan. "Okay, the football team I get. But did you notice she was hanging out with Celeste on Thursday? That seemed a little odd."

"Hmm," Alex mused. "I'm not sure what they have in common, but it's not out of the realm of possibilities for them to be friends. I wouldn't read too much into it. You're not jealous, are you?"

"Maybe a little. They went riding together. Celeste has never invited me to go riding with her."

"Have you suggested it to her?"

"We talked about it once, but I guess she forgot," I grumbled with a frown. "I wish I knew what to think about Maggie. I think she has an agenda, but I don't know what it is."

"Gracyn, don't you think you're overanalyzing things a bit? Maybe you should give Maggie a chance. It can't be easy starting at a new school in the middle of the year after something awful happened to her father."

I wished my doubts could be washed away with an explanation that simple. But Maggie knew Lucian had taken me to the farm last Saturday. I wouldn't rest until I understood how she had learned about our day and why she cared.

"I suppose you're right," I relented, knowing I could never tell Alex what really bothered me about Maggie. Even though I felt I had done nothing wrong by going to the farm with Lucian, I feared Alex would be hurt if he found out. I promised myself to find a way to make sure Maggie never said a word about it to him, only I had no idea how I would do that. Maybe I could ask Becca to put a spell on her. *Good idea*, a sarcastic voice rolled out in my head. *Like you want Becca to know you spent a day with Lucian. Maybe you should just own up to it and tell Alex before he hears it from someone else.*

I spent the rest of the ride home worried Maggie would not only tell Alex about my day last weekend with Lucian, but also embellish to make it sound like something it wasn't. By the time Alex pulled into the driveway, I was a nervous wreck.

Alex turned the Jeep around and stopped next to the porch steps. After shutting off the engine and headlights, he shifted in his seat to face me. "Here we are. At least tonight was better than the dance."

I smiled, sensing I was forgiven for wanting to go home. "Yes. We're getting better at this. I can't wait to see what happens next time."

"Me, neither," he said before cupping his hand under my jaw and kissing me.

A minute later, Alex broke away from me. "I should probably stop before your sister walks outside and sees us making out in the driveway."

I laughed. "I doubt she'll care. Besides, she likes you. She seems to think you're good for me."

"Great. I like hearing that. But I'm still not going to risk it. And I'm probably going to drop in at Ben's for a beer."

"Ah, now the truth comes out," I teased.

"You know I have a reputation to protect," he said with a smile before jumping out of the Jeep and coming around to my side. After helping me down in my high heels, he walked me up the steps to the porch.

We stopped at the door and Alex let go of my hand. "You have your key, right?"

I fished it out of my small purse and jingled it in the air. "Of course."

"Good. Now go on in and I'll call you tomorrow, okay?"

"Yes. Have fun at the party, but not too much fun."

Alex lifted his hand in a mock salute with a genuine smile before whipping around and rushing down the steps to his Jeep. After the tail lights disappeared into the darkness, I retreated into the house, grateful for the silence that greeted me. Feeling drained, I hung up my coat and headed upstairs, my sights set on curling up with a book and trying to forget Sedgewick High's newest red-haired bombshell.

— ~

The next morning, I put off my homework and rushed out to the barn to groom Gypsy. The sky was deep blue, the air cool and crisp. The golden leaves towering above the barn were beginning to fade, a sign they would fall as winter approached.

Gypsy filled me with a sense of peace, helping me forget Maggie's accusation that Lucian meant more to me than a friend. The only problem was that I feared she was right. I couldn't deny how he sent my heart spinning into motion every time he glanced my way with those green eyes.

I wanted to escape, and the barn offered me a reprieve. Gypsy stood patiently in the aisle while I brushed her red and white coat now thick and ready for winter. Dust clouded the air with every brush stroke. I thought about taking her for a ride, but fear of the wolf held me back. My best option was to wait until Becca and Gabriel returned home from brunch and ask if they wanted to head out on the trails.

Lost in my thoughts, I moved the brush over Gypsy's back and hindquarters, nearly jumping when a voice came from behind me. "How was your date last night?" Lucian asked.

Spinning around, I clutched my hands up to my chest. Lucian stood in the doorway, his long black coat falling around his jean-clad knees. The cross necklace dangled over his gray shirt, and his green eyes flashed with curiosity. "Thanks for sneaking up on me," I said. "You scared me."

"Sorry," he replied with a grin, walking into the barn and stopping in front of me. "I didn't mean to frighten you."

"What happened to calling first? Didn't we talk about that?"

"Yes," he rolled out in a long syllable. "But you haven't given me your phone number."

"Then let's take care of it right now. Got your phone?"

"Of course." He pulled it out of his coat pocket and swiped the screen. "Okay. Ready." As I recited my number, he added it to his contacts. "There," he said, sliding the phone back into his pocket. "Now I can call and text you whenever the mood strikes. Are you sure you want me to have your number?"

"I guess. Now, I expect you to call or text me before you show up."

"Why? Catching you off-guard is so much more fun."

Huffing, I turned back to Gypsy. "Well, it was getting a little old," I muttered.

"Oh, come on," he said, walking around Gypsy and watching me from across the top of her back. "You can't tell me you didn't enjoy last Saturday. It was probably a lot better because I surprised you."

My frown faltered for a moment. He had a good point. I had enjoyed the spontaneity, but now, knowing Maggie had seen us, it could never happen again. "Yes. That was fun. You know I had a good time. Except—"

"Except what?" he prompted when I didn't finish my thought.

"Do you know the new girl, Maggie?"

"The one with the red hair?"

"That's the one."

"Well, I haven't spoken to her personally, but I know who she is. She was hard to miss last week."

"I know," I said with a groan. "She said she saw us at the farm last weekend. Do you remember seeing her there?"

"Hmm," he mused, pausing thoughtfully. "No. And I'm sure I would have noticed her. She would have stood out in that crowd."

"I keep thinking the same thing. I don't get it. How does she know we were there?"

"Why do you care?" Lucian asked.

Flustered, I took a deep breath, my shoulders rising and falling. I cared because I didn't want Maggie to ruin my relationship with Alex, but I didn't feel like sharing my fears with Lucian. "It's just odd, that's all."

Lucian walked around Gypsy's hind end and approached me. He stopped inches away. "You can tell me if something's bothering you."

"No," I said, shaking my head. "It's nothing."

"Are you sure?"

I looked up at him, my eyes locking with his. Damn those gorgeous green eyes, pulling at my heart, tempting me to open up to him.

"Gracyn," a voice said behind me, breaking my attention away from Lucian and causing me to jump. "Is there a problem here?"

I whipped around to see Gabriel standing in the doorway, his blond hair shining like a halo in the bright sun. "No," I answered. "No problem."

Lucian walked past me before halting a few feet away from Gabriel. "I was just riding by and thought I would say hello. I'm leaving now."

"I thought I told you never to come back here again," Gabriel said, his icy eyes and bitter tone sending a warning.

"Did you? Because I seem to recall you slamming me against my truck and threatening me."

"Same thing. Now I'm telling you to stay off our property once and for all."

Lucian shrugged. "I haven't done anything, but if that's what you wish, I will comply."

"Be sure you do," Gabriel said.

Lucian turned his head, tossing me a faint smile. "See you, Gracyn." Then he strolled out the door, not breaking his stride, forcing Gabriel to move out of his way.

As soon as Lucian disappeared, Becca rushed into the barn. "What's going on?" she asked, heading straight for me. "Gracyn, is everything okay?" Worry lines creased her forehead, and a dark shadow raced through her eyes.

"Yes," I said. "It's fine. Look, I know you two don't like Lucian, but I'm not afraid of him. Please stop worrying about this."

Becca shook her head and looked at Gabriel, catching his eye for a moment. After they exchanged a knowing look, she turned back to me. "It's only natural for you to trust Lucian after he helped you the night your friend's stepfather dragged you into the woods, but you should still keep your distance from him."

I wanted to explain how Lucian had helped the lost little girl last weekend, but then I would have to reveal I had spent the entire day with him. Instead, I shifted my gaze to Gypsy and folded my arms across my chest. Hiding one hand under my arm, I crossed my fingers. Then, feeling like I was six years old again, I nodded. "Okay. I will."

25

onday morning, the school buzzed with chatter, the excitement stemming from the upcoming Halloween weekend. Fliers for a haunted house had been posted on every corner, but I ignored them, instead seeking out Alex in the hallway. Finding him where I expected at his locker with Derek, I wound my way through the crowd until I reached his side.

"Good morning," he said, flashing me a warm smile, his dark eyes meeting mine. Then he slid an arm over my shoulders, pulling me to him.

"Hi," I replied, enjoying his attention. He had called yesterday as promised, filling me in on Ben's party. I had apologized again for bailing on him after our dinner, but he insisted he understood why I didn't want to stay out after reliving my nightmare with Sam's stepfather. Now leaning into him, I felt a smile beaming on my face.

"Gracyn, ready for those ghosts, goblins and ghouls?" Derek teased.
I rolled my eyes. "No, thanks. I'll pass."

"Sorry, that's not allowed. You can't skip this," Derek gushed, handing me a flier. Haunted House Halloween Night was scrolled across the top in wavy letters. The hand-out promised a night of gore, thrills, and far more tricks than treats. Not exactly my cup of tea.

"This haunted house is practically famous around here," Alex explained. "Kids come from other towns just to go to it. The line will be huge, but it'll be worth it. The house once belonged to a witch who died hundreds of years ago. Some say her spirit comes back one night a year."

"And that night is Halloween," I mused.

"How'd you guess?" Derek asked.

"Kind of hard not to see that coming," I said, handing the paper back to him. "I'll think about it."

"Come on, Gracyn," Alex said. "You have to come. We always go to this. It's an annual tradition. And this is our last year of high school. Besides, the group who organizes it donates the proceeds to the local animal shelter, so it's for a good cause."

"I don't know," I replied, still not sure.

"If I promise to hold your hand and keep you safe, will you agree to it now?" Alex asked.

I took a deep breath, my resolve crumbling fast. I didn't want to be a total dud, and lately, that was all I seemed to be. "Okay," I relented. "I guess I can close my eyes through most of it."

"That's the spirit," Derek said. "You two can double with me and Maggie."

My smile turned upside down at the mention of Maggie. "Really? You're seeing a lot of this new girl. A second date already? Must be getting serious."

"We'll see," Derek said with a shrug. "The jury's still out, but so far, so good."

I groaned inwardly at Derek's smitten expression. I didn't trust Maggie, and I wondered if Derek was in over his head with her. But I said nothing, not sure it was my place to cast doubt on the girl he had his heart set on. "I'm glad it's working out for you, Derek," I said.

"Thanks," he replied with a grin.

"But Derek, how much do you really know about her?" I asked. "I mean, she appeared here practically out of nowhere. Have you met her grandparents yet? Been over to their house?"

"No. There hasn't been any reason to. And hanging out with her grandparents isn't exactly my speed."

"Oh, I don't know," Alex chimed in. "Maybe they can tell you what she was like when she was little."

Derek huffed. "And maybe we could all bake cookies and play Candyland. Maggie is no child, trust me."

"No one would ever accuse her of that," Alex said. "I'm just saying you might learn more about her."

"Speaking of Maggie, has she said anything about her dad?" I asked.

Derek shot me a confused look, his eyebrows raised, prompting me to explain. "Because of his stroke. Has she mentioned if he's getting any better? I would assume she's keeping up with his progress."

"No, she hasn't mentioned him," Derek replied, his tone defensive. "And I'm not about to ask because if he's getting worse, the last thing I want to do is to upset her."

I nodded slowly, offering a consolation smile. "Good point," I said quietly, not pushing for any more information on Maggie. It would probably be better if I forgot about her, as long as she didn't stick her nose in my business again.

Alex squeezed my hand, and I glanced at him. He gave me a knowing look before taking charge of the conversation. "Well, hopefully, she'll be up for Saturday night. We can all go to the haunted house together. It'll be fun."

"We're not dressing up, are we?" I asked. "Because I hate trying to find a costume."

"The younger kids dress up and go trick-or-treating after the haunted house, but we're probably a little old for that. So no, you don't have to wear a costume," Alex confirmed.

"Good," I said. "Then I guess I'll come. But if it gives me nightmares, I'm calling you even if it's the middle of the night."

"Sounds good to me. I can't think of a better way to be woken up than by hearing your voice." With a grin, Alex planted a kiss on my lips.

Derek took a deep breath, letting it out with a loud huff. "Okay, you two, that's my cue to run."

Alex pulled away from me, shifting his attention to Derek who backed up.

"Oh, no, don't stop on my account," Derek said. "I have to go find a certain redhead and convince her to come out with us on Halloween. See you two lovebirds later." With mischief in his eyes, Derek waved before rushing down the almost empty hall.

Alex watched him for a moment, then looked back at me. "Now, where were we?"

When he tried to kiss me again, I slipped out of his reach. "We really need to get to homeroom. The bell's going to ring any minute."

"Okay," he let out with a long sigh. "You're right. See you in Calculus." With a nod, he turned and headed in the direction of his room.

Alone, I took off down the hall, pushing the idea of sharing another Saturday night with Maggie out of my mind. It was way too early in the week to let her ruin my mood.

— ～

Nothing changed with the start of a new week. Alex was his usual charming self, warming my heart every time our eyes locked. Celeste kept a low profile, rushing from class to class without giving me a chance to say hi. The one time I almost got to her, Maggie intercepted me. She shot me a knowing look, the satisfied grin on her face unsettling me. Then she approached Celeste, engaging her in a conversation clearly meant to exclude me. I slunk away amongst the other students, my pride hurt. I had made an honest attempt to win over Celeste, and she seemed to have forgotten me.

To my surprise, Lucian smiled at me a few times in the hall and greeted me with a quick "Hello" in Art class. In spite of his softer demeanor, he still spent most of his time in between classes with Zoe, and I stayed away.

Tuesday after my fourth class, I ducked into the bathroom to find it empty. While washing my hands, I glanced down at the running water. When I looked up, a pair of yellow eyes stared back at me in the mirror.

The white wolf fluttered across the glass, the image causing my heart rate to spike at once. Fear blasted through me, and I closed my eyes.

Opening them, I took a deep breath to steady my frazzled nerves. When I lifted my gaze, Maggie was staring back at me in the mirror. "What the—" I gasped, whirling around to find the bathroom empty.

My heart thumping, I inhaled slowly, trying to get ahold of myself. My imagination was out of control. I needed to stop torturing myself with hallucinations before the madness drove me to the brink of insanity.

Slowly, I turned around to face the mirror. I peered into it, seeing nothing except the bathroom stalls behind me. Then I studied my face, shaking my head. To anyone else, I looked like a typical high school senior. A dab of makeup covered my freckles, and my hair fell in waves over my black sweater. But fear brimmed in my eyes. I had a sneaking suspicion something evil had arrived and wouldn't leave until it got what it wanted. I only wished I knew what that was, aside from tormenting me.

I leaned my hands on the edge of the sink and closed my eyes for a moment. I knew what I needed to do. This afternoon, as soon as I saw Becca, I would tell her everything. I should have done that weeks ago after the dance. Why I had thought this would just blow over was beyond me. Tonight, I would come clean. Hopefully, she wouldn't scold me for keeping it from her. But more importantly, I hoped she would know how to stop the hallucinations from haunting me.

Trying to forget the disturbing images, I left the bathroom, convinced that concentrating on my classes for the rest of the day would be a losing battle.

—◦ ◦—

Becca beat me home that afternoon. By the time I arrived, she was resting, her migraine medicine working in full force. My hopes fell, my mood darkening. Instead of telling Becca what was going on and possibly getting some answers or comfort, I added her failing health to the growing list of all that troubled me.

Gabriel had also returned home earlier in the day, but he did little to comfort me. He kept a careful watch over Becca, not allowing me near her. Frustrated, I retreated up to my room, in no mood to hang out with him and make small talk. The thought of telling him about the wolf crossed my mind, but I pushed it aside. He might think I was crazy, and I wasn't ready to deal with any judgment. Burying my fears in the back of my mind, I set my sights on finishing my homework, hoping to avoid the world that seemed to be falling apart around me.

The next two days flew by. No more visions of the wolf appeared, although I never let down my guard. Becca's headache continued on Wednesday, forcing me to wait another day to talk to her. Gabriel tended to her, making sure she was comfortable. Worry lines creased his forehead when he explained he was expected back at the hospital for the Halloween weekend. I promised to help out in any way I could, whether that meant taking care of the horses and dogs or making Becca something to eat. Either way, I hoped she felt better soon.

Celeste and Lucian were absent from school Thursday, but I didn't think anything of it. I trudged through the crowded hallways, a little surprised to see Maggie and Zoe huddled together, Zoe's smile evidence that Maggie had won her over. Ignoring them, I found Alex as often as I could between classes, grateful for his company.

When I returned home that day, heavy clouds hid the treetops and a fine mist coated my car with moisture. The damp chill in the air made me want to curl up under a blanket with a good book.

Minutes after I entered the house and placed my bag on the kitchen table, Becca blasted in through the front door. She raced across the room, her eyes alert and worried. Wispy strands of blonde hair had fallen out of her ponytail, brushing against her face. Wearing a long coat over her tan suit, she approached the table and dropped her briefcase next to my book bag.

"Becca," I said. "I didn't realize you went to work today. Are you feeling better? I'm afraid to ask if you have another headache."

"I'm fine," she replied in a distracted voice, her attention glued to her phone as she scrolled over the screen. When she stopped and looked up, the anxiety in her blue eyes sent a feeling of dread through my veins. "We have a big problem."

Chilled to the core, I drew in a sharp breath. "You're scaring me. What's going on?"

"Celeste is missing."

"What?" I asked, gasping, not sure I heard her correctly.

"She's gone," Becca stated. "Her mother texted me a little over an hour ago. Celeste wasn't feeling well this morning, so she stayed home from school. Valerie went to work not thinking anything of it, but when she got home, she couldn't find Celeste anywhere."

"Maybe she just went out," I suggested, grasping onto the feeble hope that there was a reasonable explanation.

"No," Becca said, furiously shaking her head. "Her car is in their driveway. Valerie found her phone in her bedroom, and Serenity was pacing in her stall."

"Oh," I whispered, my worst fears confirmed. Shock took hold of me, rendering me speechless for a moment. I didn't know what to say. A feeling of helplessness rolled through me. I wanted to do something, to find Celeste and make sure she was okay, but I didn't know where to begin. The wolf's golden eyes whipped through my thoughts, pitching my heart into a frenzy. So much had happened so quickly, and I hoped none of it was related. But I couldn't keep what I knew to myself any longer. "Becca, I think there's something I should tell you."

Becca shifted her attention to me, her eyes fearful and her gaze steady. After swallowing hard, I proceeded to fill her in about the wolf in the graveyard the night of the dance. As soon as the floodgates opened, I couldn't stop the words tumbling out of my mouth. I went on to describe the dead dove from a few weeks ago, the fire in the corn maze, and the hallucinations I'd seen in the mirror. When I finished, I dropped my gaze, my shoulders falling in shame, afraid of her reprisal.

"I'm so sorry," I said. "I should have told you sooner. I don't know if any of this has to do with Celeste's disappearance, but I had to tell you just in case."

Becca took a deep breath. "Gracyn, look at me."

I looked up, meeting the steady gaze in her blue eyes.

"I can tell this is eating at you. Don't blame yourself. You had no idea what you were doing."

Nodding, I hung my head like a child being scolded. "But I should have told you as soon as it happened. I tried, honestly, I did. It was on the tip of my tongue several times, but...I just couldn't. I don't know why, but I lost my nerve every time. I even came home Tuesday determined to tell you everything, but you had another headache and Gabriel wouldn't let me anywhere near you."

"I suspect you had no control over that." When I gave Becca a curious look, she continued. "Several hundred years ago, one of the witches in our coven stole something very powerful and evil. I had no choice but to banish her. She has been locked in the crypt ever since. She must have managed to get you to break the spell holding her there, something I never imagined would be possible. And if she was powerful enough to do that, I wouldn't be surprised if she also put a gag spell on you to keep you from telling anyone. I'm sure she didn't want to lose the element of surprise."

Sick to my stomach, I sat down, dropping my gaze to the floor. Feeling ashamed and riddled with guilt, I shook my head. "Oh, no. I'm so sorry. I didn't know."

Becca rushed to my side, studying me when our eyes met again. "Of course, you didn't. So stop beating yourself up. If anyone is to blame, it's me for not anticipating something like this."

"What do we do now?"

"We have to find Celeste. She's very special, and we can't afford to lose her, especially after Cassie was taken from us."

"What can I do to help?"

"Right now, I'm not sure. Valerie let Serenity loose, and there's a chance she'll find Celeste. Serenity is our best hope right now. We need to give her some time. If Celeste is close by, Serenity will find her just like Gypsy found you the night of the Harvest Festival."

"Okay." I felt like I could breathe, at least barely. This allowed me to hope Celeste would be located soon. "Will you let me know if you hear anything?"

"Of course. But I'm not going to wait around. I want to ride up to the graveyard. I need to see for myself that the chains have been broken."

"I'm coming with you," I said firmly.

Becca looked at me like she was about to object, but then her expression softened. "Very well. Be ready to ride out in five minutes. I'll meet you in the barn."

I nodded, wanting to help in any way I could. As Becca rushed off to her bedroom, I grabbed my book bag and ran upstairs, my mind spinning. I had so many questions, but there was no time to ask them. All I wanted was to turn back time and put the wolf back in the crypt. Instead, I pushed all but one thought aside. The only thing that mattered right now was finding Celeste. If she was harmed at the hands of the wolf, or the witch Becca said the wolf was, I would never forgive myself.

26

Ten minutes later, Becca and I galloped off into the woods in a race against time. The mist stung my face, but I paid it no attention. Daylight was fading fast, the low clouds taking on a rosy glow from the moon hidden behind them. The horses charged along the trail, slowing to keep their balance around the turns.

Gypsy and I followed Becca and Cadence as they shot through the woods. The saddle and bridle made me feel secure enough, the adrenaline pumping through my veins giving me the courage to push Gypsy into a gallop. When we passed the trail that led to Lucian's estate, I caught a glimpse of the stone mansion shrouded in the dense fog. My heart skipped a beat at the thought of Lucian. Celeste had feared him for months, and I couldn't help wondering if he had something to do with her disappearance. The moment my suspicions cast doubt on him, I scolded myself. *Don't even go there! Lucian is no criminal, and you know that. You should be ashamed of yourself for suspecting him. He has saved your butt countless times.* The words in my head were so true, but this time, I wasn't the one in trouble. Just because he had helped me in the past didn't mean anything as far as Celeste was concerned. She had been worried he would hurt her, and now she was gone.

My apprehension grew when Becca veered off the trail and headed in the direction of the graveyard. I ducked down close to Gypsy's mane to avoid the low-lying branches. Putting Lucian in the back of my mind because I believed with all my heart he had nothing to do with Celeste's disappearance, I focused on staying in the saddle. Gypsy made abrupt turns, dodging the trees and causing me to keep a firm grip on her mane.

A few minutes later, we emerged into a clearing. Fog swirled around the rickety picket fence and tombstones covered with dead ivy. The crypt loomed in the corner of the graveyard, the door hanging open.

Becca pulled Cadence to a stop in front of it and jumped off. Not wasting a second, she marched into the crypt. As much as I didn't want to go inside the musty building again, I stopped Gypsy beside Cadence and dismounted.

I approached the crypt and paused in the doorway. Beads of moisture clung to my face and arms and, in spite of the cold, damp fog, my blood ran hot with fear. "Becca?" I called softly.

"In here," she said, her voice sounding distracted.

I opened the door to see her kneeling on the floor, her fingers running over the chains that had tethered the wolf until my touch unlocked them.

"What is it?" I asked.

"The collar is gone," she mused, reaching the end of the chain.

"I know. It disappeared when I touched it. Do you know what happened to it?"

"No," Becca said, shaking her head. She stood up and faced me. "There's one more thing I need to see." She rushed past me, hurrying out into the cemetery. I followed her, staying close behind in the thick fog.

Becca wandered around the graveyard before leaving through the gate. Then she scanned the area between the fence and the woods until she noticed the hole I had fallen into the day after releasing the wolf. She let out a worried sigh. "I was afraid of this."

"What is it?"

Becca turned to me, the concern in her eyes whipping mixed emotions of guilt and fear through me once again. "She has her horse, which means she'll have her powers back in full force. She'll be much harder to stop now."

"Do you think this has anything to do with Celeste?"

She nodded, her eyes clouding over. "It's very possible."

"But why? What could this witch want with Celeste?"

"I'm not sure, but I have my suspicions, and it's a very long story. I'll have to fill you in after we find Celeste. There's nothing more we can do here. Come on. Let's go."

Becca rushed back to Cadence who dropped to the ground. I watched Becca swing her leg over the saddle, my feet feeling frozen for a moment. I wanted answers. I needed to know why Celeste had been targeted by the witch I had released. I would never forgive myself if Celeste was harmed in any way.

Cadence rose to her feet and charged toward me in a few strides. When she stopped inches away, Becca looked down at me, urgency written all over her face. "Gracyn, what are you waiting for? Get on and let's go."

As if my knees had been unlocked, I ran around to Gypsy who had dropped to the ground. As soon as I hopped on and found the stirrups, she scrambled to her feet while I gathered the reins. Without another word, Becca spurred Cadence into a gallop. Gypsy shot forward to keep up with her and once again, we raced through the woods.

I hung on tightly as Gypsy darted around the trees in the mist. Hours seemed to pass while we headed up and down the hills. A few times, Becca slowed Cadence to a walk and studied the fog, as if searching for clues before taking off again.

Darkness had fallen by the time we emerged onto the Hamiltons' property. The sand arena was still and quiet, the white jumps mere shadows rising up in the cloud cover.

We trotted around the ring and pulled the horses up in front of a white farmhouse. A wraparound porch was lit up by two bulbs on both sides of the front door, the wicker furniture seeming to welcome visitors.

But today wasn't a social call. As soon as Becca dismounted, the front door opened and a woman walked out. I recognized her from the day she and her husband had shown up to discuss their concern over Lucian's return with Becca and Gabriel.

"Becca!" she gushed, tears streaming down her pale cheeks. Her blonde curls hid her shoulders, and her hands were tucked into the pockets of her dark sweater. "Anything?"

"No, Valerie," Becca said softly, embracing Celeste's mother. When Becca let go, she shook her head. "I'm sorry. We scoured the woods, and there's no sign of her. I didn't see or sense a thing. I don't believe she's anywhere nearby."

"Then where could she be? If someone took her far away, Serenity won't be able to find her." More tears filled the woman's brown eyes that reminded me of Celeste's. "We knew this would happen. Tom and I told you we never should have allowed him to move back here."

"We can't jump to conclusions," Becca said. "We don't know Lucian is to blame for this."

Valerie shook her head, her curls swaying over her shoulders. Her eyes turned cold, her expression stony. "I called around this afternoon. It turns out Lucian missed school today, too. If that isn't enough to know he's behind this, I don't know what is."

A chill swept over me, my doubts about Lucian punching a hole in my heart. Taking a deep breath, I shoved my suspicions as far from my mind as I could. I prayed the wolf or the resurrected witch, whoever she was, had something to do with this because it would mean Lucian wasn't the monster everyone seemed to think he was.

"Valerie, you know in our world, anything is possible," Becca said. I waited for Becca to tell Celeste's mother about the witch I had unknowingly released, but she never did.

"You're right," Valerie replied sharply. "Like finding Celeste the same way Cassie was found, with a hole in her heart." Barely finishing her sentence, she broke down, shuddering.

Becca wrapped her arms around Celeste's mother while a lump formed in my throat. I couldn't begin to imagine that Celeste would suffer the same fate as Cassie. Tears sprang to my eyes, and I fought to hold them back. I had to remain strong, for Celeste. Whatever Becca needed me to do to help find her, I would give my all. And crying would only weaken me.

Hoof beats sounded in the distance, growing louder until a bay horse galloped out of the woods. Serenity followed, her pure white coat glistening with moisture and steam rising from her back. They pulled up next to Gypsy and Cadence, and Celeste's father dismounted.

"There's no sign of her," he said, plowing his hands through his dark hair. "We looked everywhere. Serenity tried, but I think she got confused once or twice, which can only mean one thing."

My heart plummeted. The more I learned, the worse this situation seemed to get.

Becca nodded. "Yes, I figured that out, too. This is the work of another witch. One of us would have picked up on something unless her presence was erased."

Serenity tossed her head, her mane swishing against her neck. Then she stood up on her hind legs, pawing the air with her hooves. When she landed, she spun around in a circle.

"At least we know she's still alive," Celeste's father said.

When I tossed a confused look at Becca, she explained. "Serenity will die if Celeste dies. As long as she is still alive, we know Celeste is, too."

Faint relief calmed my fear, but only for a moment.

"Tom," Becca began. "Please take Valerie inside and make her comfortable. There isn't much we can do now. Gracyn and I will return home and summon the others. We'll come back later tonight."

"Okay. But please hurry. We won't rest until our daughter is safe."

"None of us will." Becca placed a hand on his shoulder, squeezing gently, a hopeful smidge of a smile on her face.

"Thank you," he said.

She nodded. "We're in this together. I'm not going to give up on her without a fight. She's very special, and we need to find her."

"We know," he said, his eyes glimmering with moisture. Then he wrapped an arm around his wife's shoulders and led her into the house.

Becca turned her attention to me. "There isn't anything more we can do here right now. Let's get home so I can alert everyone else. Plan to return with me tonight. We're going to need all the help we can get."

As soon as Becca swung her leg over the saddle, Cadence rose to her feet. Then she and Gypsy took off into the dense fog, racing through the woods at full speed as though they understood every second counted until Celeste was found.

— ~ —

"Why didn't you tell Celeste's parents about the witch from the crypt?" I fired my question at Becca the moment we dismounted outside the barn door when we arrived home. Standing before Gypsy, not ready to lead her inside, I watched Becca run up the stirrups on her saddle. Her blonde hair and Cadence's snow white coat stood out in the darkness.

Her back to me, Becca lifted her shoulders with a deep breath. Then she turned and slipped the reins over Cadence's head. "Valerie and Tom have enough to worry about right now. I don't need to add this to their list."

"But they think Lucian did something to Celeste. It's not right to let them believe something you know isn't true. It's not fair to them, to Lucian, and even to Celeste."

"I don't know for a fact that Lucian isn't involved. I told Valerie not to jump to conclusions, and I'm telling you the same thing. There is a lot we still don't know. You released a wolf from the crypt. If she hasn't shifted back to her human form, then it's unlikely she has anything to do with this."

"It's awfully coincidental though, don't you think? Lucian has been back for two months and he hasn't gone near Celeste. I let this wolf witch out of the chains, and a few weeks later, Celeste goes missing."

"Believe me," Becca said. "I've already thought of that."

"You're going to tell everyone else about the wolf tonight, right?"

Becca dropped her gaze. When she looked up, meeting my eyes, she sighed. "That isn't a good idea. This is my problem, and I will handle it."

I shook my head, shocked Becca would hide something like this. "But—"

"Gracyn," she said, interrupting me. "I'm asking you to trust me on this. I know what I'm dealing with. She's evil, and she'll stop at nothing to get what she wants, even if it means eliminating anyone in her way. So please, leave this to me."

"Can you at least explain who she is and what exactly happened before she was locked in the crypt?"

"I would, to you only, but there is no time. I need to put Cadence away and call the others."

As frustrated as I was knowing Becca had more secrets, I didn't push for answers. Instead, I stepped toward her. "I'll take care of Cadence. You go make the calls and I'll meet you inside."

Becca offered an appreciative smile, gently touching my arm. "Thank you." Then she handed me the reins before taking off across the driveway. When I heard the door shut with a bang, I turned and led the horses into the barn.

— —

A few hours later, Becca and I drove back to the Hamiltons' farm. When we pulled into the driveway, half a dozen cars were parked along the side.

"Looks like we're the last ones to arrive," Becca said, turning off the engine. "Let's go inside."

I nodded, my eyes adjusting to the dim light. After hopping out of the SUV, I followed her up the driveway, surprised when I recognized Lucian's Range Rover in the line-up of cars. I hadn't expected him to show up, but he was part of the coven. At least if Becca had called him, she must not truly believe he was involved.

I was about to climb the porch steps when someone in the shadows caught my eye. A moment later, Lucian stepped up to the railing, coming into the soft glow of light from the bulbs burning outside the door.

Our eyes met for a moment before I whipped my attention back to the house. I rushed up the steps to the open door, stopping when I heard footsteps behind me. I turned as Lucian approached, his dark coat blending into the night. His gaze was directed beyond me, and I spun around to see a handful of people gathered in the entry hall. Candles burned from sconces nailed into the walls, flickering against the wood panels.

Without saying a word to Lucian, I walked into the house. Several sets of eyes shifted to me and the voices tapered off, the somber mood reminding me of a funeral.

"Becca," Celeste's father said, working his way down the hall to greet her in the center of the small crowd. "Good. You're the last one to arrive. We need to get started."

As she nodded, his gaze drifted past her. Anger flashed through his eyes, his worried expression turning icy. With a stony scowl, he rushed past me. I turned in time to see him charge at Lucian.

"What do you think you're doing here?" Celeste's father demanded, blocking Lucian from stepping into the house.

My heart shattered into pieces when Lucian bowed his head, shame in his eyes.

"First, you kill your own sister, and now, you show up here when my daughter is missing? Where is she, Lucian? What have you done with her?"

"I don't know," Lucian replied quietly, his voice restrained. "I didn't touch Celeste."

"Like hell you didn't," the older man hissed. "You're nothing but a disgrace to this entire coven. Murder, kidnapping. What do you want? Why did you even come back? No one wants you here. So just go back to Paris or Italy or wherever you spent the last two years and crawl back under your rock."

Lucian's green eyes locked with the older man's gaze, neither one of them backing down. "This is my home, and I will stay if I so choose."

"Fine. Obviously, I can't make you leave town. But you are not welcome in my house."

Lucian paused, his eyes wandering over the crowd, landing on me for a moment before returning to Celeste's father. "With all due respect, I took a big chance coming here tonight. Clearly, I knew I would not be well-received. I did it because I want to help you find your daughter. Regardless of what you think about me, I wish her no harm. If anything, Cassie's death has made me realize we all have to protect Celeste."

The older man's stone-cold scowl softened for a moment before hatred returned to his eyes. "We don't want your help. I already told you, you're not welcome here."

When Lucian didn't move, Celeste's father huffed, seeming ready to blow. Becca rushed in between them, placing a hand on his chest, her back to Lucian. "That's enough, Tom. We aren't going to accomplish anything fighting amongst ourselves." Her gaze was steady, her expression calming him.

Then she turned around. "Lucian, we could use your father's help. Have you been in touch with him?"

"Yes," he replied. "I spoke to him as soon as I heard about Celeste. He's making arrangements to come home."

"Good. Please ask him to contact me as soon as he gets to town."

Lucian nodded.

"Thank you," Becca said before stepping around Tom to head back down the hall.

Tom returned his attention to Lucian. "When your father arrives, tell him to come see me as well. If the law can't touch you, perhaps he will punish you."

"I didn't—"

"Don't even start. We know you weren't in school today. Celeste disappeared from her room sometime between eight this morning and four this afternoon. If you weren't at school, where were you?"

Lucian cast a hurt look at me before his bitterness returned. "Would it even matter if I told you?" he shot out. "You've made up your mind about me and you've asked me to leave. I'm out of here." With a huff, he stormed out of the doorway, disappearing around the corner. Then the door slammed shut, making me jump.

"Well," Celeste's father said as all eyes settled on him. "We don't need the likes of him here. When we find out what he did with Celeste, he'll pay once and for all."

At that point, I'd heard enough. As he ushered everyone down the hall, I remained in the foyer. I felt torn, caught in the middle. Celeste was my friend, but so was Lucian. In spite of the rumors and suspicions, I believed every word he said. It must have taken a lot of courage for him to show up amongst people he knew hated him, just to try to help them find the one girl who feared him the most. That deserved respect, not the hatred Celeste's father had just shown him.

My heart was trapped in a tug of war between showing my support for Celeste's family during this dark time and running after Lucian to tell him I believed in him. After a few seconds of deliberation, I rushed out the front door, hoping I could catch Lucian before he drove away.

27

*L*ucian had almost reached his Range Rover by the time I caught up with him. He clicked his key, and the lights flashed in the darkness.

"Lucian, wait!" I called, running down the gravel driveway. His back to me, he didn't turn around, but I was sure he heard me in the quiet night.

I approached him as he was about to open the door.

"Lucian, please don't go yet," I said, out of breath. Sliding to a halt behind him, I waited, hoping he would listen to me before taking off.

He whipped around to face me, his scowl dark and his eyes hardened. "What do you want?" he grumbled.

"Just—" I paused, searching for the right words. My pulse quickened, his angry stare flustering me. "Just to tell you I don't think Celeste's father had any right to treat you like that. You came here to help. He shouldn't have pushed you out."

Lucian stepped closer to me, his chest inches away from mine. His green eyes held my gaze, causing my breath to hitch. "Funny. You were awfully quiet in there. You didn't say a word to dispute him."

"I...I'm sorry."

"Don't be. I'm used to it. Although one day, it would be nice for someone to tell the world they believe in me."

Nodding, I felt my throat swell, choking me. Tears threatened to fill my eyes, but I refused to let them weaken me. "I do believe in you," I stated, my voice soft. "After everything you've shared with me, I know you would never hurt your sister."

"I wish you would tell them." He tossed a swift nod in the direction of the house. Before I could say a word, Lucian continued. "You know what else you can tell them? That I was home all day nursing my mother's sick horse. She was down in the morning, and I fought for hours to get her to her feet, but her colic only got worse. I tried to call my mother, but she wasn't answering her phone. I had to contact the authorities in Hawaii to check on her, and it turns out she overdosed again. She's in ICU, and this time they aren't sure if she's going to make it. I managed to get her mare to stand up, but she was struggling when I left to come over here only to be branded a monster and chased away. For all I know, they'll both be gone when I get home. I don't know why I wasted my time coming here when I have my own life and death situation at home."

"I'm so sorry. I had no idea what you've been going through today."

"Of course, you didn't. Well, go on in and tell everyone what a lousy day poor Lucian had and maybe they'll get off my back."

"I will, I promise."

He huffed, bitterness seeming to consume him. "I wasn't serious, but you can go ahead and try. By all means, see if you can get them to sympathize with me."

"Lucian," I started, my voice threatening to crack.

He stepped closer and stared down at me, his expression cold and distrusting. "You're a wonderful girl, Gracyn. Why you've been kind to me, I'll never know. But maybe you should stay away from me. You need them, and standing by my side will do you more harm than good."

"Lucian, no, I don't believe that. How can you say that?"

"When you've been labeled a monster over and over again, sooner or later, you start to believe it." Lucian flashed a longing look at me, the betrayal in his eyes breaking my heart. "Well, I need to go. I don't belong here. But you should get back inside. Celeste is your friend, and I know you're worried about her." Without saying goodbye, he turned around and slid into his Range Rover.

I backed up, giving him enough room to turn the SUV around. When the red tail lights disappeared in the darkness, I remained where I stood, staring into space, wondering if that was the last I would see of him. The idea of never having his company again, whether on a trail ride or at a pumpkin farm designed for families, filled me with a sense of loss.

Slowly, I turned and walked back to the front porch, but instead of heading inside, I sat down on the steps. Propping my knees up to my chest, I dropped my forehead on them. Turbulent emotions whirled through me. Becca was inside, letting everyone believe Lucian could be involved with Celeste's disappearance while a resurrected evil witch was at large. I considered running to Lucian's defense and explaining what he had just told me about his mother, but I suspected no one would believe me.

For what felt like an eternity, I sat on the steps. When footsteps sounded in front of me, I looked up, curious.

Derek hovered above me, his blond hair light against his black leather jacket. Without a word, he extended his hand down to me.

Grateful for a friend, I took it and let him pull me to my feet.

"Please tell me Lucian isn't to blame for your troubles," Derek said.

"No," I said, giving myself a mental kick for my little white lie. I was also worried about Celeste, so there was a smidge of honesty in my answer.

"Then why are you out here in the cold when everyone else is inside?"

"It's hard to explain."

"Okay, I'll let you off this time. But only because we have bigger matters to tend to. So, it seems like we have more in common than you probably thought possible." He flashed a sly grin, lightening the mood.

"Yeah. I guess this is a small world."

Derek nodded. "How's it been going for you? At least ever since you found out?"

I sighed. "Crazy. Definitely hard to believe. I miss my old life. It was boring and normal."

"And you miss that?"

"Yes. Because I certainly never ended up out on a school night with a coven of witches trying to find a missing friend."

Derek's smile collapsed. "You've got a point. This is crazy."

"Why are you here?"

Derek shot me a stern look, confused. "Why wouldn't I be?"

"I thought you didn't like Celeste."

He shrugged, dropping his gaze to the ground. "She's not that bad. I put up a good front at school."

"Are you trying to tell me you like her?"

"Maybe," he muttered before pausing. "Okay, I'll admit she has a good heart."

"And those other girls?"

His eyes lit up. "Are a lot of fun. I'm going to play until I have no choice but to settle down."

"You're impossible."

"I know." His smile collapsed while his gaze on me remained steady. "By the way, I think it's pretty cool you're one of us. Welcome to the club."

"Thanks. Now I have one more person I can ask about witchcraft."

"It can be pretty fun," he said, a twinkle in his eyes before he grew serious once again. "But not now. We should probably get inside and see if there's anything we can do to help."

I nodded, my thoughts returning to Celeste. "You're right."

Derek gestured to the door. "After you."

I walked ahead of him and slipped inside. We crept down the hall to the family room where the group formed a circle in front of the fireplace, their hands locked together and their eyes closed. Becca stood in the middle, clutching a sweater to her chest.

After a few minutes, everyone opened their eyes. "Anything?" one of them asked.

"No," Becca said, shaking her head. "I feel blocked. I'm not picking up a single sign of Celeste. It's like she disappeared into a black hole."

Becca bowed her head, as though ashamed she had failed. "There is only one explanation for this."

The others nodded, waiting for her to continue. "Another witch must be involved. It's the only possibility. Valerie and Tom, you need to keep a close watch over Serenity. She's the only way we'll know if Celeste is harmed."

Celeste's father nodded. "Of course."

"I feel like we're reliving the nightmare of losing Cassie," Valerie said in a low voice, causing a hush to fall over the room. She stepped out of the shadows in the corner, her eyes bloodshot and tears streaking her face. "Cassie was just like Celeste. Celeste has been terrified ever since Lucian returned to town. We should have paid more attention to her. We should have listened."

"There was no way any of us could have anticipated this," Becca stated.

"I can't accept that. We should have protected her. She knew something bad would happen. She told us over and over again, but none of us took her seriously. Now it could be too late."

"Valerie," Tom said, approaching her. "Becca's right. We never could have predicted this. I know you're going to blame yourself, and you can't do that. It's not your fault. Whatever happened to her, we're going to find her and bring her home."

"I wish I could believe that," she said, her voice trembling. "But all I keep seeing is Cassie lying in the casket." She paused, drawing in a deep breath. "I'm so scared Celeste will end up like her."

Becca rushed to Valerie's side, taking her hand. "We're going to do everything we can to find her. She's not dead. We know that. So don't lose hope. Tomorrow morning, you need to file a missing person report with the authorities."

"What will they be able to do?" Valerie asked, her voice bitter. "It's not like they were any good at solving Cassie's murder."

"It doesn't matter," Becca said firmly. "It won't hurt to have them looking for her. And how will you explain her absence to the school? You need to go on record that she's gone. We have to follow the law like everyone else."

Valerie nodded, her defiance seeming to fade away.

"Okay," Becca said. "I don't know what more we can do here tonight. We all need to remain vigilant. And keep up hope."

Whispers erupted in the room. Celeste's father wrapped an arm around Valerie while others approached her, offering their help and showing confidence that Celeste would make it home safely. Leaving Derek behind, I squeezed through them until I reached Becca's side.

"Becca," I said quietly. "I need to talk to you."

She nodded, holding up a finger. Then she placed a hand on Valerie's shoulder. "I'm heading home now. I'll have my phone on all night. Call me if you hear from her."

"We will," Celeste's father said. "Thank you for all your help tonight."

"Nonsense," Becca replied. "I don't feel like I did much."

"You're here for us, and that's all that matters," he told her, an appreciative smile curling his mouth for a quick moment.

Becca nodded, then embraced him, her eyes closing, her expression concerned. After backing away from him, she joined me and we made our way to the front door.

Without a word, we slipped outside and hurried to her SUV in the driveway. The cold air hit me, but it was nothing compared to the bone-chilling fear that swept over me when I thought about Celeste. I paused before getting in the SUV, rubbing my arms and hoping wherever Celeste might be, she was warm and comfortable.

After Becca and I jumped in the SUV, Becca turned on the engine and the headlights. Then she backed the truck up before guiding it down the driveway.

"What did you need to talk to me about?" she asked as soon as she pulled out onto the road, the headlight beams cutting through the darkness.

"I talked to Lucian before he left. He explained where he was today." I glanced at Becca, noticing the interest in her eyes before I continued. "He had a problem with his mother's horse. Apparently, his mother isn't well. He said he tried to contact her and he ended up having to ask the authorities to check on her. He told me she overdosed and she's in the hospital. I don't care what anyone says. I believe him."

"Hmm," Becca mused, her lips pursed in thought. "I'm sorry to hear that. His mother has a history of substance abuse. We tried to get her to sober up years ago, but the more she used, the more she couldn't get away from it."

"I felt really bad for him tonight. First he dealt with that, and then he came over here to try to help, only to be run off. It breaks my heart to see the way everyone treats him."

"They're afraid. Until we find Cassie's killer and justice is served, he is still a possible suspect."

"Do you honestly believe that after all he has done for me?" When Becca raised her eyebrows, I went on to tell her I had woken up in Cassie's bedroom the morning after passing out in the graveyard.

"Maybe you should have mentioned that earlier," she said, as though she was about to scold me when I finished. But then her voice softened. "Look, I know it's hard to be objective, but the fact is, we can't rule him out."

"Becca, that's not fair."

Becca swallowed hard, her eyes focused on the road. "This isn't about what is or isn't fair. We don't know what happened to Cassie, and now Celeste is gone. It's possible whoever killed Cassie has Celeste."

"I realize that. But blaming Lucian without concrete evidence is wrong. No one can be sure he's guilty."

"I'm not disagreeing with you," Becca said. "But I have to admit, I'm a little surprised at how defensive you are of him right now. What's going on?"

My heart flip-flopped at the memory of the day at the pumpkin farm. He had been a perfect gentleman, not only to me, but also to the little girl who had gotten lost in the maze. I refused to believe he was a cold-blooded killer. Not the person I had seen being kind and gentle to a little girl he didn't even know.

"Nothing," I said, not ready to explain how much time I had spent with Lucian and risk getting lectured.

"Okay, I was just checking."

"You haven't forgotten how he helped me the night Sam's stepfather dragged me into the woods, have you?" I asked, wanting her to remember the one good deed of his she had witnessed.

"No, of course not. And I can see why it would be hard for you to remain impartial after that."

"Yeah. I guess that's it," I said quietly, leaning back against the seat. I felt tired, emotionally drained from the day. It was getting late, although I suspected sleep would not come easy tonight.

"Tired?" Becca asked, as if reading my mind.

"Yes," I replied with a stifled yawn. "But I have a feeling it's going to be a long night. I'm really worried about Celeste."

"I know," Becca said, casting a glance my way. "Me, too."

"Do you think we'll find her before it's too late?" I asked, hating myself for imagining the worst possible outcome.

"I do," Becca replied confidently. "Celeste is stronger than she looks. I think she'll get through this."

"I hope you're right," I said, staring out the window at the trees passing in the headlight beams. "But until then, I don't know what to do."

"You're going to do exactly what you normally would. Go to school tomorrow and then follow through with any plans you have for the weekend."

"The haunted house," I murmured.

"Are you going with Alex?"

I nodded, my heart sinking at the idea of pretending to have fun while knowing Celeste was in trouble.

"Good. He can help take your mind off this. I will worry enough about Celeste for both of us."

"No," I said, shaking my head. "I don't want you to do that. It doesn't matter what you say, I'm not going to be able to act like everything is normal until we find her. I've never known anyone to be in trouble like this, and I've certainly never lost a friend. Nothing will be the same until I know she's okay."

Becca looked at me, her eyes glistening with moisture. "I think that goes for all of us. Gracyn, you have a very good heart. You've made me proud."

I felt a blush race across my face, and I couldn't stop a tear from rolling down my cheek. "Thanks." Then I fell silent, afraid more tears would follow if I tried to speak again.

For the rest of the way home, I remained quiet, my thoughts and prayers going out to Celeste. If I had ever wished for a miracle, to have Celeste safely returned to her family was it. Because until then, nothing else mattered.

28

The gray sky cast a dark shadow over Sedgewick the next day. By noon, the mood at school had fallen to a new low. Rumors of Celeste's disappearance had made their way through the masses, causing the excitement for Halloween to taper off. The hallways were quiet for a Friday, let alone the Friday before Halloween.

Celeste might not have been popular, but she wasn't hated, either. No one wanted anything bad happen to her. Above all else, it seemed that the memory of Cassie's murder had returned to the forefront. Other students whispered, speculating that the killer was still in town and Celeste was the next target. Lucian's absence for another day prompted many to blame him for Celeste's disappearance, much to my dismay.

Exhausted, I fought to stay alert. In Calculus, Alex reached over to tap my shoulder when my eyelids began to fall. Awakened, I opened my eyes and focused on the formulas scrawled across the blackboard, the teacher's low voice nearly putting me to sleep again. After the bell rang, Alex turned to me while the other students packed up and trickled out the door.

"You look like you're having a tough time today," he said.

"I am," I replied, shutting my notebook. "I'm so worried about Celeste. I can't believe no one has heard from her in over twenty-four hours. That doesn't seem like her."

"I know. I feel like history is repeating itself, although Cassie never went missing before her body was found. I just hope they find Celeste soon and that she's okay."

"You and me both." I stuffed my notebook into my bag, zipped it, and stood up, sliding the strap over my shoulder. "Things won't be the same until she's back."

"I know. It's pretty scary, that's for sure. I never thought we'd have to relive this nightmare again. Celeste doesn't deserve that. It seems like the nicest girls are always the ones that get hurt."

Alex and I walked up the aisle together. At the front, I turned the corner and he took my hand. Grateful to have him by my side, I let him lead me out into the hallway where we merged with the crowd. "I hope you're wrong."

"Me, too. But listen, are you still up for the haunted house tomorrow night? If you're not, I completely understand."

I wanted to take him up on his offer to skip the weekend festivities, but Becca had told me to carry on as usual. If I didn't go with him, I'd end up doing nothing but worrying about Celeste while I paced the floors all night. The haunted house appealed to me more than being cooped up at home. "That's very sweet of you, but I don't think Celeste would want us to put our lives on hold right now. Besides, I know you've been looking forward to it all week. I'm sure the people putting it on are expecting a crowd. We have to go. I like knowing the proceeds are going to an animal shelter."

"Yes, it is for a good cause," Alex pointed out. "And it will be fun. It'll give us something else to think about, at least for a while."

"I'm not so sure about that, but I'm willing to give it a try."

As Alex rambled on about the haunted house, I noticed Maggie and Zoe standing next to the lockers out of the corner of my eye. Smiling, they laughed as though nothing awful was going on. Their carefree expressions made it clear Celeste's disappearance mattered little to them.

Looking at Alex to force them out of my line of sight, I threw on a fake smile. "What time should I be ready to go tomorrow?"

"About eight-thirty. The haunted house opens at six for the younger kids, but they don't add the good stuff until around nine." When I raised my eyebrows, Alex explained, "That's when it gets really scary."

"Great. I'm not sure how much scary stuff I can handle right now."

"You'll be fine. I think you'll have a good time. Celeste wouldn't want you to miss this on her account. I may not have known her very well, but I know she never wanted to be the center of attention. I have a feeling that wouldn't change now just because she's gone."

We reached my locker and stopped. Leaning against it, I sighed. "You're right. And who knows, maybe she'll be back by then. There's an entire day between now and tomorrow night."

"Good point. I'll keep my fingers crossed. Well, I have to run to my locker. See you later?"

"Of course," I said.

Alex kissed me before heading off into the crowd, leaving me alone to get ready for my next class.

— ~

My wish that Celeste would be found safe before the haunted house was never granted. No news was reported Friday night or Saturday. Feeling restless, I tacked up Gypsy around noon on Saturday, thankful the sun had broken through the clouds. We headed out along the trail until we reached the opening to Lucian's estate. Beyond the break in the trees framed by golden leaves still clinging to the branches, Shade and his dark bay companion grazed in the pasture. The gray mare who usually joined them was missing.

I glanced at the barn in the distance, wondering if she was recovering in a stall. The notion that she hadn't survived the night struck me, sending my spirits into a nosedive. First Celeste, then Lucian's mother. Each tragedy seemed senseless, and I hoped both of them would emerge from these dark times stronger than ever.

I searched the grounds for Lucian, but saw no sign of him. Emptiness overwhelmed me, the memory of his abrupt departure at Celeste's house filling me with longing. I already missed the stolen moments we had shared, and I wondered if things between us were over.

They never really started, so how can it be over? a smug voice asked before sliding into a sad tone. *And you shouldn't even be thinking about Lucian until Celeste is found. She's been missing for two days. The longer she's gone, the greater chance there is that something happened to her.*

Knowing my inner self was right, I nudged Gypsy back into a walk. We set off at a leisurely pace along the trail, giving me time to savor the afternoon.

The anticipation that hell was about to break loose weighed on me all day. In spite of it, I tried to keep my chin up. After returning home and untacking Gypsy, I buried myself in my homework until the sun set.

Alex picked me up at eight-thirty, and we drove into town. When he turned onto a side street, cars were already parked in a long line next to the curb in front of an old Victorian house. Two jack-o'-lanterns propped up on stakes lit both sides of the walkway entrance. Pillars lined the front porch, partially hidden by fog swirling over the ground. Purple lights were twisted around the porch railing, spider webs formed crisscross patterns in every corner, and skeletons hung from the overhanging roof.

A crowd of kids wearing costumes and others dressed in jeans gathered outside on the lawn. Screams came from inside and outside the house, unsettling me even though I knew everything here was an act.

Derek approached us a few minutes after we got in the line extending from the front door. "Hey, man," Derek said, his voice low and unenthused. He glanced at me, his eyes meeting mine with a knowing look. After flashing me a faint smile, he frowned again.

"Derek," Alex said, appearing confused. "Why do you look like your dog just died? I thought you were looking forward to this."

"I was, until Maggie stood me up."

"Ouch," Alex replied, cringing. "Sorry to hear that. Did you try calling her?"

"No, I didn't have to. She called me a few hours ago to break our date. She said she wasn't feeling well."

"Oh," Alex let out with a deep breath. "So she really didn't stand you up, she just canceled for tonight. That's women for you. Maybe she'll be feeling better next weekend."

"Hey," I said, jabbing my elbow into Alex's ribs. "What's that supposed to mean?"

Alex smiled, giving my hand a gentle squeeze. "Don't worry. That doesn't apply to you. You're the best."

"Thank you," I said. "So are you."

"Oh, no," Derek groaned. "Do you two have to be so happy? I practically got dumped. I'm not sure I can handle you lovebirds tonight."

"Cheer up, Derek," Alex teased. "In a few days, either Maggie will be back or you'll find some other poor girl to lick your wounds."

Derek's face lit up. "Hmm, now that could be interesting."

I laughed, shaking my head. "Well, I've got to hand it to you two. You sure know how to take my mind off where we're about to go." When Alex and Derek looked at me as though they had no idea what I meant, I nodded toward the house. We had inched up to the front porch as kids left the house, their pale faces and wide eyes making me think twice about entering. *You can't chicken out now,* I told myself. *You're here, and you're going in. Besides, nothing in that house could be scarier than what you've dealt with lately.*

Alex and Derek continued their banter while we waited patiently. But as each dazed kid emerged from the house, my courage began to fade. Real or not, I wasn't sure I wanted to find out what lurked inside, even if it took my mind off Celeste.

We had reached the porch steps when Mr. Wainwright walked out of the house, his hands stuffed in the pockets of his fleece-lined denim jacket. His hair was disheveled, his jaw covered in scruff longer than usual. He stopped in front of us, smiling weakly. "Alex, Gracyn, and Derek," he said, his words clear.

I was mildly surprised to see he wasn't drinking, at least not yet.

"Hi, Mr. Wainwright," Alex said. "What's it like in there?"

Mr. Wainwright shook his head. "Pretty intense. Might give me nightmares."

"Great," I said with a groan.

"What's the matter?" he asked, directing his question at me. "Don't have a strong stomach?"

"Something like that," I admitted.

"If that's the case, you might want to think twice before you enter," he said seriously before grinning. "I'm only kidding. You'll be fine, Gracyn. Have fun and just remember, it's all for a good cause."

I nodded, knowing he was right.

"You three have a good night. I'm headed back to town. Got a bourbon and Coke with my name on it at the Brew. Anything to keep those nightmares at bay tonight." After glancing my way one last time, he headed down the sidewalk to the street.

At the door, Alex paid for our tickets, refusing to let me cover mine when I offered. As soon as we entered the house with a group of about ten others, the door slammed shut with a bang behind us, making me flinch. Cackling came from an overhead speaker in the dark foyer. Then a trap door in the ceiling opened, and a severed head dropped, hanging suspended in mid-air.

"You have dared to enter a house haunted by an evil spirit. Prepare for the fright of your life. And good luck. Not many who enter will leave alive," it said from a recording before laughing.

After the message ended, the head was reeled back up into the ceiling compartment. A woman wearing a white gown splattered with blood, an open gash around her neck, stepped into the entry hall. "This way," she said.

For a moment, Derek and Alex challenged each other to go first. Finally, Derek stepped up to the plate, letting me and Alex trail behind. I was more than happy to be last. Maybe then I could keep my distance from the displays. All I wanted was to get through this. I had never found blood and gore entertaining, and I had a feeling tonight wouldn't change my sentiments.

The floorboards creaked as we followed the group down the hall and into the family room. The leader swept her arm out at the scene before us. A fire roared in the brick fireplace while a man and a woman rocked peacefully in their chairs. "This house was built by Benjamin and Ruth Sutton. When they first moved in, it was a dream come true. They couldn't wait to have children and raise them right here." She paused before dropping her voice. "But what they didn't know was that the land under this home had once been an ancient burial ground. They accidentally summoned the souls of those buried here, not just bringing them back to this world, but also angering them, setting themselves up for a lifetime of torture and pain."

The woman gestured for us to move into the kitchen. "The first sign that something was wrong came when Ruth fixed dinner for her husband."

Another woman sat at the table lit only by a flickering candle. Before I had a chance to study the room, the lights flashed, illuminating a bloody severed arm on the table next to a plate of meat. Sickened even though I knew none of it was real, I shut my eyes for a moment.

We continued through the house, exploring room after room filled with blood and gore. My stomach turned, making me queasy. I couldn't enjoy the horror even if it was Halloween. I started to worry about Celeste, hoping these grisly sights wouldn't become her reality.

Upstairs, we were led into another room of torture and pain. Two people, their faces ghastly white, had been chained to the walls. Stakes impaled the man's chest, and he groaned. A noose circled the woman's neck, but her eyes were open as if she begged for mercy.

I gasped, unable to take any more. "Alex," I whispered.

"You probably shouldn't talk in here. Could get us killed, or worse," he teased.

"I'm serious."

His grin fading, he wrapped an arm around my shoulder, pulling me close. "Okay, sorry. What is it?"

"This really isn't my thing. I can't get into it, especially with Celeste missing. Can I wait for you outside?"

"You sure? It's probably almost over."

"Yes. I don't want to see one more room of torture. It's too much for me." Without waiting for his response, I shifted my attention to the guide. "Do you mind if I excuse myself?"

She frowned with a deep sigh. "I'm not supposed to let anyone leave the group, but I'll make an exception this one time. Please go straight to the front door and slip out. If anyone says anything, tell them Tracy said it was okay."

"Thank you," I replied with relief before flashing a weak smile at Alex.

Stepping away from him, I slipped out into the dark hall, the only light coming from a purple bulb plugged into the outlet. Disoriented, I wasn't sure which direction would lead me to the stairs. Turning left, I cringed as the floorboards groaned beneath my feet. Running my hand along the wall, I crept down the corridor until it ended where a mirror hung in the corner. I paused, noting from my pale complexion in the glass that I looked as sick as I felt.

With a sigh, I spun around, ready to retrace my steps when the door to my right opened. "I've been waiting for you," a honey-smooth voice said. "Come in, my dear." Fog filled the room, hiding the woman who had spoken.

"Please save it for the next person. I'm just looking for the stairs."

When I started to walk away, a hand reached out and grabbed my wrist. "But I have a present for you. Don't you want to find out what it is?"

My heart took off at an alarming rate, and I ripped my arm out of her hand. Peering through the doorway, I still couldn't see anyone through the fog. My nerves frazzled, I gulped back my fear. "I think I'll pass," I said, my tone firm. Forcing someone to experience the haunted house seemed to be taking things a bit too far.

I took one step before hearing a familiar voice. "Help me," it called out softly.

"Celeste?" Shocked, I rushed into the room, waving my arms to clear the air.

The door slammed shut, trapping me. My eyes started to adjust to the hazy glow as a figure emerged from the shadows. Her fiery red hair was unmistakable. "Maggie?" I whispered, my heart hammering in my chest.

"Yes. Recognize me?" she asked, her eyes turning yellow while her face shifted to that of the white wolf.

"So, it was you," I stated, holding on to every ounce of composure I had left and refusing to let her see my fear.

She laughed, her human form returning. Wearing all black from her leather jacket and skin-tight pants to her boots, she appeared dressed to play the devil.

"Derek said you weren't feeling well," I said calmly. "What are you doing here?"

"Waiting for you, of course. A friend of yours would like to say hello." Maggie waved her hand to the side, clearing the air. Behind her, Celeste sat in a rocking chair, her expression dazed as though she had been drugged.

"Celeste!" I ran to her, immediately picking up her wrist. She felt cool and clammy, but the faint beat of her heart pulsed through her veins.

I dropped Celeste's hand and turned to Maggie, glaring at her. "What have you done? I swear, if you hurt her in any way, I'll turn you in so fast you won't know what hit you."

"Calm down. She's fine. A little sleepy maybe, but that's all."

"What do you want with her?"

"Absolutely nothing. It's Becca I want, but Becca isn't as easy to get to." Maggie stepped toward me, her calculating eyes narrowed. "Tell Becca to meet me at the crypt at midnight. And tell her to bring me what I want."

"What is that?"

Maggie shook her head. "No need to say what it is. Becca will know. And tell her to come alone, or your precious Celeste won't live to turn another feather into a dove."

"I'm sure she'll give you anything if you let Celeste go. Please, let me take her home. She doesn't look well."

"I told you she's fine. She's staying with me until this is over. Midnight at the crypt. Make sure Becca knows I'll be waiting." A sly smile crossed over Maggie's red lips. "It feels good to be in charge again. It's been way too long. I've waited a lifetime to come back."

"You won't get away with this," I said.

Maggie huffed with a wicked smile. "You're young, and you know nothing. Leave the real witchcraft to those of us who know how to use our power." Maggie skirted around me until she reached Celeste's side. Then she picked up Celeste's hand. "Well, this has been fun, but it's time for us to go. Enjoy the rest of the haunted house. It looks like a good time. I might have enjoyed it if I didn't have more pressing matters to tend to."

I didn't have a chance to respond. At once, Maggie and Celeste disappeared. Just like that, they were gone, leaving me alone.

29

Standing as though frozen, my heart thundering in my chest, I took a few deep breaths. I had never trusted Maggie, and I wasn't surprised to learn she was involved in Celeste's disappearance. But what she wanted from Becca kept me guessing.

The fog cleared quickly after their departure, revealing a twin bed against the back wall, a dresser and mirror, and a rocking chair. As I expected, there was no sign of Maggie and Celeste in the stillness.

A muffled scream echoed through the house, breaking me out of my trance. Reality setting in, I rushed out into the hallway. I ran down the stairs and flew past the people in the entry hall, not even flinching when the head dropped from the ceiling. The haunted house seemed silly and fake now compared to Maggie's threat to kill Celeste if Becca didn't comply.

Once outside, I ignored the chill in the air as I squeezed through the crowd to make my way down the sidewalk, relieved when I passed the end of the line. I scanned the yard, wondering if Maggie and Celeste were near. *Of course not,* a voice declared in my head, rising above my fears. *They're probably halfway to the graveyard by now. What are you waiting for? Call Becca!*

My nerves on edge, I pulled my cell phone out of my pocket and dialed Becca. The other line rang four times before dumping into her voice mail. As soon as her greeting ended, I left a message. "Becca, it's Gracyn. Call me as soon as you get this. It's urgent. It's about Celeste."

Frantic, I hung up and then sent her a text. Hopefully, she would get one of my messages within the next few minutes.

A few seconds later, Alex and Derek walked out of the house, a dazed look in their eyes. They caught sight of me and headed over as I composed myself, ready to pretend nothing was out of the ordinary. Celeste's life was on the line, but I couldn't breathe a word about Maggie to anyone other than Becca.

"How was it?" I asked, my fingers wrapped around my phone. *Any second now, Becca. Any second,* I thought, praying she would call me back right away.

Derek shrugged. "I've seen scarier ones."

"Yeah, right," Alex teased. "You should have seen the look on your face when that girl flew off the wall."

"She came right at me," Derek shot out. "I thought she was going to hit me. It might be Halloween, but I'm not about to get blood, even fake blood, all over me. It's not like you took it in stride, either. You turned as white as a ghost."

"Then I guess we're even," Alex said.

"Sounds like it," I added. "But you both beat me because at least you went through the whole thing."

"You've got a point," Derek said. "So, what's next? I'm hungry. Anyone in the mood for pizza?"

"You're kidding, right?" Alex asked with a huff. "After all that?"

"I didn't eat before I left tonight," Derek explained. "I was too disappointed when Maggie ditched me."

The mention of Maggie made my skin crawl. I wanted to burst Derek's bubble with the news that Maggie was pure evil, but I had a feeling he wouldn't believe me.

"Okay," Alex agreed with a sigh. "I guess we could join you. I'd never forgive myself if I made you eat alone on Halloween after getting stood up. How about it, Gracyn? Are you in?"

Without considering his offer, I shook my head. "I'm going to pass. The haunted house, well, the parts I saw, made me pretty sick to my stomach. Can you drop me off at home first?"

Alex took a deep breath, disappointment sweeping over his expression. He nodded with a weak smile before turning to Derek. "Guess both of our girls are bailing tonight," he said. "Meet you in town in twenty minutes?"

"Sounds good," Derek said with a grin. Then he glanced my way. "Sorry the haunted house didn't agree with you. I guess it's not for everyone."

"That's okay," I replied. "I gave it a shot, right?"

"Absolutely. And that's all that counts." Derek gave me a quick wink, but he wasn't fast enough to hide it from Alex.

Alex draped an arm over my shoulders, as if protecting what was his. "Hit the road, Derek. I'll catch up with you soon."

"Got it. But if you're late, I'm ordering without you. See you, Gracyn." Derek turned, heading down the sidewalk along the endless line-up of cars.

"Getting rid of him is sometimes a bit of a chore," Alex said, a twinkle in his eyes.

"I've noticed. You're a good friend. He's lucky to have you."

Alex gave me a gentle squeeze. "And I'm lucky to have you."

I smiled for Alex's sake while a voice in my head ranted. *Stop letting him take his time! You need to get home and find Becca. If she doesn't show up at the crypt on time, there's no telling what Maggie will do to Celeste!*

Before I could say a word, my phone rang. I held it up, relieved to see Becca's name flash across the screen. "Finally!" I whispered, swiping the phone.

"Becca?" I asked, tossing a glance at Alex. I held up a finger and mouthed, "One minute."

When Alex nodded, I ducked around a huge oak tree, dodging the skeleton dangling from its branches.

"Gracyn? I just got your message. What's going on?"

"I know where Celeste is, but I can't talk about it right now. Are you home?"

"Yes, but—"

"I'll be there in ten minutes. We're leaving now. Wait for me."

Before she could push me for answers, I hung up and rushed back to Alex. "Sorry. That was Becca."

"Everything okay?" he asked, taking my hand and threading his fingers through mine as we walked back to the Jeep parked on the side of the street.

"Yes," I said, not sure how convincing I sounded. "Why?"

"Because you don't look so good."

"I told you the haunted house made me feel a little sick. That's all, I promise," I replied, squeezing his hand.

My performance seemed to work because Alex smiled. Then without any more questions, he drove me home.

— ~

As soon as Alex dropped me off, I flew up the porch steps. The door flung open before I could reach for the handle and Becca stood under the frame, her face pale and her expression deeply worried. Wearing jeans and a black sweater that reached her hips, she didn't look anything like a witch on Halloween.

"Where is she?" Becca asked.

"At this moment, I'm not exactly sure. But I know who has her." In as few words as possible, I explained everything from the day Maggie had shown up at school to the demands she made less than an hour ago in the haunted house.

"Maggie isn't her real name," Becca said when I finished.

"It's not?"

"No. Her name is Marguerite. And she's ruthless. I have no doubt her threats are real. Wait here. I need to get something, and then we'll go."

"We?" I asked. "She said for you to come alone."

"I'm sure she did, but she's not going to get everything she asks for. I know what she wants, and she wouldn't care if I brought an army as long as I have it."

"Okay. I'll go. I'll do anything if you think it will help get Celeste home safely."

Becca disappeared into the house, leaving me to wait alone. Guilt trampled through my mind, my thoughts drifting to the night of the dance when I had released the wolf. In spite of Becca's belief that I'd had no control over the situation, I felt as though it was all my fault. I would do anything to get Celeste back, even if it meant offering to take her place.

Becca returned moments later, and we raced across the driveway to the barn. After bridling the mares, we climbed onto them from the mounting block outside. Grabbing a fistful of Gypsy's mane, I prepared for a tough ride without the saddle. Then we took off into the dark woods at a full gallop, as though every second counted.

The horses seemed to know exactly where to go. They followed the trail, their hoof beats thundering in the silence. Soon after passing the gateway to the Dumante estate, we turned right and headed up the hill. The mares dodged the trees, the dark shadows and branches whipping by in a blur.

At the top, we entered the dense fog and the mares slowed to a walk. The air grew colder, the brutal chill reaching inside my jacket and biting at my cheeks. I shivered as the horses marched through the leaves, taking us closer to the cemetery. Cadence led the way, her white coat easy to see in the dark.

Minutes later, we entered the graveyard. Tombstones rose above the mist rolling over the ground. The horses weaved around them until we reached the stone building on the far side. After halting in front of the door, Cadence and Gypsy stood patiently while Becca and I dismounted. Leaving the reins to rest on Gypsy's withers, I approached Becca, my eyes focused on the building. Moss grew in between the stones, and a padlock hung from the latch, holding the door shut.

When I opened my mouth to ask where Celeste could be, Becca held a finger up to her lips, silencing me.

My eyes open wide, I arched my eyebrows. Leaves rustled in the distance, causing me to look in the direction of the noise. But I only saw a veil of black beyond the fog.

Holding my breath, I waited as the sound grew louder. Within seconds, a horse as white as a ghost emerged from the mist. I drew in a sharp breath until Becca relaxed and offered the animal a smile. "Serenity," she whispered, reaching out to let the horse sniff her hand. The mare's nostrils rippled from a few deep breaths, her eyes worried.

Dropping her hand away from the horse, Becca looked back at me. "Celeste must be close."

I pointed to the crypt. "Maybe she's in there."

Without waiting for Becca to answer, I marched over to the door and tugged on the lock. Unlike the night of the dance when it opened from my touch, it remained secure, not budging. I pulled a second time, but only succeeded in bruising my fingers on the cold metal. "Ow!" I cried, wincing as I shoved my hand between my side and my arm, holding pressure on it in an attempt to stop the throbbing.

"What were you doing?" Becca asked, confused.

"This might sound crazy, but the last time I was here, when I touched the lock, it opened."

"Hmm," she mused. "Nothing surprises me when it comes to Marguerite."

Annoyed that Maggie was nowhere to be found, I whipped my hand out from under my coat sleeve and pounded on the door. "Celeste? Are you in there? Answer us, please!"

When I gave up, silence took over again. I turned to Becca, feeling tears of frustration filling my eyes. I had hoped to find Celeste as soon as we arrived, and yet there was no sign of her. I refused to believe she had been harmed, but fear snuck inside me, giving me no control over my emotions. "What if something happened to her? She could be dead, and this could be a trap," I said frantically, searching Becca's expression for a glimmer of hope.

Before Becca could respond, a cool voice rang out behind us. "She's fine. And you should know that since her horse is right here, alive and well. I keep forgetting how new you are to our ways."

Becca and I spun around at the same moment. Marguerite stood tall and confident, her booted feet slightly apart and her hands on her hips. The fog cleared around her, revealing her black leather clothing and long red curls.

"Marguerite," Becca said, her eyes settling on the other woman.

"We meet again, mother," Marguerite drawled out.

I sucked in a deep breath, my heart thumping against my ribcage. Not sure I'd heard Marguerite correctly, I waited, hoping to find out it wasn't true.

"Where is she?" Becca demanded, ignoring Marguerite's reference to her as mother.

"What? No hello? How are you? I missed you? Don't you think I deserve a little more than that?" Marguerite asked.

"Stop with the small talk. You and I both know we have more important matters to discuss here," Becca said.

A coy smile slid over Marguerite's face. "Yes, we do. Where is the script?"

"Where is Celeste?"

"She's safe, and that's all you need to know."

"Do you honestly think I'm going to take your word on this?" Becca asked calmly. "I want to see her."

"And I want the script," Marguerite repeated. "Funny thing about books. They're worthless without the words."

"Don't worry," Becca answered without missing a beat. "Of course I have it. I'd be a fool to come here in the middle of the night without it."

Marguerite flashed a satisfied smile. "Good. Then you may see her." She held up her hand, her blue eyes deepening to the color of sapphire. The lock on the door broke open, slid out of the latch and hurled across the fog into Marguerite's hand as if pulled by a magnet. Then the latch snapped to the side and the door whipped open, flapping back until it hit the stone wall.

Celeste lay in a crumpled heap on the cement floor. Her white blouse was ripped at the elbow, her jeans dirty. She had no jacket or blanket to keep her warm. Her dark hair covered her pale cheeks, rippling every few seconds when she exhaled.

"Celeste!" I gasped, rushing toward her. When I reached the doorway, I slammed into an invisible wall and fell to the ground. The impact caught me off-guard, and pain shot through my back from a rock buried under the leaves.

"No!" Becca screamed. In a flash, she was kneeling beside me, helping me up to a sitting position.

Dazed, I whispered a quick thank you.

An evil laugh cackled behind us. "You didn't think I'd give Celeste back that easily, did you?"

I glanced at Celeste, her still body in the same fetal position from moments ago.

Becca rose to her feet beside me. "That was uncalled for, Marguerite," she said.

"No, it was my insurance policy. Now that you've seen her, tell me where the script is."

Becca reached into her pocket and pulled out the amber paperweight from her study. "The script," she said. "Is locked in this stone."

The gem sparkled in the darkness, as if charged by electricity. I shivered, remembering the shock it sent through my veins when I touched it weeks ago. I couldn't take my eyes off of it. It shone in the night, the soft yellow light glowing in Becca's hand.

Marguerite stared at it, satisfaction lurking in her eyes. "You brought it," she whispered. Her gaze locked on it, she approached Becca.

As soon as Marguerite reached for the stone, Becca closed her fingers over it and pulled it back. "Let Celeste go first. Then I'll release the script."

Marguerite snapped her gaze away from the stone and shot an evil smile at Becca. "No script, no Celeste."

Then the door to the crypt slammed shut, locking Celeste in the cold dungeon once again.

30

uming, Marguerite locked her eyes on Becca, sparks flying from them. Becca stood tall, her shoulders square as she met Marguerite's gaze, not once flinching.

"We had a deal," Marguerite said, her calm voice dripping with ice.

"I don't believe I agreed to anything," Becca replied.

"You showed up here, so I assumed you had." Marguerite looked at Becca, smiling as though in charge. "But it's your choice. If you don't unlock the script, I'm not giving Celeste back. I'll keep her here as long as it takes to get what I want. And I'm not sure how comfortable that will be for the poor girl. It's only going to get colder."

"Fine," Becca said. "I'll give it to you. But first prove you'll hold up your end of the deal."

"How do you propose I do that?" Marguerite asked.

"You figure it out."

Marguerite took a deep breath before raising her hand. The door to the crypt swung open in slow motion, revealing Celeste who still huddled on the floor. Putting her hand up to her chin, Marguerite's lips formed a circle and she exhaled. Fog rolled out from her mouth in waves, reaching Celeste and caressing her.

A few moments later, Celeste opened her eyes, blinking a few times. She let out a low moan before sitting up and pushing her hair out of her face. Her brown eyes shifted to us, and she looked at me, seeming worried. "Gracyn?" she whispered.

Without thinking, I ran to the doorway, slowing when I approached it. I held my hands out, relieved when they passed into the crypt, the invisible shield gone. Then I walked inside and knelt beside Celeste. "Yes, it's me."

Barely a second passed before I heard Becca's voice cut through the silence. "Gracyn, no!"

I whipped around, and the wicked grin sliding across Marguerite's face made my heart fall into my stomach. I jumped up to my feet and ran back to the doorway. Stopping, I reached out and felt a solid force trapping me in the crypt.

"Becca!" I cried, pounding on the wall.

Becca turned to Marguerite, her confidence fading. "That was uncalled for."

"No. It was a perfect opportunity. Now you have two reasons to restore the script to the book."

Becca paused, glancing at me and Celeste and then back at Marguerite. I held my breath, hoping she had a plan to get us out of the crypt. Seeming to be on high alert, Gypsy lifted a foreleg into the air before pawing at the ground. Leaves and dirt went flying behind her as she snorted, the whites of her eyes showing.

Becca ignored Gypsy and shifted her attention to Marguerite. "I won't do anything until you release Celeste and Gracyn."

"Fine. Throw the stone up into the air. I'll let the girls out before it lands."

Becca took a deep breath, her displeasure obvious. With a frustrated sigh, she tossed the amber stone up, sending it high above the treetops.

The stone glowed like a shooting star as it rose into the heavens. When it reached its summit, Marguerite held her hand out toward the crypt. "The shield is now gone. You two are free to go."

Without hesitating, I grasped Celeste's arm and helped her to her feet. As soon as we ran out of the crypt, Gypsy and Serenity charged toward us, halting within an arm's reach. Celeste wiggled out of my grasp and ran to her mare, wrapping her arms around Serenity's neck. I stopped next to Gypsy, my attention shifting to Marguerite who reached out to catch the stone.

Her fingers curling around the gem, Marguerite shrieked and collapsed onto the ground. She kept a firm grip on the rock as smoke rose from her hand. The scent of burning flesh filled the air, turning my stomach.

After a few seconds, she dropped the stone and clutched her hand to her stomach. "You bitch!" she yelled at Becca before jumping up to her feet. "What have you done?"

"It's protected. I'm the only one who can touch it."

"You know as well as I do if there's a spell, there's a counter spell to reverse it. I'll find it and use it."

Becca stooped down and picked up the stone. Standing up, she placed it in her pocket. "Go ahead and try."

"You know I will, and I'll succeed. But for now, I'll take my insurance policy back." Marguerite held her hand out in Celeste's direction and chanted something unrecognizable.

Celeste screamed out in pain, putting her hands up to her ears and falling to her knees. Her mare whinnied sharply before pacing and nudging Celeste. But nothing she did seemed to help Celeste.

I couldn't bear to watch Celeste suffer. Remembering how strong I had been against Sam's stepfather on that stormy night, I rushed toward Marguerite, preparing to knock her to her knees. Before I reached her, Becca called out. "Gracyn! No!"

A force unlike anything I'd ever felt slammed into me. I was launched about twenty feet into the air before falling. I landed against a tombstone, the impact sending a crushing pain through my back as though I had just been hit by a truck. I let out a scream, tears filling my eyes. Weak, I felt like a rag doll that had been tossed about, and I couldn't find the strength to rise to my feet.

"Enough!" Lucian's voice called out through the night.

My eyes wide open, I searched the night until I saw him at the edge of the graveyard. His black clothing blended into the shadows, and he held the reins of a chestnut mare. She tossed her head, her mane swaying against her neck. Prancing, she tried to pull away from him, but he held on tight, jerking the bit in her mouth.

"What are you doing here?" Marguerite hissed. "This is a private matter."

"I don't think so. Let Celeste go."

"No."

Lucian smiled as though he was in total control, his green eyes narrowing. "I'm only going to ask you one more time. Release Celeste. If you don't, there will be consequences."

Marguerite laughed. "You sound like you know what you're talking about. I'm the one calling the shots here, and I'm not giving her up until Becca does what I've asked."

"What is that?" Lucian asked.

Remaining silent, Becca watched Lucian. Celeste had fallen to the ground, her hands still clutching her head in pain. I wanted to do something, but Marguerite had proven she was far too powerful for me.

"None of your business," Marguerite replied before turning her attention to Becca. "I'm waiting, mother."

"Don't give in, Becca," Lucian said. "I'll take care of this." He pulled a silver dagger out of his inside coat pocket and raised it to the mare's throat.

"No!" Marguerite cried, throwing her hands up in defeat. "Don't!"

Lucian held the knife steady, his eyes locked on Marguerite. "You know what you need to do. Do it now, or your horse is history. And that means you are, too."

Surrendering, Marguerite removed her invisible hold on Celeste. Celeste sat up at once and removed her hands from her head, the painful glaze in her eyes gone.

"There. Happy now?" Marguerite asked.

"Yes," Lucian answered, lowering the dagger. "For now." As soon as he let go of the reins, the mare charged over to Marguerite and halted, standing like a soldier ready for battle.

Marguerite turned to the horse, instructing her to drop to the ground. After climbing onto the mare's back, Marguerite gripped the reins as her horse stood up. Then they whipped around, circling back to Becca and Lucian.

"You may have won the battle, but the war is just beginning," Marguerite stated. Without waiting for a response, she kicked her heels into the mare's sides. In a flash, they galloped away, their red hair a blur until they disappeared into the shadows.

My back still aching, I got up and walked over to Celeste as she rose to her feet. After giving her a gentle hug, I stepped back. "I'm glad you're safe. We were all so worried."

She gave me a faint smile, her eyes still appearing dazed and weak. "Thank you. But I don't understand. How did I get here?"

Becca approached us, placing a hand on Celeste's forearm. "Maggie put you under her spell. Do you remember anything?"

Celeste shook her head. "No. Not since she stopped by the house Thursday after school to ask how I was feeling," she explained, her gaze landing on Lucian for a moment. Seeming confused, she looked back at Becca. "The next thing I knew, Gracyn woke me up here."

"The important thing is that you're safe," Becca said.

"Yes," I added in agreement. "And you're going to have to be more careful when choosing your friends from now on."

"I will," she replied. "I never saw it coming, that's for sure."

Becca squeezed her arm before letting go and turning her attention to Lucian. "Thank you," she said. "I was running out of options. You proved your loyalty here tonight."

He dipped his head, not seeming to know how to respond. Looking up, he smiled. "I only did what any one of the others would have done."

"How did you know we were here?" Becca asked.

"I saw you and Gracyn riding through the woods about twenty minutes ago. I didn't think the two of you would be out for a pleasure ride this late, so I followed you."

"Well, we're glad you did," Becca said with an appreciative smile.

"Who was that? I'm guessing Maggie is no ordinary high school student," Lucian mused.

"No, she's not," Becca replied.

"Care to elaborate?" Lucian asked.

Becca's gaze drifted to me before returning to Lucian. "Not now. I need to get Celeste home. I don't want her going alone because she's probably exhausted."

Lucian studied Becca, as if not ready to let her leave without giving him the explanation he expected. "With Cassie, you numbered three. Now you're down to two, and Celeste might be safe for now, but if she could be at risk again, the rest of us need to know why she's being targeted."

"I know, Lucian," Becca said quietly. "Give me a day or two."

"My father is on his way home. I suggest you start by telling him what this is all about as soon as he gets back to town."

Becca nodded. "I will. But for now, I need to go." She shifted her gaze to Celeste. "Your parents have been very worried about you. Can you ride?"

"Yes," she answered weakly. "I think so."

"Good. Go ahead and get on. I'll ride home with you. Lucian, would you please see that Gracyn gets home safely?" Becca asked.

"Yes, of course. But what about you?"

"I'll be fine," Becca assured him. "Marguerite will wait at least a few days before she tries something else."

"Just be safe," he added, sounding concerned.

Becca's eyes met his for a moment, and she tilted her head with a silent acknowledgement before making her way to Cadence who lay on the ground, waiting for her. She slid onto the mare's back and nudged her sides. The horse rose to her feet and walked a few steps to join Celeste and Serenity.

They set off into the woods at a brisk walk, the shadows quickly swallowing up the pair of white horses.

Alone with Lucian, I shifted my gaze to him, but he wouldn't meet my eyes. Instead, he gestured to Gypsy. "Get on. We should be going," he said, his tone cold and business-like, as though taking me home was nothing more than a job to him.

His solemn mood crushed any hope I had that things between us would return to the way they had been. Forget the ride to the rock, waking up in his sister's room, and the day at the family farm. Lucian clearly wanted nothing to do with me.

A lump forming in my throat, I forced it back, refusing to let him see my emotions get the best of me. As soon as Gypsy dropped down, I slipped onto her back. By the time she stood up, Lucian sat astride Shade who had emerged from the woods. Without a word, Lucian spun Shade around and took off down the hill at a canter. Gypsy surged forward to keep up, the sound of her hooves crashing through the brittle leaves all that could be heard.

When we arrived home, Lucian halted Shade at the edge of the driveway. Gypsy passed them before stepping onto the gravel, her hooves clattering on the stones. We were halfway to the barn when I realized we were alone. I whipped Gypsy around only to find Lucian and Shade gone without a trace.

My heart heavy, I guided Gypsy to the barn, prepared to unbridle her and wait for Becca. The questions I had would take my mind off Lucian, at least for a little while.

31

I was waiting inside the house with the dogs who slept on their beds, oblivious to the turmoil the night had brought, when Becca returned. As soon as she shut the front door, I spun around on the island stool, my ginger ale on the counter forgotten.

"How is she?" I asked as Becca placed her coat on the couch and approached me.

"She's fine. A little tired, but definitely happy to be home."

"I'm sure she is. I'm glad she's safe, but I really want to know Marguerite's story. What does she want?"

Sighing, Becca sat down on the stool next to me. "Oh, only spells that hold the power to cause widespread destruction, not to mention manipulate and control others."

"Destruction? As in—"

"Floods, fires, drought." Becca paused, her grave expression sending a wave of fear through me. "A few hundred years ago, she stole The Book of Darkness. The name doesn't do it justice, trust me. It's not just dark, it's pure evil."

"Great," I muttered with a huff, not sure I wanted to know anything more.

"When the book went missing, I cast a spell to remove everything written in it, rendering it useless. I also used my magic to trace the book to the witch who stole it. As soon as I confirmed it was in Marguerite's possession, I banished her to the crypt. Her punishment should have been for eternity, but she was clever and must have protected herself with a counter spell."

"Is that how she turned into a wolf? Or is that something we all can do?" I cringed inwardly at the idea of being a werewolf as well as a witch. Although it sounded absurd, at this point, nothing would shock me.

"No, it's not, at least not without the right potion. She must have consumed wolfsbane before I banished her. The wolf's form probably protected her in the crypt for all those years."

"Did you ever check on her? I mean, you knew where she was all this time."

"The spell I placed on the crypt to lock her in didn't allow anyone, including myself, to open it."

"Then how did I do that?"

"I wish I knew."

I frowned, frustrated because nothing seemed to make any sense. Changing the subject, I asked, "Is she really your daughter?"

"Yes," Becca admitted quietly.

"And Gabriel is her father?"

Becca shook her head. "No. Her father passed away several hundred years ago. Gabe and I have only been together for about twenty years."

"Oh. So what happened to Marguerite? I mean, she seems nothing like you."

"I know. Unfortunately, my values never seemed to sink in with her. She's clever and powerful. But she's also greedy and manipulative. The worst possible combination, at least for a witch. I tried to raise her right, but I failed."

"Becca," I started, not willing to let her take the blame. "You didn't fail if you tried. There comes a point when Marguerite has to make her own decisions. You can't control her."

"I keep trying to tell myself that. I wish I knew how she strayed from our ways. As soon as she turned sixteen, she became very self-centered. Then she learned about the book. It was given to me to keep it out of the wrong hands, and that's exactly where it ended up."

At that moment, I put two and two together. "Oh," I said, exhaling. "Now I know what she meant." When Becca shot me a confused look, I explained that Maggie had confessed to stealing a book the night she and Derek crashed my date with Alex. "I had no idea what she was talking about."

"Of course, you didn't," Becca said. "I searched high and low for the book as soon as I banished her. I tried every spell I could think of to locate it, but nothing worked. She must have protected it before I locked her away. She's very strong and good with magic. Even better than most witches, possibly because she's my daughter." Becca shifted her eyes down and took a deep breath. "I never expected a child of mine would defy me as she did."

"I'm sorry," I said when no other words came to mind.

Becca snapped her attention back to me. "You shouldn't be. You have done nothing wrong. But this is a really bad situation. I'm afraid Marguerite will be hell-bent on unlocking the spell that removed the words from the book. If she can't do it, then—" Becca's voice trailed off, a worried look crossing over her face.

"Then what?"

"Then her only option will be to remove anyone in her way."

I was afraid to ask, but my mouth didn't heed the warning in my mind. "Who is that?"

"Me," Becca replied. "If I die, then the spell will be broken and the script will be restored to the pages. The only one who can reinstate the spell to protect the book from being used is Celeste. But if she does that, then she'll be in danger. Lucian was right. We already lost Cassie. If we lose Celeste, then there could be serious repercussions."

Confused, I gulped back the apprehension settling over me. "I don't understand. What was so special about Cassie? I mean, of course, every girl is special in her own way, but I've heard these references to Cassie a few times."

"Cassie, Celeste and I are the three chosen ones. We are the purest of hearts, and we are marked by our white horses. We exist to watch over the coven, to protect the innocent and ensure that others like us with supernatural powers abide by a code of morality. Witches have the power to do great harm to people and the world. The three of us, or rather two of us now, are here to make sure that never happens."

My jaw fell open, my thoughts spinning. No wonder so many of the others, including Celeste and her parents, held such hatred toward Lucian. I had heard Celeste compared to Cassie often, and I never would have guessed their connection. "That explains why Celeste has been afraid of her own shadow."

Becca nodded. "Yes. She's worried she'll be next. I will admit, I'm worried about her, too."

Silence swept over the room when Becca paused. The reality sunk in, pitching my heart into despair at the thought of losing either Becca or Celeste. "What can we do to stop Marguerite?"

"I don't know right now, but I'm not about to give up. Everett Dumante is on his way back to town. Next to me, he's the oldest, and that makes him very strong and powerful. He will help. In fact, he probably won't leave town again until we clean up this mess. He lost Cassie, and I'm sure he's not about to let us lose Celeste. He has connections to other covens. He may be able to enlist their help as a last resort."

"Really? Do you think it could come to that?"

Becca offered a faint smile. "There's no way to know right now. Marguerite is very strong. I'm not sure how she got her strength back so quickly."

"Lucian could have taken her down tonight. Why didn't he do it when he had the chance? If he had slit her horse's throat, the world would be rid of her now."

"Killing is usually not the answer," Becca said. "He was acting with a moral conscience as he should."

I glanced at Becca. "I suppose we should respect that." Silently, I realized now more than ever he couldn't possibly have killed his sister if he couldn't take down a witch guilty of kidnapping. "But—"

"He doesn't know about the book," Becca said, practically reading my mind. "None of them do. It was given to me by a Salem witch before she was convicted in the trials. She told me to protect it with my life. And then she transferred her power to me. I kept the book safe for over two hundred years, and I never told a soul about it, not even Gabriel."

"Don't you think you should have?"

"No," she said, shaking her head. "It was too risky to let anyone know."

"How did Marguerite find out?"

"I don't know, but I wish I did."

As Becca paused, another thought crept into my mind. "How are you feeling? Is tonight giving you a headache?" I asked, realizing the events of the last few hours were slightly reminiscent of the night Becca had dealt with Sam's stepfather.

"I didn't even think about that. I'm fine. I must not have used much power tonight."

"Well, I'm glad. I hate seeing you in pain. Maybe you're getting better."

She nodded. "That would be nice, but I'm not going to hold my breath." With a deep sigh, she stood up. "You must be exhausted."

"Yes, I am. Although I don't know how I'm going to sleep tonight after all this."

"You should at least try. It's after midnight, and you need your rest."

"Okay," I relented, slipping off the stool. "But if I can't sleep, I might come back downstairs to watch TV."

"That's perfectly fine," Becca said before hugging me. "Goodnight, Gracyn." After I returned the sentiment, she turned and headed down the hallway leading to her room.

Alone with the dogs, I dumped what was left of my ginger ale in the sink and placed the glass in the dishwasher. Exhausted, I turned out the lights and retreated upstairs, hoping I would feel more optimistic in the morning.

— ⁓

I woke up the next morning with Lucian on my mind. Once again, he had saved the day, but this time I didn't want to wait several days to thank him. At noon, after dressing in jeans and a black shirt, I grabbed my parka from the coat closet and hurried outside. The air held a bitter chill to it, matching my somber mood.

Choosing to drive, I pulled into his driveway a few minutes later and turned off the engine. His Range Rover was parked outside, and I hoped he wasn't out riding. I hated showing up unannounced, but he had done it to me more times than I could count. Hesitating in the driver's seat, I gazed at the stone mansion under the gray sky. The sun hid behind the clouds, the overcast day lowering my spirits.

After getting out of the car, I hurried up the sidewalk to the mahogany doors. "Please be home," I muttered, ringing the doorbell. At once, Diesel charged into the foyer, his muffled barking growing louder inside.

A minute later, the Doberman hushed and the door opened. Lucian slipped outside, the silver cross hanging over his white T-shirt smudged with black paint. He didn't say a word. Instead, he nodded, watching me with those green eyes that had haunted me since the first day of school.

"Hi," I said, flashing him a small smile.

"Hi," he replied, his glare flustering me. "What are you doing here?"

"I...um...I came to thank you for helping me and Becca last night. I don't know what we would have done if you hadn't shown up when you did."

"Don't mention it." He paused, his gaze shifting away from me. "If that's all you came to say, then you should probably head back home. I don't want anyone to worry about me hurting you."

"Is that why you're giving me the cold shoulder? Well, I don't care what anyone else thinks. I'm here because I want to be."

Lucian shook his head, contempt in his eyes. "Doesn't matter. They'll turn you against me one day. I'm no good for you. You might as well stay away like everyone else."

"What's gotten into you? You know I'm not like them. I'm not afraid you'll hurt me because I don't believe you hurt your sister."

Lucian took a deep breath, his expression solemn. No emotion played across his face, and his cold stare unnerved me. "You don't seem to get it. When anything goes wrong around here, I'll be blamed. I'm bad news. For you, for Celeste, for everyone. So let me tell you again, for your safety, stay away."

"Lucian, I don't know what you're talking about, but I don't believe you. If I thought those things, I never would have gone riding with you weeks ago or accepted your invitation to take me out when you wouldn't tell me where we were going." I touched his arm, causing him to lift his gaze and meet mine. "I mean it, too," I stated with conviction. "I see the good in you, and I don't care if the others don't see it now. As soon as we find out who killed Cassie, they will."

Moisture glistening in his eyes, he swallowed. At first, I thought he was going to step toward me, and all I could think about was wrapping my arms around his shoulders. But the moment ended abruptly. He drew in a sharp breath, blinking away the tears. "My father is on his way back to town, and I need to get ready for his arrival. Thank you for stopping by, Gracyn, but I have to be going."

Before I had a chance to say goodbye, he shut the door. The sound of the lock clicking was like a slap in the face. The cold wind blew, whipping a shiver through me. A tear escaped from my eye, and my heart ached for Lucian and the pain he must feel from constantly being accused of killing his sister, a crime I couldn't believe he committed.

All I wanted to do was knock on the door and tell him I believed in him again, but I had a feeling I wasn't welcome. Instead, I turned and retraced my steps back to my car, the trees in the distance a blur beyond my tears. I refused to believe Lucian had written me off forever, but only time would tell.

32

I arrived at school Monday morning with a heavy heart. Lucian hadn't left my mind since the previous day. His cold green eyes and stony expression had lingered in my thoughts, filling me with sadness every time I took a break from my homework. I tried to distract myself, often by thinking about Marguerite. But the memory of her sinister eyes and wicked smile shot fear through me, making me wonder when, not if, she would make another move to get what she wanted.

The gray sky matched my mood as I walked between the cars in the parking lot on my way to the school. The leaves were nearly gone, the bare branches forming a dark web in the distance. I wasn't sure what today would bring. I doubted I would have a chance to talk to Lucian, and I hoped Maggie wouldn't show up. I wanted to warn Derek about her, but I had no idea what to say to him, especially if she dared to return to school. Trying to push all that troubled me out of my thoughts, I entered the school, grateful for the noisy chatter filling the halls.

The day was exactly what I expected. Alex greeted me with a smile and a kiss, keeping me company between classes and making sure I stayed focused in Calculus. Celeste darted through the crowd, keeping a low profile as usual. Rumors circulated about her disappearance, speculating she had run away but didn't have the courage to stay out in the world on her own. I spoke to her a few times, happy to see her in a fairly good mood.

To my relief, Maggie was gone. Derek reported that her father had recovered, allowing her to move back to Boston earlier than expected. But I knew the truth, and her departure from school didn't comfort me at all. I suspected she was close by, watching Becca and waiting to strike again.

Lucian kept to himself that day. I stole glances at him every chance I got in the hall, shocked to see Zoe huddled with a group of girls far away from him. More than once, she cast an icy glare his way before looking back at her friends. Her distance from him came as a surprise, but I warned myself not to jump to conclusions. Whatever had happened between them was none of my business.

Art class was particularly painful. I smiled at Lucian, but his frown made me cringe. I felt like I had jumped back in time to the first week of school, as though all the hours we had spent together never existed. Conflicting emotions of fear and sorrow merged in my heart, keeping me on the edge of my seat for the entire period.

After class, I rushed to my locker, grateful to get away from Lucian. Unsettled, I reached for my parka and book bag when I felt a hand on my shoulder. "I'm in the mood for pizza," Alex said. "How about a spontaneous study date?"

My jacket in hand, I turned around to meet his dark eyes. His smile instantly lifted my spirits. "I would love that," I replied.

"Really?" he asked, seeming surprised.

"Yes," I assured him. "Just let me finish getting my things." I dropped my book bag and slipped my jacket on. Then I grabbed the books I needed for the night and tucked them into my bag. As soon as I finished, I shut the locker door and spun around to face Alex. "Okay. I'm ready. Pizza and Calculus, perfect for a cold Monday afternoon."

"My thoughts exactly," he said, draping an arm over my shoulders.

Side by side, we wound our way through the crowd until we reached the doors. Once outside, we headed down the steps to the sidewalk.

"How about if I drive? I can bring you back to get your car later," Alex offered.

"That sounds great," I said as we stopped at the curb.

Before we had a chance to walk across the traffic lane on our way to Alex's Jeep, red and blue lights flashed in the distance. Two police cars raced into the parking lot and jerked to a stop in front of us. The lights spinning, the engines still running, four uniformed policemen jumped out.

"I'll take the front," one of them said. "The rest of you cover the side and back doors. We'll find him."

All movement seemed to stop as if frozen in time. The chattering came to a standstill, all eyes glued to the officer approaching the double doors. As if on cue, Lucian walked out of the school, his head bowed and his hands shoved in the pockets of his long black coat. When he looked up, his gaze locked on the policeman in front of him. Lucian halted, his expression void of any emotion other than pure defeat.

I felt like the world was crashing down around me. Swallowing the lump in my throat, I listened to the officer. My heart seemed to stop, and everything became hazy, like that of a dream. Only I knew it was real. I closed my eyes, wishing this wasn't happening. But when I opened them, I heard the policeman loud and clear.

"Lucian Dumante," the officer said, holding up an official document. "We have a warrant. You're under arrest for the murder of Cassie Dumante."

Don't miss
GYPSY BLOOD

Book Three of The Gypsy Magic Trilogy

Coming in 2017

Acknowledgments

want to start this section by thanking everyone who has emailed me, stopped by my table at an event, or picked up one of my books to read. Thank you for your interest and taking the time to read my stories!

To my mom, thank you for you for reading this book in its most horrible rough draft form. I thoroughly enjoyed getting your opinion as I worked through the painful revisions to turn it into something that could be shared with the world.

To Lisa, thank you for making time in your schedule to proofread this book. I know I asked at the last minute, and not only did you find the time to work it in, but you did a great job!

To Veronica, thank you for being an awesome friend and beta-reader! I know you've taken time out of a very busy schedule to help me with proof-reading and editing, and I can't thank you enough! But more than that, thank you for letting me vent occasionally. This journey has been one of ups and downs, and having a friend I can turn to when the going gets tough means the world to me!

Once again, to Jennifer Gibson for the beautiful cover and bookmark designs. Your talent is amazing. Thank you for putting up with my last minute requests and working your magic as quickly as it was needed. Just knowing you're there to finalize the covers at the last minute is a huge help!

Lastly, to my family, coworkers, and friends as well as everyone mentioned above. Thank you for listening and supporting me. It's been an incredible journey and it wouldn't be nearly as special if I didn't have all of you to share it with!

About the Author

Tonya lives in Northern Virginia with her husband, son, two dogs and two horses. Although she dreamed of writing novels at a young age, she was diverted away from that path years ago and built a successful career as a Contracts Manager for a defense contractor in the Washington, DC area. She resurrected her dream of writing in 2013 and hasn't stopped since.

When she isn't writing, Tonya spends time with her family. She enjoys skiing, horseback riding, and anything else that involves the outdoors.

More information about Tonya and her writing can be found at www. tonyaroyston.com.

Made in the USA
Lexington, KY
28 May 2017